Domestic Affairs

DOMESTIC AFFAIRS

By

EILEEN GOUDGE

Vanguard Press
A Member of the Perseus Books Group

Published by Vanguard Press
A Member of the Perseus Books Group

Set in 12.5 point Centaur MT

Goudge, Eileen.
  Domestic affairs / by Eileen Goudge.
     p. cm.
  ISBN 978-1-59315-475-2
  1. Housekeepers—Fiction. 2. Master and servant—Fiction.
  3. Domestic fiction. I. Title.
  PS3557.O838D66 2008
  813'.54—dc22

                                                    2008005070

Vanguard Press books are available at special discounts for bulk purchases in the U.S. by corporations, institutions, and other organizations. For more information, please contact the Special Markets Department at the Perseus Books Group, 2300 Chestnut Street, Suite 200, Philadelphia, PA 19103, or call (800) 810-4145, ext. 5000, or e-mail special.markets@perseusbooks.com.

10 9 8 7 6 5 4 3 2 1

To my mother,
who is no longer with us
but who I know
is smiling down from heaven

ACKNOWLEDGMENTS

First off, a big kiss to my publisher, Roger Cooper, and his trusty crew at Vanguard Press. I've never met anyone in publishing who works harder than Roger. He's my not-so-secret weapon, a true Energizer Bunny when it comes to encouraging, promoting, and most of all believing in what I do. Any risks I've taken with him have been amply rewarded.

I'd also like to thank the following people, who were so generous in sharing with me their time and expertise. Bob Poole, cameraman par excellence and world traveler, who, in addition to reminding me of just *how* sedentary my job is, gave me a glimpse of the world through his lens, so to speak, by taking me on a guided verbal tour of some of his adventures in documenting wildlife and the various efforts to preserve it. Katie Carpenter, for putting me in touch with Bob, and also for her work as a documentary filmmaker, from which the planet has benefited as well as I. Dr. George Lombardi, my doctor and medical adviser, who gave me the information I needed to create what I hope is an authentic portrait of a cancer patient and who gave up his lunch hour to do so. My new friend, Thomas Rosamilia, a cancer patient himself, provided some insight into the emotional aspect of that journey.

Thank you to my dear husband, Sandy Kenyon, and my agent (and friend), Susan Ginsburg, who have been with me every step of the way;

also to Francine LaSala, for a respectful and thorough job in editing the manuscript.

A special thanks, as well, to two people who gave me what is perhaps the greatest gift of all to a writer: solitude. By allowing me to hole up again in their guesthouse for more than a month, Valerie Anders and her husband, Bill, provided me with the freedom in which to write uninterrupted. I wish every author could have such generous patrons as they. This work wouldn't have been nearly as good (or finished nearly on time) without their support.

Last but not least, I'd like to thank my readers, many of whom validate my efforts on a daily basis through e-mails. For anyone wishing to contact me, my address is eileeng@nyc.rr.com. You can also visit my website at www.eileengoudge.com. I'd love to hear from you.

I was in my own room as usual——just myself, without obvious change: nothing had smitten me, or scathed me, or maimed me. And yet, where was the Jane Eyre of yesterday?——where was her life?——where were her prospects?

——FROM *JANE EYRE*, BY CHARLOTTE BRONTË

The minute I heard my first love story
I started looking for you, not knowing
how blind that was.

Lovers don't finally meet somewhere.
They're in each other all along.

——JALAL AD-DIN RUMI

PROLOGUE

GREENHAVEN, GEORGIA, 1982

The last day at 337½ Vermeer Road began like any other. Abigail's mother rose before dawn and headed over to the main house to make breakfast. It was a Sunday in August, and Mr. Meriwhether liked to eat early on weekends in order to take his morning ride in the relative cool of the day, so she was gone by the time Abigail tumbled out of bed. Abigail usually hurried to join her—it was her job to make coffee and set the table—but on that particular morning, she took her time getting dressed, choosing her outfit with care: her most flattering shorts and a sleeveless blouse that showed to advantage her breasts, which had recently emerged into a bona fide bosom. She dabbed on cologne. She peered into her bureau mirror, trying to coax a curl into her stubbornly straight hair.

Abigail had a secret. A secret that glowed like a jewel at her center, warming her and casting a rosy glow over her surroundings. The hideous landscape over the bed, painted by some long-dead Meriwhether aunt, might have been a Rembrandt and the old chifforobe that listed to one side the magic portal to Narnia. She was giddy with nervousness, wondering what was in store today. How would *he* act when she saw him at breakfast? Would it be as if last night had never happened, or was her life about to change?

I

Until now, life had been fairly predictable. Her mother kept house for the Meriwhethers, and she and Abigail lived in the caretaker's cottage out back, in what remained of the old pecan grove. It was the only home Abigail had known in her fifteen years: four small rooms sided in white clapboard, with an asphalt shingle roof that sagged in the middle like the backbone of an aging plow horse. But it had its own separate address, the fraction tacked onto the street number on Vermeer Road, with its suggestion of old money and gilded ancestral ties, like a dropped glove, a casually discarded silk scarf (or, as she would come to think of it in later years, as in half as good, less than whole).

From her bedroom window she had a partial view of the main house, a handsome Greek Revival mansion dating back to the Civil War era. There had never been a time when it hadn't been occupied by Meri-whethers. The original owner, Colonel Meriwhether, who'd lost a leg at Appomattox, had lived there with his wife and their six children until his death at the then ripe old age of sixty-eight. He was succeeded by his eldest son Beauregard, a successful entrepreneur who'd promptly bought up the surrounding land, fifty acres in all. By the time his grandson Ames took up residence, in the early 1960s, a good chunk of the land had been sold off, leaving the remaining acreage, a lush emerald veld of whispered wealth discreetly dotted with fountains and statuary, to grow into itself like the roots of a hothouse orchid coiled inside its pot.

As she strolled along the path to the main house, beneath a bower of ancient oak trees festooned in Spanish moss, Abigail thought back to more carefree days, when she might have been on her way to play tennis or swim in the pool, or go horseback riding with the Meriwhether twins, Vaughn and Lila, before she'd become old enough to start helping her mother out after school and on weekends.

She'd always taken it at face value whenever Mr. or Mrs. Meriwhether would proclaim, in response to a raised eyebrow or murmured comment from one of their friends, "Why, Rosalie and her daughter are like fam-ily!" For hadn't they always been treated as such? Vaughn and Lila were the closest Abigail had to a brother and sister. She took meals with

Vaughn and Lila when their parents were out and often slept in the spare bed in Lila's room. To the casual observer, watching them play croquet on the lawn or splash around in the pool, Abigail and the twins, born in the same year, might have been family, except that they looked nothing alike. Abigail was tawny-skinned and long-limbed like her mother, with large dark eyes and thick hair the color of sorghum, while Vaughn and Lila were both fair and blue-eyed as a pair of lion cubs: Lila fine-boned and dainty, Vaughn fleet of foot and possessed of a fearless athleticism that by age sixteen had landed him in the hospital a few times with broken bones.

When she was younger, Abigail hadn't been aware of any class distinction. If anything, it was a badge of honor that her mother kept house for the Meriwhethers. No other home was as grand in her view and no other family as fine. If Mrs. Meriwhether drank too much and often took to her bed and Mr. Meriwhether wasn't home much due to the long hours he put in at his law office, it did nothing to diminish their stature in her eyes. It wasn't until they were thirteen and Lila and Vaughn enrolled in the exclusive Hearne Academy that the difference in social status became apparent.

Even so, the twins went out of their way to include her. They made sure to invite her to their parties and often asked her along when going out with their other friends. When they were alone together, Lila pretended to be envious of Abigail's greater freedom in attending public school and she mocked the airs put on by her snootier classmates. And woe unto any guest of Vaughn's who directed a derogatory comment at Abigail: Not only was he never invited back, but one boy found himself leaving with a bloody nose.

Vaughn was like an older brother to Abigail and Lila, never mind they were the same age. Whenever they climbed the water tower out by the old sugar refinery, he always insisted on going last, prepared to catch either of them should they fall. Diving into the quarry, where they picnicked in summer, he was the first one in, to make sure the water was deep enough to keep them from cracking their skulls. And Abigail's sophomore year, when she didn't have a date for the Christmas dance, Vaughn gallantly offered to escort her, making her the envy of every other girl there. Floating into the auditorium in a crimson velveteen dress she'd made herself, from a Vogue pattern, she felt every eye on her and the tall, un-self-consciously handsome boy at her side—eyes in which she saw the two of them reflected in an entirely new light, one that brought the blood rushing to her cheeks and made her suddenly and acutely aware of his arm circling her waist. As he guided her onto the dance floor, she was barely aware of her feet touching the ground.

Lila, for her part, became skilled at the art of giving things away without its seeming like charity. Casually, she'd toss Abigail an item of clothing out of her closet, saying, "It's missing a button, and you know I can't sew to save my life," or "Stupid me, I caught it on a nail. You barely notice the tear, but Mother will kill me if she sees it." And though Abigail recognized it for what it was, she didn't mind, because Lila was always so good-natured about it . . . and because secretly Abigail coveted those things. How else could she have owned sweaters of kitten-soft cashmere, skirts from Marshall Field's, and blouses made of real silk, not the cheap polyester kind worn by the girls in her school?

She arrived at the house to find Mr. Meriwhether breakfasting in the morning room. No one else besides her mother was up and about. A tall, buff-colored man with thinning blond hair and militarily erect posture, Ames Meriwhether, in addition to being one of Atlanta's eminent trial lawyers, was every inch the proud descendent of his great-great-grandfather, the Confederate cavalryman. In private, though, he was relaxed and affectionate. When the children were little, he'd get down on all fours and have them straddle his back, bouncing them up and down until they squealed with delight. His affectionate nickname for Rosalie was "the General." If a child wanted permission to do something, he'd say, with a wink, "You'll have to ask the General," or, slipping Abigail a bag of treats, "Don't let on to your mama, hear. I don't want to get into trouble with the General."

Abigail's mother knew more about his habits than did his wife, Gwen, who slept in most mornings, sometimes until noon, and had little to do with the running of the household: that he liked his eggs over easy but still runny and his bacon extra-crisp; that he was in the habit of losing buttons off his shirt cuffs and that his pants usually ended up in the laundry basket with their pockets full of loose change, crumpled receipts, and scraps of paper scribbled with phone numbers; that he was a fitful sleeper, his bed, in the room next to his wife's (she suffered from chronic migraines and couldn't abide his presence during those bouts), such a tangle of sheets and blankets Rosalie had once joked that if he were ever to wrestle the devil for his soul, there was no doubt who'd win.

"Take it away before I eat them all," Ames groaned, pushing away the plate of biscuits before him. To Abigail, he commented with a chuckle, "If I'm fat, it's because your mother's too good a cook." He patted his belly, which had thickened a tad with middle age. Except for that, he might have been an older version of Vaughn, with his enviable physique and keen, blue-eyed gaze.

"Fat? You're no such thing," Rosalie protested. Her hill-country twang, sanded down by the years of working for quality folks, carried but a faint echo of her hardscrabble youth. "Wouldn't I be the first to know if your pants needed letting out?" She spooned onto his plate a second helping of scrambled eggs. "Besides, a man has to keep his strength up. I don't know anyone who works as hard as our Mr. Meriwhether," she remarked to Abigail, as if she herself hadn't been toiling away since sunup.

Ames Meriwhether's expression briefly clouded over. He had to be thinking the same thing as Abigail and her mother: that there was a reason other than his crushing caseload for why he spent such long hours at the office. It had been evident for some time that his marriage wasn't all it should be. Not that he and Gwen fought, at least not openly. Just the opposite: They went to elaborate lengths to be polite to each other in front of Rosalie and the children, which was worse in a way. It was like watching actors in a play that you knew from the outset wouldn't have a happy ending.

"Well!" Ames exclaimed in an overly hearty tone when he'd finished what was on his plate. "Thank you, Rosie, for another fine meal."

He turned to Abigail, as he was pushing back his chair, saying with a twinkle in his eye, in an exaggerated drawl such as the old Colonel might have used, "Ab-beh, will you please tell huh royal highness, when she deigns to make an appearance, that huh fah-ther's in the barn saddlin' up."

"Too late, sir; she beat you to it," Abigail informed him. Lila had gotten up earlier than usual to take her new gelding for a ride. The horse had been a gift from her parents when she and Vaughn had turned sixteen the month before, and since then she'd spent nearly every waking hour with him. (Vaughn, who preferred the kind of horsepower that came under a hood, had been presented with a brand-new Dodge Ram pickup in a shade of red that ought to have been illegal, given the effect it had on Abigail whenever it came roaring up the drive, Vaughn at the wheel.)

"What's with the *sir?*" Ames growled with mock sternness. "I thought I made it clear there'd be none of that."

Aware of her mother's eyes on her, Abigail struggled not to smile. Rosalie was strict about how Abigail should address her employers, however relaxed she was with the twins. "I'm sorry, s—Mr. Meriwhether. It won't happen again," she said with feigned seriousness.

He leaned in, his breath pleasantly smoky from the six slices of extra-crispy bacon he'd put away, to whisper, "Between you and me, I prefer Ames. But we don't want to upset the General."

He and Rosalie exchanged an amused glance as he went out.

Minutes later Vaughn padded barefoot into the kitchen on his way to the morning room, yawning and tucking in his shirttail, his eyes heavy-lidded from sleep. (To Rosalie's eternal vexation, he always took the back stairs, seldom bothering to make a proper entrance.) At the sight of him, Abigail's pulse quickened and she was flooded with memories of the night before. She struggled to keep her gaze averted, fearing it would betray her, as she set out a napkin and cutlery.

It had begun innocently enough. They'd gone into town to see *ET*, which had just opened at the Rialto. Lila was supposed to come, too, but when it was time for them to leave she was nowhere to be found.

"She probably went for a ride and lost track of the time," speculated Vaughn, as he was digging his car keys from his pocket. He shook his head in bemusement, as if to say, *Typical of my sister.*

Abigail responded with a shrug, leaving the impression that she'd done a thorough search, when it had been cursory at best. Deep down, hadn't she *wanted* to be alone with Vaughn? she thought, feeling a pang of guilt as they started down the driveway. This way, she could pretend it was a date. And, as it turned out, she didn't have to work too hard at pretending. All evening, she was almost excruciatingly aware of his presence: his hand lightly cupping her elbow as he steered her through the crowd at the entrance; during the movie, his forearm resting on the armrest separating their seats, tickling the tiny hairs of her bare arm; his buttery fingers brushing against hers when he reached into the popcorn box just as she was doing so.

Nevertheless, she read nothing into it when, on their way home, Vaughn pulled onto the old quarry road instead of heading toward the house. It was early yet, and these days he seldom missed an opportunity to put his new set of wheels to the test. As they barreled down the dirt road, dust boiling up around them and the tape deck cranked up to full volume, blasting Van Halen, she let go of any trepidation she felt at the speed with which Vaughn drove and gave herself over to the sense of abandon that he never failed to generate in her. Vaughn, it seemed, had been born with the inverse of gravitational pull, and as he raced along, expertly guiding the pickup over bumps and potholes, the wind streaming in through the open windows making a tornado of his sun-streaked hair, she was infected by the thrill of it as well.

When they could go no farther, they got out and went the rest of the way on foot, picking their way over rocks and down a slope that after a dozen or so yards ended in a steep drop-off. Below, the waters of the quarry gleamed blackly, pricked with the reflections of stars.

Vaughn turned to her with a grin. "How about a swim?"

It was a warm night, the air soupy and sluggish as the water below was cool and inviting, but she hesitated even so. Where once they'd run

around each other half naked, lately she'd become self-conscious with
Vaughn. It had started the night of her school dance, when in the span of
a few short hours he'd gone from being her surrogate brother to someone
capable of breaking her heart. These days, whenever she was around him,
she felt as if an invisible band were constricting her chest. It was difficult
to speak without having to stop every few seconds to catch her breath.

But she didn't want him to know her feelings toward him had changed,
so she tossed back casually, "Why not?"

They stripped down to their underwear, as they had countless times
before, only this time it was different. Abigail turned her back as she hur-
riedly peeled off her T-shirt and jeans, glad for the cover of darkness.

As always, he was the first to dive in. She quickly followed, the shock
of the cold water against her sweaty skin causing her to cry out, a cry
that ricocheted against the quarry walls and sent Vaughn splashing his
way toward her, hooting in laughter as he attempted to dunk her. They
wrestled briefly underwater, his limbs slippery against hers, his hand
grazing her breast at one point, before they surfaced with breathless
whoops. It was too cold to stay in for very long, and minutes later
they were stroking their way toward the rocks, Vaughn scrambling onto a
wide, flat boulder, then grabbing her by the wrist and hauling her up
alongside him.

She stretched out on her stomach, soaking up the warmth of the
boulder, which had retained some of the day's heat. She was shivering,
and her flesh felt shrink-wrapped from the goose bumps that covered
every inch of her. "Ooof! I don't remember the water being this cold!"
she exclaimed.

"That's because we never went skinny-dipping at night."

Vaughn lay on his back, his fingers laced behind his head, gazing up at
the starry sky. Extremes in temperature didn't bother him as they did
most people; he was like a wild animal that way, adapting to changes in
climate with the ease of a creature naturally suited to the outdoors.

"I wouldn't exactly call this skinny-dipping." She brought her head up,
propping her chin on her folded arms to peer at him. A three-quarter

moon shone overhead, casting a glow that turned the boulder on which they lay the dirty white of a salt lick. She could see the braided muscles in his arms and chest, glistening with droplets of moisture. His briefs clung to him like a second skin, leaving little to the imagination. She quickly averted her gaze, but not quickly enough. The humid night air grew warmer, and she felt the tightness of her goose-pimply flesh ease.

He laughed. "You say that like there's something wrong with it."

"No. All I meant was, we're not little kids anymore. I'm a little old to be parading around in my bra and panties." She cringed inwardly as soon as the words were out. Oh, God. Why was she drawing attention to the fact? Why didn't she just shut up about it?

"So I've noticed."

He rolled onto his side so that he was facing her, lifting himself onto one elbow. The moonlight reflecting off the water made his face appear to shimmer. His eyes, normally a pale, almost unearthly shade of blue, were as dark as the surrounding shadows. She felt a sense of gathering momentum, though neither of them had moved so much as a muscle. Even the air was as still as a held breath.

When he leaned in to gently kiss her on the lips, it caught her by surprise nonetheless. She drew back with a sharp intake of breath. "Why'd you do that?" She'd fantasized about it often enough, but now that it was happening, she didn't trust it: Suppose he was only fooling around, the way boys were known to do? (Not that she'd had much experience in that department, having been on a grand total of two dates before now.) Suppose it meant nothing more to him than scratching an itch? The thought was unbearable.

He didn't help matters by answering, with a shrug, "I don't know. I just felt like it, is all."

"You're still doing it," she said hoarsely as he nuzzled her cheek, toying with a damp lock of her hair. Heat traveled through her like a fire through pitch pine. She could feel the feather movement of his lips all the way down in her crotch, where the wet fabric of her panties clung.

"Do you want me to stop?" he murmured, nibbling on her ear.

Abigail didn't answer. What was there to say? *I'll die if you don't stop, and I'll die if you do.* Death from the thousand cuts that would be inflicted by watching him with other girls, once he'd tired of her. Already she was in over her head, and for once she couldn't rely on Vaughn to protect her. He was the reason she was drowning.

They kissed some more, alone in the dark with only the chittering of nightjars and the rustling sounds of some larger creature, a possum or a raccoon, making its way through the underbrush. There was something dreamlike about the whole thing, as if in shedding their clothes they'd stepped out of their bodies as well, becoming different people. When he rolled over so he was on top of her, the wet imprint left by his body on the rock seemed to belong to the other Vaughn, the Vaughn she'd known only as a brother; as if he were still stretched chastely alongside her and the moist, warm flesh pressing against hers, the mouth hot against her face and neck, belonged to someone else entirely. A beautiful stranger she desperately wanted to get to know, but a stranger nonetheless. Already they had passed a point of no return, though. Whatever happened next, there would be no going back to the easy familiarity they'd known.

She stiffened briefly as he fumbled with the hooks on her bra, but she didn't protest. It occurred to her briefly that she should tell him to stop. She'd only been kissed once before, by Bif Wannamaker after the homecoming dance, and then with an awkward tentativeness that had left her more embarrassed than anything. Now here she was doing things the girls at school talked about in whispers, things her mother and Sunday school teacher had *warned* against, and she didn't feel the least bit inclined to hold back. Was there something wrong with her for wanting this as much as he? Some sort of internal brake system that asserted itself in other girls, at this point, that was missing in her? If so, it must be in her blood. Look at her mother, who'd been only a year older than Abigail when she'd gotten pregnant. *I was born bad,* she thought. So why fight it? Why not just let nature take its course? When her bra fell away and he gathered her breasts in his hands, bending to take one of her nipples in his mouth, she only arched her back, shivering with pleasure.

He placed her hand over the thing poking up, rigid as a tent pole, over the elastic waistband of his briefs. "Yeah, that's it . . . like that," he whispered as she began to stroke it, tentatively at first, then with increasing boldness. Moments later, she felt it spasm, and something warm and wet spilled over her fingers.

He drew away, muttering, "I'm sorry. I didn't mean for that to happen." He sounded almost angry.

Was he angry at *her?* she wondered. Had she given in too easily? Had he expected her to be more demure?

"It's okay." Abigail knew about such things from Sex Ed, but experiencing it was something else altogether. She felt embarrassed, not sure how she was supposed to act. Were there rules of etiquette about this sort of thing? When he didn't reply, she managed to stammer, after an awkward moment of silence, "I . . . I guess we should be going. It's getting late."

Neither of them spoke as they got dressed. There were none of the affectionate touches or kidding remarks she was used to from Vaughn. Had he belatedly come to his senses and realized what he'd be getting into? God knew she was nothing like the girls he normally dated. Like their neighbor Ginny Clayson, the daughter of a state senator . . . and last year that pretty blond he'd met skiing with his dad in Aspen, who'd come for a visit, some sort of heiress whose father owned half the oil wells in Texas. Maybe Abigail was only good enough to be his friend but not his girlfriend. After all, she'd been willing to go all the way without so much as a halfhearted protest, which made her little better than a common slut.

Driving back, though, he acted as if nothing were out of the ordinary. They talked about their favorite scenes in the movie, the trip he was taking to St. Simons Island with his family on Labor Day weekend, and what his football team's chances were of making the division playoffs next year. Before she knew it, they were pulling into the driveway. The only indication that a profound change had taken place came when Vaughn, as he was saying good-night, brushed his lips over hers instead of giving her the usual peck on the cheek.

Now, as Abigail carried a plate of bacon and eggs out to Vaughn on this first morning of her new and not necessarily improved life—a life like an upended boxful of puzzle pieces scattered every which way—she thought, *What now?* She was trying to remain cool, but it was difficult with her heart racing a mile a minute and her cheeks on fire.

But Vaughn had his head buried in the newspaper; he wasn't even looking at her. She wondered what he was thinking, or if he was thinking about her at all. Maybe he just didn't know how to act. It was an awkward situation, the two of them all but living under the same roof and having to pretend everything was normal. Some might say it was downright *weird.*

Her hand trembled as she poured his juice, and some of it dribbled onto his place mat. "Sorry," she murmured. Vaughn glanced up from his newspaper then, and she saw, from the expression on his face as his gaze met hers, that he'd only been pretending to read. As she reached for a napkin to mop up the spill, she felt the light brush of his fingertips against the inside of her wrist. The same fingers that last night had fondled her breasts. That had pushed her damp panties down around her thighs.

"You don't have to do that," he said.

"I don't mind." She aimed for a normal tone but couldn't hide the quaver in her voice. Her cheeks were so hot, they felt scalded.

"Well, *I* do. Don't you have anything better to do than wait on me?" He spoke in a playful tone no doubt meant to break the tension. But all it did was remind her that it was her *job* to wait on him. And what had he meant, anyway, by touching her like that? Had it been some sort of secret signal, his way of letting her know that last night was only the beginning . . . or merely a way of telling her he was sorry, that it wouldn't happen again?

He stayed at the table just long enough to bolt his breakfast before heading out. Minutes later, Abigail heard the roar of his pickup's engine in the driveway. She let go of the breath she'd been holding and turned her attention to preparing Mrs. Meriwhether's tray.

"No, not like that. Do it the way I showed you," Rosalie gently corrected as Abigail arranged toast triangles on a plate. Abigail suppressed a sigh. Her mother had schooled her so well that by the age of twelve, Abigail could iron a collar that would stand up and whistle Dixie. She knew that old linen, made from flax grown tall and stout, was more durable than new, that soaking a tablecloth in milk got out red wine stains, and that ants wouldn't cross a chalk line drawn across a stoop or windowsill. But her mother still didn't trust her with this simplest of tasks.

Rosalie fussed over Gwen Meriwhether as she would a child in delicate health. When Gwen was laid up with one of her "headaches," Rosalie brought her breakfast in bed. The rest of the day she tiptoed in and out of Gwen's room bringing cold compresses and warm solace.

When she wasn't looking after her employer, she was filling in for Gwen by acting as surrogate mother to Lila and Vaughn. She'd been the one to remind them when they were growing up to take their vitamins and to zip up their jackets on cold days, to phone home if they were going to friends' after school. Abigail knew her mother secretly worried that Ames would one day leave his wife. Wasn't that what men did? When Rosalie was just nine, her pa had gone out for a pack of cigarettes one evening, never to return. And hadn't Abigail's father left Rosalie when he'd found out she was pregnant?

"Like this?" Abigail rearranged the toast triangles in a fan shape. Rosalie nodded in approval, maintaining a careful watch out of the corner of her eye as Abigail spooned homemade strawberry preserves into a little porcelain dish, fragile as an eggshell. Alongside it she placed a small sterling spoon engraved, in worn but still decipherable curlicues, with Mrs. Meriwhether's initials. The spoon gleamed as though newly minted in the sunlight that filtered in through the curtain sheers. It might have been Rosalie's own wedding silver for the pride she took in keeping it polished.

When everything was to her satisfaction, Rosalie lifted the steaming kettle off the stove and poured boiling water over the two heaping teaspoons of Ceylon tea in the Limoges teapot. The final touch was a single pink rose, its petals still beaded with dew, tucked into a sterling bud vase.

Had Rosalie ever verbally declared her devotion to the Meriwhethers it would have been an embarrassment to all concerned. It was the care she took in anticipating their every need that expressed her sentiments more eloquently than any words. Like Gwen's breakfast tray, with its attention to every detail, down to the crisply ironed linen napkin tucked into a silver napkin ring. It was Rosalie's way of letting the Meriwhethers know that she considered them more her family than she did her own kin. Sixteen years ago, they'd taken her in, pregnant and penniless, and when Abigail was born they'd embraced her as well. How could she feel anything but love for them?

"Why don't you have something to eat while I take this up to Mrs. Meriwhether," Rosalie said, hefting the tray with a faint, musical chiming of the porcelain teacup in its saucer.

"I'm not hungry," Abigail replied in a lackluster tone. Her stomach was still in knots over the encounter with Vaughn, which had left her more confused than ever.

Rosalie paused to smile at her in a way that made her feel suddenly self-conscious. "It won't always be this way, you know."

"What?"

"Boys."

Abigail blushed, realizing how transparent she was even as she replied innocently, "I have no idea what you're talking about."

"Oh, I think you do." Her mother's calm, steady gaze gave no quarter. Clearly she hadn't missed the way Abigail had been mooning around Vaughn. What she didn't know was that it had since crossed over into another realm. "But don't let it worry you. Before long you'll have them eating out of your hand. And believe me," she said, her tone turning ominous, "that's when your real troubles begin."

Rosalie's expression was that of a woman who knew all too well where that kind of trouble could lead. Pregnant at seventeen, she'd been cast out by her deeply religious mother and stepfather and probably would have starved, or worse, if she hadn't happened into this job. Now, at thirty-four, she professed to be done with men and all their "nonsense." The one time

Abigail had floated the idea of her mother's getting married one day, Rosalie had scoffed at it. "What do I need with a husband?" she'd said. "Don't we have everything we could possibly want right here?" She seemed to go out of her way to discourage any potential suitors by downplaying her looks. While still relatively young and pretty, with eyes the color of the aged bourbon Mr. Meriwhether had a glass of every night before supper and thick brown hair shot through with coppery highlights, she dressed like a spinster, in below-the-knee skirts and sensible, low-heeled shoes, blouses buttoned to the neck, and little or no jewelry, her one good dress reserved for church and her only makeup the occasional touch of lipstick.

"It doesn't seem to have hurt Lila any," Abigail observed grumpily.

Lila was popular with boys and girls alike. Never mind they were only six months apart in age, Abigail felt like a kid sister in comparison. A *dorky* kid sister, half a foot taller and with none of Lila's social graces. If it hadn't been dark when they'd stripped down last night, Vaughn probably wouldn't have looked at her twice.

"It's different for everyone," Rosalie said gently, meaning that not everyone was as blessed as Lila.

Abigail sighed. "It's not fair."

Her mother's expression settled into one of flat resignation. "Well, life's not fair. The sooner you accept it, the better." With that, she pushed her way through the swinging door into the stairwell beyond.

When she returned a short while later, one look at her ashen face told Abigail that something was terribly wrong.

Rosalie dropped into a chair at the table, burying her face in her hands.

Abigail rushed to her side. "Mama! What is it? What's happened?"

Rosalie only shook her head, too distraught to reply.

Was it Lila? Abigail wondered. Could she have suffered a fall while out riding? At the image of Lila lying crumpled on the ground, Abigail felt as if she'd had the wind knocked out of *her*. But the notion was quickly dispelled. "It's . . . it's Mrs. Meriwhether," Rosalie said haltingly when she'd finally recovered her voice. "You know the diamond necklace Mr. Meriwhether gave her on their anniversary? Well, it's missing. She . . .

she seems to think I took it." Rosalie lifted her head, and the look in her eyes was awful to behold, for Abigail saw more than the shock and horror of someone wrongly accused. She caught a furtive glint. There was more to the story than her mother was telling.

Had her mother taken the necklace? Not intending to keep it, of course. Maybe she'd only borrowed it, planning to put it back before it was discovered to be missing. But even that was so completely out of character, Abigail immediately dismissed the idea. If her mother found so much as a nickel in a pants pocket while doing the laundry, she returned it. She would never have borrowed anything without asking, especially something so valuable.

"She must have misplaced it," Abigail offered. "It's got to be somewhere in the house. I'll help her look for it."

She was turning to go when Rosalie seized hold of her wrist. "No! It's too late for that."

Abigail eyed her in confusion. "Mama, what are you saying?"

"The police are on their way over." Her mother's eyes were like two holes burned in parchment.

The police! Oh, God, this was more serious than she'd thought. All at once Abigail felt deeply afraid. The feeling that her mother was withholding some vital piece of information became stronger than ever. "Mama, what on earth is going on here? Whatever it is, I want to know. Please."

"Yes, why don't you tell her, Rosalie?"

Abigail spun around at the sound of Gwen Meriwhether's soft, lilting voice. Her mother's employer stood in the doorway, dressed in a pink satin robe and matching slippers, her platinum hair, normally smoothed into a pageboy, sticking out in stiff clumps. Her face was pinched and grayish, the way it got when she was having one of her migraines. A fine-boned, aristocratic face that, however pretty it had been in her youth, showed the ravages of time and ill health. From this distance, Abigail could see its myriad of fine lines and the tiny broken veins that webbed her patrician nose like the cracked glaze on the Limoges teacup that had graced the tray so lovingly prepared by her housekeeper.

Rosalie jerked to her feet, her cheeks flushing a hectic red. The beseeching look she gave her employer was that of a family dog that's been kicked, wary but still steadfastly loyal. Abigail cringed inwardly, silently vowing to never, ever subordinate herself that way before another human being, however much she might love that person. "Abby was just volunteering to help look," Rosalie offered timidly.

"Well, then, perhaps we should start with the cottage." Gwen's normally honeyed voice was cold. Abigail had never heard her address Rosalie in this manner. The effect was chilling. She realized that, though she'd been around Mrs. Meriwhether all her life, she didn't really know her. Gwen was the distant sun around which the rest of the household orbited: at once constant and removed.

Rosalie just stood there clutching her elbows and shivering, as if it weren't 90 degrees outside.

An awful suspicion crept in: Could this have something to do with her and Vaughn? Mrs. Meriwhether might have gotten wind of last night's activities and decided to nip it in the bud by firing Rosalie. It was one thing to bestow the honorary status of "family" on hired help and another to risk their one day becoming just that. She might have concocted this setup as a sure way of getting rid of Abigail. But how could she have known? It was inconceivable that Vaughn would have confided in her. Unless . . .

What if he'd told Lila and she'd said something?

In horror, Abigail watched as Gwen Meriwhether advanced toward them, silent as a stalking cat in her satin slippers. She was staring at Rosalie in a way that made her seem slightly deranged. Maybe she *had* lost her mind. Maybe that was what this was all about: Rosalie covering for the fact that Gwen had gone mad. Abigail felt a sick sort of relief at the realization that this might not have anything to do with her after all.

At last, Abigail's mother replied in a low, trembling voice, "I would never steal from you. You know that."

"Why don't you tell it to the police? They'll be here any minute." Gwen's thin lips stretched in a mirthless smile. "Meanwhile, I suggest you start packing your things." Her gaze softened slightly as it fell on Abigail. "I'm sorry you had to get caught in this, Abby. I know it's not your fault."

Abigail watched her mother's eyes go wide with panic. "Where would we go? This is our *home.*" It was less a plea than a cry of lament. Rosalie looked vaguely unhinged herself at the threat of their being kicked out, as she stood there swaying on her feet, clutching the back of her chair for support.

"You might have thought of that before you took what didn't belong to you," Gwen said, her pitiless gaze showing no mercy.

Abigail couldn't believe this was happening. If last night was a dream, this was a nightmare. She couldn't shake the suspicion that it had something to do with her. And now, because of what she'd done, her mother was going to lose her job and they'd be homeless. She couldn't let that happen. She had to *do* something.

Mr. Meriwhether, she thought. *He won't allow this. He'll put a stop to it.*

She dashed outside in search of him. But when she reached the stable, out of breath, with a stitch in her side from having run as though her life depended on it—which, in a way, it did—he was nowhere in sight. There was only Lila, seated on the bench by the tack room, tugging at one of her boots. "I swear, my feet must have swelled two sizes since I put these on," she said through gritted teeth. "It's this damned *heat.*" She managed to yank off the boot before she straightened to fan herself, her cheeks pink with exertion, ringlets of blond hair pasted to her sweating forehead. Then she took note of Abigail's expression and all at once grew still. "Oh, Abby, what is it? You look like *death!*"

Abigail struggled not to give in to her panic. First she needed to get to the bottom of this. "Did Vaughn say anything to you after we got home last night?" she burst out without preamble.

Lila's delicately arched brows drew together in a frown. She seemed vaguely put out. "I haven't seen him since yesterday afternoon. Really, I should be angry at you two, taking off like that without me."

"We couldn't find you." Abigail felt a guilty flush spread through her cheeks, though technically it wasn't a lie.

"Well, you couldn't have looked very hard. I was here the whole time," Lila said, as though it should have been obvious. "What *about* Vaughn, anyway? Are you two up to something I don't know about?" She shot Abigail a darkly speculative look.

"No, of course not," Abigail said, too quickly, hoping her inflamed cheeks wouldn't betray her.

"What, then?"

"It's . . . it's your mother." Abigail didn't bother to explain the connection. There was no time.

Lila visibly tensed. "What about her?"

It wasn't something they'd ever discussed, but Abigail knew that Gwen's drinking was a source of embarrassment to Lila. At the same time, she'd defend her mother to the death were anyone to suggest she had a problem. Mindful of this, Abigail found herself downplaying the situation as she explained, "She's missing a piece of jewelry—the diamond necklace your dad gave her for their anniversary. She seems to think it was stolen."

"I don't see how that's possible. As far as I know, there aren't any burglars skulking about. And we're the only ones who know where she keeps her jewelry box." All at once a horrified expression dawned on her face. "Oh, God. She's not accusing *you*, is she?"

Abigail shook her head. "Not me. My mom." Even saying the words made her feel sick with shame, as though there might be some truth to Gwen's accusation.

"That's the craziest thing I ever heard! She's just confused, that's all." Lila scrambled to come up with a logical explanation for her mother's irrational behavior. "She gets that way sometimes when she's having one of her headaches."

The Meriwethers never made reference to Gwen's drinking; when she had too much wine at dinner and suffered for it the next day, it was always filed under the general heading of migraine. "Don't worry. We'll get it straightened out. Does Daddy know?"

"Not yet. We have to find him." Abigail cast a panicked glance around her.

"Well, I'm afraid it'll have to wait until he gets back from his ride. We'd never catch up with him on foot, and Maverick lost a shoe, so he's out of commission for the time being." Lila gestured toward her horse, in his stall contentedly munching on hay, before she bent to tug off her other boot. "Don't worry," she assured Abigail once more. "Daddy will deal with it as soon as he gets back." She didn't sound overly concerned.

"What about Vaughn? Do you know where he went?" asked Abigail in mounting desperation.

"I told you, I haven't seen him." Lila glanced up at her, looking annoyed, as if at being reminded of how she'd been stood up the night before. Then her expression softened. "Look, I know you're upset, but I promise it'll be okay. Like I said, it's probably just some silly idea Mother's gotten into her head. Five minutes from now, she'll have forgotten all about it."

"It's more serious than that." Abigail struggled to keep from losing her cool, with her heart pounding and her stomach up where her throat ought to have been. "She's phoned the police."

"She *what?*" Now Lila did look alarmed.

As if on cue, Abigail heard the crunch of tires in the driveway. Peering out the stable door, she saw a police cruiser slow as it approached the house before pulling to a stop in front of the pillared portico. Something lurched in her chest, Lila's assurances scattering like so much dandelion fluff in the wind. Her mother would be arrested . . . or evicted . . . or both. It was her word against Mrs. Meriwether's, and whom were the cops going to believe? Her only hope now was Lila. If Lila could somehow persuade her mother to see reason . . .

She turned to find Lila hobbling her way toward her, the one boot still stubbornly wedged onto her foot. "Come on, help me with this. I can't get the damn thing off."

Years later, Abigail would burn at the memory of her kneeling to pry off Lila's boot—an innocent gesture that would be transformed into a humiliating act of servitude in light of what came after. But in that moment all she felt was gratitude. Lila led a charmed life, true. Nothing bad had ever happened to her, certainly nothing as bad as this. But that didn't mean she wouldn't stick up for those she loved. Maybe it really would be all right.

She gazed up at Lila, loving her and envying her at the same time. Lila, slender as a willow switch and so light on her feet she scarcely seemed to touch the ground, with eyes the blue of a cloudless sky and hair a natural shade of blond that women paid hundreds of dollars to achieve. It wasn't just that she was beautiful. At sixteen, she already possessed formidable social skills: She could have conversed charmingly with a brick wall, in French as well as in English, and she could throw a party with as much ease as any society matron; most of all, she had every young male from here to the Mason-Dixon line vying for her attention, never mind she seemed to prefer hanging out with the horses or with Abigail and Vaughn.

By the time they got to the house, the two policemen, a burly salt-and-pepper-haired veteran and his younger, skinnier sidekick, were seated in the front parlor with Mrs. Meriwhether. She was giving them her version of events while Rosalie stood meekly to one side, amid the antique furnishings so lovingly dusted and polished by her hand. It was obvious from their deference, which bordered on obsequiousness, that Gwen's would be the only version that mattered. Rosalie must have known it, too, for her head hung low and she said nothing in her own defense. She managed to look both wrongly accused and guilty as charged.

Abigail wanted to shout at her mother to stand up for herself. Why was she taking this lying down? She was on the verge of speaking out when Lila piped up.

"Mother, what on earth is going on? Abby's just told me the most unbelievable th—"

Gwen didn't let her finish. "Stay out of it, dear. This doesn't concern you." She spoke softly, in her creamiest patrician tones, but it was clear from the sharp glance she cast Lila that she wasn't going to tolerate any interference.

Lila shut up at once. She just stood there, staring at Gwen in wide-eyed astonishment. Clearly, this was a side of her mother she'd never seen. Usually Gwen was either "indisposed" or on her way to becoming so. She rarely took an interest in household affairs, preferring to let her husband handle any crisis that might arise. Right now, though, she was not only stone-cold sober but clearly in charge.

A search was conducted of the cottage. It didn't take long for the necklace to turn up, in one of Rosalie's dresser drawers. Abigail wasn't all that surprised to see the skinny policeman emerge from the bedroom, necklace in hand. "Lookee here at what I found," he crowed, casting a nasty, knowing look at Rosalie. Mrs. Meriwether was summoned. She didn't look surprised, either. When asked if she cared to press charges, she replied with a queenly wave of her hand, "That won't be necessary." Now that she had the necklace back, she would settle for having the "culprit" clear out at once, she said. She gave Rosalie an hour to pack her things.

Abigail appeared to be the only one who saw through Mrs. Meriwhether's act. The whole thing was so obviously a setup. It was like a scene out of a hokey detective show. The only thing she couldn't figure out was *why*. Why would Gwen want to frame her mother? Wasn't she always saying, *What would I do without Rosie?*

Abigail was nearly done with her packing when Lila showed up. She looked as if she'd been crying. "I'm sorry," she said in a low, cracked voice.

Abigail stared down at the clothes neatly folded inside the suitcase that lay open on her bed, many of them castoffs of Lila's. An open cardboard box sat on the floor, filled with books and old report cards; a pink music box her mother had given her for her tenth birthday, with a ballerina that twirled to the tune of "Tiny Dancer" when you opened the lid; a crepe-paper lei Vaughn had brought her back as a souvenir the year the Meriwhethers had gone to Hawaii on vacation; ticket stubs from the concerts she'd attended with Lila and Vaughn; a trophy she'd won in a districtwide spelling bee. None of which meant anything anymore. It was just junk.

She took slow, careful breaths. She herself was beyond tears. Now that her panic had burned off, all that was left was anger, like a thick cloud of volcanic dust, filling her throat and lungs, choking her. Anger entirely focused on Lila right now. Because she'd believed Lila was her friend, and Lila had let her down in a way that was so profound, even now Abigail had trouble believing it.

She turned on Lila. In her righteous fury, she felt ten feet tall. "Why didn't you say something? Why did you just *stand* there?"

Tears rolled down Lila's cheeks. "I tried," she said weakly.

Abigail gave a scornful laugh. "You *tried?* What kind of lame excuse is that? I've seen how you act when it's *your* reputation at stake. That time Lainie DuMarche was spreading those lies about you and Timmy Jordan? She was in tears after you reamed her out. And God forbid anyone should lay a hand on your precious horse. You'd knock them flat. So don't insult my intelligence by saying you tried."

"Think what you like." A note of defiance crept into Lila's voice. "But the fact is, even if I'd said something, it wouldn't have done any good. Mother clearly wasn't in the mood to listen."

Abigail's eyes narrowed. "Or maybe you *believed* her story."

She saw from the sheepish look on Lila's face that she wasn't far from the mark, even as Lila protested, "Of course I don't think your mom would ever do anything like that on purpose. But maybe she . . ." Lila floundered, trying to come up with an explanation that wouldn't incriminate Rosalie. "Well, she could have borrowed it and forgotten to put it back."

"She wouldn't do that, not in a million years." Abigail felt a prick of guilt for having thought the same thing herself, if only fleetingly. Coldly, she added, "Anyone with eyes in their head could see it was a setup."

Lila looked aghast. "Are you suggesting that Mother *lied* to the police?"

"I wouldn't know," Abigail replied in the same coldly derisive tone. "Why don't you ask *her?*"

Now it was Lila's turn to grow indignant. "You're out of your mind. That's insane!"

"Then I guess it all boils down to who you're going to believe. The woman who practically raised you, or the one who calls herself your mother."

Abigail was aware that she'd crossed a line even before she watched the color rise in Lila's cheeks, saw her eyes flash and her chin tip up in a haughty pose worthy of her mother, but she was too angry to care. She slammed the lid down on her suitcase. When she looked up, Lila was gone. She'd left without even saying good-bye.

Ames Meriwhether was another one. She heard him come back from his ride while she and her mother were loading the car, but any hope that he would come to their rescue was soon crushed. He never even showed his face. Abigail lingered a few minutes longer, praying he would intervene . . . that Vaughn would show up . . . but in the end there was no one to see them off when they finally rolled down the driveway of 337½ Vermeer Road. Abigail thought she saw a flicker of movement behind the window of the upstairs bedroom that was Lila's, but it could have been merely a reflection playing against the glass.

Rosalie had placed a few frantic calls, and now they were on the way to an aunt and uncle whom Abigail had never even met. They lived in the hill country up north, in a town called Pine Bluff. All Abigail knew about Aunt Phyllis was that she had taken their mother's and stepfather's side when they'd booted Rosalie out after learning she was pregnant. What it must have cost Rosalie to swallow her pride and phone her sister, Abigail could only imagine.

They were at the railroad crossing on their way out of town, waiting for a freight train to pass, when the strain finally became too much and Abigail broke down. "*Why*, Mama?" she asked, weeping. For a long moment there was only the rhythmic *rickety-rack-rack* of the train wheels and the strobe-flicker of light and shadow reflecting off the dusty windshield of their '72 Dodge Dart. The sun was high, and the moist heat blowing in through the vents swirled lazily as stirred soup.

Rosalie sat there, gripping the wheel and staring straight ahead. Her face was as lifeless as that of someone who'd died and hadn't yet caught on to the fact. "It wasn't what she thought," she croaked, in a voice as lifeless as her expression. "I didn't love him, not that way. I did it for *her*. I did it to keep him from leaving."

1

NEW YORK CITY, PRESENT DAY

Lila had saved the storage bin for last. It was all the way down in the basement of their Park Avenue apartment building, along a concrete corridor lined with identical steel-mesh cages, seemingly a world away from the walnut-paneled lobby with its antiques and tasteful floral arrangements, just one floor up, and quite frankly, it gave her the creeps. There was all that stuff to weed through, too: skis and snow gear to remind her of their family vacations in Aspen and Telluride; beach blankets, coolers, and a well-used picnic basket; the antique regulator clock out of their cabin at Lake Mahopac, which she'd brought home years ago, meaning to have it repaired, and which had been languishing down there ever since; stacks of photo albums; Neal's baby clothes and old toys, plus twelve years of her son's school report cards and various certificates and awards; and, last but not least, the scrapbook of press clippings documenting her husband's meteoric rise to the top, which seemed richly ironic to her in light of their present circumstances. Heading down in the elevator, she felt a familiar clutch in her stomach at the thought.

The first thing that greeted her when she unlocked the door and switched on the overhead fluorescents was the set of Mark Cross luggage, monogrammed with her initials: LMD—Lila Meriwhether DeVries— a wedding gift from her late mother. Shrouded in plastic, it sat wedged against the steel-mesh divider separating their unit from the adjoining one: a three-piece matched set in burgundy leather that looked back at her like a reproach. It must have cost a small fortune, money her mother could ill afford at the time, but Lila had used it just the one time, on her honeymoon in the south of France. It had made her feel conspicuous, not to mention it was highly impractical for anyone who didn't travel with a valet. Now it seemed a liability as well, those initials stuck to her like something nasty she'd stepped in and couldn't scrape off.

She tried not to think about all that as she threw herself into the task at hand, separating everything into piles: one for all the stuff that was to be given away or thrown out, another for those items that were to be placed in storage along with the rest of their things, packed in readiness upstairs for tomorrow's move. It was mid-September, and the city was experiencing a heat wave that had turned the storage unit, where the ducts that kept the rest of the building temperature-controlled year-round were noticeably absent, into an oven. Before long she was sticky with sweat, her eyes and throat itchy from the dust.

Lila didn't mind. The busier she kept, the dirtier and more physically demanding the job, the easier it was to cope with what was going on in the rest of her life. For whole minutes at a time, she didn't have to think about the reason for all this upheaval. She didn't have to dwell on the fact that her darling, brilliant, handsome husband was currently upstairs in their thirty-second-floor penthouse with a monitoring device strapped to his ankle and that tomorrow he was being transported to the Fishkill Correctional Facility to begin his ten-year sentence. As she pried open box lids and tossed things into trash bags, the nightmare of the past eighteen months—the grand jury indictment, Gordon's perp walk on national TV, the endless rounds of meetings with his lawyers, culminating in the lengthy and very public ordeal of the trial—was like the wail of a siren off in the distance, registering only peripherally on her consciousness.

Of course, the reality of her new existence eventually reasserted itself, as it always did. Coming across the engraved brass plaque Gordon had received at the Vertex Leadership Association banquet in his honor three years ago, she paused to reflect on the precipitous drop in their fortunes since then. He'd been the golden boy of Vertex Communications, the architect of the merger that had sent stock prices soaring. Wall Street loved him, political bigwigs courted him, and he and Lila were much sought after on the social scene. Theirs had been among the famous faces at every blue-chip function, regularly featured on society pages, Lila always in glittering jewels and the latest couture, Gordon the handsome young Turk in his bespoke tuxedo. She recalled watching him move with ease among his fellow titans of the business world, as though he'd been born to it, and how proud she'd been, not so much of his outward achievements as of his greater accomplishment in having risen, Proteus-like, from the murky waters of his humble beginnings. He'd triumphed over adversities that would have hobbled or soured a lesser man, all without sacrificing his essential decency (or so she'd believed at the time). Others in his shoes might have had their heads turned by such early success, but not Gordon. Through it all he'd remained not only a devoted husband and father but a good man, one who seldom passed a homeless person on the street without opening his wallet.

Then, seemingly overnight, it had all come crashing down.

Even now, after the fact, Lila could scarcely fathom it. It was like some twisted practical joke. How could her smart, savvy, loving husband be headed for prison? How could they be nearly broke? Almost their entire net worth—bank accounts, stocks, limited partnerships, their Park Avenue apartment and the cabin in Mahopac—had vanished like so much smoke from a burning pyre. Everything that hadn't been seized had gone to the lawyers. The only thing the government and creditors hadn't been able to touch was Gordon's IRA. It wouldn't amount to much, given the penalty for cashing in early, but if she were very, very careful, it should be enough for her and Neal to squeak by. Their son wouldn't have to drop out of college, and Lila would have a little time to establish a career of some kind. What sort of career she had no idea. The only salaried job she'd ever held had been back in college. What would her résumé even look like, if she had one?

Company wife (1988–2008)

> Twenty years' experience in planning parties and entertaining at a high level.
> Responsible for managing several homes, making travel arrangements, and, most
> recently, acting as legal adviser.

Mother (1990–present)

> Served two years as president of the Buckley School Parents' Association and
> eight years as chairman of the school's Book Fair Committee. Organized fund-
> raisers for the Knickerbocker Greys and Madison Avenue Presbyterian, where son
> attended kindergarten. Reasonably skilled at basic first aid, sewing costumes,
> baking large quantities of cupcakes, refereeing, and SAT tutoring.

Daughter (1966–2006)

> Acted in the capacity of unofficial diplomatic liaison during parents' divorce.
> Saw mother through final (and protracted) illness and, prior to that, a nervous
> breakdown and several rehabs. Provided emotional (and occasionally financial)
> support to father through his second and third divorces, as well as the subsequent
> squandering of his fortune on said ex-wives, until his death in 2006.

Sister (1966–present)

> Skilled at corresponding with peripatetic brother, who, when last heard from,
> was embarking on an expedition to the Galapagos Islands.

Thinking of Vaughn, Lila pulled from a box a batch of his old letters,
tied together with string. They were from all over the globe, addressed to her
in her brother's slapdash hand: Bombay, Marrakech, Abidjan, Lima, Mom-
basa, Ho Chi Minh City. The most recent one—they had stopped coming
regularly once e-mail had become the preferred mode of communication—
was from two years ago, postmarked Anchorage, Alaska, where her
brother had been based while filming a documentary in the Aleutian
Islands. Lila settled back on her heels as she riffled through them, indulging in a small, ironic smile.

Their parents had despaired of her twin brother's ever settling down
and pursuing a "real" career, whereas in their view Lila had fulfilled her
destiny (and their aspirations) by marrying Gordon and producing a
grandchild. Until recently Lila had shared that view, but it seemed laugh-
able now. Vaughn, on the other hand, had attained something far more
worthwhile than any material success. He was doing what he loved;
he was living a life that wasn't some castle in the sky. She envied him

for that, and at the same time a small part of her was resentful over the fact that, while he'd been off traipsing around the world, she'd been the one cleaning up the family's messes. It had been left to her to deal with the fallout from their parents' ugly divorce and their father's equally ruinous second and third marriages. She'd had the job of caring for them when they'd become ill as well—first their mother, who'd died of cancer, then two years later their father, who'd succumbed to a heart attack. Any support Vaughn had provided had mainly been from afar.

Still, hadn't he been there for her when it had counted most? Following the virtual overnight collapse of Vertex, when Gordon and several other senior officers had been charged with falsely inflating stock prices, among a host of other crimes, her brother had flown in from Botswana to be at her side. She'd been on the verge of collapse herself, besieged by reporters and the flow of increasingly dire news. Her normally solicitous husband was too frantic with his own worries to soothe hers, and her teenaged son was asking questions she wasn't remotely equipped to answer. Her friends stopped returning her calls, and she couldn't walk from the front entrance of her building to her hired car without being swarmed by the press. It was Vaughn who acted as chief facilitator and bodyguard in those first crazed weeks, fielding the flood of phone calls, helping her dig through old records that might help Gordon's case, fending off the media, calming the worst of her fears.

"Why is this happening? *Why?*" she railed at one point, after a frightening incident in which she'd come close to being knocked over by a paparazzo as she was climbing out of her car (an action the man had occasion to regret when Vaughn caught up to him, pinning him against the side of the car and nearly wrenching his arm out of its socket). "I'm not a bad person, am I?"

"No, you're not a bad person," Vaughn soothed, putting his arms around her. They were in her apartment, behind closed doors, safeguarded from prying eyes and intrusive reporters, yet her brother seemed the only thing standing between her and the world. "It was just a shitload of bad luck, that's all. But you'll get through this. I promise." He drew back to look at her, his blue-eyed gaze like a fixed point on a compass in the rugged landscape of his deeply suntanned face. "We're made of strong stuff, you and me. I've survived everything from armed rebels to snakebite, and you'll survive this."

Since then he'd kept in daily contact, the only one besides her son whom she could rely on for total, unquestioning support. The rest of the family was of little help. She'd kept in only sporadic touch through the years with the various aunts, uncles, and cousins, and Gordon's brothers were a dissolute pair who'd shown more interest in Gordon when he'd been in a position to lend them money. As for her and Gordon's friends, all but a few had abandoned them. They hadn't needed a judge or jury to tell them Gordon was guilty; as far as they were concerned, the facts had spoken for themselves. No doubt they questioned, too, how Lila could've been so blind to her husband's misdoings.

Lila didn't know which was worse: being judged a fool or an accessory to a crime. The latter would have put her in jail along with Gordon, but at least she wouldn't have appeared a clueless nincompoop. (Lady Macbeth, whatever else you could say about her, had been nobody's fool.) In fact, her only crime had been in remaining loyal to her husband. Whatever anyone might think, Lila had been as roundly duped as the rest of the shareholders. Even now, a small part of her—the part that, as a child, had stubbornly clung to the myth of the Easter Bunny and Santa Claus long after she'd been old enough to know better—still believed in Gordon's claim, in the face of compelling evidence to the contrary, that he was the innocent fall guy. The same man who was presently upstairs putting his affairs in order. Gordon couldn't even venture as far as the basement, to help pack up the storage bin, without the device on his ankle emitting a silent alarm that would bring the cops running.

Lila experienced a surge of anger. How could he have done this to her? To Neal? Not to mention all those poor, trusting shareholders, many of whom had lost their life's savings. And to what end? So she and Gordon could dine in expensive restaurants three nights a week and vacation at four-star resorts? Fill their closets with designer labels and buy a new luxury car every other year? All of which had ended up costing them more than a fortune: It had cost Gordon his freedom and the respect of his peers, the future he should've had with her and Neal.

Had he truly believed that money would buy them happiness? That she'd have loved him any less had he been earning a modest salary working nine to five? Was *she* somehow to blame? No, she thought. Her husband was driven in a way that went beyond a mere desire to provide his family with all the things he hadn't had growing up. Their lifestyle had been a validation of sorts: proof that he was Someone. The irony was that he hadn't needed to play fast and loose; he'd have made it on his own merits. But Gordon had been impatient. Why wait when he could have it all *now*, simply by bending a few rules?

She thought back to when they'd first met, in their junior year at Duke. Her first day of a class in Shakespearean literature, she was scribbling notes when she happened to glance up and see a dark-haired boy gazing at her unabashedly. She was used to being stared at by boys; what made this one different was that he didn't look away when she caught him at it. His lips curved up in a faint smile instead, as if he and Lila were in on a private joke. Lila was intrigued. For the remainder of the hour, she found herself sneaking glances at him. He was different in other ways as well, more mature-seeming. Also refreshingly clean-cut, in a reverse-cool sort of way, in his snug-fitting jeans and polo shirt, his dark hair cut short but not too short, compared to the boys around him—the sons of the privileged who went out of their way to look as derelict as possible.

In the days that followed, she found herself noticing other things about him as well. Like the fact that he seldom took notes, yet whenever he was called on in class, he made the most intelligent, incisive remarks. It was obvious that he hadn't just studied the material; he'd given it a great deal of thought. Lila found herself shying from raising her own hand after Gordon had delivered one of his brilliant insights, fearing that she'd sound stupid in comparison. Thus, she was taken off guard when he approached her after class one day to comment, "I liked what you said about Julius Caesar. About its being no less of a betrayal because Brutus felt conflicted."

"I'm not so sure Professor Johns agreed with me," she said as she gathered up her books and notepad. "I just happen to have my own views on the subject." She had a Ph.D. in the subject of betrayal, after all. Hadn't she betrayed her best friend and the woman who'd practically raised her? Even all these years later, Lila was haunted by the memory: Abigail mutely beseeching her as Lila had stood rooted in place, unable or perhaps unwilling to speak up in Rosie's defense. And even when she could have made amends, had she lifted a finger to do so, written a single letter? No. That she would have to live with for the rest of her life.

"'O pardon me thou bleeding piece of earth!'" Gordon intoned in a stagy British accent before adding in a normal voice, "Do you think he was appealing to God or Caesar, or both?"

"Maybe he was asking forgiveness from himself."

He cocked his head, eyeing her with keen interest. She found herself noticing the little flecks of gold in his wide-set hazel eyes and the whorl at his hairline, above his right eyebrow, like a thwarted cowlick. "I like the way you think." He paused to stick out his hand as they made their way out of the lecture hall. "Gordon DeVries," he introduced himself. "Listen, if you don't have another class to get to, do you want to grab a cup of coffee?"

As it happened, she was on her way to another class: a course in quantitative analysis, which she was semifailing and could ill afford to skip. But she found herself replying nonetheless, "Sure, why not?"

They lingered in the cafeteria for the next hour or so. She learned that Gordon had grown up poor, in the hills of Tennessee, the eldest of three boys, all with different fathers, and that he'd been raised by his grandparents after his mother had run off to join a commune when he was just six. "I don't even know who my father is." His tone was matter-of-fact.

"Aren't you at all curious?" she asked.

He shrugged. "Not really. You don't miss what you never had to begin with." His expression turned thoughtful as he sat idly running his thumb over the edge of his Styrofoam cup. "Though every now and then I'll be passing a strange guy on the street, someone who looks a little like me, and I'll think, 'Is he the one?' How weird would that be, coming across your own father and not even knowing it was him?" He wore a small, contemplative smile.

Thinking of her own parents, whom she'd loved dearly but who were the source of much grief and aggravation in her life, it was on the tip of Lila's tongue to reply, *Trust me, you're better off.* But she knew it would come across as insensitive. All she said, when Gordon asked about them, was, "If you've read Tennessee Williams, you know the story."

Gordon's upbringing made hers seem idyllic in comparison. As if being abandoned by both his parents weren't enough, his grandfather had died when Gordon was sixteen, after which his grandmother had had a debilitating stroke. "We couldn't afford outside help, so it became my job to look after her," he went on in the same matter-of-fact tone, clearly not wishing to paint himself as any kind of hero. "My brothers did what they could, but I was the eldest, so most of it fell on my shoulders. It wasn't easy, I'll admit. I was holding down two jobs at the time while busting my ass to keep my grades up in order to qualify for a scholarship. But I wouldn't have had it any other way. It would have been awful, Gran's being in some state nursing home. At least she got to spend her last days at home, with me and Billy and Keith."

"You must have loved her very much." Lila, moved by his story, wondered if she would have performed as admirably under the same circumstances.

He smiled, his expression turning tender. "She was the only mother I knew."

Lila thought once more, with fleeting sadness, of Rosie, who had been far more than their housekeeper. She'd been like a second mother. "Well, I'm sure she'd have been proud of you," she said.

Gordon shrugged once more. "All she ever wanted was for me to be happy. She used to say, 'Gordie, if playing the banjo on street corners was what you felt you were born to do, I'd be the proudest granny of a banjo player you ever saw.'"

"You don't strike me as the banjo-playing type," she said.

"Couldn't pick a tune to save my life," he freely admitted.

"So what *do* you want?"

"Oh, the usual. To make my first million by the time I'm thirty," he replied with a lightness that belied the steely intent behind his mild, smiling gaze.

Later, Lila thought that if she could pinpoint the exact instant when she fell in love with Gordon, it would be that moment, as she'd sat across from him in the cafeteria, nursing her coffee and listening to him talk about his dreams for the future. Dreams shaped out of molten desire, by the anvil of hard circumstances, like those of the great men of history who'd triumphed against adversity. *A biography will be written about him someday,* she remembered thinking. She couldn't have known how eerily prescient that thought was, except she'd been wrong in one sense: Much would be written about Gordon at the end, but none of it good.

Within days they were lovers. By the time they graduated, they were engaged. They were married the summer after graduation. By then Gordon was already on his way up the ladder, recruited by Vertex right out of college and rapidly making his mark. When Neal came along two years later, Lila felt she was leading the charmed life that had eluded her parents.

Now, alone amid the flotsam and jetsam of that life, she was engulfed by a flood of sorrow. Love wasn't something you could turn off like a faucet, and in spite of all that had happened, she still loved Gordon. He might be a thief, and he was most certainly a convicted felon, but he was still her husband and Neal's father. Guilty or not, there was a part of her that would always see him as the idealistic man she'd fallen for that long-ago day in the cafeteria. She knew that her friends, as well as the vast majority of the public, judging from the mail she'd received, thought she'd be better off divorcing him, but Lila couldn't do that. A long time ago she'd turned her back on people she'd loved in their time of need, and she'd never forgiven herself for it. She wasn't going to repeat that mistake.

Swept up in the tide of memories, Lila rocked back and forth on her haunches, moaning softly to herself as tears rolled down her cheeks and dripped off her chin. With Gordon and Neal she kept up a brave front, and she would have died rather than shed a tear in public. It was only in private moments like these that she allowed herself to fall apart.

When she felt she could move again without crumbling, she resumed packing. She was sorting through a box of loose photos when she came across a recent snapshot of Gordon, taken at Neal's high school graduation. No one could have mistaken them for anything other than father and son, they looked so alike, both tall and lanky, with the same dark curls and seawater eyes. They shared other traits as well. They had the same quirky sense of humor and intense drive. They were harder on themselves than on anyone else—like his dad before him, Neal sweated over his grades as if his very life depended on it. But what struck her most now, looking at the photo, was the proud expression on Gordon's face. All the love that would have been spread among other children, had they been so blessed, was channeled into his only son. She knew it had to be tearing him up inside, knowing that the next time he laid eyes on Neal, it would be under the watchful eyes of guards, where he would be allowed only limited physical contact.

As if on cue, Lila's cell phone trilled. It was Neal.

"Hey, Mom. You'll never guess where I am."

At the sound of her son's voice, Lila felt her heart break all over again. "I don't know. Where are you, sweetie?" she replied in what she hoped was a normal tone.

"Here, in the lobby." He broke away briefly to give a muffled greeting to Carlos, the doorman. "I decided to come in a day early. PJ was driving into the city, so I hitched a ride with him." Neal's roommate at Wesleyan, a Pakistani boy named Prakash Johar, lived nearby with his parents, on Lexington and East 72nd, and the two boys had often exchanged rides. That is, until Neal had had to give up the brand-new Jetta she and Gordon had leased for him. Now PJ did all the driving.

Lila felt herself tense up. The one thing Gordon had been adamant about was that Neal be spared tomorrow's emotional farewell. He wouldn't be happy that Neal was here. "Don't you have school?" she asked.

"Relax, Mom. I can afford to cut a few classes. You didn't really think I was going to miss seeing Dad off?" He struck a breezy tone, but Lila wasn't fooled. Neal never cut classes if he could help it. Growing up, he'd been the opposite of the stereotypical kid, insisting he wasn't sick even when running a temperature so as not to miss a day of school. "Where are you? I tried the apartment, but all I got was the machine."

"I'm in the basement, cleaning out the storage room." Lila wondered briefly why Gordon hadn't picked up. Probably because he wasn't in the mood to talk to anyone, even Neal. He'd been so depressed lately. All these months he'd kept up a good front, holding out hope until well into the eleventh hour, but he was finally cracking under the weight of despair. He had no appetite these days, and he didn't sleep more than a few hours each night. "I'll be up in a sec. I just need to clear away some of these boxes." Lila glanced at her watch, surprised to see that she'd been down here for several hours. "I'm not sure what there is to eat, but you can check the fridge."

"Not to worry. I picked up bagels and cream cheese on my way over. And some of that Scottish salmon Dad likes." Lila's eyes misted over. Wasn't that just like Neal? He was like his dad in that respect, too. Gordon never forgot an occasion. Every birthday and anniversary, he'd gone to extraordinary lengths to get her the perfect gift. Like on their tenth anniversary, when he'd whisked her off to the airport for a surprise trip to Morocco, a place she'd always wanted to visit. Without her knowing it, he'd had her bags packed, arranged for a babysitter, and rescheduled all her appointments. Now it was his father's voice she heard as Neal said, "I brought a bottle of wine, too. The good stuff."

"What are you doing buying liquor? You're underage!" She tried to sound like a concerned parent, but it was painfully obvious, to her at least, that she was only going through the motions. She hadn't been much good to Neal or anyone since this whole ordeal had begun.

"I never told you about my fake ID?" Neal gave a wicked laugh. "I just hope you haven't packed up all the glasses." From his tone, it might have been a celebration he had planned, but she heard the underlying cracks in his voice, the faint warble of fear.

"We're in luck. I left the kitchen for last. I was going to tackle that tonight," she told him. "In fact, you can help."

Tomorrow morning the movers would arrive to cart off all their stuff. Then she'd be on her way to Hopewell, about two hours' drive north of the city, where she'd rented a small house, not far from Fishkill and near enough to Gordon so she'd be able to pay regular visits. It wasn't fancy, but it would suffice. In fact, relocating to more modest digs was the part she minded the least. As their income had dried up, she'd learned to make do on less and had found, to her surprise, that she didn't miss the luxuries she'd once thought essential. In some ways, too, it would be a relief to get away from the city, where she was surrounded by uncomfortable reminders of a lifestyle for which they'd all paid dearly.

After she hung up, Lila finished stacking the boxes and tidying up before she locked the storage bin. Moments later, waiting for the elevator, she happened to catch her reflection in the mirror by the laundry room. It was with a small shock that she recognized the haggard face looking back at her as herself. Gone was the sleek, stylish woman who'd once graced *New York* magazine's society pages. She'd lost so much weight her bones jutted like those of a famine victim and her eyes appeared sunken. She hadn't been to her stylist in so long that the layers of her hair had grown out; they lay flat against her head, frizzy with split ends, as if she'd been caught in a downpour and it had been left to dry without the aid of a blow-dryer. In the harsh glare of the overhead fluorescents, her once porcelain complexion was the chalky white of toothpaste.

As she stepped into the elevator, she said a silent little prayer of thanks that it was unoccupied. Her luck held out, and it didn't stop at any of the other floors on its way up to the penthouse. Lately she lived in dread of running into other people in the elevator. They either felt obliged to murmur some polite pleasantry or they simply stared silently into space, pretending not to recognize her. It would have been almost a relief if for once someone had voiced what they were surely thinking: *He got what he deserved. And so did you.* It wasn't just that she and Gordon had been found guilty in the court of public opinion; they made people like them nervous. They were a constant reminder of how swiftly one's fortunes could turn. Weren't they all just one catastrophe away from the brink?

Getting out at the penthouse level, she paused at her door before inserting her key into the lock. Did it look as though she'd been crying? It wouldn't do for these last precious hours with her husband to be spoiled by her weepy mood. She straightened her shoulders and took a deep, steadying breath before she unlocked the door and stepped inside.

Their building, at Park Avenue and East 72nd, was one of the Upper East Side's more venerable prewars and the penthouse its crown jewel. With views stretching on either side all the way to the East and Hudson Rivers, spacious rooms with twelve-foot ceilings, and a wraparound terrace, it had been the ideal stage for the numerous parties she and Gordon had thrown, most in an effort to further Gordon's career. Only now, stripped of its decor, with what was left of its furnishings—the more valuable pieces having been sold—swaddled in quilted packing blankets and bubble wrap, the memory of those festive occasions, the front room alive with conversation and laughter, music and the clink of glasses, waiters gliding about with trays of artfully displayed canapés, was a distant one. She felt as if she were walking into a tomb.

"Gordon?" she called.

There was no answer. That was odd. Where could he have gotten to? And where was Neal? He'd said he was on his way up, and that had to have been at least fifteen minutes ago.

She felt a strange sense of foreboding. The parquet floor, with its rugs rolled up, echoed with her footsteps as she made her way through the vestibule and down the hall into the living room. There was something very wrong here. She could feel it in her bones.

She found Neal huddled on the floor by the sofa, his knees tucked against his chest. He was staring blankly ahead, shivering uncontrollably, his face drained of all color.

Lila gasped and sank into a crouch before him. That was when she noticed the smudges of blood on his sneakers and the faint but discernible trail of bloody footprints on the floor leading up to him. A wave of panic crested inside her. "Honey, what happened? Are you hurt?" She felt woozy at the thought, her heart banging lopsidedly in her chest, like a piece of machinery missing a cog.

Neal wore a strange, unfocused look, the muscles in his face slack and his eyes staring sightlessly ahead. He appeared almost drugged. His lips were moving, but only a strangled croak emerged. At last he managed to unlatch his arms from around his knees and lift a trembling finger toward the arched entrance leading to the hallway beyond.

Lila's panic instantly congealed into a heavy, sinking dread. She could feel a pulse thumping in the pit of her stomach, and the world went a little gray as she rose shakily from her crouched position, already half knowing what she was going to find at the other end of the hallway.

"Gordon?" she called softly as she made her way down the hall.

No answer.

The door to Gordon's study was cracked open. As she approached it, time seemed to slow to a standstill. She could see dust motes swirling lazily in the band of sunlight that angled across the polished floor where the Bokhara runner had been rolled up, and she became aware of violin music playing softly inside the study. Beethoven . . . or was it Brahms? Her husband's love of classical music was a source of both wonderment and amusement to him. "Amazing, isn't it? I grew up listening to Merle Haggard saw on the fiddle. I wouldn't have known a violin sonata from a cat with its tail caught in a door," he would often remark with a bemused chuckle.

Now, as Lila entered the study, the sweet sounds rose to a crescendo, then hung, suspended, on a single, achingly pure note. For the rest of her days she would be unable to listen to that particular piece of music without feeling a cold trickle down her spine. Or without picturing the blood. Her husband's blood. Pooled on the floor where he lay dead, his stiff fingers clasped loosely about the .38 revolver with which he'd shot himself in the head.

2

"*Ink,*" *Abigail barked* over the phone to her secretary. She frowned. "No, not as in incorporated. Ink, as in what you write with. I'm going to need stamp pads, half a dozen, six each of red and black, for my *A.M. America* segment." During which she'd be demonstrating a clever way to design wrapping paper using cookie cutters. "No, not today—it's next week. But see that the stylist gets on it right away." She hung up, ex-pelling a deeply aggravated breath. "Honestly, am I expected to do every-thing myself?"

The Bluetooth headset more or less permanently affixed to Abigail's right ear emitted a pulsing light as she paced back and forth, her high heels tapping out a frenetic rhythm on the tile floor of her kitchen, where at the moment her husband and daughter were having breakfast and their live-in housekeeper, Veronique, was preparing an omelet at the restaurant-grade Garland range.

Abigail wondered if it was too soon to fire someone she'd only just hired. Well, technically, *she* hadn't done the hiring. She'd long since ceded that job to her executive director, Ellen Tsao. Didn't Abigail have enough to oversee as it was, with her catering business, books, and me-dia appearances? And now the line of bed and bath linens soon to be launched in twelve hundred Tag superstores nationwide—the next step in a well-orchestrated campaign that would make Abigail Armstrong a household name. A light chill, part anxiety and part delicious expectation, rippled through her at the thought.

"I was going to ask if you wanted my omelet, but I can see you'd rather sink your teeth into something more substantial," observed Kent. She turned to find her husband regarding her with a wryly arched brow over the top of his newspaper. "How about another cup of coffee instead?" He put down the newspaper and got up to fetch the pot.

"Just what I need." She was already so wired, she could have run a marathon. "Sorry if I'm a little on edge," she apologized as he filled her mug. Kent shrugged, as if to say, *What else is new?* "I have a meeting with the Tag executives later today. They want to talk about a marketing campaign, and I don't even have a final ship date yet."

There had been one problem after another at the factory in Mexico, and now they were seriously behind schedule. Her fault—she'd insisted on maintaining full control and ensuring top revenue by taking on the manufacturing herself. She should have anticipated the difficulties in dealing with a Third World country. Now, as a result of the delays, she'd had to ask her foreman, Señor Perez, to step up production, even if it meant hiring extra people and having everyone work double shifts. Even then, if they were able to get the first shipment out on time, it would be by the skin of their teeth.

"Relax; it'll be fine," Kent assured her.

"What makes you so sure?"

"Because I know you. You always deliver. Either that, or you'll die trying," he said with a smile. Something in his tone made her wonder if he'd meant it as a compliment.

"I'd rather not put it to the test. I'm already half dead as it is." It wasn't just a figure of speech: She hadn't slept more than a few hours last night, and for the past four days she'd been subsisting on diet sodas and protein bars. She noticed that Kent was dressed in his civvies: faded jeans and his favorite Irish fisherman's sweater. "You taking the day off?" she asked.

Kent thought nothing of canceling his appointments for the day if there was a school event of Phoebe's to attend or if one of his pet charities required his presence. It was the reason he'd chosen to join a medical practice here in Stone Harbor rather than remain on staff at Columbia-Presbyterian. While Abigail thrived on pressure, Kent found it soul-destroying.

He nodded, helping himself to a banana from the fruit bowl. "There's some stuff I need to do around here." She sensed that he wasn't being entirely forthcoming, but she didn't press him.

She was distracted by the sight of her seventeen-year-old daughter hunched over the kitchen table—an old workbench out of a turn-of-the-century woolen mill, which Abigail had lovingly refurbished with her own hands—pushing bits of scrambled eggs around her plate with her fork in an attempt to disguise the fact that she wasn't eating.

"Something wrong with your food?" Abigail asked pointedly.

"No." Phoebe kept her gaze lowered.

"Then why aren't you eating?"

"I'm not hungry."

"That's because you don't eat. Look at you, you're wasting away."

"I eat," Phoebe protested weakly.

"Good. Then you won't have a problem finishing what's on your plate."

Phoebe shot her a resentful look and went from rearranging her eggs to tearing up bits of toast and feeding them to their English sheepdog, Brewster, parked in his usual station underneath her chair. Was it a coincidence that while Phoebe wasted away, their dog seemed to grow fatter?

A sliver of worry worked its way in. Did her daughter have an eating disorder? Or was it just the anxiety surrounding college applications? Phoebe had applied for early admission to Princeton, her father's alma mater—a long shot despite the fact that her grades were good, with the competition being so much tougher than in Kent's day—and she'd been on edge, waiting to hear back. Which gave way to another discomforting thought: Phoebe would be leaving home in less than a year. Hard to imagine, looking at her now. In her baggy sweatshirt and cargo pants that sagged down around her slender hips, her black curls cropped in a pixie cut that accentuated her cheekbones and enormous brown eyes, she looked more like a poster girl for Save the Children than someone college-bound.

Abigail was opening her mouth to suggest they make a date to go clothes shopping in the city later this week, maybe get an early dinner afterward—she'd rearrange her schedule if need be—when another call came in, this one from Rebecca Bonsignore, the producer for her *A.M. America* segment. By the time Abigail got off the phone, any thought of spending a leisurely afternoon with her daughter had vanished along with the coffee she was draining from her mug.

She sat down at the table. Kent had left the front section of the *Times* neatly folded at her place, knowing she seldom had time to do more than scan the headlines. "Nothing for me," she said to the housekeeper in response to the inquiring look Veronique gave her as she delivered Kent's omelet to the table. Abigail was too wound up to eat.

Veronique frowned disapprovingly. She had old-fashioned ideas about what constituted a nutritious breakfast, and she was certain that one consisting solely of caffeine didn't qualify. A trim, fine-featured Haitian woman with skin the color of the third cup of coffee into which Abigail was now pouring a generous dollop of milk, Veronique had old-fashioned ideas about a lot of things, such as proper work attire. Today she was as stylishly dressed, in a wraparound print dress and low-heeled pumps, as if headed for a job in an office. Abigail wished all her employees took as much pride in their appearance.

A front-page headline caught her eye. "I see they buried the son of a bitch," she remarked.

Her husband looked up from the English muffin he was buttering. "Who?"

"Gordon DeVries."

Kent shook his head. "Sad business, that."

"You should save your sympathy for the Vertex shareholders," she replied irritably. "I'm sure plenty of those folks thought he got off easy, taking his own life."

Kent cast a sharp glance at her. "I was thinking of his family. I saw his wife on the news the other day. She looked as shell-shocked as if she'd just come out of a battle zone."

"Widow," Abigail corrected. She felt a moment's knee-jerk sympathy for the former Lila Meriwhether, whom she hadn't seen or spoken to in twenty-five years. But it was quickly consumed by the bitterness that had been smoldering inside her like banked coals for as many years.

"You ought to drop her a line," he said. "Didn't you two used to be friendly?"

"A million years ago. She probably wouldn't even remember me."

Abigail had been vague with Kent about that whole period in her life. All he knew was that she'd grown up on the Meriwhether estate, where her mother had been employed as a housekeeper. She'd told him little about Vaughn and Lila, leaving the impression that they'd moved in a separate sphere from hers. As for the reason her mother had been let go, she'd chalked it up to the fact that Rosalie had been ill, though in truth she hadn't been diagnosed with cancer until months later. Abigail had told no one, not even Kent, that it was because her mother had been sleeping with Mr. Meriwhether. It would have reflected badly on Rosalie. Who would believe that she'd been motivated not by lust but by the self-sacrificing, if extremely misguided, desire to hold the family together by preventing Mr. Meriwhether from straying outside the home?

When her mother had died a year later, officially of natural causes, Abigail had known that she'd really died of a broken heart.

The Meriwhethers, whom Rosalie had considered her true family, had cut her off without so much as a phone call. The only one who had cared enough to reach out to them was Vaughn. Eight weeks after arriving in Pine Bluff, Abigail received a letter from him in which he wrote to say how shocked and saddened he was by her and her mother's abrupt departure. He would have gotten in touch sooner, he said, but it had taken him a while to track down her address. He hoped she was well and that they would see each other again one day. Sadly, that day had never come, though they'd kept up a correspondence over the next few years. They wrote about mundane stuff mostly, never any reference to what had happened that night out at the quarry, but those letters had been her lifeline, the only thing that had kept her from utter despair during that bleak period of her life.

Some years after they'd stopped corresponding regularly, Vaughn had sent her a newspaper clipping with an account of Lila's wedding, which looked to have been the social event of the season in Greenhaven: a lavish three-day affair attended by everyone of any importance, including the governor of the state. Looking at the photo of Lila, radiant in her beaded silk gown and veil, posing beside her new husband, a dark-haired, intense-looking man, Abigail had experienced a resurgence of the old bitterness. Bitterness that might have faded with time if Lila and her husband hadn't relocated to New York City shortly after they were married. In the years since, it had seemed that Abigail couldn't open a newspaper or a magazine without seeing a photo or mention of her former friend in some society column. That is, until Lila and Gordon had become tabloid fodder.

"Still, maybe a condolence note—" Kent started to say.

"Damn." Abigail frowned down at her watch. "Where *is* that man?" Of all the mornings for her driver to be late! She had a nine o'clock meeting, and if she didn't leave soon, she wouldn't make it into the city in time.

She looked up to find Kent eyeing her in a way that she didn't much care for. "Will you be home in time for supper?" The casualness with which he spoke didn't match the look on his face: that of a husband who'd been left to his own devices once too often.

She felt a pang, remembering how different it had been in the early days of their marriage. They'd been living in a converted artist's studio in Bronxville that was so small one couldn't move without bumping into the other, and still they hadn't been able to get enough of each other. Back then, they'd both been working long hours and money had been tight— Kent had been in his fourth year of residency at the time, so their main source of income had been the money Abigail had been earning from her then fledgling catering business—but none of that had mattered. On the rare occasions when his days off coincided with hers, they usually wound up in bed. The rest of the time they took long walks, went to movies, and wandered around the Village or Chinatown in search of cheap eats. And although they couldn't afford big-ticket items, Kent often surprised her with little gifts: an antique carriage clock he'd picked up at a flea market, a box of her favorite French-milled soaps, a photo he'd taken of her that he'd had framed. Occasionally, when she was short-staffed on a night that he had off, he even pitched in, donning a jacket and tie to play bartender or pass out canapés. (Which led to several amusing incidents of his being recognized by people he'd treated in the ER, who eyed him curiously, no doubt wondering what the young doctor who'd stitched them up or set their broken bones was doing serving them drinks.)

Kent was still that man. But if his caring nature occasionally crossed over into fanaticism when it came to causes he was passionate about, and if he'd embraced his country-doctor persona to the point where he could be downright judgmental at times of those, like her, with less noble aspirations, at least he wasn't one of those husbands who cheated on their wives or, like the late Gordon DeVries, allowed greed to get the better of them.

She took in his long, lean face and gray eyes the color of a rainy day, which when they lit up were like the sun coming out from behind the clouds. She remembered how she used to love running her fingers through his thick brown hair, cropped short now and flecked with gray. That was back when they would linger in bed, making love or talking over future plans on mornings like this, instead of her rushing from pillar to post. How long had it been since they'd done that? She couldn't recall. Nowadays, their time together was as fractured as it was filled with promises, from her, that never seemed to materialize. *It won't always be this way,* she would tell him. As soon as she got a little bit ahead at work they would take that trip to Europe . . . go on that cruise . . . look into summer rentals on Fire Island. Promises that Kent had heard so many times, he no longer believed them. And why should he?

Next time, she wouldn't say anything. She'd simply spring a couple of airline tickets on him. He had a birthday coming up. What better way to surprise him than with a long weekend in Paris? As soon as she got to the office, she'd see about arranging it.

Her thoughts were interrupted by the discreet honk of a horn in the driveway.

She leaped to her feet. "I have that cocktail reception at Gracie Mansion, an hour tops. I promise to come straight home after that," she told him, dropping a kiss on his cheek on her way out.

"What about the community board meeting?"

"Oh, that. I completely forgot." She smacked her forehead with the heel of her hand. Though how was she supposed to remember every one of Kent's causes? There were so many, he ought to be anointed the patron saint of Stone Harbor. This latest had to do with a proposed halfway house for the mentally ill, to which there was a fair amount of local opposition. The community board was voting on it tonight. "Why don't you go ahead without me?" she said. "I'll join you if I make it back in time."

Kent cast her a veiled look that left Abigail feeling momentarily unsettled. But, with the day looming before her like a mountain to be climbed, she couldn't allow herself to be sidetracked.

She was retrieving her coat from the hall closet when she felt a gentle tap on her shoulder. She turned around to find Veronique eyeing her anxiously. "I'm sorry to bother you, Mrs. Whittaker, I know you're in a hurry . . ." she began in her precise, accented English. Veronique was the only person who addressed Abigail by her married name.

Abigail was eager to be on her way, but she put on a smile nonetheless. She might scream at her office staff, but she always treated her domestic help with the utmost respect. She hadn't forgotten what it had felt like when the shoe was on the other foot. "Can it wait until I get back?" she asked, as pleasantly as she could with her internal motor racing a hundred miles a minute.

"No, I'm afraid not." Veronique regarded her dolefully. "It's my sister in Haiti. She's very ill."

Abigail couldn't recall Veronique ever before mentioning a sister. Maybe it had just slipped her mind. "I'm sorry to hear that," she murmured in sympathy.

"She has no one to take care of her or her children," Veronique went on, visibly distressed. "I must go to her. I'm sorry to give you such short notice, but it was all very sudden."

Abigail felt her impatience flare once more. Why did she have to deal with this *now*, when she was running late? But she reined in her annoyance. It wasn't Veronique's fault. These things happened. "Of course. Take as much time off as you need," she said. "Do you have enough money for the plane fare? I can have Dr. Whittaker write you a check."

This only served to heighten Veronique's distress. "Thank you, that's very kind. But you've been too good to me as it is." Her eyes shimmered with unshed tears. "I will never forget you or your family."

Abigail was getting a bad feeling about all this. "You talk as though you're never coming back," she said.

"I'm sorry." Veronique lowered her head.

It took a moment to register that their housekeeper of ten years was actually leaving them for good. Immediately Abigail slipped into damage-control mode. "There's no need for drastic measures." She spoke firmly but reassuringly. "We'll just find someone to fill in for you while you're away. Don't worry; your job will be waiting for you when you get back."

Veronique shook her head again. The tiny gold hoops in her ears flashed in the morning light filtering in through the fanlight over the door. "I can't say when that will be." Her eyes pleaded with Abigail for understanding. "It would be best if you made other arrangements."

Abigail was momentarily at a loss. Veronique had been with them since Phoebe was a little girl. How would they manage without her? She made one last attempt to salvage the situation. "Can it wait until tonight, at least? We'll sort it all out then, I promise."

"I'm afraid not. My flight leaves at one o'clock," Veronique informed her with regret. "Dr. Whittaker has very kindly offered to drive me to the airport."

"Dr. Whittaker knows about this?" Abigail asked in surprise. It made sense now, his taking the day off from work and how evasive he'd been when she'd asked about it. But that didn't explain why she was only just now hearing about this. "Why didn't you come to me sooner?"

Veronique hesitated before replying, "You were busy. I didn't wish to disturb you."

Abigail felt a fresh surge of guilt. Once again, she'd been too self-absorbed to know what was going on in her own household. She stood there a moment with her coat half on, the other sleeve dangling limply at her side, until a glance out the window at the Town Car idling in the driveway reminded her that she had other, more pressing commitments at hand.

As she hugged Veronique good-bye, she worried about how Phoebe would take it. This would affect her most of all. Veronique had been like a second mother to her. Or was it the other way around—that Abigail was the second mother?

Her throat was tight when she drew back. "If you change your mind, the offer is still open. You can have your job back anytime."

Moments later she was sinking into the backseat of the Town Car, sparing but a single backward glance at the house now receding in the rear window—a house that had once been the center of her universe but which had lately come to seem like a satellite distantly orbiting around the planet that was her career. Six years ago, when she and Kent had purchased the estate, with its twenty-two overgrown acres and nineteenth-century manor house that had been in such disrepair it was practically falling down, what might have seemed a money pit to some had been, for them, a dream come true. A dream they'd shared. They'd spent nearly every spare moment working to restore it to its former glory, doing much of the labor themselves. Backbreaking work, to be sure, but looking back, she realized that those had been among the happiest days of her life. And now that Rose Hill was a showcase regularly featured in magazines, it was her family life that was falling into disrepair. But where were the tools to fix a faulty marriage? An unhappy child? Where did you begin when you had no blueprint to guide you? Her own childhood, riddled as it was with lies and delusions, had left her ill-equipped to deal with such matters.

It was easier to cope with crises at work. *That* she could handle because it didn't require any soul-searching; it was simply a matter of figuring out the best way, or finding the right person, to get the job done.

Cruising along the Henry Hudson Parkway, Abigail reflected on the long, twisting road that had brought her to this point. Eight years ago, her big break had come when a holiday gift basket of hers had been featured in that year's December issue of *Country Living*. Overnight, orders had begun pouring in, and she'd landed several high-profile accounts, including Ralph Lauren. Her catering business went from pulling in a modest five figures to netting a quarter of a million annually. A cookbook deal soon followed, and before she knew it she was on the circuit, traveling around the country, appearing at food festivals and trade shows and on local TV. The cookbook had sold out its modest first printing, but it wasn't until she began making regular appearances on *A.M. America*, where her relaxed-seeming approach made even the most elaborate cake or tart, or intimate dinner for ten, seem a cinch, that it began flying off the shelves. *Abigail Armstrong's Secrets of Successful Entertaining* had ended up selling nearly two hundred thousand copies.

Suddenly she was a celebrity, in demand by companies wanting to sign her as their spokesperson and besieged with requests for speaking engagements. The press couldn't get enough of her. She was featured in the *New York Times* and *People* magazine, *Ladies Home Journal* and *House Beautiful*. Her inspiring story about having grown up poor, raised by a single mother who'd died when Abigail was in her teens, became the stuff of legend. She never mentioned the Meriwhethers by name, referring to them only in passing as "the family my mother worked for." She talked instead about how, in high school, she'd peddled her homemade cakes from door to door to earn money, and how in later years, after moving up North, she'd worked as the personal chef of a wealthy family in Greenwich, Connecticut, before starting her own business selling quiches and tarts at farmers' markets. Fare that had proved so popular, she'd soon been making items to order, and before long catering dinner parties.

Just as she rarely mentioned the Meriwhethers in interviews, there were whole chunks of her years in Pine Bluff with her aunt and uncle that she either left out or glossed over. She didn't talk about the trips her uncle Ray had forced her to go on and what she'd had to endure while on those trips. She'd blocked out that period of her life as surely as if she'd taken an editor's red pencil and drawn a line through it, replacing it with a Horatio Alger tale that was the American Dream with whipped cream on top. The public gobbled it up.

Now there was one more goal to achieve: the branding of Abigail Armstrong. Once she was a household name, she'd be in a position to start her own magazine and, down the line, her own production company. She warmed at the prospect. Her husband and daughter, Veronique and her ailing sister, were far from her mind just then.

Her thoughts returned to Lila. All these years, what had spurred her on was the desire to prove she was the equal of Lila and her kind. Not just equal but *better than*. Now, with the death of Lila's husband following his very public disgrace, Abigail was struck by the irony of their situations being reversed: she the successful, secure one . . . and Lila alone and financially ruined. She wouldn't have wished such a ghastly fate on anyone, not even Lila—she wasn't heartless. But she wouldn't cry any tears, either.

At eight-forty-five on the dot, the Town Car was pulling up in front of her building at One Park Avenue. Stepping out onto the sidewalk, Abigail felt as if she were coming home. Her stride was brisk as she pushed her way through the revolving door into the lobby. She caught her reflection in the glass as it spun past: a confident woman in a mink-trimmed coat, her body toned from hours at the gym, her forty-year-old face showing none of the fine lines, in that brief glimpse, against which she did daily battle with an armory of expensive treatments and creams. She rode the elevator up to the twenty-fourth floor, where she passed through the reception area of Abigail Armstrong Incorporated—done up to look homey, with comfortable furniture upholstered in Ralph Lauren plaids and cozy little touches like the collection of vintage cookbooks and cookware displayed in the antique bookcase against one wall—before heading down the hall. No sooner had she stepped into the inner sanctum of her office than there was a knock on the door. Before she could answer, her executive director, Ellen Tsao, slipped inside.

Ellen wasn't normally given to unannounced visits. One of the reasons Abigail had hired her was because Ellen was good at taking care of the myriad details that Abigail didn't wish to be bothered with. Ellen was in charge of overseeing the catering end of the business, run out of a commercial kitchen in Long Island City, as well as facilitating production on both Abigail's books and the line of how-to trade paperbacks, penned by a carefully selected stable of writers under her name, that she packaged—*Housekeeping for Dummies*, it had been dubbed by one snarky reporter—and more recently the bed-and-bath line, which currently had them in long-distance, Third World hell. In short, it was Ellen's job to make the trains run on time.

A five-foot-two dynamo, the product of a Scottish mother and Chinese father, Ellen had freckles and dark brown hair that bore unmistakable traces of red. She usually had the unflappable air of a Zen master, but right now she looked worried. That alone was enough to make Abigail's stomach clench. She had never seen Ellen look this way.

"We have a problem," Ellen said in a dire tone, as in *Houston, we have a problem.*

Abigail slipped off her coat and tossed it over a chair. "Don't we always," she said, with a sigh.

"It's the factory," Ellen continued in the same ominous tone.

"What now?" There was always a problem with the factory. Nothing in Abigail's considerable range of experience had prepared her for the endless delays, miles of red tape, and countless palms to be greased in dealing with a Third World country. Never mind the intermediaries who were supposed to handle all that. But she could see from Ellen's expression that this wasn't about another broken piece of equipment or official snafu. It was something worse. Now she listened in horror as her executive director delivered the bad news.

"There was a fire last night. The place was gutted. I don't have all the details yet, but we do know . . ." Ellen swallowed hard, looking as if she were on the verge of tears. "There was at least one fatality."

3

LAS CRUCES, MEXICO

"When I go to America, I'll live in a nice house, with a garden. Eduardo says the rich *Americanos* he works for, they all have fruit trees—lemon, orange, grapefruit. They don't eat the fruit; it's just for show." Milagros shook her head at the peculiar gringo ways. Her brown eyes danced with anticipation, even so. She was counting the days until she could join her husband, Eduardo, in the Promised Land.

Her mother, Concepción, shifted her cloth bag from one hand to the other as they trudged along the road to the factory where, *gracias a Dios*, they both had jobs. The bag contained the extra sewing she took in. She would deliver it to Señor Perez, the boss of the factory, to take home to his wife, as she did every Monday morning.

"All that is very well," she said, "but first you have to get to America. And how do you propose to do that when you have no money?" Even if she were able to save enough, Concepción went on to point out, everyone knew that the *coyotes*, who charged unheard-of sums to smuggle you over the border, were thieves who would just as soon leave you to die out in the middle of nowhere.

The light in Milagros's eyes dimmed. "Eduardo would send more, if everything up North didn't cost so much. Two dollars for a loaf of bread!

And even when there's work, he gets half what the gringos make, and sometimes he doesn't get paid at all. Gringos have no scruples, Eduardo says." She sighed. Forgotten for the moment were the fruit trees and shiny car and nice house with a washing machine that she dreamed of owning one day.

Concepción's heart went out to Milagros, even as it selfishly wished for another year, another two years, with her only child. "Ay, *mi hija*. And this is where you wish my grandchildren to be brought up? In a country where they steal your money and leave fruit to rot on the ground?" Concepción hated the idea of her daughter's living so far away, in a country where she wouldn't be able to visit. It was selfish of her, she knew. Who was she to dictate to a married woman? But she'd lost so much already— her parents, a husband, and three babies that had never even drawn breath. When the time came, how could she bear to lose her only child, the daughter she had named Milagros for the miracle that she was?

"So now you're worrying about grandchildren not even born?" teased Milagros, her characteristically sunny nature reasserting itself. In her daughter's wide, sparkling eyes and the jaunty sway of her hips, Concepción saw no fears about the future, only the boundless optimism of youth and the unblemished love for a husband she had yet to become disillusioned with. Milagros and Eduardo had been wed only a short while before he'd been forced to seek work up North after losing his job. The time they'd spent living together as man and wife numbered in weeks and months, not years.

So, yes, Concepción worried. She worried about the inevitable disappointments and heartbreaks to come. What did her daughter, a mere nineteen, know of life? Of men who betrayed you and babies who died for no reason? How would she manage when she arrived in America to find that the streets weren't paved with gold and that the only way of gaining access to those fine houses was with a mop and pail? With that in mind, Concepción had been putting a little bit of money aside each week for Milagros, so that she would have a cushion, however small, against the hardships ahead. For however loath Concepción was to be parted from her, she was determined that her daughter be given every advantage when that day came. And someday, God willing, her grandchildren would have all the things that had been denied her own child: the chance to go to college, to earn a good wage.

Concepción perked up a little at the thought. She told herself that if she dreaded the prospect of being parted from her daughter, it was only natural. It had taken her this long to get used to Milagros's being somebody's wife. Even now, she wondered why this beautiful young woman, who'd had half the boys in Las Cruces bewitched with her slim hips and shiny black hair to her waist, her lively black eyes and cheekbones worthy of a Mayan princess, had chosen to marry Eduardo: a man ten years older than she, who in Concepción's view was no prize. But there was nothing sensible about love, she knew. Hadn't she defied her own parents in marrying Gustavo? Though she wished now that she had listened to them. Once the enchantment had worn off, she'd seen Gustavo for what he was: a man whose only love was for the bottle and who'd preferred the company of easy women and *borrachos* like himself to that of his wife. On the other hand, if she hadn't married him, she wouldn't have borne this child who was more precious to her than anything in the world.

She gave Milagros a small, apologetic smile. "*No escúchame, mi corazón.* I'm an old lady, sick at the thought of losing her only child."

"You? Old?" Milagros laughed. It was a well-known fact, she went on to say, that Concepción could have her pick of the unmarried men in the village. Why, just the other day, Señor Vargas, from the *abogado*'s office, where Milagros earned extra money cleaning nights and weekends, had been asking after Concepción.

Concepción dismissed the notion that the widowed Vargas had his eye on her, though she knew it to be true. He'd come calling a few times when Milagros wasn't around, blushing like a schoolboy and tripping over his words. She'd politely pretended not to notice, but she hadn't encouraged him, either. He was attractive enough, she supposed, and he made a good living as a lawyer, but he wanted a wife, and even though she was now free to marry—word having come, five years ago, of Gustavo's death, from drink, nearly two decades after having run off to Culiacán with another woman—she had no interest in doing so. At forty-three, Concepción was done with all that. What had sweet-talking men, with their mouths full of promises and hands offering nothing but empty pleasures, ever brought her but heartache? After Gustavo had run off, when Milagros was a baby, Concepción had still been young and naive enough to believe that she'd merely chosen badly the first time, that with another man it would be different. But she'd been wrong about that, too.

A year later, Angel had come into her life. Angel, with a face to match his name and a smile like the noonday sun, lighting up everything around him. He'd been new in town, a stranger passing through on his way north to look for work. He'd picked up a few days' labor at the tannery, where Concepción had been employed at the time, and it had been love at first sight. Angel extended his stay from one week to two, then indefinitely. They began seeing each other outside work. Angel never showed up at her house empty-handed, and though the gifts were modest—a handful of wildflowers he'd picked, a *dulce* or a loaf of bread from the *panaderia*, a small toy for Milagros—they might have been diamonds and rubies as far as she was concerned. It had been so long since she had even felt like a woman, much less a desirable one, that she blossomed like a cactus in the desert after a cloudburst. And how like gentle rain were his words to her parched soul!

"Someday, when I have enough money saved, you and Milagros will join me in America," he would say as he dandled the one-year-old Milagros on his knee, cooing to her, "You'd like that, wouldn't you? For me to be your *papi?*"

Milagros had gurgled happily in response, while Concepción had looked on with her heart full to bursting. Listening to him talk of their future together, and seeing how tender he was with her little girl, it had been easy to imagine a life with him. It wasn't just words, either. He'd seduced her with his hands and mouth as well, doing things to her in bed that made her blush now to remember them.

But in the end, he, too, had broken her heart. Ironically, she'd been on her way to church to ask Father Muñoz about the possibility of an annulment, which would have left her free to marry again, when she had run into her old friend Esteban, whom she hadn't seen in a while. They'd chatted for a bit, and she'd happened to mention that they'd hired a new fellow at the tannery, a man named Angel Menezes from El Salto. Other than that, she'd given no indication that she had any particular interest in Angel—she'd intended to wait until after she'd spoken to the priest before making their courtship known. But it was an idle remark for which she'd paid dearly . . . and which at the same time had saved her from certain humiliation, or worse. For it turned out that Esteban had a cousin in El Salto, and that was how Concepción had learned that Angel already had a wife and child back home.

Esteban's words had rendered her mute for a moment. She'd felt as if she had been struck by lightning, standing there in the village square under the cloudless blue sky. Then she'd become aware of a hand on her arm and Esteban's face had loomed close, peering at her with concern. *"Está bien?"* he'd inquired.

"Sí," she'd lied. "Just a cramp in my leg. There, it's gone." She'd forced a smile that felt hammered in place before wishing him a good day and continuing on her way.

It was a blow from which she'd never fully recovered.

Since then, the gateway to her heart had remained fiercely guarded. It wasn't just that she was protecting herself from being hurt; she'd also seen enough to know that marriage wasn't all it was cracked up to be. Vargas's intentions toward her might be serious, and he might have a big house and money in the bank, but those things didn't necessarily make for a good life. Concepción had spent the better part of the past two decades observing the marriages of those around her, noting how servile many of the wives were with their husbands, watching their inner light dim a little more with each passing year. Few of those wives were as happy as on their wedding day, and none enjoyed the freedom she did. Concepción regularly congratulated herself on having chosen a different path, even though it hadn't been easy raising a child on her own. It was only on occasion, late at night when she was feeling blue, or after the rare glass of spirits, that she wondered if, in barring the door to her heart, she was denying herself as much as she was the men whom she kept at arm's length.

Nonetheless, it secretly pleased her that she was still considered desirable. The glow of youth may have faded, but she hadn't lost her looks. No threads of gray had invaded her long, black hair, which she wore in a thick braid coiled into a bun at the nape of her neck, and except for a slight thickening about the waist, she was as slender as her daughter.

The dirt road they were making their way down was on the outskirts of town, the same one Concepción used to travel in taking her daughter to school, only yesterday, it seemed. It was lined with shanties, some with satellite dishes sprouting absurdly from their corrugated roofs, interspersed with the occasional open-air vendor, offering the usual assortment of boxed and tinned goods: rust-speckled cans of processed meat and fruit cocktail, Fanta soft drinks, packets of crackers and cookies. Chickens pecked in the dusty grass alongside the road, and two old men perched on folding chairs in front of a taco stand, playing checkers, nodded to her and Milagros in greeting as they passed. Concepción smiled at several women she knew who were on their way home from working the midnight shift at the factory, their slumped shoulders and glazed eyes telling an all-too-familiar tale of long hours without a single day of rest. Even on Sundays, you were expected to work, and though in theory you were free to take the day off, those who'd been foolhardy enough to do so had returned to work the following Monday to find that they'd been replaced.

The factory was a godsend to the community in many ways, Concepción thought. It provided much-needed jobs that, in some cases, made the difference between starving and being able to put food on the table. Yet she sometimes saw it as more of a curse than a blessing, one that had them yoked like oxen to a plow that was putting far more money into the pockets of the rich Americana who owned it than into theirs. Seeing it in the distance, a sprawling cinder-block building, its corrugated roof glowing like a griddle in the red glow of the rising sun, she found herself slowing, her load growing a little heavier with each step.

She prayed that today would bring relief from the *jefe*'s constant riding. For the past month, ever since production had been brought to a near standstill for several crucial weeks by a faulty piece of equipment, the boss, Señor Perez, and his foreman had been on the workers like fleas on a dog. They were given no breaks, except twice a day to use the lavatory. Lunchtime had been reduced to a mere fifteen minutes. And illness was no longer an excuse for missing a day's work. Last week, when Ana Saucedo had complained of pains in her arms and chest, she'd been sent home and told not to return.

But if there was grumbling among the ranks, no one had dared to voice a complaint. They were all too afraid of losing their jobs. It was hard work, yes, but it was work, and the wages were decent compared to the pittance they would have eked out elsewhere. And if the rich Americana who employed them, known to them simply as the Señora, had yet to show her face, her largesse was well-known. Weren't they reminded of it daily by Señor Perez? He seldom missed an opportunity to tout the efficiency of their modern equipment and their "unheard-of" wages, which he claimed were absurdly generous compared to those at other manufacturing plants. All this while he cracked the whip and docked the pay of anyone reckless enough to sneak off for a quick smoke or an unauthorized visit to the lavatory.

They arrived just as the air horn let out an ear-splitting blast, announcing the start of their shift. They were punching their time cards when Ida Morales, a plump older woman who made it her business to know everyone else's, sidled up to Milagros. "What, no baby yet? Someone should tell that husband of yours he'd do better filling his wife's belly than getting rich up North," she teased, patting Milagros's flat stomach.

"I'll tell him myself when I see him. Which will be soon," replied Milagros with a carefree toss of her head. Concepción knew, though, from the color blooming in her daughter's cheeks, that she'd taken the old busybody's comment to heart. No one was more eager for a child than Milagros. It was just one more thing she'd had to defer.

"The sooner, the better. A wife without a husband to look after her is a recipe for trouble. Look what happened to poor Maria Salazar." Ida clucked her tongue at the fate of the unfortunate Maria, who'd taken up with another man while her husband was up North looking for work. By the time he'd returned home, Maria had been heavy with a child that wasn't his. Some had said that it was a blessing she'd lost the baby at birth.

Concepción brushed past Ida, suddenly in a hurry to get to her station. Talk of losing babies always seemed to her a bad omen, and she protectively made the sign of the cross.

Bent over her sewing machine, she quickly settled into a rhythm. If the work had one advantage, it was that it was unchanging, hour upon hour of stitching the exact same seam on the exact same length of cloth, one after another, the ceaseless rhythm allowing her mind to drift. Even the noise of a hundred sewing machines whirring simultaneously at a deafening pitch, punctuated by the mechanical thump and whuff of the steam presses, became tolerable after a while. She ceased to notice, too, the closeness of the air, swarming with particles of dust and fabric, and the bits of thread stuck to every part of her. (When she was an old woman, long retired, Concepción didn't doubt, she'd still be plucking stray threads from her hair and clothing.)

It came as a jolt to her senses when the noontime whistle sounded. She and Milagros took their lunch outdoors with the others, seated cross-legged on the grass feasting on the *sopas* and *pollo tinga* that she'd brought from home. Just as greedily, Concepción drank in the open air, which, even with the sun high in the sky, was like a cool mountain breeze compared to the stifling atmosphere indoors. Before she knew it, it was time to head back to her station. Concepción rose with a sigh, brushing crumbs from her lap.

She was six hours into her ten-hour shift when she caught the first whiff of smoke. At first she took little notice of it. Probably just Candelaria Esperanza sneaking a cigarette, she thought. Candelaria had been reprimanded twice before for the same offense. But the odor quickly intensified, turning acrid, and when she looked up from her sewing, she saw that the air was hazy with smoke. Concepción dropped the cloth she was stitching and leaped to her feet in alarm.

Just then, she heard a shrill voice cry, "Fire!"

The factory erupted in chaos. Workers cried out in panic as each person scrambled for the nearest exit. Concepción strained to catch a glimpse of Milagros amid the thickening smoke, but all she could see was a writhing mass of limbs. She stumbled off in the direction of Milagros's station, coughing from the smoke that filled her lungs and calling out her daughter's name until she was hoarse.

Amid the frantic cries of those around her, she could hear the sound of fists hammering futilely against the exit doors. Ever since the step-up in production, the *jefe* had kept them chained shut during work hours to prevent slackers from slipping outside for unauthorized breaks. In all the confusion, no one had thought to unlock them.

Concepción was gripped with a paralyzing panic. They were all going to die, trapped in here like rats! But a part of her, the part that had refused to give up in the wake of all the tragedies she'd endured thus far—the deaths of both her parents, the stillborn babies before Milagros, and the betrayals by her husband and Angel—came to the fore now, commanding her sharply to remain calm. If she succumbed to panic, she might very well die. And she would be of no use to her daughter dead.

Without stopping to think, she snatched a half-sewn pillowcase from a basket on the floor. Holding it over her nose and mouth to filter out the worst of the smoke, she forged on in search of her daughter. But even with a layer of protection, each breath was a searing attack on her lungs. Worse was the panic clawing inside her like a caged beast. It was all she could do to stay focused on her goal of finding her daughter and, if need be, guiding her to safety. For Milagros, she would have headed straight into the flames of hell.

And hell was where she appeared to be right now. Amid the ever-thickening smoke, she could now see flames leaping, orange tongues licking greedily at the piled-up scraps of fabric around her. As she stumbled blindly about, her eyes burning and the tiny hairs on her arms crackling with the heat, the cool voice of reason in her head instructed her to get down on her hands and knees. Then she was crawling over the concrete floor, where the smoke wasn't quite so dense. She negotiated her way through a thicket of table legs and the iron pedestal of a steam press, as big around as a tree trunk. Dimly through the smoke, she could see the people gathered by the nearest exit, men and women bawling like frightened cattle as they kicked and pounded in an effort to batter down the door. A chair sailed by overhead, and she heard the shattering of glass as a window gave way. But the windows were all secured from the outside by wire mesh, so it was to no avail: The desperate move only succeeded in letting in a gust of air that sent the flames ever higher.

Concepción gasped for breath, fearing for her own life now. Long ago, after burying the last of her stillborn babies—a little boy—she had imagined that she would welcome death. At the time, she'd had nothing to live for but a husband who'd stagger home from bars only to impregnate her with yet another baby that wouldn't survive to draw its first breath. But that had been before Milagros. The day she'd become a mother to a perfect, healthy child, she'd begun to see death as the enemy. The one time Concepción had been seriously ill, after a cut on her foot had become badly infected, she'd had but one thought in her head: *Who will raise my daughter if I die?* And that alone had been enough to send her crawling from her sickbed, gritting her teeth from the pain as she'd hobbled off to see to her child.

Now she sent up a prayer—*Ayudame, Dios!*—that she would find Milagros among those clamoring at the exit. For it seemed that hope wasn't lost after all. Amid all the shouting, she heard the rattle of a chain, followed by the sound of metal scraping over concrete as the door was shoved open.

At that moment, she faded from consciousness. In some distant recess of her mind, she was dimly aware of a hand roughly grabbing her by the arm and dragging her across the floor. The next thing she knew, she was outside, lying on the ground, staring up at the sky and gulping in fresh air. Her eyes and lungs burned, and the flesh on one side of her body was scraped raw. All around her, people in similar states of dishevelment and confusion lay sprawled on the ash-strewn grass. Others wandered aimlessly about, their eyes staring whitely from soot-grimed faces as they watched the factory, and their livelihoods, go up in flames.

Concepción ran from one person to the next, crying hoarsely, "Have you seen my daughter?"

No one had seen Milagros.

No one knew where she was.

At last she came across the *jefe*, looking on in dull-eyed disbelief as the whole rear section of the building collapsed in a shower of sparks. Señor Perez didn't look so puffed up with self-importance now; he looked more like a wet rooster, with his oily hair in strings and sweat pasting his khaki shirt to his fat belly.

Concepción seized his arm. "Did everyone get out?"

Woodenly, he shook his head in response. *"Espero que sí."* I hope so. The words only heightened her fear. He didn't have to add that anyone still inside would have perished by now.

Still, she clung to the hope that Milagros was alive. Maybe she was wandering about in a daze somewhere nearby. Concepción prayed to God that it was so as she hurried off to continue her search.

But the God to whom she'd prayed wasn't the God of mercy, as it turned out. He was the same heartless God who had taken all her other children. Once the fire was under control and a head count taken, it was determined that all the workers had made it to safety. All but one. By the time the body was recovered, it was barely recognizable as human remains.

Immediately after the funeral, Concepción took to her bed. Her days became a dark tunnel through which she passed without any sense of time or purpose. Concerned neighbors brought food, for which she had no appetite. They lit candles, which burned unheeded. She neglected to bathe, and the glossy black hair in which she'd once taken pride grew dull and matted. One day, she happened to glance in the mirror and was startled to see a stranger looking back at her—a crazy lady, a *bruja*. She attempted to draw a comb through her hair, but it was too tangled. So she took a pair of scissors and hacked it all off instead.

Dios, why didn't you take me instead? she cried inwardly.

In time, the grieving mother began to wonder if the reason she was still alive was because God wasn't done with her yet. Perhaps He had a purpose for her. It wasn't until Señor Perez came to call one day that she discovered what that purpose was.

She looked at the *jefe* seated across from her, his hair slicked back and his fleshy fingers splayed over his knees. It might have been the heat causing him to perspire, but for some reason he appeared nervous, as though he found her presence unsettling. And why wouldn't he? She herself would have run from anyone who looked as she did. She was a wraith, alive only in the corporeal sense, her hair, what was left of it, sticking out in clumps and her sunken eyes like two nails pounded into her death mask of a face.

The *jefe* handed her an envelope. Inside was a thick sheaf of bills. "The Señora wants you to know how very sorry she is for your loss, as are we all." He was quick to add, "And though she is under no obligation to do so, she was good enough to insist on my giving you this, to cover the cost of the funeral as well as any lost wages."

For a long moment, Concepción merely sat there staring wordlessly at the envelope full of bills before she passed it back to Perez. "Tell her she can keep her money," she said with contempt. "I don't want it."

Perez appeared at a loss. He'd clearly never encountered anyone who'd refused such a large sum of money. "Now, *señora*, let's not be hasty. It may be some time before you're able to return to work, and in the meantime you'll need—"

"I don't need anything from you or the Señora," she cut him off.

He licked his lips nervously. "I assure you, the Señora is only acting out of the goodness of her heart," he insisted, addressing Concepción as if she were a willful child he was attempting to reason with. "But if you need more than this, perhaps I can—"

"This isn't about money."

Something in her expression must have told him it wasn't just the talk of a woman too unhinged by grief to know what was good for her, because she heard the wariness in his voice as he inquired, with false solicitude, "What *is* it you want, then?"

She looked him hard in the eye. "Justice."

Seeing that this unfortunate matter wasn't going to be settled easily, Perez began to sweat in earnest. "You don't know what you're saying.

You're beside yourself. Perhaps I should come back another time, when we can talk about this more sensibly."

He got up as if to leave but was instantly brought to a halt when she commanded sharply, "*Siéntate!* We will talk now." She might appear crazy, but in fact, she was thinking clearly for the first time in weeks. "You can start by explaining why there has been no investigation."

He shrugged, spreading his fat-fingered hands in a helpless gesture. "It was an accident. What more is there to say?"

As she leaned toward him, she had the small satisfaction of watching him shrink from her. "The fire might have been an accident, but my daughter's death was not. *You* are responsible, Perez." She jabbed a finger in his direction. "You and the Señora, whose praises you are so quick to sing. You had us penned in like cattle, with no regard for our welfare. No, even cattle are treated more humanely."

He sighed heavily, reaching into his pocket for a handkerchief with which to mop his perspiring brow. "Whatever mistakes were made, they weren't intentional," he hedged by way of apology. "What good would it do to bring more trouble when there has already been so much?"

"In other words, I should just keep my mouth shut," she said.

"No one is suggesting you don't have a right to be upset. But—"

"I would like the Señora to look me in the eye" she said scornfully, not letting him finish, "and tell me how sorry she is for my loss."

"Be reasonable," Perez cajoled. "She's a busy woman. You can't possibly expect her to come all this way. Besides, if you stir up trouble, you'll only make it worse for us all. Our people depend on the Señora to put food on the table. Think what a disaster it would be if you forced her to rebuild somewhere else."

But Concepción wasn't swayed. She knew he was only playing on her sympathies in order to protect himself. "In that case, you leave me no choice but to go to her." With a determination that gave her renewed strength, she rose to her feet, letting him know he was dismissed. "Now, if you'll excuse me, Señor Perez, I have business to attend to."

4

The woman was giving her the Look—the one that said, *Don't I know you from somewhere?* Recognition would click in next: *Oh, that's Lila DeVries.* Widow of the infamous Gordon DeVries. Lila had been down this road with so many prospective employers these past weeks that she was steeling herself against yet another rejection even as Ms. Scordato of the Sterling Employment Agency went through the motions of interviewing her.

"Do you have any computer experience, Mrs. DeVries?"

"Some," Lila answered. She had found that when gilding the lily, it was best not to elaborate. Especially when one's only computer experience was e-mail and online shopping.

"Are you familiar with Quicken and Excel?"

"No, but I've signed up for a course." *Attitude is everything*, she'd read in one of the self-help books she'd checked out of the library. "I should be up to speed before too long."

Ms. Scordato frowned at her application. "It says here that you type sixty words a minute. Would you say that's fairly accurate?" A large woman in her early fifties, with sculpted blond hair, she bore an uncanny resemblance to Lila's sixth grade teacher, Mrs. Lentini (who'd specialized in a particular form of sadism that had involved forcing the offending party to write their crime on the blackboard fifty times, in front of the other students). Lila stared at the brooch, the size of a door knocker, pinned to the lapel of the employment agency director's kelly-green jacket, which was complemented by—*accessorize! accessorize!*—the requisite Hermès knockoff scarf swirled around her neck. Ms. Scordato seemed impatient for this charade to be over so she could get on with her *real* business.

Lila felt herself reddening. "It's just a rough guess. I've never really timed myself."

Ms. Scordato peered at her dubiously over the rims of her reading glasses. "Any bookkeeping experience? Double-entry systems, et cetera?"

"Um . . . no, actually." Did balancing one's own checkbook count?

The woman studied her application, frowning, before she seized upon something that caused her to brighten unexpectedly.

"Ah, I see you worked for the Lincoln Center for the Performing Arts."

"Not *for* Lincoln Center exactly." Lila was careful to set her straight. "I chaired a committee that raised money for the jazz festival. Last year alone, we raised more than three hundred thousand—"

"So it was volunteer work?" The spark in Ms. Scordato's eyes went out.

Lila felt a familiar ooze in her armpits. She had thought it would be easier getting her foot in the door at an employment agency after having failed miserably with a number of companies and firms, but apparently she'd been wrong.

As she had been about so many other things.

"Yes, but you see . . ." She aimed for an upbeat tone—*attitude is everything!*—while keeping her smile epoxied in place. "I never really needed to . . . that is, my husband . . . well, I'm on my own now. It's just me and my son. So even though I know I'm getting a late start, I'm a hard worker, and I'm willing to learn."

She would have laughed at the irony if it weren't so painful: the idea that they'd hit rock bottom with Gordon being sentenced to prison. Now that ordeal seemed like relatively halcyon days compared to the hell she'd been through in the weeks since Gordon's death. Back then, at least she'd had the comfort of knowing her husband would return to her one day. Also, there had been the cushion of his IRA. Or so she'd thought until she'd been horrified to discover, in going through her husband's papers, that the account had been cleaned out: No doubt in some last-ditch attempt to spare himself a prison sentence. But what difference did it make how it had been spent? The money was gone. There would be no umbrella for the rainy day that had become a downpour. She'd had to give up the rented house in Hopewell, and there was no question of her being able to make next semester's tuition bill: Neal would have to drop out of college at the end of this semester. Partly his choice, yes—she'd urged him to apply for a student loan, but he'd insisted on looking for work instead so he could contribute financially. Still, that didn't make it any easier. In some ways, it made it worse: She now had to feel guilty for being dependent on her son, when it should have been the other way around, she taking care of him.

But even with whatever Neal could contribute, the fact was they'd be homeless if she didn't find a job, and soon. She'd known it wouldn't be easy, but she hadn't been prepared for just *how* hard it would be: a quest that had become a daily exercise in humiliation. In addition to being a social pariah, she was a modern-day Rip Van Winkle, it seemed, too late to the game, at forty-one, to compete with eager beavers half her age and three times as qualified.

She couldn't rely, either, on the few friends she had left. There had been no shortage of helpful suggestions, but no one had gone so far as to offer her a job. Not that she blamed them. The vast majority of her and Gordon's social circle had been made up of those either in the financial world or with ties to it, and as far as they were concerned, the widow of the late Gordon DeVries was radioactive. The only one who'd offered anything substantive had been Birdie Caldwell, whom Lila had known since Neal and Birdie's son, Wade, had been best friends at Buckley. Early on, Birdie had given her the name and number of a friend of hers in human resources at Bergdorf Goodman. Unfortunately, when it came time for the interview, Lila had learned that the only openings available were in sales, so she'd demurred. Most of the women she knew shopped at Bergdorf's, and she hadn't been able to bear the idea of waiting on those with whom she'd once socialized.

Now, after weeks of fruitless job hunting, she regretted that lost opportunity. Pride, like so many other things she'd once taken for granted, was a luxury she could no longer afford. And now time was running out. Birdie and her husband had generously allowed Lila the use of their Carnegie Hill apartment while they were in Europe, but they would be returning at the end of the month. If Lila didn't find other accommodations, she'd be literally out on the street. She couldn't ask her brother for any more money, though he'd gladly have lent it to her. Already she was so deeply in debt to Vaughn, she didn't know how she'd ever be able to repay him. Besides, he was far from wealthy. The only reason he had money socked away was because he spent so little on himself.

"Have you ever worked in retail?" Ms. Scordato inquired hopefully.

"The summer after my freshman year in college, I clerked in a dress shop," Lila informed her somewhat reluctantly. A job she'd gotten through her roommate, a girl named Irina Kolinsky whose family owned a string of upscale fashion boutiques in Atlanta. It wasn't on her résumé because she'd thought it would look pathetic that her one and only paying job had been a summer job back in college. It was so long ago, bar scanners hadn't even been invented; she'd worked an old-fashioned cash register, and that alone classified her as antediluvian.

Not surprisingly, Ms. Scordato appeared unimpressed. "Nothing since?"

Lila shook her head. "Not unless you count volunteer work. I was in charge of the annual book fair at Buckley during the years my son was in school there. It was a fair amount of responsibility, and believe me, I wasn't shy about rolling up my sleeves. So you see, even though I may not be experienced . . . well, *technically*, that is . . ." Lila faltered, taking note of the woman's tight expression. At once, she realized her error: She might have been boasting not that she was a hard worker but that her son had gone to an exclusive private school, one the likes of Ms. Scordato could ill afford.

It was no surprise when Ms. Scordato abruptly concluded the interview. "Unfortunately, Mrs. DeVries, I don't have anything for you at the moment. And even if you were to get up to speed . . ." She paused before continuing, more frankly, "Needless to say, any company that hired you would be subjecting itself to a fair bit of media scrutiny. Perhaps if you wait a bit for the smoke to clear, you'll find people more receptive."

Lila felt herself stiffen. Yet wasn't Ms. Scordato only stating what the politically correct drones of human resources, fearful of a lawsuit, were careful not to voice? That given the bad press she'd generate, she'd be more of a liability to them than an asset? Let's face it, to the ruined shareholders of Vertex, she was Marie Antoinette and Imelda Marcos rolled into one.

"I'm afraid I can't wait that long." Lila swallowed what was left of her pride to level with Mrs. Scordato. "I need a job *now*. Any job." She tried to sound highly motivated rather than hard up, but it was no good. She felt her eyes well with tears.

Ms. Scordato's expression softened somewhat. "I'll tell you what, why don't you brush up on your computer skills and check back with us in a few weeks? Maybe we'll have something for you then," she said a bit more kindly.

Lila rose to her feet and politely shook Ms. Scordato's hand, thanking her for her time. But she knew that if she were to come back in two weeks . . . a month . . . a year . . . the answer would be the same.

Making her way out of the office, she felt the full weight of her circumstances settle over her. She'd been so thoroughly stripped of her identity, there was almost nothing left of the old Lila. Amnesia would have been a welcome alternative at this point. At least there would have been no regrets, no memories. None of this creeping sense of failure.

In the subway on her way back to the Caldwells' apartment at Madison and 92nd, she was leafing idly through a back issue of *New York* magazine that someone had left on the seat next to her when she came across an ad for an escort service. She thought, *I wouldn't even cut it as a call girl.* Not that she wasn't desperate enough to try almost anything at this point, but who wanted a call girl with crow's-feet and stretch marks?

No, she thought, there was only one thing left to do. She'd put it off as long as she could, not so much out of pride as out of shame, but she'd run out of other options. She would have to make the call she'd been dreading, to the one person who had the power to make this happen for her . . . to turn Lila's life around with a mere snap of her fingers . . . and who, among all the people she knew, would be the least inclined to do so.

Abigail.

"That's why rich people have secretaries and unlisted numbers, to screen out all the so-called friends hitting them up for favors." Vaughn's voice crackled over the satellite phone. He was calling from somewhere in Namibia, where he was filming the movements of a herd of rare desert elephant.

"I wouldn't be doing this if I weren't desperate," she told him. "Anyway, it's not as if I'm looking for a handout."

"Look, Sis, I know you see this as the last chopper out of 'Nam, but don't you think Abby might be a tad, shall we say, bitter?"

It wasn't just speculation on her brother's part: He and Abigail had corresponded for years. Vaughn had never shared the contents of those letters with Lila, but she didn't need him to tell her that Abigail had every reason to be bitter.

"You're right. I owe her an apology," she was quick to admit. "And the way I see it, this is my chance to do what I should have done years ago." She was well aware of how disingenuous that must sound, given the fact that, as far as Vaughn knew, she hadn't made the slightest attempt to get in touch with Abigail before this. He didn't know about all the letters she'd started and never finished. But what did it matter now? It was so long ago, and the fact was, she'd never sent a single one of those letters— they'd only ended up crumpled in her wastebasket. Bottom line, Lila had abandoned Abigail when the chips were down. And now their situations were reversed. So, yes, she supposed any attempt to make amends would come across as self-serving, but that was a risk she was going to have to take. What other choice did she have?

"Anyway, this could be good for Abby, too," she went on with a conviction that sounded forced even to her own ears. "I may not be your typical applicant, but I *do* have something to offer. It doesn't have to be a one-way street."

"That's one way of looking at it, I suppose," he replied dubiously. "But just put yourself in Abby's shoes. You don't hear from your best friend in more than twenty years, and then suddenly she pops up out of the blue, hat in hand, to tell you how sorry she is for ruining your life. Oh, and by the way, you wouldn't happen to have a job for her?"

Vaughn, as usual, saw straight through Lila. It was one of the things she loved most about her brother: He knew her better than anyone, and he always gave it to her straight. However supportive he'd been throughout her ordeal, he'd never babied her or minced words. When it had become apparent to him that Gordon was going down, he'd cautioned her to get her ducks lined up. Advice that would have stood her in good stead if her ducks hadn't already flown south by then. But though normally she appreciated his honesty, right now it was tough to hear.

She heaved a sigh. "I see your point. But aren't you exaggerating just a little? I didn't exactly ruin Abby's life. It was Mother who fired Rosie; I was just an innocent bystander. Okay, I admit I handled it badly, but that doesn't make me a terrible person, does it? I was just a dumb kid."

"I won't argue that," he said with brotherly affection. "And, no, you weren't the only one to blame. Whenever I think about that whole disgusting episode, it makes me sick to my stomach. Whatever Rosie did or didn't do—and, believe me, I have my doubts about the official version—Abby shouldn't have had to suffer for it."

"It wasn't just Mother. It was Dad, too," Lila reminded him. "He could've done something about it."

"The reason he didn't was because it would have been the same as admitting that Mother was too wasted to know what the fuck she was talking about," Vaughn replied with disgust.

It wasn't just that their mother had been a hopeless drunk. Vaughn blamed their dad for being too weak to see the situation for what it had been and to grapple with it head-on. Instead, he'd simply bailed out. Worse, he'd left their mother to marry another woman—his secretary, who had been nearly twenty years his junior, and who, it turned out, had only been after him for his money. But that wasn't the only reason Vaughn was bitter. In their father's absence, the responsibility of caring for their increasingly dependent mother had fallen onto Vaughn's and Lila's shoulders. There had been no one else; none of the housekeepers hired to replace Rosie had lasted more than a few months. Once they'd taken stock of the situation, they'd hightailed it out of there. Who in their right mind wouldn't have? Even Vaughn had cut out to join the Peace Corps as soon as he'd turned eighteen, leaving Lila in charge of running the household from afar while pursuing her studies at Vanderbilt.

Looking back, she saw Rosalie's dismissal as the catalyst for her family's long, slow disintegration. And yet the real reason for it remained a mystery to this day. Even if Rosalie had stolen the necklace, which was unlikely, given that it would have been totally out of character, what use would she have had for it? It wasn't as if she'd needed the money. Lila's parents had been generous in that regard; they'd even offered to pay for Abigail's college education. But if Rosie had been innocent, how had the necklace ended up among her things? Had Lila's mother had something to do with it, as Abigail had hinted darkly at the time? And if so, why? There would have been no earthly reason for her mother to want to get rid of someone she'd depended on so heavily. None of it made any sense.

"I wish I could go back in time," Lila said with a sigh of regret. "I'd have done it all differently, knowing what I know now." It wasn't just the guilt that had plagued her all these years. Her recent hardships had given her a new appreciation of what it must have been like for Abigail and her mother, cast out of the only home they'd known.

"Look," Vaughn said. "If it's money you need, I can have my bank wire some into your account. Seriously, Sis, I *want* you to have it. This is no time to go all stubborn on me."

They'd been through this before, but though the offer was tempting, Lila remained firm. She might have sacrificed her pride, but she still had some common decency left. It simply wouldn't be fair to her brother. He might need that money for a rainy day of his own. "Thanks, but no. You've done too much already."

"The money's just sitting there," he insisted. "Really, it's no big deal."

"Well, it is to *me*," she told him. "Don't think I'm not appreciative, because I am, more than you know. But I'm a big girl. I can't be sponging off my brother the rest of my life. I have to start fending for myself at some point." Brave words that did nothing to ease her fears.

"I wish I could offer you a place to stay, at least. But I'm sort of between places at the moment."

Vaughn was perennially "between places." Sometimes she thought he'd be happiest living out of a tent, and not just when he was on the road, filming in some godforsaken locale. In another life, her brother must have been a hermit crab.

"Don't worry, I'll figure something out," she told him.

But a week later, she was no closer to a solution. She'd left several messages at Abigail's office, to no avail. Under ordinary circumstances, Lila would have let it go at that—honestly, could she blame Abigail for not returning her calls?—except that she was rapidly running out of road. Birdie and Whit Caldwell were due back from Europe in a little over two weeks. Lila would have to be out by then.

In desperation, she put another call in to Abigail. This time, she was placed on hold. It seemed an answer to her prayers when moments later, Abigail's voice came on the line—richly modulated, with just a trace of a southern accent, and so honed by years of media exposure, it was barely recognizable as that of Lila's childhood friend. "Lila. My goodness, this is a surprise." As if it weren't Lila's fourth attempt to reach her. "It's been a long time, hasn't it?"

Lila had been braced for a cool reception, and now she felt some of the tension drain out of her. From Abigail's breezy tone, she might have been any old friend checking in after a long absence. "I've been meaning to call," she said somewhat sheepishly. "But you know how it is, one thing after another. The years go by so quickly."

There was a low chuckle at the other end. "Don't I know it! I've been pretty busy myself."

"No kidding. I've seen you on TV. Congratulations, by the way. I always knew you'd be a success." Even as a kid, Abigail had had that drive. Lila recalled the scrapbook Abigail used to keep. It had been filled with pictures cut from magazines of the fantasy life she'd dreamed of. Beautiful clothes . . . fancy homes . . . luxury cars . . . red-carpet events.

"And you?"

Lila hesitated before replying with chagrin, "I'm sure you've heard." Who hadn't? Her life was an open book at this point.

Abigail murmured the requisite condolences. "Yes. I'm sorry about your husband. Such a tragedy, and so young. It must have been hard for you."

"Thank you. Yes, it's been difficult." Lila didn't elaborate. Her grief was still too raw. And she couldn't lose sight of her purpose, which certainly wasn't to pour her heart out to Abigail, at least not over the phone.

Moving right along, Abigail inquired, "And your parents, how are they?"

Lila felt herself start to tense up again, but she didn't detect any animosity in Abigail's voice. "Both passed away," she replied. "Mother died of cancer about five years ago and Dad of a heart attack a couple of years after."

"Sorry to hear it." All at once, Abigail's tone turned businesslike. "So. What can I do for you?"

"Actually, I was hoping we could meet for coffee," Lila answered tentatively.

"Hmmm . . . let's see." Abigail paused as if to consult her BlackBerry. "I'm afraid I'm all booked up through the end of the month." Lila's heart sank, and she was already wracking her brain for an alternative plan, when Abigail suggested, "Why don't you come out to my place this weekend? I know it's a bit of a schlep, but I'm afraid it's the only time I have available. Say, two o'clock on Sunday?"

Relief poured through Lila. "Sounds good. Let me check my calendar." Seated at the antique escritoire in Birdie Caldwell's study, she let a moment or two elapse while she stared emptily at Birdie's red leather address book from Smythson before chirping, "Yes, that's fine. Sunday it is." It wouldn't do to appear too eager. Abigail might get a whiff of her desperation.

She carefully copied down the directions. By the time she hung up, she felt more hopeful than she'd felt in weeks. But she cautioned herself not to read too much into the invitation. She was far from an offer of employment.

The following Sunday, heading north along the Henry Hudson Parkway in the ten-year-old Ford Taurus she'd gotten off a used-car lot, a trade-in for her BMW, Lila wondered nervously what was in store for today. Abigail had been nice enough over the phone, sure, but the real proof would be in the reception Lila got when she arrived at the house. And something told her they weren't going to be reminiscing about old times over coffee and cake. The woman with whom she'd spoken, the sleek, successful entrepreneur seen on magazine and book covers, bore little resemblance to the funny, irreverent, unsophisticated girl Lila had known. The girl with whom she'd shared endless confidences and with whom she'd danced in her room, lip-synching the tunes of Pat Benatar and Kim Carnes, using a hairbrush as a microphone. They used to giggle themselves silly, and if one of them was blue, the other would always manage to cheer her up. Like the time, in the seventh grade. when Abigail had been upset because she hadn't been asked to a party being thrown by a girl in her class. "We'll have our own, then," Lila had said. And so they had, Lila and Vaughn inviting all of their friends and Rosalie supplying the refreshments. Abigail had declared afterward that it had been the best party ever.

Lila hoped it wasn't too late to rekindle some of that goodwill.

Inching her way toward the first of the toll booths, just beyond the George Washington Bridge, Lila observed that the trees along the parkway were nearly bare. Somehow autumn had come and gone with her scarcely noticing. Now she watched with a kind of wonder as a handful of the remaining leaves were torn loose from their branches by a gust of wind and sent scuttling through the air like a flock of scattered birds. She felt like someone emerging outdoors for the first time after a lengthy and debilitating illness.

It was late November, and even with the windows rolled up all the way, Lila could feel the chill of the approaching winter. Inside the Taurus, it was cold enough to keep a carton of ice cream from melting. Stupidly, she hadn't thought to test the heater before driving the car off the lot. She'd bought it back in May, when the weather had been warmer, and to be fair, she'd had far bigger concerns at the time. Now, without the funds to get it fixed, a functioning car heater was just another item on the long list of things she'd learned to do without.

It amazed her, the things she'd once taken for granted—designer clothes, dining at four-star restaurants, limousines to ferry her to various venues in the city. All of which belonged to another era. The collapse of Vertex might have been the fall of the Roman Empire as far as she was concerned. Her entire world had crumbled in its wake. The first wave had taken out her personal trainer, masseuse, and four-hundred-dollar haircuts, not to mention those romantic weekends she and Gordon used to enjoy at the Point and Twin Farms, where a single night cost more than an entire month's rent on the house she'd been forced to relinquish. But that had been only the first notch in tightening her belt. Hardship, she now knew, wasn't having to wear last season's fashions or riding the subway instead of taking taxis. It was wondering how you were going to survive from one day to the next. And Neal . . .

She couldn't think about her son without choking up. He'd been stoic about having to drop out of school, insisting it was what he wanted, but she knew it was hard for him.

How like Gordon he was! Her husband, until the very end, had always striven to care for his family, to shield them from the buffets of any ill wind—even, as it turned out, at a cost that had brought them all down. Now it was Neal assuring her, in the midst of his own grief, "It's no big deal, Mom. Seriously. I don't want you to have to go through this alone. I can always go back to school when you even out a bit. Anyway, it's not the end of the world if I take a year off."

Lila wasn't fooled. She hadn't missed the dark circles under his eyes or the worry lines on his forehead. "Honey, I know it's hard, but it won't be this way forever." She reached out to put a hand on his arm, to console him, but instead of the warm pliancy of flesh as familiar to her as her own, she met with stone. Neal was so tense, it might have been the arm of a statue she was touching.

She didn't need the psychologist her son had been seeing to tell her that Neal was bottled up—so bottled up, he was on the verge of imploding. Worse, there was little she could do to help. For wasn't she partly to blame? She should have recognized the warning signs with Gordon; she never should've left him alone that day. If she had, he might still be alive, and Neal . . . well, Neal wouldn't have had to witness what no child ever should.

With any luck, time would heal those wounds. The more immediate concern was figuring out how they were going to survive, starting with a place to live. Manhattan, with its obscene rents, was out of the question, but she might be able to find something affordable that was within commuting distance, say in Brooklyn or Queens. The only thing she knew for sure was that, if she didn't find a job soon, they'd be living out of her car.

An hour later, she was pulling into Stone Harbor. Cruising along the main drag, she was struck by how little it had changed in the eight or nine years since she'd last visited, on a weekend antiquing trip with Gordon. The quaint turn-of-the-century village lay just outside easy commuting distance to the city, which was no doubt the reason its Victorian homes and public works dating back to the WPA era hadn't been torn down years ago in the name of progress. Except for a scattering of tony boutiques and gift shops where old mom-and-pop establishments had been, it was pretty much as she remembered.

Driving past the bed-and-breakfast she and Gordon had stayed in, a two-story gingerbread house perched on the riverbank, with a wide deck that jutted out over the water, she indulged in a memory of the two of them making love by firelight, fueled by the complimentary bottle of champagne that had come with the room—a bittersweet reminder of the life they'd once shared, like the taste of something delicious lingering on the tongue after the last bite has been swallowed.

Once she'd passed through town, the landscape became more rural. Lila wound her way down country roads lined with trees that formed one long, continuous tunnel, broken only by the occasional field. She didn't see many houses; most were tucked back from the road. This was gentleman-farmer country, province of the landed gentry and wealthy second-home owners. Gated entrances were as far as you got unless you were there by invitation.

At last, she came to a graveled drive whose location matched the one in the directions Abigail had given her. There was no sign, but the gate stood open, as if in anticipation of her arrival. She turned down it without bothering to announce her presence into the intercom.

She'd seen magazine spreads of Abigail's estate, but nothing had prepared her for the sight of it firsthand. On either side of the meandering drive were gently sloping pastures so bucolic she expected to see sheep and horses grazing. She drove past a vegetable garden the size of a truck farm's, mulched over for the winter, with an orchard beyond that rambled for what seemed like acres. Just past it was a duck pond, with a white lattice gazebo gracing its banks in which a wicker table and four chairs sat in readiness, as if for an impromptu tea or picnic. It seemed almost too perfect to be real, like the set of a Merchant and Ivory movie. An impression that was only heightened by the house when it finally came into view: an impeccably restored colonial revival, its white clapboard and blue trim gleaming as if newly painted. Smoke curled invitingly from the chimney, and on the grass out front there was scarcely a fallen leaf or twig in sight.

Moments later, Lila was standing on the porch, ringing the doorbell. Her heart was in her throat and her mouth dry, despite the entire liter of water she'd drunk in the car on the way over. She couldn't remember the last time she'd felt this nervous. Maybe on her wedding day, but that had been joyful anticipation, not the sweaty palpitations she was experiencing now.

She was momentarily thrown off guard when Abigail answered the door herself. *It must be the housekeeper's day off,* she thought. Abigail, for some reason, seemed equally surprised to see her.

"Lila?" There was an awkward moment in which Abigail stared at her, as if at a stranger, before she broke into a smile that didn't quite reach her eyes. "Well, come on in. You look half frozen."

Lila hadn't realized she was shivering. "It's good to see you, Abby." She gave Abigail a light kiss on the cheek as she was ushered inside, feeling her stiffen a bit before she drew back.

Lila stepped into a sunlit vestibule. A vase of the most exquisite purple gladiolas sat atop an Arts and Crafts chest, over which hung a nineteenth-century portrait of a severe-faced woman in a mutton-sleeved dress, with her hair pulled back in a bun. The painted floor beneath the rug had a border stenciled around it resembling a leafy garland. Farther down the hallway she caught the buttery gleam of polished woodwork and the graceful curve of a staircase.

"How was the drive?" Abigail inquired as she took her coat.

"Not bad. There wasn't much traffic."

"You're probably wondering why anyone who works in the city would want to live all the way out here," Abigail commented, with a rueful smile. "But really, the commute's not bad. If I leave early enough, I can usually make it in just over an hour, door to door."

"I can see why you love it here. It's so peaceful," Lila remarked.

"It is, isn't it?" Lila saw a closed, unreadable look flit across Abigail's face as she turned to lead the way down the hall, and wondered what it meant. "Can I get you some coffee or tea?"

"Tea would be nice." In the living room, Lila settled onto the long sofa facing the fireplace, where a fire was burning, its pleasant crackling the only sound other than the muffled tread of Abigail's footsteps as she retreated. Lila glanced around the room, which was tastefully decorated in muted shades of yellow and blue, with bold prints as accents. A large mirror inside a painted frame reflected the cozy seating arrangement and artfully placed Early American antiques. Sunshine poured in through a bank of windows looking out on the pool and patio beyond. Abigail certainly had good taste, she thought. But despite its coziness, she felt strangely uncomfortable. Though furnished in another style, there were echoes of the house in which Lila had grown up. It was almost eerie, like going back in time.

Abigail returned a short while later with a tea tray and a plate of what looked to be freshly baked scones.

"Pear-ginger," Abigail said when she noticed Lila eyeing them. "Made with pears from my own trees."

"They look delicious." Lila helped herself to a scone after Abigail had poured her tea. She was too nervous to eat, but she nibbled on it anyway, to be polite. "Thanks for agreeing to see me on such short notice."

"Not at all. What are old friends for?"

Lila thought she detected a note of irony in Abigail's voice, but it might have been her imagination. Watching Abigail settle into the wingback chair across from her, Lila was struck by how much lovelier she was in person than on TV. She'd grown into the lanky frame she'd so despaired of as a teenager, blossoming into the elegant, streamlined woman seated before Lila now—a woman to whom the years had been more than kind; Abigail appeared ageless. Anyone who didn't know her history would have found it hard to believe that she hadn't always led a privileged life. She appeared the essence of refinement while at the same time achieving the parlor trick of coming across as down-to-earth and approachable. Her makeup was so expertly done it didn't look as if she was wearing any at all, and her glossy, shoulder-length hair was cut in a way that looked at once utterly natural and unattainably chic. In her tailored slacks and a wide-lapelled cream silk blouse, a cashmere cardigan the color of cinnamon butter draped over her shoulders, she brought to mind Katharine Hepburn in *The Philadelphia Story*.

"Still, it was nice of you to make time on a Sunday," Lila said.

"Don't mention it. My husband and daughter went sailing, so I have the afternoon off." Abigail reached down to give the English sheepdog that had wandered in to plop at her feet, like a furry ottoman, an idle scratch between the ears. "I'm sorry you won't get to meet them. They won't be back until later this afternoon."

"Maybe another time?" Secretly Lila was relieved. She hadn't come all this way to make polite chitchat with strangers. There was a moment of strained silence before she said softly, "It really is good to see you, Abby. It's been a long time."

Abigail acknowledged this with a pensive nod. "Too long." There was a slight but discernible edge in her voice. "I must say, you're looking remarkably well under the circumstances."

"Sackcloth and ashes aren't exactly my style," Lila replied in a lightly ironic tone. She'd taken care getting dressed for this meeting; she'd even splurged on having her hair done, though not with her regular stylist but at Supercuts. "Besides, it's amazing how far a designer label and a little lipstick will carry you." Not that she didn't have her moments. Days when she burst into tears at the slightest provocation. Nights, lying awake in bed, when she vacillated between thinking that if Gordon were still alive she'd save him the trouble of killing himself and wondering how she was going to survive without him. Sometimes she would be up until dawn and then be too exhausted to drag herself out of bed until later in the day. But she'd never told that to anyone, not even Vaughn.

Abigail smiled. "I see you haven't lost your sense of humor."

"It comes in handy when you're swallowing your pride."

Abigail studied her a moment, her expression coolly assessing. "So, what is it you wanted to see me about?"

Lila felt her stomach clench, as it used to in gym class when she'd been standing on the high dive, staring down at the water that had seemed a million miles away. But she'd always forced herself to take the plunge, and she didn't back away from it now. "I . . . well, the thing is . . ." She smiled nervously, saying into the napkin she was smoothing over her lap, "I suddenly find myself in need of employment." She struck a light tone, not wanting to appear desperate. "And I thought . . . well, I *hoped* . . . that in a big outfit like yours, there might be a place for someone with my, um, talents. An entry-level position, anything at all— I'm willing to learn. I've done lots of charity work, so believe me, I know how to work the phones, and I'm taking a class to brush up on my computer skills."

She looked up to find Abigail staring at her. "Why me?" she asked, wearing a small, perplexed frown. "You must have lots of other friends."

"None who are in a position to hire me."

"And what makes you think *I'd* want to?"

Lila realized, with a sinking sense of despair, that it had been a mistake to come here. Even so, she made one last attempt to appeal to

Abigail in the name of friendship. "I know I don't have any right to expect it, after what happened with your mom." She'd been waiting until the time was right to apologize, but she could see from the look on Abigail's face that there would never be a good time. "I should have come to you years ago. Or at least written. There's no excuse, so I won't bother giving one. I just want you to know how sorry I am. I let you down when you needed me most, and I've felt terrible about it ever since."

"So now it's forgiveness you're after?" Each word was like an ice cube dropping into a chilled glass.

"I don't blame you for being angry at me."

Abigail gave a scornful laugh. "Angry? I'm not angry. That would imply I cared enough to be angry."

Lila felt as if she'd been slapped. With that single sentence, she'd been put in her place more surely than if Abigail had hurled accusations at her. She realized there was no point in sticking around. She was a stranger to Abigail. And Abigail, *this* Abigail, was a stranger to her.

Lila set her cup and saucer down on the coffee table and rose stiffly to her feet. "In that case, I won't waste any more of your time. Thank you for the tea. I'll see myself out."

She was turning to go when Abigail called after her, "Wait." Lila swiveled to face her. "I might have something. It's not the kind of work that you're used to," she went on in a hurried tone, as if rushing to get the words out before she could change her mind. "In fact, you'd probably consider it a step down. But I'm afraid it's the only thing I have at the moment."

Lila regarded her uncertainly for a moment before giving a wary smile. "Like I said, I'm willing to learn. Though I'll be honest with you, my typing needs some brushing up."

"You won't have to worry about that. I don't need another secretary."

"Then what—?"

"The opening is for a housekeeper."

Housekeeper? At first, Lila wasn't sure she'd heard correctly.

"It's a live-in position. Five hundred a month, plus meals, and your own separate quarters over the garage," Abigail went on, ticking off all the perks. "Thursdays and Sundays off and half days on Saturdays."

For a moment, Lila was too stunned to reply. She felt as if she'd been punched in the gut. Was Abigail looking to punish her, or was this some twisted form of charity?

"It . . . it wasn't quite what I was expecting," she managed to stammer at last. "Can I think about it?"

"Of course, but don't take too long. I need someone right away, and I have a long list of applicants."

It wasn't until Lila was being ushered out the door that the shock finally wore off. She paused on the threshold, turning to face Abigail. "Why are you doing this?"

Abigail regarded Lila a moment, her eyes dark and unreadable, before replying cryptically, "Let's just say it's out of friendship."

But what kind of friendship was it, Lila wondered, that would have her mopping Abigail's floors and washing her dirty underwear? "I'll let you know tomorrow," she said in a dull voice that seemed to come from somewhere outside her. Every instinct urged her to walk away before it was too late, but she didn't have that luxury. It wasn't just her. She had Neal to think of.

"Call me at my office. Say, ten o'clock." Abigail gave Lila a business card with the number for her private line. Her trademark smile was firmly in place as she shook Lila's hand. "Whatever you decide, I wish you the best. No hard feelings."

No hard feelings? What a joke. Abigail had no sooner shut the door than she collapsed against it, trembling all over as if wracked with fever. The truth was, she wanted to see Lila suffer. Just as Abigail and her mother had suffered as a result of the Meriwhethers' coldhearted disregard. If she'd felt any flicker of affection toward her childhood friend just now, Abigail likened it to the ghost sensation of an amputated limb.

As for her offering Lila the job left open by Veronique's ill-timed departure, it had been pure impulse. Curious as to Lila's reason for wanting to see her, Abigail had intended to do no more than hear her out, if only for the satisfaction of seeing her humbled. Now she wondered what could have possessed her. What did she hope to gain? Certainly not a viable replacement for Veronique. Lila wasn't exactly cut out for domestic work. She probably hadn't made her own bed since college. And it wasn't as if she needed to be brought down a peg or two. Life had already taken care of that. Thanks to her husband, she now knew what it was like to be scorned and humiliated, to feel as if you hadn't a friend in the world.

The old bitterness rose in Abigail once more. Where had Lila been when it had been Abigail in need? No one in the family except Vaughn had even sent condolences when Rosalie had died. The weight of those memories pressed down on her until Abigail felt her legs give way. She slid slowly to the floor, where she sat hugging her knees, shivering uncontrollably. It occurred to her that, in re-creating herself, she'd failed in one crucial respect. She hadn't been able to excise her anger, which had become rooted over time and was now a part of her, like an inoperable tumor. Maybe this was what she needed in order to be free of it: the chance to reenact the past, this time with the tables turned—*she* the one in a position of authority and Lila at her mercy.

The beauty of it was that she hadn't even sought it out. The opportunity had landed like a fat plum in her lap. What was it if not poetic justice?

She didn't doubt that Lila would accept her offer. Abigail was on intimate terms with that kind of desperation. She could easily picture the scenario: the friends who'd deserted Lila in droves, the potential employers who'd shied away due to the threat of bad press, the ever-shrinking reserves of money that had left the proverbial wolf not just at her door but gnawing its way through it. So, yes, Lila would do whatever it took to survive. Just as Abigail had all those years ago, after her exile to Pine Bluff.

An old memory surfaced. Uncle Ray bending over her, his face inches from hers, the smell of the mints he sucked on to help him quit smoking so strong she could almost taste it—a smell she'd come to loathe. She heard him rasp, in his gravelly smoker's voice, "The way I see it, girlie, you're lucky to have us looking out for you, your mama being so sick and all." She could feel his breath tickling her ear. "If it weren't for me and your aunt Phyllis, you'd be shit out of luck. Now, ain't that right?"

She'd feared and despised her uncle from the very first moment she'd laid eyes on him. No sooner had they walked in through the door than he was sizing her and her mother up with a long, slow look that had held a world of contempt, as if they weren't his wife's kin but just another pair of mouths to feed. And in the weeks that followed, he did nothing to dispel that negative first impression. Though her aunt and uncle were fairly affluent by Pine Bluff standards, their modest ranch house a palace compared to the one-room shack Uncle Ray had grown up in, he was as coarse and crude as his moonshine-drinking pappy before him (about whom they'd had to listen to stories ad nauseam). Out in the world, Uncle Ray played the part of all-around good guy: the dependable husband who went off to work each morning in a suit and tie, to the offices of Farmer's Mutual, where he was chief claims adjustor; the good neighbor who kept his lawn trimmed and who was quick with a smile and a handshake or the offer of a cold beer. But at home, he was a foul-mouthed tyrant, barking orders at Rosalie and Abby when he wasn't yelling at his wife, as if they existed for the sole purpose of seeing to his every need. At the same time, he seldom missed an opportunity to remind them of the debt *they* owed him. He'd taken them in when no one else would, he'd say. Where would they be if not for his generosity?

Aunt Phyllis, a weak, washed-out woman, was too intimidated to stand up to him. It must have been somewhat of a relief to her that, with the arrival of her sister and niece, she was no longer the sole person at the receiving end of her husband's abuse. The only true respites the women enjoyed were when Uncle Ray went away on overnight trips, to assess the damage caused by some catastrophe in a neighboring county, as he frequently had to do in his line of work.

The first time he asked Abigail to accompany him on one of those trips, she did her best to wriggle out of it. But Uncle Ray insisted that he needed her to spell him on the driving—she had her driver's license by then—so she had no choice but to go along. If Aunt Phyllis saw through his ruse, she was too cowed to offer any objection. And Abigail's mother was so ill by then that every ounce of her energy was devoted to simply getting through each day. Looking back, Abigail could see that Uncle Ray had timed it perfectly.

She should have had some inkling of what was in store when he booked a double room at the motel that night, instead of two singles. But she was so naive, her only sexual experience to date that one time with Vaughn—which by then had come to seem as if it had taken place in another lifetime—that she didn't see the handwriting on the wall.

Uncle Ray didn't try anything that first trip. He lay in wait until the next time he coerced her into going out of town with him. On that occasion, she was half asleep in bed, lights out, when she felt him crawl in next to her. Even now, more than twenty years later, she physically recoiled at the memory: Uncle Ray, his bony knees poking her under the covers, a scrawny arm hooked about her middle, while she lay there, too frozen with shock to move so much as a muscle. A slightly built man with a head too large for his body and a rattle in his lungs from having smoked two packs a day from the time he was a teenager, he couldn't have outweighed Abigail by much, but he was wiry and strong as an old cockfighting rooster. Had she put up a struggle, there was no question as to who would have won.

Nothing happened that night. He gave her time to get used to the idea, as if she were supposed to think it was the most natural thing in the world for a grown man to get into bed with his sixteen-year-old niece. He didn't make his move until the following night. They'd spent the day wading through the wreckage caused by a flood in nearby Tull's

River, which had left many of Farmer's Mutual's policyholders either homeless or under several feet of water, and by the time she hit the sack, Abigail, who hadn't slept more than a wink the night before, was so tired she was scarcely able to keep her eyes open. She was sound asleep when she woke to him spooned up next to her, rubbing himself against her backside with slow, undulating movements.

She cried out and attempted to push him away. But he only clamped his arm more tightly about her. "You know what happens to ungrateful little bitches who bite the hand that feeds them?" he hissed. "You get your poor, sick mama kicked out into the cold, and it'll be on your head, girlie."

He had her right where he wanted her. She would have endured anything for her mother's sake. Even that.

She'd never told a living soul about those nights in the motels with her uncle Ray. Not the therapist she'd seen for a short while after moving to New York; not even her husband. Rationally, she knew that she hadn't been to blame. You had only to watch *Oprah* to know that. She'd been victimized, plain and simple. Still, even after all this time, she couldn't shake the sense that she'd been at fault somehow, that she could have done something to prevent it if she'd been smarter or braver or more devout. Every so often the old shame would sneak up on her, triggered by some reminder of the past, and she'd be forced to confront the beast slumbering within. A beast she feared would one day awake.

In the meantime, she had more pressing matters at hand. Such as Lila. And the fire that had destroyed her factory in Las Cruces.

Her thoughts turned to the poor girl who'd died in the fire. Only nineteen! Just a few years older than Phoebe. A shudder went through her at the mental image of her daughter being consumed by flames. But no one else had perished or been seriously injured in the blaze, so they'd been lucky in that sense. Small consolation to the girl's family, she knew. And from what she'd just learned from her Mexican middleman, there was reason to believe the fatality might have been prevented. Certain measures had been taken to ensure that the workers remained at their stations for the duration of their shifts, Perez had belatedly informed her.

Measures he'd taken the liberty to implement *only* after she'd ordered a step-up in production, he'd hastened to underline. When asked if those measures could have caused a delay in evacuation after the fire had broken out, he grudgingly conceded that it was possible.

"Why wasn't I told about this before?" she demanded.

"I didn't wish to concern you. It seemed a minor matter," he said.

"Minor matter! A girl is dead."

"Yes. Most unfortunate," he murmured sympathetically.

"Who else knows about this?"

"Only the workers, and they'll keep quiet about it. They're too afraid for their jobs." Señor Perez sounded nervous, even so. "The girl's mother, on the other hand . . ." He let the sentence trail off.

"You think she'll make trouble?"

"Who can say if the ravings of a grief-stricken woman are to be taken seriously?" he said.

"Do you think it would help if I spoke with her myself?"

"No, no!" Señor Perez was quite firm on that point. "Let me handle it, Señora. I know this woman. I can reason with her. You'd merely be giving credence to her accusations."

And so, against her better judgment, Abigail had left Perez to handle the matter. There was no sense in her mixing in if it was only going to cause more trouble. And right now, she needed to concentrate on the home front. The company had taken a hit, and some serious damage control was in order. For one thing, she'd had to delay the planned launch of her bed-and-bath linen line. The Tag executives hadn't been happy about it. Marty Baumgarten had even gone so far as to say they were considering backing out of the deal altogether.

As a result, her team at Goldman Sachs had decided to postpone filing an application with the SEC for Abigail Armstrong Incorporated to go public, at least until the dust had settled. They didn't have to tell her what it would do to stock prices should potential shareholders get wind of any illegal activity, even on the part of a middleman acting on her behalf. Especially if said activity were connected to a fatality. The fact that it had taken place in a Third World country would only make her look worse. She'd come across as a heartless exploiter of the poor and disenfranchised. Every international rights group would be all over her like white on rice. The media would have a field day.

And none of it would bring back that poor dead girl.

She was busy preparing supper when Kent and Phoebe walked in. Phoebe, her eyes bright and her cheeks flushed, looked livelier than she had in weeks. The fresh air and exercise must have done her good. Kent appeared energized as well—ruddy and tanned, his tweed-colored hair scuffed from the wind. She felt a moment's regret that she hadn't joined them on the boat. But she'd had so much to do, and there had been Lila. . . .

"I'm making pasta," she announced. "Would anyone like to volunteer to set the table?"

"I'm not hungry," Phoebe said pointedly as she squatted down to let Brewster give her a wet, doggy kiss.

"We had burgers at the club," Kent explained somewhat sheepishly. "We didn't know you'd be making supper."

"What do you mean? We always eat together on Sundays!" Abigail's voice rose on a peevish note.

"I know, but we figured that with Veronique gone . . ." He shrugged off his North Face parka and tossed it over the back of a chair. "Anyway, it's not the end of the world, is it? Won't it keep until tomorrow night?" He peered into the pot of pasta bubbling on the stove.

"It won't be the same." Abigail didn't know if it was the spaghetti marinara or the missed opportunity to dine with her family she was referring to. "Couldn't you at least have phoned? I wouldn't have gone to all this trouble if I'd known you were eating at the club."

"Sorry. It was an honest mistake." He slipped an arm around her shoulders, delivering a cool kiss to her forehead. He smelled of damp wool and sea air. "Anyway, you said you had a meeting. We thought you'd be tied up with that. How did it go?"

"What?"

"The meeting." He gave her a funny look.

"Oh, that. Yes. I was going to tell you about it over dinner. I hired a new housekeeper today." She spoke casually in an attempt to downplay it.

"You did *what?*" Phoebe yelped, so loudly that their dog cowered as though it were something he'd done.

Kent eyed Abigail with a somber expression. "I thought we agreed it would be a family decision."

"She's very nice," Abigail went on in the same mild tone, as if they hadn't spoken. "In fact, she's someone I've known for a very long time." The less they knew about the true nature of her and Lila's relationship, the better.

"Who?" Kent wanted to know.

"Lila DeVries."

"The wife of that guy who offed himself?" Phoebe shot to her full height, staring at her mother in disbelief.

Kent looked similarly taken aback. "Abby, I don't know if this is such a good—"

Abigail didn't let him finish. "*You're* the one who suggested I reach out to her." He didn't need to know it had been Lila who'd contacted her. "Well, I did. And she happened to mention she was looking for work. So I offered her the job."

"Something tells me it wasn't the kind of job she had in mind," he said, eyeing her warily.

Abigail shrugged. "Work is work."

"Couldn't you have found her something at the office?" Kent asked.

"Maybe, but I didn't really think it through. She needs a job and we need a new housekeeper. It just seemed the natural next step. Frankly, I thought you'd be pleased." Abigail turned away, so Kent wouldn't see the guilty expression on her face, and dumped the contents of the boiling pot down the disposal. The marinara sauce would keep, but the pasta wouldn't. "Anyway, I'm not even sure if she's going to take it. She's supposed to let me know tomorrow."

Kent settled heavily into the chair over which his jacket was slung. It was always this way when they argued. The angrier he got, the quieter and more über-reasonable he became. Good qualities in a doctor; not so good in a husband. "Let's say she does take the job," he reasoned in that slow, ponderous way of his, as if she weren't his wife but one of his patients. "Have you given any thought to what will happen if the press gets hold of this?"

"Yeah, Mom. Aren't things weird enough around here as it is?" Phoebe demanded. "Besides, how do we know she's not as bad as that creep she was married to who stole all that money?"

Truth to tell, Abigail hadn't given any thought at all to the possible ramifications of hiring Lila. Now the wheels in her head began to spin. Was there a way she could turn this to her advantage? Use the publicity to make her appear the champion of the downtrodden, even if the downtrodden in this case happened to be a Park Avenue socialite fallen on hard times, not a disenfranchised Mexican?

She looked up to find Kent and Phoebe eyeing her with identical looks of reproach. Often she had the disquieting sense that her husband and daughter were somehow joined in conspiracy against her. As if, in her frequent absences, they'd formed a closed corporation, from which she was more or less excluded. For one thing, Kent was the only one who could have gotten Phoebe to eat an entire burger. And even if it had been only half a burger, it was still more than Abigail had lately seen her consume in one sitting. Even when Phoebe had been younger, it was her daddy whom she'd called for whenever she'd had a "boo-boo" or couldn't get back to sleep after a nightmare. And Phoebe and Kent's Friday night ritual of pizza and a movie had withstood even the storms of adolescence. Often Abigail didn't get home until too late to join them, but on the occasions she had, she'd gotten the distinct impression, though nothing had ever been said, that they weren't too happy about her "crashing" their little party.

"I'll deal with it when the time comes," she told them, feeling a heaviness settle over her, like when she'd been up half the night going over mockups or page proofs. "In the meantime, I think you could both show a little more support. I was only doing what I thought was best."

"You should have consulted us. That's all we're saying." Kent eyed her wearily, as though tired of going over the same old ground. As if it mattered less and less what she did, except where it directly involved him or Phoebe.

The realization made her suddenly fearful. What if he were to leave her? But she dismissed the fear as irrational, saying, "Well, it's too late now. If she decides to take the job, you're just going to have to deal with it."

A loaded silence fell. *Nothing good will come of this,* whispered a familiar voice in her head. Her mother's voice. But who was she doing this for, if not her mother?

Out of the blue, she thought of Vaughn. She hadn't heard from him in ages. All she knew was that he traveled the globe as a freelance cameraman—when she'd Googled his name, up had come a number of cable shows and documentaries for which he was credited—but now she wondered what *he* would make of all this. Would he suspect her motives had been less than pure in offering his sister the job? And if so, would he despise her for it? It was strange, because she hadn't laid eyes on the man in more than twenty years, but the thought was almost enough to make her think better of her decision where the combined efforts of her husband and daughter had failed.

5

It had been a long trip. Three days just to get from Namibia to Johannesburg, beginning with the nearly four-hundred-mile jeep ride from the crew's desert camp to the capital city of Windhoek, where he'd caught a lift on a transport plane headed south. Following that had come four days of medical tests at the hospital in Johannesburg before his flight to JFK. Now here he was, at six-thirty in the morning, in a taxi bound for Manhattan, all one hundred and sixty-five stripped-down, bloodshot, beard-stubbled pounds of him.

The sun was just coming up, revealing a gray November sky streaked with cirrus clouds, like a dirty window that had been given a few halfhearted swipes with a cloth. Vaughn had beaten Old Man Winter, but not by much. The trees along the access road down which they were currently traveling, the cabdriver having taken a detour to avoid the traffic on the Long Island Expressway, were skeletons on which only a few dry leaves rattled, and high overhead a flock of migrating geese sketched a dark, slow-moving chevron against the lightening sky.

He gazed out at the houses lining the aptly named Horace Harding Expressway. (*Who the hell was Horace Harding, anyway?* he thought.) Ranging from shabby to well kept but all fairly uniform in size, with identical patches of khaki lawn and identical views of the traffic crawling along the LIE, they made him think of packing boxes on a stalled conveyer belt.

He wondered about the occupants of those homes. How did you end up in a place like that, looking out every day at the same view of cars zipping by (or in this case crawling) and breathing in the fumes from their exhaust? Was it by choice or through a slow process of elimination? Were those people content to stay put, or did they ever itch to explore the world beyond?

Vaughn had been born with an itch. He couldn't recall a time when he hadn't longed to explore distant lands. As a boy, he'd immersed himself in the writings of Thor Heyerdahl and Peter Matthiessen, Jan Morris and Paul Theroux, dreaming of one day seeing those exotic places for himself. As soon as he'd turned eighteen, he had signed up for the Peace Corps. After a two-year stint in the Mariana Islands, where he'd taught rudimentary English to the natives, he'd returned home to find his sister engaged to be married, his father headed to the altar for the third time, and his mother headed off to her fourth or fifth rehab (he'd lost count by then).

He'd moved in with a couple of buddies from high school and had subsequently managed to talk his way into a job as production assistant at CNN's Atlanta headquarters. Within two years he'd acquired the skills necessary to become a cameraman, and before long his natural fearlessness and facility for languages had gotten him dispatched to various hot spots on the continent and abroad. He'd developed a reputation for navigating quickly to the front line of any action and always nailing the operative footage—in '83, he'd been among the first to capture the carnage of the marine barracks in Beirut after a suicide bomber's attack. In war zones, he'd become adept at dodging gunfire, land mines, and diplomatic snafus. It wasn't until he'd narrowly missed being hit by a sniper's bullet in Somalia that he'd lost his stomach for what his buddy Matt McFettridge called the "bang-bang."

Vaughn had parted ways with CNN shortly after that, picking up freelance work wherever he could and restlessly sitting out the periods between gigs like a wild animal deprived of its natural habitat. The rise of cable TV had opened up new opportunities, primarily in the form of the National Geographic and Discovery channels, where previously there had been only PBS and the BBC, with the occasional documentary film thrown in. For the past fifteen years, Vaughn had been more or less constantly on the move, his only fixed address a post office box in Grand Central Station and his true home whichever corner of the globe he happened to be in at any given time. This was his first trip back to New York since his brother-in-law's funeral.

And quite possibly it would be his last.

But he wasn't going to think about that right now. Such dark musings were best tackled on a full stomach, after a good night's rest, he reminded himself. At the thought of food, his stomach muttered in complaint. He hadn't eaten since yesterday morning, having slept straight through the meal service on the plane. He'd grab a bite in the city before heading over to his sister's temporary digs. He didn't want to be banging on her door at this hour; she might still be asleep.

They took the Triborough Bridge, and soon they were rattling over the familiar streets of Manhattan. Vaughn asked the cabbie to drop him off at the corner of Madison and 89th, tossing off a few phrases in Arabic that prompted the man to glance over his shoulder at him in surprise. From the huge smile that broke out on the cabbie's seamed brown face, the ten-dollar tip Vaughn slid him might have been a fifty. He jumped out of the driver's seat to liberate Vaughn's luggage from the trunk before Vaughn could get to it himself: a backpack and olive-drab duffel bag, both of which had seen more miles than a Boeing 747 and which constituted the sum total of Vaughn's worldly possessions, apart from the HD camera and various cases of equipment he'd had shipped.

Vaughn clasped the man's hand in parting. "Stay well, my friend," he said in Arabic.

"May Allah be with you," replied the beaming cabbie.

Vaughn found a cafe that was open twenty-four hours and ordered a full breakfast of eggs, sausage, pancakes, and hash browns, which he washed down with copious amounts of black coffee. He caught the waitress glancing at him a bit curiously from time to time, probably wondering how anyone who consumed such gut-busting quantities could stay so lean. *Lean* wasn't the word; he'd grown downright scrawny—the result of a recent bout with amoebic dysentery that had melted ten pounds from his already rangy frame. He might have been someone newly sprung from a POW camp. Certainly, he didn't look as if he were from around here. His longish blond hair was bleached nearly white from the sun, and his deeply tanned face, into which lines were carved like rills on a barren hillside, stood out in marked contrast to the pasty complexions around him. In his travel-worn fatigues, he could hardly have been mistaken for an early-rising businessman catching a bite to eat on his way to work. These days, he felt more a stranger in his own land than in any of the far-flung places he'd roamed.

He paid the check, tipping the waitress handsomely. Hanging on to money was another habit, like settling in one place or staying with the same woman for very long, that he'd never really acquired. Earning a wage was no problem—he got paid quite well, in fact, for doing what he'd just as happily have done for free—but for him, it was little more than a means by which to take care of life's boring little necessities. Thus it had a way of accumulating: in his pockets and drawers, in half-forgotten money market accounts, and occasionally in the form of uncashed checks.

He'd gladly have given every cent he owned to his sister, but she'd stubbornly refused to take any more than he'd lent her already. "Who knows? You might need it yourself one day," she'd said in that lightly ironic tone she always used when making reference to his inability, or perhaps refusal, to plan further ahead than booking his next flight. Words that seemed prescient now.

Duffel bag in hand and backpack slung over one shoulder, Vaughn walked the three blocks to where Lila was staying. As eager as he was to see her, he dreaded giving her the news that would only add to her already onerous burden, so he ambled along the sidewalk at an unhurried pace. Besides buying time, it allowed him to acclimate to the city's rush and tumble, the blare of horns and squall of traffic. All the while, as he strolled along, he found himself traveling back in time to other places he'd known. Marrakech, with its ancient, mazelike warrens and the ululating cries of the muezzins summoning the faithful to mosque. The Marianas, where villagers made less in a year than most of the people scurrying past him now probably made in a week, yet were far more content. In his mind, he saw the sun coming up over the Greek isle of Limnos, where he'd been on assignment around this time last year, setting fire to a sea of such achingly pure turquoise translucence that it had seemed almost a sin that the fishermen onshore, hauling in their nets, were oblivious to it.

He would miss all that. He'd miss waking up to the crowing of roosters and falling asleep at night to the chirping of crickets or peeping of tree frogs. He'd miss the giddy sense of possibility he always felt walking down the streets of an unfamiliar town or city for the first time, a feeling that was a little like falling in love. He'd miss the street food in Ho Chi Minh City and the home-brewed tequila in San Juan de Alima. He would miss the women as well, no two of them alike and each beautiful in her own right, with whom he'd been privileged to share a bed through the years.

Hunched inside his well-worn aviator jacket, its sheepskin collar pulled up around his ears, Vaughn thought ahead once more to the difficult conversation he was going to have to have with his sister. Poor Lila. Hadn't she endured enough already? But he would put that off until after they'd had a chance to catch up. He hadn't seen her since the funeral. Why spoil it the minute he walked in the door?

He found the address she'd given him, a tony building where the smartly uniformed concierge phoned upstairs to announce his arrival. Minutes later, he emerged from the elevator, on the thirtieth floor, to find Lila waiting for him. She flung her arms around him, hugging him so tightly that Vaughn, laden as he was by his bag and backpack, was momentarily thrown off balance. When she finally drew back, it was to scold him affectionately.

"Look at you, nothing but skin and bones. What did you live off over there, roots and berries?"

"More like lizards and insects," he replied with a roguish grin.

"Ugh." She made a face.

"And you? I was expecting the wreck of the *Hesperus*. And here you are, looking almost like your old self." She was thinner than he would have liked, but she was no longer the walking dead.

"It's only because I knew you were coming. God, it's good to see you!" She hugged him again, quick and fierce, before pulling back to wrinkle her nose. "Good Lord. When was the last time you bathed?"

"Water's pretty scarce out in the desert," he replied impishly.

"In that case, you can shower while I get breakfast on the table. I know you prefer living out in the bush, but civilization does have its compensations."

Vaughn groaned inwardly at the mention of food. He should have known that Lila would insist on feeding him. Now he'd have to find room in his already full belly, or she would be miffed that he hadn't come to her straightaway.

"Nice place," he remarked, stepping into the apartment. But he barely glanced at the art deco furnishings or bold minimalist canvases on the walls as he crossed the living room, heading straight for the picture window with its panoramic view stretching all the way to the East River.

"Too bad it's only on loan."

He turned away from the window to find Lila gazing sightlessly ahead, wearing a preoccupied look. "When are your friends due back from Europe?" he asked, careful to strike a conversational tone. The last time they'd spoken, she hadn't had anything else lined up, and if that was still the case, he didn't want to spoil the moment by making a big deal of it.

"The end of the week," she told him. Just four days away.

"So where to next?"

She grew suddenly fidgety, bending to straighten the already neat stack of magazines on the glass coffee table. "I'll tell you all about it over breakfast," she replied evasively.

She showed him to the guest room, where he dumped his belongings on the bed and immediately headed for the shower. Standing under the showerhead with his eyes closed and the hot water sluicing over him, he felt the knots in his shoulders from the long hours of being crammed into his seat in cabin class start to ease and the black clouds on his internal horizon recede.

By the time he emerged from the guest room, freshly showered and shaved and wearing his only change of clothing, jeans and a button-down shirt over a long-sleeved jersey, Lila was in the kitchen setting out food: toasted bagels and sliced Nova Scotia salmon, containers of scallion cream cheese and whitefish salad. He noted, from the discarded wrappers, that it was from Zabar's, and was touched that she'd gone to the effort of trucking over to the West Side to buy his favorite New York fare.

Helping her carry the food to the table, he had a chance to observe his sister more closely as she moved about, setting out plates and utensils, pouring coffee. She seemed more than just preoccupied; there was a grim look of resolve about her, evident in the tightness around her eyes and mouth and in the firmness with which she placed each thing on the table, as if she expected it to sprout wings and fly off otherwise. The only improvement in her appearance, other than the gain of a few much-needed pounds, was her new, casual look. In the old days, Lila's idea of casual had been designer jeans paired with a tailored blouse or cashmere sweater, and a piece of tasteful but expensive jewelry to complete the outfit. It was refreshing to see her in jeans and sneakers, wearing no makeup, her hair tousled, and her only jewelry the small silver pendant on a chain around her neck. To Vaughn, it was a positive sign that she was letting go of the past, even if Lila might not see it that way.

"How's Neal?" he asked as they sat down to eat.

"Good." After a moment she went on to elaborate, with a sigh, "Good at pretending, anyway. He always *says* he's fine."

"He still seeing that therapist I hooked you up with?" Vaughn had gotten the name of someone who'd come highly recommended by a producer friend of his.

"He was until a few weeks ago."

"Oh?" Vaughn maintained a low-key tone. He didn't want Lila to know how concerned he was. The few times he'd spoken with Neal over the phone, he'd sensed that his nephew was seriously troubled.

"It wasn't Neal's fault," she explained. "I couldn't afford Dr. Goldman's fees anymore."

Vaughn gave her a stern look. "Lila . . ."

She threw up her hands. "I know what you're going to say, and yes, for my son's sake, I would gladly swallow my pride and let you foot the bill. But when I suggested as much to Neal, he told me he'd been planning to quit going anyway. He said he was sick and tired of having, quote unquote, 'some shrink digging around inside his head with a dental drill.'"

Vaughn winced. "Ouch."

"I know. I told him I'd speak to you about it, but he wouldn't budge."

"Maybe I should talk to him myself."

Lila nodded thoughtfully, blowing on her coffee before taking a careful sip. "It might help, but you should probably do it in person, and he won't be home until semester break." She gave Vaughn a cautiously hopeful look. "Will you be around then?"

He gave a noncommittal shrug, not yet ready to share his news. Instead, he asked, "What about *you*? Are you planning on staying in New York?"

She hesitated before answering, without much enthusiasm, "Actually, that's what I was going to tell you. I found a job."

He broke into a grin. "Hey, that's great news! Talk about burying the headline."

Lila didn't seem too excited about it, though. "It's not exactly what I was hoping for."

"How bad could it be?" Even an entry-level position was better than being unemployed.

"Oh, it's not without its perks," she replied in a faintly sardonic tone. "It includes housing, for one thing, so at least I won't have to worry about finding a place to live."

"What kind of job these days includes housing? Don't tell me you're running away to join the circus?" he teased.

"Not quite."

"What, then?"

"Abby offered me a job." Lila took a deep breath before adding portentously, "As her housekeeper."

Vaughn sat back, stunned. "Wow. That's . . . well, I don't know what to say." It certainly wasn't what he'd been expecting to hear.

"Yeah, I know. You're probably wondering the same thing I am. Is she doing this to humiliate me, or is it just that she's dying to have me around?" Lila gave a dry laugh. "Who knows? Maybe a little of both. All I know is that I'm in no position to turn it down. It's not like I have an alternative."

"What about Neal? Is he going to be living with you?"

Lila sat up straight, and he saw her eyes spark with some of their old fire. "He goes where I go. That was part of the deal."

Vaughn cast about for something positive to say. "Well, at least you won't be homeless."

"No, but I'll be stuck out in the middle of nowhere, where I won't know a soul except Abby. Did I forget to mention it's an hour's drive from here?" She sighed, her gaze drifting to the window. "Not that there's anything left for me here, just a lot of memories."

He reached across the table to put a hand over hers. "Don't stress about it too much. It's just temporary, until you find something better."

Lila nodded, her jaw clenched as she fought back tears. "Yeah, I know. I just wish I didn't have to feel such a loser in the meantime."

"You're not a loser. You're a fighter. Look at you; after all you've been through, you're still on your feet, still swinging."

That managed to coax a small smile out of her. "Funny how things work out, isn't it? When Gordon and I got married, I was planning on going back to school and earning my master's degree."

"You never told me that."

"No? It must not have been a huge priority, then."

"What happened?"

She shrugged. "Life. I got pregnant; then after Neal came along, it was one thing after another. Now it seems I'm not qualified to do anything except mop floors for a living, and I'm not even sure how good I'll be at that."

"I wasn't good for much either after I got out of the Peace Corps," he reminded her.

"You were twenty. I'm over forty. Believe me, there's a difference. Besides, you weren't a pariah."

"That's just the media stirring things up. It'll die down soon, if it hasn't already."

"Maybe. But I'll still be persona non grata." Gordon might have been the one convicted, she told him, but in the court of public opinion, she was guilty, too, if only by association. "No one wants to hire the widow of the man responsible for depriving a bunch of old people of their life's savings. Especially not if she drives around in a BMW and owns more pairs of shoes than Imelda Marcos."

"You do?"

She gave him a withering look. "Of course not. I'm just quoting the tabloids."

"You're not responsible for what Gordon did," he reminded her.

"Not directly, but I certainly enjoyed the benefits of all those ill-gotten gains. That must make me guilty of something—if nothing else, of keeping my head buried in the sand. It's not the first time, either. It was the same when Mother fired Rosie. I took the coward's way then, too. So maybe I'm only getting what I deserve. What goes around comes around, right?"

"That's a pretty fatalistic view, don't you think?"

"What can I say? I'm feeling pretty fatalistic these days." Lila fell silent, as if contemplating her fate. Then, with a sigh, she reached for the pot of coffee on the table. "How about a refill?"

"No, thanks, I'm good."

She eyed the plate he'd pushed aside. "That's all you're eating?"

"I stopped for a bite on my way over," he confessed.

"Why didn't you say something?"

"After you'd gone to all this trouble?"

"It was no trouble. How often do I get to see you? And who knows when you'll be back? Tomorrow or the next day you'll be off again to some far-flung place where I can't even reach you by phone . . . and where I can't—" Abruptly, she burst into tears.

He jumped to his feet and came around to where she sat, pulling her into his arms. "Who said I was going anywhere?" he soothed.

"You always leave. That's what you do," she muttered tearfully into his collar. She drew back to eye him accusingly, a look that quickly dissolved into one of resignation. "Not that I blame you. I wouldn't want to be anywhere near me, either, if I were you. Look at me—I'm a mess."

"I'm not going anywhere," he repeated.

But she wasn't going to be consoled so easily. "Not today, maybe. But tomorrow or the next day."

Vaughn realized that he could no longer put off telling her why he was here, that this wasn't just another pit stop on his way to another remote locale. "I'm here for a while. A few months at the very least."

"You mean *here?* In New York?"

He nodded. "Gillian said I could crash at her place. You remember Gillian?"

"The artist? Sure. Didn't you two used to date?"

"A million years ago. We're just friends now."

Lila was staring at him, wearing a puzzled frown. "I still don't get it. You never stick around more than a few weeks at a time. Is there something you're not telling me?"

For a long moment, he remained silent. When he finally answered, he found himself directing his words at the wall behind her. He couldn't bear to look his sister in the eye, to see the pain he knew he was causing.

"I'm sick, Lila. I have cancer. Non-Hodgkin's lymphoma, to be precise. The doctor in Johannesburg did a biopsy, to be sure. That's why I came back, to get treated here in New York."

He brought his gaze back to Lila, who was staring at him in disbelief. "No." She violently shook her head. "That's impossible. You? You're the healthiest person I know. They must have gotten your results mixed up with somebody else's."

He took hold of her hand and squeezed it, speaking to her as gently as he once had when they were children, the day she'd come home sobbing from Sunday school because the minister had told her that ponies didn't go to heaven. Her beloved Shetland, Popcorn, had just been put down, and she'd been inconsolable. It had been left to Vaughn to assure her—though he knew no such thing—that Popcorn was up in heaven at that very moment, grazing in greener pastures. "It's not a death sentence, Lila," he reassured her now. "The oncology department at New York–Presbyterian is supposed to be the best there is. And the doctor in Johannesburg said I stood a good chance of a full recovery."

She went on staring at him while slowly shaking her head. "Oh, God. I feel so terrible. All this time I've been going on about my own problems and you . . ." She started to choke up again.

"I *want* you to come to me with your problems," he told her. "Whatever it is, we're in it together. That goes both ways." Their parents used to joke that they'd come out of the womb attached to a single cord, and it wasn't far from the truth.

"But I won't be here. Who's going to look after you?" she asked plaintively.

"I've been doing a pretty good job of looking after myself for the past forty-some years," he reminded her. "Anyway, I won't be all by myself, if that's what's worrying you. Gillian will be around if I need anything."

"I could tell Abby I changed my mind. It's not too late for me to back out."

"No," Vaughn said firmly. "I won't have you putting your life on hold because of me. Besides, if you don't take this job, where would you go?"

"A compelling point. But you don't have to be so damn noble about it. You're making me look like a crybaby in comparison." She managed a small, teary-eyed smile.

"Who's comparing? Anyway, I won't be feeling so noble when I'm losing all my hair and puking my guts out."

"I bet you'll look cute bald."

"You ought to know. I was bald in all my baby pictures."

They stood there, each contemplating their own and the other's peculiar fate. He'd never felt closer to his twin sister than he did at that moment. He wondered if he could have known this deep, wordless companionship with a wife, and he felt a mild pang of regret that he hadn't loved any of his girlfriends enough to marry one. Now, though, he thought he understood the appeal: Marriage, for whichever one went first, meant you didn't have to be alone at the end.

"Don't think you're going to be rid of me," Lila said after a bit. "I'll be coming around so often, you'll be sick of looking at me."

"Believe me, I'm counting on it," he said.

"All right, now that that's settled, what do you feel like doing? We have the whole rest of the day." She spoke with forced cheer, as if determined not to let this ruin his visit. "We could go for a walk or just hang out here. What's your pleasure?"

"Honestly? What I'd really like is to get some sleep." Vaughn struggled to suppress a yawn.

"Say no more." Lila took his hand, leading him down the hall and into the guest room as she might a sleepy child. She lowered the blinds while he removed his shoes, and he was nodding off almost as soon as he stretched out on the bed. "Sleep tight. Don't let the bedbugs bite," she whispered, pulling a blanket over him before bending down to kiss him lightly on the cheek.

Vaughn, as he drifted off to sleep, thought that bedbugs were the least of his worries.

6

"You'll find everything you need in here." Abigail led the way into the laundry room, gesturing toward the open shelving against one wall, which held a wide array of cleaning supplies. On the opposite wall was a pocket door, which she slid back to reveal a closet filled with brooms, mops, vacuum cleaner, and some sort of machine that looked vaguely industrial. She caught Lila eyeing it curiously and said, "Floor waxer. Twice a year I get the floors and carpets professionally waxed and cleaned. This is just for touch-ups in between."

In between. That phrase could easily be used to describe her life right now, Lila thought. She was caught between the broken-off end of her old life and the one to come, whatever that might be. Surely she wasn't meant to spend the rest of her days washing someone else's dirty clothes! Especially since there was another, darker reason Abigail had hired her, she suspected. It frightened Lila more than a little to think of how long Abigail's resentment must have been smoldering, like one of those underground fires that burn for decades.

Lila had spent her final weekend in New York packing up her few remaining belongings, having sold off the bulk of what was in storage. Everything she owned was crammed into her Taurus, which was currently parked out by the garage. An errant thought sneaked in: *I could still back out. It's not too late.* But once again, the reality of her situation asserted itself. Where would she go? What would she do? And Neal would be joining her soon. So, really, there was no alternative. She wasn't going anywhere unless Abigail decided to fire her.

"If you run out of anything," Abigail went on in the crisp, businesslike tone with which she might have addressed a junior staffer, "I keep petty cash on hand for supplies." She pulled open a drawer, showing Lila a tin stuffed with small bills and change. "For groceries, you'll use our account at L'Epicerie," she said, referring to the gourmet market in town. "I think that covers just about everything. Any questions?"

Just one, Lila answered silently. *Are you enjoying this as much as I think you are?* Clearly, Abigail wanted to see her eat crow, a dish she no doubt had a hundred ways of serving up.

They'd gone over the rest of the house, top to bottom, Abigail showing her where everything was and letting her know what was expected of her, such as the weekly dinner menu, which Lila would be preparing ahead each day, and various duties in addition to cooking, cleaning, shopping, and running errands.

Lila's head was reeling, but she managed to reply with a certain degree of confidence, "I think I have a handle on it."

"Well, in that case, I'll leave you to it." Abigail consulted her watch. It was early yet, the rest of the household not yet up, but she was on her way to work, dressed to the nines in a Donna Karan jacket and silk tank top, midcalf wool skirt, and high-heeled leather boots. A strand of chunky amber beads added the perfect downtown touch to an outfit that might otherwise have looked too put-together.

They headed back down the hallway into the kitchen, where the sunlight slanting in through the windows stretched in long slats over the terra-cotta-tiled floor. Copper pots and pans gleamed on the hanging rack over the butcher-block island. Beside the stove, a professional-grade Garland, various food items were laid out on the spotless granite counter— a carton of eggs, butter, English muffins, a bag of select Cuban coffee beans (available only by mail order, Lila had been told; the procurement would be another of her duties)—reminding her that she was supposed to fix breakfast for Abigail's husband and daughter when they finally made an appearance, which presumably would be any moment.

Lila wondered what they were like. The only member of the household whom she'd met so far, besides Abigail, had been the family dog. At least he was friendly. Brewster had jumped up to give her a big, sloppy kiss before Abigail had scolded him into slinking off.

Abigail was heading for the door when she paused to add, "Oh, by the way, I won't be getting in until late tonight, and Kent's eating at the club, so don't bother with supper. Unless Phoebe wants something, which I doubt. She eats like a bird, that girl." A look of motherly concern momentarily softened her features, allowing Lila a brief glimpse of the Abigail she'd once known and loved.

Lila followed her out into the vestibule. "Um, Abby?"

Abigail paused as she was pulling on her coat and gloves. "Yes?"

"About my day off . . . I was wondering if it would be all right if I took Wednesdays instead."

Every Wednesday for the next three weeks, between the hours of two and four, Vaughn would be getting his chemotherapy at New York–Presbyterian, and she wanted to be with him on those days.

Abigail hesitated just long enough to make her annoyance known. "I suppose so," she said. As if it could make the slightest difference to her. From what Lila could see, one day was the same as the next as far as her schedule was concerned.

"I wouldn't ask if it weren't important," Lila felt obliged to add. "You see, my brother—" She broke off, not sure she wanted Abigail to know every detail of her private life. But it was too late. Abigail seized upon it.

"Vaughn's in town?" She tried to make it sound like a casual inquiry, but Lila couldn't help noticing the way her cheeks colored. She wondered if what she'd suspected as a teenager was true, that Abigail had secretly been in love with Vaughn.

With the cat halfway out of the bag, Lila was forced to reply, "He flew in last week."

"Will he be around for long? I'd love to catch up with him one of these days."

Lila gave a noncommittal shrug. "With him, you never know."

Abigail lingered in the doorway. She seemed on the verge of saying something more, but she must have thought better of it—or feared it would reveal too much—because she swept off to the chauffeured car idling in the drive, leaving a slipstream of Chanel-scented air.

Alone at last, Lila retreated to the kitchen, thinking she could take advantage of this brief spell before the rest of the household was up to become familiarized with its layout. In the early years with Gordon, she had done all the cooking. She recalled a few disastrous meals in the first months of their marriage, like the time she'd made creamed tuna over mashed potatoes, instead of rice, which had been about as appetizing as wallpaper paste. The memory brought a smile even while causing her to wince inwardly. Over time, she'd mastered the basics, but once they'd been able to afford full-time help, the domestic duties had been relegated to others. And since Gordon's death, she'd been too preoccupied with urgent matters to be bothered with meals. The most she could manage was to boil an egg or heat up frozen lasagna. Now she found herself praying she still knew her way around a kitchen.

She was peering into the cupboard over the sink when a deep voice startled her into swinging around.

"Good morning. You must be Lila."

A man around her age, medium height, with hair the scruffy brown of a terrier's coat and an open, friendly face ruddy from the outdoors, stood in the doorway. He was wearing khaki trousers and a corduroy sport coat over an open-necked shirt that showed his suntanned throat. His intelligent gray eyes regarded her with lively interest.

"Good morning. You must be . . ." She hesitated, wondering how she ought to address him—by his first or last name?—before deciding on the latter. "Dr. Whittaker." This wasn't a cocktail party, after all. She was the *maid*.

"Kent." He walked over to her, offering his hand. "I'm only Dr. Whittaker to my patients."

"It's nice to finally meet you. I've heard a lot about you." His handshake was dry and firm. Lila had seen photos of him in magazines, posed alongside Abigail, the two of them looking like the ideal couple, enjoying the ideal lifestyle. He was much handsomer in person, she thought.

"Likewise," he said. "Welcome aboard. I take it you've been given the grand tour?"

"Yes. I hope we didn't wake you."

"Not at all. I was up, I just wasn't dressed. Everything meet with your approval?"

Since when did her approving or disapproving have anything to do with it? Lila wondered. But she put on a pleasant, neutral expression. "Yes. You have a lovely home." She felt awkward chatting with him like this, however much his demeanor seemed to invite it. If they'd met socially, she'd have known how to act, but in her new role as hired help, the old rules didn't apply. Watching him amble over to help himself to a glass of juice from the fridge, she remembered to ask, "Would you like me to fix you something to eat?"

Kent seemed to sense her discomfort. "I have an even better idea," he said. "Why don't I fix breakfast for us both? It's your first day, and I still have some time before I have to leave for work."

"Oh, I don't—" Lila grew even more flustered.

"We won't tell anyone," he said with a conspiratorial wink. Before she could utter another word of protest, he was scooping coffee beans into the grinder. "This is going to be an adjustment for us all, so why don't we just play it by ear? I don't know if Abby told you, but our last housekeeper was with us for a number of years. Phoebe, especially, was devoted to her."

"I'll be sure to keep that in mind," Lila murmured in response.

"You haven't met Phoebe yet, have you? She should be down soon. That is, if she wants a ride to school," he said, turning to frown at the clock on the wall before he dropped a pat of butter into the skillet on the stove.

"No, but I know how she likes her eggs—over easy." Abigail had filled her in on everyone's food preferences.

"Speaking of which, how do you like yours?" Kent cracked a couple of eggs into the now sizzling skillet.

"Sunny side up."

"Ah, a girl after my own heart." He tipped her another wink. Minutes later, he was sliding two perfectly cooked eggs, sunny side up, onto a plate, to which he added a toasted English muffin and some cut-up strawberries before presenting it to her with a flourish. "Bon appétit."

They sat down to eat in the breakfast nook, which was tucked between two sets of bookshelves holding Abigail's vast array of cookbooks. "I understand you have a son who'll be joining us soon," Kent said, as he buttered his English muffin.

"Yes, he's around your daughter's age. His name's Neal."

"I look forward to meeting him." Abigail's husband took a bite of his muffin, chewing thoughtfully for a moment before adding, "I wonder what it'll be like having two teenagers underfoot. Currently, we have our hands full with just one." His tone was mild, but she sensed an undercurrent of something more than parental exasperation at a teenager's high jinks. "Oh, don't get me wrong, Phoebe's a darling girl. It's just . . . she's been kind of closed off lately. Don't be offended if she comes across as a little standoffish."

"Believe me, I know the territory," Lila commiserated, thinking of how moody Neal had been lately. The news that they'd be living out in the boonies, far from all his friends and former hangouts, had sent him into a funk. There was no longer even the pretense of putting on a brave face. He'd gone from doing his best to please her to making her life even more miserable.

"You, too?" Kent eyed her in solidarity. "Well, I suppose some of it's to be expected. Though I don't remember being that way when I was their age."

"What were you like?" she asked, curious about him all of a sudden.

He shrugged. "Pretty dull, actually—your typical overachiever. I suppose I was born too late, in one sense. I missed out on the radical '60s, which, according to Abby, would have brought out my true nature. In case she hasn't told you, I'm a bit of a crusader. Though she sees it more as tilting at windmills." Again, Lila sensed an undercurrent in the fleeting look that crossed his face.

"You're a doctor," she said. "Doesn't it go with the territory to want to fix things?"

He cast her a grateful look, as if he wasn't used to being praised for his efforts, or at least not around here. "An excellent point," he said. "But back then, all I cared about was what would look good on my college résumé. It wasn't until I graduated from med school and started my internship that I figured out there was more to life than being the best at everything." He set his fork down, his gaze momentarily turning inward. "It was all those patients, you see. They'd wash in and out of the ER every day, like a tide. A lot of them didn't have insurance. Hell, most didn't even speak English. I remember thinking how lucky I was and that I'd never truly realized it, because I'd been so hell-bent on meeting my goals. It was then that I decided I wanted to do something more meaningful with my life."

"Very admirable," she said, meaning it.

"I didn't do it to be noble. At the risk of sounding like a do-gooder, I really enjoy helping people. Okay, so being a country doctor isn't exactly a UN relief mission, but even out in this neck of the woods, there's real need—you'd be surprised. For one thing, a lot of our old folks are too sick or infirm to make it into my office and too proud to admit they need help. It's my job to see that they get it."

"You must be the last doctor in America who still makes house calls," she observed with a smile.

"It's not just that," he said. "I see patients who can't afford insurance or who've maxed out their policies. I get my share of pregnant teens, too—not much for kids to do around here, and you know what happens when they get bored." He rolled his eyes. "A lot of them are too scared to go to their parents, but for some reason they trust me."

"You have that kind of face."

"Do I? Funny, my wife doesn't seem to have noticed."

Despite his joking tone, Lila wondered if there was some truth to his words. Was Abigail's much-vaunted home life all it was cracked up to be . . . or were there cracks in the marriage that had been painted as ideal in all those magazine articles she'd read? Lila had only just met Kent, but already she could see how different he was from Abigail. She wondered how they'd ever gotten together in the first place.

But she didn't spare much thought for Abigail as she and Kent sat chatting over breakfast. She found herself lingering over a second cup of coffee, thinking how nice it was, enjoying a quiet moment with a husband on his way to work, even if that husband wasn't hers.

Apparently she'd met with Kent's approval as well, for he announced as he was pushing away his empty plate, "Well, Lila, I think you're going to work out just fine. Oh, I admit I had my doubts at first, but that was before I had a chance to get to know you a bit."

"I suppose you were expecting someone who was afraid to get her hands dirty," she said with a laugh, feeling more at ease now that it appeared she had at least one ally. "Okay, I confess I wear rubber gloves, but I'm not too proud to get down on my hands and knees with a scrub brush, and I don't think it takes a rocket scientist to know how to operate a vacuum."

He regarded her thoughtfully for a moment, frowning slightly, before he ventured, "Look, I hope you don't think I'm being too personal, but there's no sense in ignoring the eight-hundred-pound gorilla since we'll all be more or less living under the same roof. So I'm going to come right out with it: I know you've been through a lot. And I give you a lot of credit for the way you've handled it. A lot of people would have cracked under that kind of pressure."

It had been so long since Lila had been paid a compliment by someone who didn't have a vested interest in cheering her up that she found herself fighting back tears. "Thank you. That's very kind of you." It was all she could manage at the moment.

Kent clinked his coffee cup against hers. "Well, here's to success, however you define it."

While they cleaned up in the kitchen, he told her a bit more about his practice, which was located in a storefront downtown, the site of a former shoe store. "It's not the Mayo Clinic," he said, "but since my partner and I are pretty much the only game in town, we don't get a lot of complaints."

Lila's thoughts turned to Vaughn. "My brother could have used someone like you. Most of the places he travels to, the nearest doctor is hundreds of miles away. Maybe if he'd seen someone sooner—" She caught herself before she could blurt out her latest woe.

But Kent was too quick for her. "Your brother's sick?"

She gave a solemn nod. "He just found out he has cancer. Stage two lymphoma. He starts chemo the day after tomorrow."

"I'm sorry to hear that." Kent sounded genuinely sympathetic. He must have seen the worry on her face, for he added, "But you know, Lila, it's not a death sentence."

"That's what he keeps telling me."

"Who's his doctor?"

"Guy named Grossman. He's with New York–Presbyterian."

"Paul Grossman? Yes, I know him well. We were in residency together at Columbia. He's one of the best," Kent assured her. "Your brother's in excellent hands."

She felt her anxiety ebb the tiniest bit. "That's good to know."

"I'd be happy to speak with Paul, if you'd like. That way, if there's something you don't understand, I could explain it. Sometimes it's hard to make heads or tails of all that medical mumbo jumbo, and as I recall, Paul didn't get high marks for his bedside manner."

"Would you? That would be wonderful." Lila felt a wave of gratitude wash over her, which caused her to choke up again. She quickly turned away so Kent wouldn't see the tears in her eyes.

He laid a gentle hand on her shoulder. "Think nothing of it."

For a moment, Lila was almost lulled into forgetting the reason she was here. But she told herself that she couldn't lose sight of the fact that this very kind man, however sociable, was her employer. With that in mind, she shooed Abigail's husband out of the kitchen and set about the task of acquainting herself with the house. A house that suddenly didn't seem so hostile anymore.

That is, until she encountered Phoebe.

"So you're the new replacement."

Lila, on her knees in the master bathroom, scrubbing the Jacuzzi, looked up to see a teenaged girl standing over her. Pretty but much too thin, with curly dark hair cropped short and huge brown eyes that made her think of Bambi. She sat back on her heels. "And you must be Phoebe." Abigail's daughter hadn't made it down for breakfast, and the house had been so quiet ever since that Lila had simply assumed she'd slipped out the door without making her presence known. Now she raised a rubber-gloved hand in greeting. "Hi, I'm Lila. Sorry for not introducing myself earlier, but I didn't know anyone was home. Aren't you supposed to be in school?"

"I told my dad I was sick."

"You don't look sick."

"I'm not." Phoebe spoke flatly, offering no explanation. She eyed Lila askance, her arms crossed over her chest. "So what's your story? My mom says you two knew each other when you were kids."

Lila nodded, wondering what else Abigail had told her. She decided to play it safe and volunteered only, "Her mother worked for our family."

"Seriously?" Phoebe's dark eyes glittered with sudden interest. "So did you two used to, like, hang out together?" Clearly, Abigail hadn't told her daughter much about that period in her life.

Lila was a bit taken aback to learn that she'd become a mere footnote in Abigail's history, but she rallied. "We practically grew up together. It would have been hard not to," she replied, doing her best to be circumspect.

"Yeah? Well, I kind of got the impression she doesn't have such happy memories of those days."

Lila didn't dispute this. She merely shrugged and said, "We all remember things differently."

"It must seem weird. That you're working for her now."

"It *is* a little weird," Lila admitted. There was no use denying it. One look at her, and you could see that she and Mr. Clean weren't exactly on intimate terms.

Phoebe was silent for a moment. "I read about you in the papers," she said after a bit.

Lila gave a tight smile, as if to say, *Who hasn't?*

"So were you, like, seriously rich?" Phoebe pressed on.

"You could say that."

Phoebe appeared unimpressed. "Mom says you have a son my age."

"Yes. His name's Neal. He's a little older than you, actually."

"What's he like?"

"He's nice." *Unlike you.* "You'll see when you meet him."

"When's he coming?"

"In a few weeks. Soon as the semester's over."

"Cool," Phoebe replied indifferently. She turned to peer out the window, which overlooked the driveway in back. "So is that your car? The one with all the boxes in back?"

"I haven't gotten around to unpacking yet," Lila said somewhat defensively.

"Well, it looks like you're going to need some help with that. I'll give you a hand later on, if I'm not doing anything else."

Phoebe's offer took Lila by surprise. She didn't seem the type to knock herself out on another person's behalf, especially when that someone was getting paid to wait on *her*. Lila replied as nicely as she could, "Thanks, but I think I can manage." She didn't want it getting back to Abigail that she'd had Phoebe do her dirty work. She resumed her scrubbing, and when she looked up again a few minutes later, she was surprised to find Phoebe still standing there. "Do you need anything?" she asked pointedly.

"No." Phoebe picked at a hangnail. There was a long pause before she asked in a soft voice, "I was just wondering . . . what was she like back then?"

Distracted, Lila asked, "Who?"

"My mom."

"Oh. Well. Let me see . . ." Lila had to stop and think about it. At last her face relaxed in a small, remembering smile. "She was sweet and funny. Pretty fearless, too. There was a pecan tree that grew alongside the house she and her mother lived in, and she used to climb out onto her roof to collect the nuts that dropped onto it. There was this one time she slipped and fell and probably would have broken her neck if a branch hadn't caught her on the way down. We all thought she'd be scared of heights after that, but the very next day she was back up there again."

The memory sparked a tiny flame of remembered affection that sputtered, then took hold. They'd had their share of adventures, hadn't they? However unforgiving Abigail was now, nothing could alter that.

"Just think, if she *had* broken her neck, neither of us would be here now."

Lila looked up at Phoebe, somewhat startled by the morbid turn her thoughts had taken. But she sensed that Phoebe was only testing her, to see how she would react, so she replied evenly, "I'm not sorry. Are you?" She'd rather be here, on her knees scrubbing someone else's bathroom, than have taken the unthinkable route Gordon had chosen.

Phoebe didn't answer. She merely stared at Lila, scrutinizing her in a manner that was less than friendly but not outright rude. Lila could see how vulnerable she was under her tough-girl facade: a sad little girl in a young woman's body. Finally Phoebe announced, "I'll be in my room if anyone wants me. And don't bother trying to get in to clean it." She cast a pointed glance at the bucket of cleaning supplies at Lila's feet. "It's off limits."

With that, she spun around and was gone.

Even without Phoebe's bedroom to clean, it took Lila the rest of the morning to finish the upstairs. Making Kent and Abigail's bed alone was a daunting task. It was king-sized, with numerous layers of blankets, a duvet, shams, pillows, and throw pillows, which took forever to assemble in what she assumed was the correct order and nearly caused her to throw her back out in the process. Lila felt a tiny stab of guilt, remembering the bed she and Gordon had shared in their Park Avenue penthouse, which had been similarly elaborate. Her housekeeper, Martina, had never once complained, but had Lila truly appreciated the amount of work involved in making it every morning? She might have dispensed with a few of those shams and throw pillows if she had.

By the time she'd cleaned the entire house top to bottom, hours had gone by, and every muscle in her body ached. She wondered how she was going to survive a week of this, much less longer than that. She'd never worked this hard in her life. Back in the day, she could've saved at both ends had she dispensed with both her housekeeper and personal trainer and done Martina's job herself.

Lila felt ashamed now to think that she'd ever imagined the going rate she'd paid her housekeeper had been enough to compensate Martina for all her hard work, not to mention the extra jobs Martina had taken upon herself to do without being asked. Maybe this was punishment, Lila thought, not for her sins against Abigail but for those against the underclass.

She was stowing away the cleaning supplies when she remembered that she still had to unload her car and unpack her things. She quickly headed out back, while it was still light out. Grabbing a cardboard carton out of the backseat, she lugged it up the steep flight of steps to the maid's quarters above the detached garage, where she and Neal would be living. Abigail had pointed it out to her earlier, but Lila had yet to see what it was like inside.

As soon as she walked in, her heart sank. It was so small! It consisted of a living room with a kitchenette at one end, a tiny bedroom, and a bathroom. Neal wouldn't even have his own room; he'd have to sleep on the convertible sofa in the living room. But at least it was a roof over their heads, she reminded herself after she'd had time to adjust. It would be a tight squeeze, but they'd manage. On the bright side, there wasn't much to clean.

Lila was back downstairs wrestling the heaviest of the boxes from the Taurus's trunk when a deep, accented voice spoke behind her.

"Let me help you with that."

She straightened and turned around. Standing before her was a man dressed in grass-stained trousers and a sweatshirt. He was around her age, muscularly built, with dusky skin and tight brown curls that hugged his skull like a cap of Persian lamb. He had the most beautiful brown eyes she'd ever seen, long-lashed like a girl's, only there was nothing remotely feminine about him. She watched him hoist the box as easily as if it had been filled with Styrofoam peanuts.

He carried the box upstairs and lowered it onto the living room floor. "Karim Najid," he said, straightening to introduce himself.

She shook his hand, which was work-hardened but at the same time surprisingly long-fingered and supple, that of an aristocrat. "Lila DeVries. I'm the new . . . housekeeper." She stumbled a bit over the word. *Housekeeper.* She'd spent the entire day cleaning Abigail's house, but she still hadn't quite gotten used to her new role.

"I know. I was told to look out for you." His Middle Eastern accent had a British inflection to it, she noted. He must have lived abroad before coming here. "I take care of the grounds. But any of the heavier work you need done around the house, please don't hesitate to ask."

"Thanks," she said. "I don't know what I would've done if you hadn't showed up. You really saved me."

"My pleasure," he said, inclining his head in a courtly little bow.

Together, they carried up the rest of her things. The only pieces of furniture were the small end table and bentwood rocker that had been her grandmother's, which Lila had been unable to part with when she'd sold the rest of her furnishings.

"That's it," she said, stacking the last of the boxes atop the pile on the living room floor. "I'll say one thing, this sure was a lot easier than my last move. That one took four moving vans."

"When I arrived in this country, I had only one suitcase."

She turned to find Karim regarding the boxes with a small, ironic smile.

"Where are you from originally?" she asked.

"Afghanistan." He hastened to add, "Not the Afghanistan you Americans know. There were no bombed-out buildings and rifle-toting *mujahideen* back then. It was beautiful, with trees and flowers, and people who smiled at each other on the streets." His expression turned wistful. As he gazed out the window, momentarily lost in thought, she studied his face in the light of the setting sun, which had temporarily anointed the modestly appointed room with a gilded glow that rendered it almost inviting. With high cheekbones and hawklike nose, his profile was like those carved on ancient bronze coins.

"Have you been in this country long?" she asked.

"Long enough."

He brought his gaze back to her, and she saw written on his face a story that would probably have taken all night to tell. But she had no wish to coax it out of him; she was tired and hungry and wanted only to unpack her things before she called it a day. "Well, thank you again," she said, seeing him to the door. "You've been a big help."

"Let me know if there's anything else you need," he said as he was turning to go. "I'll be around a little while longer. I don't get off until six."

Not wanting to impose, she hesitated before replying, "There is one thing. Do you have a hammer I could borrow? There's a painting I'd like to hang." She indicated the framed watercolor, a seascape, propped against the sofa. It could easily have waited until tomorrow, but she knew it would bring her comfort to see it hanging on the wall—a small touch of home in an otherwise cheerless space. She remembered when she'd first seen it, in a gallery in Carmel, where she and Gordon had been vacationing at the time. She'd instantly fallen in love with it, but Gordon had been less enthusiastic. It wasn't until he'd surprised her with it on their anniversary, a month later, that she'd realized he'd only pretended not to like it. The memory brought a familiar tug of longing. Her husband might have fooled a lot of people, including her, but he'd loved her—*that* had been genuine.

Karim nodded and took off, returning several minutes later with a hammer and a box of picture hooks. "Please. I would be honored if you would allow me," he said, bending to pick up the painting. "Just show me where you would like it to go." His courtly manner was oddly endearing, bringing to mind knights in armor and gentlemen of yore.

Lila felt herself blushing. "Oh, I didn't mean—I wouldn't want you to go to any more trouble—"

He waved aside her objection. "I'm happy to be of service."

To have sent him on his way would've been rude, so she smiled graciously and said, "In that case, how can I refuse?"

She chose a spot on the wall where the painting would be displayed to its best advantage, and while Karim was hammering the hook into the wall, she returned to the carton she'd been in the midst of unpacking when he'd showed up. She was leafing through an old photo album she'd pulled out of the carton when she glanced up to find him peering over her shoulder.

"Your family?" he asked, pointing out a photo of her and Gordon posing on a beach, Gordon with their sandy-haired toddler in his arms.

She nodded, swallowing against the lump forming in her throat. "That was taken in Sag Harbor. We used to go there every year for the Fourth of July. It was our tradition," she mused aloud, using her thumb to smooth a torn edge of the photo. In it, she and Gordon were grinning into the camera, their hair windblown, and their faces aglow. Neal must have been around three, still chubby with the baby fat that had melted off by the following summer.

"You look happy," Karim observed.

"We were." If ignorance was bliss, she'd been among the happiest people on the planet. She paused before adding in a soft voice, "My husband passed away a couple of months ago."

Karim gave a solemn nod. "I'm sorry to hear that. Was it sudden?"

"Yes, very." She was quick to change the subject, not wanting to get into a long, painful discussion. "What about your family? Did they come over to this country with you?"

Karim shook his head, his face clouding over briefly. "Both my brothers had died in the war by then, and my father was killed by the Taliban.

When they confiscated our house, my mother took my sisters and fled to the countryside. The only reason I was able to get out was because I had a friend, a former student, who worked in the ministry." He explained that he'd been a professor at the university in Kabul. When the Taliban had banned all books except religious ones, it had been the end of Karim's teaching career. To have continued, even in secret, would have gotten him thrown into jail. Or worse. "They murdered my father," he told her, his expression turning grim. "They shot him in cold blood, simply for daring to speak out against their insane policies."

Abruptly, he turned away, but not before she caught the flash of some deep, banked emotion in his eyes.

So he was a victim of harsh circumstance, the same as she. They might be from different cultures, she thought, but they had that in common at least. "It's terrible what they did to your country," she said. She'd watched in shock, along with the rest of the country, the news coverage of the stone Buddhas at Bamiyan being dynamited. And from what Karim was telling her, that hadn't been the worst of it.

"It wasn't just the Taliban," he said. "It was the Soviets, the British, the Turks, the Arabs, and the Mongols before that. Now it's the warring sects killing each other off. Our young people can't recall a time when the country hasn't been at war. They have no memory of Kabul as it once was, when it was a place of culture and learning."

"Maybe it's better that they don't," she said. "Some things are too painful to remember."

"You asked about my family," he said. "What I regret most is that I didn't have the chance to say good-bye. My mother and sisters were gone by then, and I had to move quickly or I would have been arrested. We write to each other and speak on the phone, but it's not the same."

"How long has it been since you've seen them?"

"Eight years." He pondered this, as if digesting an improbable fact.

"Do you think you'll ever go back?"

"One day, perhaps." The wistful expression on his face made her wonder if he'd left more than his mother and sisters behind. Was there a wife? She noticed that he wasn't wearing a wedding ring, so perhaps it was a sweetheart for whom he pined. Before she could delve into it, he gave a small, contrite smile, saying, "Forgive me. We've only just met, and here I am burdening you with my sorrows. You must think I'm very rude."

"Not at all," she assured him. "Anyway, I can certainly relate. I lost my husband and pretty much everything I owned, all in the space of a year. In case you were wondering, that's how I ended up here." Her mouth thinned in a mirthless smile. "Ironic, isn't it? Me, with my Park Avenue digs and my full-time housekeeper, cleaning up after other people." She felt safe confiding in Karim for some reason, though, as he'd pointed out, they had only just met.

"It's honest work, at least," he said. "And I can think of worse places to be."

Yeah, she thought, *like Afghanistan under the Taliban's rule.* "You sound just like my brother," she told him. "He keeps reminding me that it won't be forever, that I have options. I just wish I had a clue what those options were."

Karim gave her a gently encouraging smile. "It's only your first day. You don't have to decide overnight."

Her first day. Lila realized, to her amazement, that she'd gotten through it somehow and that it hadn't been a complete disaster. Plus, she'd made at least one friend. Two, if you counted Abigail's husband. She had yet to win over Abigail's daughter, and there was Abigail herself, who would be an even tougher challenge. But all in all, however backbreaking, it wasn't shaping up to be the total exercise in humiliation that she'd imagined it would be.

Maybe . . . just maybe . . . there was hope for her yet.

7

"No, no, no!" Abigail swooped down to snatch up the centerpiece. "I specifically told you *no poinsettias!*" Never mind that it was that time of year, Christmas just three weeks away, Abigail loathed poinsettias. At her mother's funeral, the church had been awash in them. She thrust the flowers at the hapless production assistant, snapping, "Next time, pay attention when I give instructions!"

"Of course. I'm so sorry," the young woman apologized as she hurried off, red-faced, to find something to replace the offending flowers.

Abigail frowned as she rearranged the table, where the beauty shot—the dessert she was preparing for this morning's broadcast of *A.M. America*—would be displayed at the end of her segment. Damn it, where was the stylist? What did the network pay these people for, if not to be on top of such things?

Abigail had arrived at the studio with little time to spare before this morning's appearance, so she hadn't had a chance to go over everything well in advance, as she was in the habit of doing. She'd been late getting out of the house, thanks to Lila's having put the clean laundry away in all the wrong drawers, and then traffic on the Henry Hudson had been backed up due to construction. She'd hurried onto the set to find all in readiness, her prep laid out for the miniature cranberry-mascarpone tarts she was to prepare as part of a holiday entertaining segment, along with the finished tarts. The one false note had been the poinsettias.

Another person might have been willing to overlook it, but Abigail wasn't like other people. Being a stickler for detail was what had made her who she was. Whether it was catering an event, putting together a book, or doing a media appearance, she stayed focused on the small stuff as well as the big picture: remembering not to serve blueberries at a buffet where they were apt to roll onto the carpet when the guests helped themselves (a mistake she'd made once back when she was a novice), catching a typo in page proofs, or noticing when so much as a hair—or a flower—was out of place on a set.

Now, as she headed off toward hair and makeup, the last line from a nursery rhyme popped into her head: *All for the want of a horseshoe nail . . .*

It was the story of her life in reverse. She'd started with nothing and built her business inch by inch, nail by nail, thus winning the battle against those, like her uncle, who would have torn her down. From her mother, she'd learned that if you wanted to stand out, you had to work harder and do whatever it was you did that much better than everyone else. So Abigail had always looked for ways to distinguish herself. She'd launched her catering business during a time when miniquiches, which had been all the rage, were on the verge of becoming passé and had quickly developed a reputation for fresh, innovative hors d'oeuvres— Moroccan cigars of rolled phyllo pastry stuffed with asparagus and morels, hamachi with a sprinkling of bonito flakes set on a Chinese soup spoon, grilled octopus crostini, and miniature foie gras brûlées. The events Abigail had catered were like no others, and consequently, she'd been in great demand.

But occasionally, things happened that were beyond even her control. Like the fire in Las Cruces. As she settled into her chair in the makeup room, she felt her stomach clench at the thought. During the day, she was usually too consumed with work to agonize over it. It was mainly at night that she was haunted by thoughts of the poor girl who'd perished in the fire. As a result, she slept fitfully. While Kent slumbered maddeningly beside her, she would often slip from their bed and go downstairs to read or watch TV. Last night, she'd only had about four hours' sleep. If she was short-tempered, was it any wonder?

Still, that was no excuse for biting that young and clearly inexperienced PA's head off. Abigail had regretted it almost as soon as her outburst was over. Hadn't it been her cracking the whip that had led, if only indirectly, to the tragedy in Las Cruces? On the other hand, she thought, the trouble with young people these days was that everyone, from their parents on down, coddled them incessantly, constantly telling them they were special, showering them with praise even when they'd done nothing to deserve it. Sometimes a kick in the behind was just what was needed. *Welcome to the real world.*

Abigail's introduction to the real world had been more like a dive off a suspension bridge. Within days of her mother's death, she was on a bus to Connecticut, where she already had a job interview lined up. She'd been plotting her escape for some time, having spent countless hours in the public library scouring want ads in big-city newspapers. When she'd spotted the ad in the *New York Times*, for personal chef to a family in Greenwich, it had leaped out at her. Desperate to secure an interview, she'd lied about her age, saying she was twenty-one. Luckily she'd looked older than seventeen, and she knew her way around a kitchen, thanks to her mom's careful tutelage and the cakes Abigail had sold door to door. Her luck held, for when she arrived at the Henrys' Tudor-style mansion on the aptly named Gateway Drive, it was to find Mrs. Henry at her wits' end, the caterer she'd hired for a big party she was throwing that weekend having bailed on her due to some mix-up in scheduling. With a cool that surprised even herself, Abigail stepped right in, confidently assuring Mrs. Henry that she could handle it, though she'd never catered a party in her life. Her only experience in that area had been careful observation of the various parties hosted by the Meriwethers during her mother's tenure with them. Mrs. Henry hired her on the spot.

And now look at her. Abigail had a career most people would kill for. A handsome husband who was accomplished in his own right. A daughter who was smart and beautiful. So why wasn't she more content? Why did every little thing seem to rub her the wrong way?

Partly it had to do with Kent. There was no use denying that they'd grown apart. Her husband used to say that they were like swans, mated for life. But these days Abigail would have likened them more to a pair of goldfish, swimming around and around each other without ever really connecting. She couldn't remember the last time they'd even had sex. She wasn't entirely to blame, either. Kent devoted so much of his time and energy to his patients—not to mention his pet causes—that he was often out when she arrived home from work (though he seemed to have short-term memory loss in regard to that). Case in point: The night before, she'd gotten home early, having hinted to him that morning that she was in an amorous mood, only to be greeted by a note stuck to the refrigerator, saying he probably wouldn't be getting in until late and that she shouldn't wait up for him. It was close to midnight by the time he rolled in. He'd spent the evening at another one of his rabble-rousing town hall meetings. By then, she'd been too tired for sex. What made it so aggravating was that she wasn't even allowed to express her annoyance. Kent was doing "good works," while she was serving the gods of commerce. There was no comparison, in his view.

She still loved him, though, and hoped he still loved her. Once this whole hideous business with the factory had been straightened out, she would make good on her vow to arrange a trip to someplace romantic. Paris . . . or maybe Venice, where they'd gone on their honeymoon. Venice, yes, she thought dreamily. What better place to rekindle their passion?

She closed her eyes as the makeup artist, an older woman named Candace, powdered her nose and applied shadow to her lids. Usually Abigail spent the time in hair and makeup gossiping with Candace, who'd been in the business long enough to accrue a lifetime's worth of stories that would "curl your hair without any help from me," as she liked to joke. But today Abigail remained quiet, indulging instead in a fantasy of her and Kent ensconced in a suite at the Gritti Palace. She was picturing them having breakfast out on the terrace after a morning of mad lovemaking when her reverie was rudely interrupted by another mental image, which popped up out of nowhere: Lila scrubbing the kitchen floor. Which was precisely the scene Abigail had encountered when she'd arrived home from work yesterday.

For some reason, the sight of Lila on her hands and knees with a scrub brush, like some latter-day Cinderella, had only served to irritate her. "Is that really necessary?" she asked, stepping around Lila to fetch a wineglass from the cupboard.

"Isn't this what you wanted?" Lila paused to gaze up at her innocently. She was wearing a print dress that Abigail recognized as a vintage Lily Pulitzer, her hair tied up in a scarf and diamond studs sparkling in her ears—Brooke Astor meets Carol Burnett's scrubwoman.

"Yes, but there's no need to take it to extremes. This isn't a theatrical production. Wouldn't a mop do just as well?" She couldn't help feeling that Lila was playing her new role to the hilt in order to elicit sympathy. But that was silly, wasn't it? Lila couldn't have known she'd be home early.

Lila shrugged, replying in a tone that verged on insolent, "Whatever you say. You're the boss."

Abigail thought, *She'll bend, but she won't break.*

Lila always did what was asked of her, giving no cause for complaint, but Abigail hadn't missed the prideful tilt of her chin or the defiant glint in her eyes. It wasn't helping matters, either, that Kent treated her like a family friend who was merely helping out around the house, or that Brewster jumped all over her, tail wagging, whenever she walked through the back door. Even Phoebe was coming around. It wasn't just that she tolerated Lila; she actually seemed to like her.

Abigail had half a mind to let Lila go. She might have done just that if a new wrinkle hadn't presented itself: The other day, Kent had said something in passing, as they'd been getting ready for bed, about some doctor friend of his to whom he'd spoken about Lila's brother.

At the mention of Vaughn, Abigail's heart rate ratcheted up, though she managed to reply in a normal tone of voice, "What about Lila's brother?"

Kent paused in the midst of pulling on his pajama bottoms. "Lila didn't tell you?" He seemed mildly surprised. Of course. He wasn't privy to her complicated history with Lila.

"Tell me what?" she asked.

"He has cancer."

"Cancer?" It had been decades since she'd had any contact with Vaughn, but for some reason the news hit hard. She felt as if the wind had been knocked out of her.

"Non-Hodgkin's lymphoma," Kent went on. She must have appeared shaken, for he paused to peer at her with concern. "Abby, are you all right? You look as if you've seen a ghost."

"I . . . I'm fine," she stammered. "It's just that I didn't know he was ill."

Kent gave a somber nod. "It's stage two, so his chances are good. But he's got a long road ahead of him."

"Poor Vaughn," she murmured, shaking her head as she lowered herself onto the bed, the hairbrush in her hand resting forgotten on one knee.

Kent shot her a puzzled look. "I didn't realize you and he were close."

Abigail didn't know how much to tell him—he'd wonder why she'd withheld it until now—so she settled on a partial truth. "Vaughn was always nice to me," she said, letting it go at that.

It had been preying on her mind ever since. She couldn't stop thinking about Vaughn and the fact that he was ill. Though it had been more than two decades since she'd last seen him, she knew she couldn't let any more time elapse; she might not get another chance.

Easier said than done. She'd had a devil of a time prying his whereabouts out of Lila. At first all she'd been able to glean was that he was staying with a friend in the city.

"Why don't I give him your number?" Lila hedged. "That way, he can call you when he's feeling up to it."

"Or I could leave him a message."

Lila gave her a flat look that Abigail recognized, from when they were kids, as her digging her heels in. "I don't think he wants his friend's machine tied up with a lot of calls for him."

"Doesn't he have a cell phone?"

"Who, Vaughn?" Lila gave a derisive snort. "You're talking about a guy who spends most of his time in places that don't even have running water, much less cell-phone service. When he calls, it's usually from a sat phone."

Abigail felt herself losing patience. "Fine, whatever. So just give me the number of where he's staying. Really, Lila, I don't see the problem. It's not like I'm going to be pestering him at odd hours. I just want . . ." She paused. What *did* she want? ". . . to see how he's doing."

"I told you, he's holding up just fine. Better than expected, as a matter of fact."

"I'd like to see for myself, if you don't mind."

"Right now, the only people he's seeing are his friends," Lila said pointedly.

Determined not to let Lila's little power trip get to her, Abigail replied breezily, "Well, then, I'm sure he'll be delighted to hear from me."

In the end, she'd managed to wrangle from Lila the address and phone number where her brother was staying. For all the good it had done her. Abigail had left several messages, none of which had been returned so far. Was Vaughn really so sick that he couldn't pick up the phone? The uncertainty nibbled at her like tiny rodent's teeth. What if he wasn't do ing as well as Lila had said? What if he needed some kind of help, something that was in her power to provide? A private nurse? Money to tide him over until he was back on his feet? Whatever it was, she'd be there for him, just as he'd been for *her* when she'd needed it. Vaughn hadn't turned his back on her like the rest of the Meriwhethers. Now it was her turn to repay the favor.

After a restless couple of nights she'd decided that, if Vaughn wouldn't return her calls, she would just have to drop in on him unannounced, even if it meant catching him at a bad time. In fact, she planned to head over there as soon as her segment wrapped.

Contemplating that prospect, she made her way back to the set, freshly coifed and powdered, to find Dana Zeigler, the host for her segment, conferring with the director, Tim Graberman. Tim resembled a

large stick insect, all arms and legs and protruding eyes, while Dana, with
her fiery red hair, stood out like an Olympic torch amid the small army
of cameramen and sound engineers mobilizing around her. She spotted
Abigail and broke into a grin, waving to her as if they were old friends.
Which, in a way, they were. In the eight years that Abigail had been doing regular guest spots on *A.M. America*, she'd seen other anchors and pro-
ducers come and go, while she and Dana had remained fixtures.

Nothing lasts forever, whispered the old voice of insecurity in Abigail's
head. What if the public were to learn that she'd been partly responsible
for the death of that poor girl in Las Cruces? If the guilt she felt was any
indication of what the public backlash would be, it could spell the end
of her career. She felt a cool trickle of unease at the thought.

It took all of Abigail's media savvy to keep the stress and sleepless
nights from showing on her face when, minutes later, the cameras rolling,
Dana launched into her thirty-second intro. It wouldn't do to let the
viewers see any cracks in her facade, she thought, for them to know that
underneath this calm, smiling exterior she was as fallible as they.

She chatted as easily with Dana as if they were in her own kitchen at
Rose Hill as she pressed pastry dough into tart pans and whisked the
cranberry juice reduction into the softened mascarpone, then folded it
into the whipped cream. While spooning poached cranberries over the
finished tarts, she filled the viewers in on her upcoming projects, which
included a book on wedding planning and a food festival to raise money
for an orphanage in Bangladesh, in which she'd be participating along
with a number of other chefs.

It wasn't until Abigail was wrapping up, with a tip on holiday party
decor, that Dana ambushed her, interjecting with a staged coyness,
"From what I hear, you'll be getting some help this year from someone
who knows a little something about entertaining herself."

Abigail was momentarily thrown. How had Dana found out about
Lila? With Gordon's suicide, there had been a last flurry of the media
frenzy surrounding the DeVrieses, but in the weeks since, with Lila out
of the public eye, there had been no mention of her in the press. Dana
must have her own sources.

Abigail quickly recovered her wits—wasn't her catchphrase "When life gives you lemons, make lemon meringue pie"?

"You must mean my dear old friend Lila DeVries. Yes, we're lucky to have her," she replied without missing a beat. She carefully positioned a cranberry atop the tart, smiling as though she and Lila were indeed the best of friends.

Dana clued the audience in. "For any of you who've just dropped in from another planet, we're talking about *the* Lila DeVries, widow of the late Gordon DeVries, who was convicted earlier this year in the Vertex scandal. If you were wondering where she'd disappeared to, I'm here to report she's alive and well and working for Abigail. *As her live-in housekeeper.*"

Abigail seized the opportunity to spin a negative into a positive. Fortunately, she'd anticipated being questioned about Lila—just not this soon. "Yes, and I tell you, Dana, she's been a godsend. In fact, I don't know what we would have done without her. You see, my old housekeeper had to leave suddenly because of a family crisis, and we were in a real pickle. When Lila found out, she took pity on us and insisted on helping out—that's the kind of person she is. Oh, I know how she's been portrayed by the press, but she's nothing like that. Which only goes to show, you can't believe everything you read in the papers."

"'Selfless' isn't exactly a word that comes to mind with Lila DeVries," Dana lobbed back at her. "Does it concern you at all, given the negative publicity she's gotten, that this might tarnish your own image?"

"Not in the least," Abigail replied smoothly. "Besides, what are friends for, if not to look after each other in times of trouble?" She smiled serenely into the camera, as if her words weren't sticking in her throat like a spoonful of dry cornmeal.

"Well, we wish you both a happy holiday." Dana moved to wrap things up with Tim Graberman signaling wildly to her off camera, adding with a sly chuckle, "One thing's for sure: It's going to be an interesting one in the Armstrong house this year."

You can say that again, Abigail answered silently. She flashed Dana a dirty look as she unclipped the mike from her lapel, letting her know that she hadn't appreciated being blindsided, but all in all she was confident that she'd managed to salvage the situation, even if it had meant having to lie through her teeth on national TV.

On her way to her dressing room, she spied the PA snapped at earlier, scurrying down the corridor just ahead of her as if she were trying to escape her notice. Feeling a fresh pang of regret, Abigail called out to her, and the girl—thin and dark like Phoebe, though not nearly as pretty—slowed to a halt, looking as if she expected to get yelled at again. But Abigail only said sweetly, "I just wanted to thank you for doing such a nice job. I'm sorry if I was a little hard on you earlier. Let's just say it's been one of those mornings."

The girl relaxed visibly. "It won't happen again, Ms. Armstrong." Color rose in her cheeks, and she hastened to add, "The poinsettias, I mean. I'll remember the next time."

Abigail smiled and touched her arm. "I'm sure it won't. And please, call me Abigail."

The girl looked as if she'd been handed a door prize. "Between you and me, they're not my favorite flowers, either," she confided. "My grandma always gets those huge ones in tubs, and her cats use them as litter boxes. The whole house stinks to high heaven."

"In that case, I have an excellent recipe for potpourri. It makes a nice gift, and it'll mask the odor," Abigail said, leaning in slightly, as if in confidence. "It's in my holiday craft book. Why don't you e-mail me your address, and I'll send you a copy?"

The girl was glowing as Abigail swept off down the hall, as if she'd received a papal blessing instead of the promise of a book she could have easily purchased in any store.

A short while later, Abigail was heading across town in a chauffeured Town Car, on her way to see Vaughn. It was still early, so there was a good chance of her catching him at home. Even so, she felt strange about showing up unannounced. Would he be happy to see her . . . or would she only be intruding? Would he even recognize her as the girl he'd known all those years ago? And Vaughn—he had to have changed, too. Would the forty-one-year-old man bear any resemblance to the boy she remembered with such affection? Would they have anything in common other than their shared past?

The car pulled up in front of a converted loft building on West 22nd, between Fifth Avenue and Avenue of the Americas, and Abigail climbed out. She found the correct button on the intercom by the front entrance, where the name "Rinaldi" was penned on a strip of curling adhesive tape, and was about to press it when a man came barreling through the door. Abigail seized the opportunity to slip in after him.

She took the ancient, creaking elevator to the fourth floor, where she knocked on the door to 4B. "Coming!" cried a female voice from within. Seconds later, the door swung open to reveal a thirty-something woman, so petite that Abigail might have mistaken her for a kid if not for her spiky hair that stood up like the feathers on a baby duck—platinum blond with crimson tips—and her green eyes that, in contrast, appeared world-weary. Eyes that looked Abigail up and down, taking in her sheared mink coat and Christian Louboutin heels before instantly dismissing her as someone who had no business being there.

"What can I do for you?" she asked none too politely. Her voice was unexpectedly throaty, with a Demi Moore–like rasp.

"I'm looking for Vaughn Meriwhether," Abigail told her.

"He expecting you?" She squinted at Abigail suspiciously, as if she already knew the answer. She couldn't have been much younger than Abigail, even if she dressed like someone closer to Phoebe's age—barefoot, with her jeans so full of holes they were like some intricate denim web and her baby-doll top made of some flimsy fabric through which her small breasts were faintly visible.

"Just tell him an old friend from Greenhaven is here to see him." Abigail was used to being recognized by strangers when she was out and about, but clearly this woman didn't know her from Adam.

The old Armstrong charisma didn't seem to be working, either, for the woman deliberated a moment before replying, "Wait here." She turned and padded off down the hallway, reappearing after a minute or so to usher Abigail in, somewhat grudgingly, it seemed.

Abigail stepped into a huge, light-filled space with exposed brick walls and plank flooring so marred and unevenly worn that it had to date back to the days when the building had been a factory. It was so roomy, what little furniture there was looked marooned almost, like that of someone just moving in or in the process of moving out. What saved it from looking too spare were the large, abstract sculptures positioned throughout. One in particular caught her eye, a sort of totem pole constructed out of what looked like knotted towels.

Seated on the sofa by the bank of floor-to-ceiling windows, an open book facedown on one knee, was a lanky, blond-haired man. A man who was a stranger to her but at the same time brought a shock of recognition.

Vaughn was so lean that he seemed stripped of all but muscle and bone. Other than that, she wouldn't have known he was ill. His blue eyes were as vivid as ever, even more so against the deeply tanned contours of his face, in which the lines carved into it formed a kind of rugged topography. Even if she hadn't known what he did for a living, she'd have pegged him as an adventurer. He had the look of someone not content to stay put for any length of time. Yet unlike his self-appointed bodyguard, he didn't appear world-weary. The lively expression he wore was that of someone, sick or not, who was deeply engaged in the business of living.

Vaughn seemed to be trying to get a fix on her as well. It wasn't until she drew nearer that he broke into a grin, leaping to his feet so abruptly that his book was knocked to the floor.

"Abby? Is that you?" He enfolded her in a quick, hard embrace—a fleeting impression of hard muscle and bone—that left her struggling to catch her breath. He stepped back to grin at her. "I can't believe it. How did you even know where to find me? Lila, right?"

Abigail nodded. "I hope you don't mind my barging in on you like this, but you never answered any of my messages. . . ."

She watched him glance in confusion at his friend, who gave a shrug. "I must have erased them by mistake," she said.

Abigail had her doubts. From the possessive way Vaughn's friend was hovering at his elbow, it seemed more likely that she'd erased the messages on purpose.

Vaughn must have come to the same conclusion, for he gave his friend—or was it girlfriend?—a wry look bordering on reproach, saying, "Abigail, meet Gillian, my unofficial nurse. She insists on treating me like a dying man, even though I keep telling her I feel perfectly fine."

"A good thing, too." Gillian turned to Abigail, saying without a hint of apology, "If it weren't for me, he'd spend his days hanging out with his friends or roaming the streets like some nomad instead of getting the rest he needs."

"Well, you're obviously doing a good job because he looks to be in excellent shape. But I'm sure you could use a break, so why don't you let me take over for a bit?" Abigail proposed, hoping for some time alone with Vaughn.

Gillian got the hint. She flashed Abigail a veiled look before announcing to Vaughn, "I'll be in my studio if you need me." With that, she sauntered off, her twelve-year-old's behind twitching in her torn jeans, her shock of platinum hair bristling like the fur of a small but feisty dog whose turf was being threatened.

"Gillian's a sculptor," Vaughn explained.

Abigail nodded, glancing around at the artwork, each piece more bizarrely arresting than the next. "So how do you two know each other?" she asked.

"We used to date," he said in a matter-of-fact tone. "A long time ago. We're just friends now." Something told her he'd been the one to break it off.

Typical of a man, Abigail thought. They always imagined it was a mutual decision when they ended a relationship, and that as long as the woman didn't cry or make a scene, there was no reason they couldn't remain friends. But from what Abigail had seen, it was a moot point whether or not he and Gillian were sleeping together. She was obviously still in love with him.

The thought brought a small dart of jealousy. Though why she should feel even remotely jealous of Gillian was beyond her. It wasn't as though she and Vaughn were or had ever been romantically involved, not counting that one night out at the quarry, which over time had come to seem more like something she'd dreamed.

"Do you plan on staying here for the time being, or will you be getting your own place?" she asked.

He shrugged. "I haven't made any long-range plans. My life isn't my own at the moment—it's in my doctor's hands." He made a face. "Don't get me wrong, I trust the guy. But it's a weird feeling, I can tell you. Like being a little kid again, having your parents deciding everything for you."

"How's that going?" She was fearful for some reason of saying the dreaded word: *cancer.*

"Not bad. I seem to be weathering the chemo okay. I'm told it gets worse, but so far the only side effect has been some nausea. That, and I'm tired all the time, even though mostly all I do is lie around and read." He bent to retrieve the book that had fallen onto the floor—a battered copy of Jack Kerouac's *On the Road*—and placed it on the coffee table.

"You don't look it," she commented. "In fact, overall, I'd say you look amazingly well."

"For someone with a life-threatening illness, you mean?" he replied with an ironic twist of his lips.

"That's not what I meant."

"No, but it's the truth."

"People recover from cancer all the time."

"So I'm told." He must have seen that he was making her uncomfortable, for he was quick to move on. "Listen, can I get you something to drink? There's coffee and tea, and some juice I think, though I'm never sure what's in the fridge. Gillian does all the shopping."

"No, thanks. I can't stay long," she told him.

"Well, make yourself comfortable, at least. You can stay a few minutes, can't you?" He helped her off with her coat. When she was seated on the sofa, he sank down beside her. "So, how have you been, Abby?" He looked deeply into her eyes, as if he truly wanted to know.

"Compared to what you're going through, I have no complaints." He didn't need to know that she'd been a wreck ever since finding out about the fire in Las Cruces.

"I've known worse than this," he said with a laugh. "Try spending two weeks in a cave, knee-deep in bat dung, with bugs crawling all over you."

She made a face. "Is all your work that . . . interesting?"

"I've had my share of adventures." His tone was that of someone for whom adventuring was second nature. "Most of what I film is wildlife, so I've been to some pretty remote places. Last year around this time, I was shooting in the Congo basin for a National Geographic special on the ivory poaching that's wiping out the elephant population there."

"Ever been attacked by a wild animal?" She felt a low, uneasy thrill at the thought.

"I was once charged by a gorilla—an eastern lowland gorilla, to be exact. Not the gentle creatures of Gorillas in the Mist. These guys, their only experience with man is getting shot at, so they don't take kindly to anyone invading their turf. Fortunately, I knew what to do to get him to back off."

"What was that?"

"Crouch down and act submissive."

She smiled and shook her head. "Somehow, I can't picture you being submissive."

He shrugged. "You do what you have to in order to survive. Though I don't know if that makes me smarter than the next guy, or if I'm just plain lucky."

"Maybe a little of both?"

"The truth is, the threat of attack from wild animals is vastly overrated," he went on. "You're more apt to meet your maker trying to get around in Third World countries where the roads are dicey and the native drivers even dicier. I can't tell you how many times I've seen my life flash before my eyes taking a hairpin turn on a steep mountain road. Choppers, too—it's easy to fly in too low and have the blades nearly get tangled up in a treetop."

"Sounds risky."

"Not as risky as run-ins with poachers. They won't hesitate to take a shot at you if they catch you sniffing around. Sometimes it's just to chase you off, but if they think you're going to end up cutting into their action, they won't think twice about putting a bullet in you."

"Have you ever been shot at?" She leaned toward him in fascination. This was the Vaughn she remembered, only even bolder and more colorful—an *Indiana Jones* movie come to life.

In answer, Vaughn hiked his right leg up onto the coffee table and lifted the cuff of his jeans to reveal a faded purplish scar on his calf, like a small puckered mouth. "A little souvenir from an armed guerrilla in Darfur, where we were filming the migration of the wildebeest. He took a potshot at our helicopter while we were flying in low. Luckily, it was only a flesh wound or I probably would've bled to death." He paused to shake his head, as if at the irony of it. "Funny, I always figured that when my time came, it'd be something like that—a bullet, or a plunge off a mountain road. I never imagined I'd go out with a whimper."

"This," she reached over to lightly brush her fingertips over the puckered scar tissue, a sensation that sent a low-voltage charge up her arm and down to the pit of her stomach, "is proof that someone up there likes you. So I wouldn't worry too much if I were you. You'll beat this, too." She spoke with an assurance she didn't feel, and prayed that it would be true.

He sat back to regard her thoughtfully. "And you, Miss Abby. Look at you, all grown up and with everything you've ever dreamed of. I just hope it's made you happy."

She frowned slightly. Was he mocking her? "You say that like it's all for show."

"Not at all. I was just wondering why a woman who has the world on a string would feel she has something to prove."

His tone seemed to carry a faint note of reproach, which instantly put her on the defensive. "What makes you say that? Was it Lila? Did she say something to you?"

"No, but since you brought it up, what's with you and my sister? Did you hire her to make a point, or is this your backassward way of burying the hatchet?" His blue eyes cut through her like a blowtorch. She saw no accusation in them, not yet, just a wish to understand. She wished she fully understood it herself so she could offer an explanation.

"No one forced her to come work for me," she said.

"According to her, she didn't feel she had a choice. As I recall, she was pretty desperate at the time."

"Well, she's not the only one who knows what it's like to be desperate." Abigail felt the old bitterness creep up on her. "I lost my home and everyone I loved, all in one fell swoop. You were the only one who didn't turn your back on me." She felt the prickle of impending tears and willed herself not to cry. She didn't want Vaughn's pity. Hadn't she come here to offer *him* comfort? "You don't know how much it meant to me, those letters you wrote. There were times when they were the only thing that kept me going."

"I don't remember what I wrote, but knowing what I was like back then, I'm sure it was pretty boring stuff." He looked pleased but somewhat embarrassed. "If I'd known it would mean that much to you, I'd have at least tried to come up with something less mundane."

"It didn't matter *what* you wrote. It was the fact that you wrote to me at all."

He reached over to lay his hand over hers, a light touch that she was acutely aware of. "Don't punish Lila because of what our parents did. I know she let you down, but she was just a kid."

So were you, Abigail thought. But she bit back the retort, knowing how protective he was of his sister. "I don't blame her for that," she said. She'd been hurt and angry at the time, yes, but the main source of betrayal was what had come after—Lila's inexplicable lack of communication, which had left her feeling utterly abandoned. "Actually, there's more to the story than you know."

Vaughn arched his brow in a questioning look. "I always suspected as much," he said. "So are you going to tell me what really happened?"

She hesitated a moment before replying, "It has to do with my mom and your dad." She paused, wondering if she'd be destroying any illusions he might still have about his father. But from the look on Vaughn's face, she got the feeling that he wouldn't be all that shocked by her revelation. "They were sleeping together," she went on. "Your mother must have found out. I guess that's why she cooked up that whole story about the stolen necklace, so she wouldn't have to confront your dad." She hastened to explain, "It wasn't that Mama was in love with him. I don't think he loved her, either. They were *fond* of each other, but it was more complicated than that." The whole sorry tale had unraveled in the months before her mother's death; Rosalie's need to unburden herself had been so great that it had outweighed her better judgment in revealing it all to her young and impressionable daughter. "You know what she was like. How devoted she was to your family. She would have done anything—even *that*—to keep it together, keep your dad from straying outside the home. Oh, I know it was terribly misguided of her, and believe me, she paid the price. But, as strange as it might seem, her intentions were good." Rosalie hadn't been a duplicitous person by nature; it was just that her boundaries had become so blurred that she'd lost sight of where she left off and the Meriwhethers began.

Vaughn sat there in silence, taking it all in. At last, he sat back and let out a breath. "Wow. That's quite a tale."

"Are you sorry I told you?" she asked somewhat sheepishly.

"Just the opposite. I'm glad you did."

"Even if it makes your father out to be a cad?"

Vaughn's mouth flattened in a mirthless smile. "I didn't need you to tell me that. And if you're worried that it might have had something to do with my parents getting divorced, don't be. They'd have split up no matter what."

"So you don't hate my mother?"

"Hate her? No, I could never hate Rosie. She was like a second mother to me." Vaughn's expression softened, a look of affection crossing his handsome, weathered face.

"And you were the son she never had." Abigail smiled, remembering how her mother had doted on Vaughn.

"She loved Lila, too."

He was reminding her that, in Abigail's place, Rosalie would have forgiven Lila long ago. In fact, she *had* forgiven her, as she had Ames and Gwen, never once blaming the Meriwhethers for their shabby treatment of her at the end. Her mother's heart might have been in the wrong place at times, but there had been no room in it for bitterness.

Instead, she'd left her daughter to become the receptacle for all that.

Now, looking into Vaughn's clear blue eyes, in which she saw herself reflected in a pure light untainted by the passage of time, as the innocent girl she'd once been, Abigail wished with all her heart that she could be that girl, free of all the resentment she'd accumulated like radioactive waste through the years. She had hoped that Lila would provide the key to some sort of understanding, but it wasn't exactly working out that way. If she and Lila were playing out some sort of psychodrama, it was shaping up to be a battle with no clear winner.

"I'm not heartless," she said in her own defense, but it sounded weak even to her own ears.

"I don't think that. The girl I knew, the girl who answered every one of my letters, she wasn't heartless." Vaughn spoke softly, holding her pinned with his gaze.

"Maybe that girl doesn't exist anymore."

"Oh, I think she does. I think she's in there somewhere." Lightly, he brought a finger to her chest, his touch sending a warm shock through her. "Keep looking and you'll find her."

A memory surfaced. In her mind, she saw herself peering through the living room curtains in anticipation of the mailman's arrival, hoping he would bring another letter from Vaughn. Then the thrill when she'd open the mailbox to find an envelope with Vaughn's handwriting on it, the delicious feel of the crinkly stationery in her hand, and the way her fingers had trembled tearing it open.

But she could only bear to remember so much at a time, and with Vaughn, the memories were coming too fast and thick. She drew the curtain over them for the time being, withdrawing into her safety zone, where she wouldn't have to feel so much.

"Thank you, Dr. Freud. But, just to set the record straight, I came here to see if there was anything *I* could do for *you*," she told him.

"As you can see, I lack for nothing." He gestured about him. "There's only one thing I want from you."

"Name it," she said.

"Come see me again."

Moved by the obvious sincerity with which he spoke, she was unable to reply for a moment. "That's it?"

He laughed. "You were expecting more?"

"I thought I could be of use to you in some way. You know, your every wish is my command." She spoke lightly so he wouldn't view it as charity, but at the same time, she wanted him to know that she had deep resources.

"I don't need a genie," he said, "but I can always use a friend."

Abigail smiled at him. Far from her mind just then was any thought of Lila, or her shaky marriage, or the pressing problems at work. She realized that all these years she'd been carrying an idealized version of Vaughn in her head. But she very much wanted to know the living, breathing man seated beside her now, however much time he might have left on this earth.

"In that case, I shall return," she said. "Right now, though, I should get going. I don't want to overstay my welcome, or Gillian might have me thrown out." Reluctantly, she rose to her feet.

He gave a knowing chuckle even as he came to Gillian's defense. "She's really nice once you get to know her."

Somehow, I don't think I'll ever be given that opportunity, she thought. She was reaching for her coat when some impulse made her ask, "It's none of my business, but were you ever in love with her?"

"You're right, it's none of your business," he said with a laugh.

She hugged him good-bye at the door. He smelled not of sickness but of the outdoors. He must have gone for a walk earlier. She imagined him bundled up in his jacket, tramping along the sidewalk, no particular destination in mind. How long since she'd done that herself? Since she'd taken the time to appreciate the joy of simply being alive?

Reflecting on it as she rode down in the elevator, Abigail knew she would most certainly be back. As often as Vaughn would have her. Not just because she wanted to get to know the person he'd become—she wanted to reconnect with the person *she'd* been.

It wasn't until she stepped outside into the chill air that she was reminded of the person she was today—a woman whose business might be on the brink of ruin—by the shrill ringing of her cell phone.

It was Señor Perez. "I'm afraid I have some rather disturbing news to report," he said in a somber tone after bringing her up-to-date on the progress in rebuilding the factory. "The girl's mother—Señora Delgado—appears to have vanished."

"Vanished?" In that moment, with her mind still wrapped up in thoughts of Vaughn, Abigail couldn't think of a reason why the girl's mother would have disappeared. "Where could she have gone?"

"I can't say for certain, but I have a strong suspicion it was a *coyote* that carried her off." Perez's voice was heavy with portent. Abigail shuddered at the image of the woman being devoured by a wild animal before she realized that he meant the two-legged variety—men who extorted large sums of money to guide those desperate to get across the border into the United States by any means necessary. "If that's the case, she'll be lucky to make it across the border alive," he said ominously.

Abigail had the awful suspicion that he wouldn't shed any tears should that prove to be the case. "And if she does?" Shivering, she pulled her coat more tightly around her.

"I can't say, Señora," he said darkly. "All I know is that she's a formidable woman, this Concepción Delgado."

8

By noontime, it was well over 100 degrees in the shade. What little shade there was. The only relief from the sun in all that blasted expanse of desert was the scant protection provided by the paloverde trees that straggled along the banks of the arroyos and by the boulder formations that dotted the landscape like remnants of a lost civilization. Except for that, as far as the naked eye could see, there were only endless stretches of baked hardpan dotted with scrub and cacti and the mountains, shimmering in the distance like the fabled city of Cibola, which never seemed to grow any closer. None of the creatures that slithered and skittered about in the relative cool of the mornings and evenings were stirring at this hour. The only thing moving was the ragged band of travelers trudging with weary, numb, mindless determination on their way to God knew where, their stunted shadows trailing in defeat alongside them under the harsh noonday sun.

Concepción had never known heat such as this. Not as a girl toiling under the hot sun on her family's farm in San Juan de Córdoba. Not as a young wife selling mangoes and papayas by the side of the road to earn extra money after her husband had spent all of his in bars. Not in all the years of working in poorly ventilated factories amid the collective heat of so many other bodies. That was a warm breath compared to this. This sun was merciless, unrelenting, pummeling her into submission. Even death had come to seem a welcome alternative. The only reason she was still alive, she was sure, was because God wasn't ready for her to die. She had almost no strength left in her body. She was weak from lack of food and so parched that her swollen tongue felt like a foreign object in her mouth. What else could it be but His grace guiding her steps, coaxing her onward?

When they'd first started out, there had been ten of them. Now there were only seven. Elena Gutierrez had been the first to go. Overweight and not in the best of health to begin with, she had sickened and died before they'd even reached the border, crammed into the airless back of the truck along with the others. There had been times, bumping along those endless roads, breathing in dust and exhaust fumes, when Concepción had wondered if she herself would survive the trip. But she'd only to remind herself of her purpose in coming in order to strengthen her resolve. Unlike the others, she wasn't driven by the prospect of work in the land of the Norte-Americanos. What she wanted was justice.

The Señora, whose greed had cost Concepción's daughter her life, had to be made accountable.

They'd laid Elena to rest in a ditch by the side of the road. The *coyote* was a hard man named Hector González, his face pitted with old acne scars and his eyes like two holes bored into his head. He'd refused to let them give Elena a decent burial, insisting that it would only slow them down. The most Concepción could do was offer a prayer as they'd covered the body with rocks and brush, marking the spot with a small cross fashioned out of two sticks. At least Elena had fared better than Milagros, who'd died in agony, burned almost beyond recognition.

They'd arrived at the border in the dead of night, some miles west of Nogales, a place far from any known road, accessible only by the dirt track—little more than a trail in spots—over which the truck transporting them had bumped and lurched for the better part of an hour. Hector had cautioned them to keep an eye out for the border patrol, nonetheless. Off-road vehicles and helicopters regularly patrolled this stretch, he'd warned. With that, he had given them what remained of their meager supply of food and water and wished them luck.

Santos Nuñez, just shy of seventeen, with a mustache struggling to take hold on a face as smooth as a baby's bottom, grabbed the *coyote* by the arm as he was turning to go. "You can't just leave us here. You promised to take us to America!" he cried. Concepción heard the fear in his voice.

Hector shot him a look of contempt before hawking up a great gob of spit, which he aimed at the boy's feet. "That," he said, pointing out at the great shadowy expanse beyond the wire fence in front of which they stood, where the only sound was the rustling of the wind, and the mountain range in the distance wasn't so much a shape as an even blacker void against the nighttime sky, "is America."

The others had merely grumbled and shuffled their feet, not wanting to anger the one person who seemed to have any idea which direction they should head. Concepción was the only one who'd dared stand up to Hector. "You're a liar and a thief. Worse than the *gabachos*," she'd hissed, thrusting her face close to his, so close that she'd caught the sour whiskey smell on his breath.

But the *coyote* had only laughed in her face. "You can turn back, if you like. Or take your chances out there," he said with a contemptuous flick of his wrist. "*Como se quiere.*" Suit yourself.

Concepción had chosen to continue on, as had the others. They'd come this far; why turn back now? Desperation will make a lunatic out of a sane man, she knew. And they were all desperate. The men desperate to find work up North so they could send money to their wives back home. Their women desperate for a fresh start in the Promised Land. But what they hadn't counted on was just how brutal the elements would be. Had they not arrived under cover of night, had they known the full extent of what lay ahead, would they have chosen to go on? Concepción couldn't speak for the others, but she knew nothing would have made her turn back. Her life was of little consequence to her now. All that was left for her was to accomplish what she'd set out to do.

That first night they'd walked until dawn, the sunrise a bloody gash along the horizon before they'd stopped to rest. Alberto Muñoz, their self-appointed leader in Hector's absence, stated that they were now far

enough into the desert to keep from being detected by the border patrol's infrared devices. He'd made this crossing once before and was now
positioning himself as an authority in the matter. Though Concepción
couldn't help wondering why, if he knew so much, he hadn't spoken up
earlier, when everyone had been so fearful of the *coyote*'s leaving them to
fend for themselves.

When Alberto suggested that they rest for a few hours before continuing, she reasoned, "Wouldn't it make more sense to keep going while
it's still cool out and rest when the sun is high?"

"I'm tired and my feet hurt," Guadalupe Reyes complained. A small,
sallow woman with bad teeth, Guadalupe had been complaining ever
since they'd left Las Cruces, while her long-suffering husband, a sad-eyed
man with drooping jowls, had mostly sat silent. She was thirsty, she was
hungry, she couldn't move her bowels. She'd whined until Concepción
had wanted to slap her.

The others were tired, too, so they voted in favor of saving their
strength for the even longer trek ahead. It wasn't until the sun was high in
the sky that they had reason to regret that decision. For it wasn't the
bountiful sun of Las Cruces that coaxed seeds into sprouting and buds
into flowering; this was a cruel sun that withered everything in its path
and sucked the moisture from your very flesh. There was no escaping it,
either. No shaded doorways or awnings under which to duck. No trees,
even, except those clinging stubbornly to the banks of the arroyos,
scrawny-looking things scarcely fit to shelter a bird. The sun beat down
with a relentlessness that rendered you mad before crushing you under
the hot iron of its wheel, as it had Luis Fernández.

Luis, a farmer whose crops had dried up in the drought that had
held their region in its grip for the past two years in a row, had been on
his way north to seek work in the fertile fields of the San Fernando
Valley, where he'd heard a man could earn enough picking fruit in one
week to feed his entire family back home for a month. The trouble was
that Luis wasn't a young man. The intense heat, coupled with the lack
of food and water—by then, they'd nearly run out of both—was testing

even the hardiest constitutions, and for the sixty-year-old Luis, it had proved fatal.

In the beginning, the genial farmer had kept them distracted with his jokes and stories, but by the end of the second day, he'd fallen silent. So it came as a shock when, as they were crossing an arroyo, he ground to a sudden halt, bellowing, *"Dios! Donde está?"* He stood swaying on his feet like a *borracho*, legs spread to keep from being pitched off balance, shaking his fist up at the pitiless sky. "Show your face, you rotten bastard!"

"It wasn't God who abandoned us," young Santos growled in response. "It was that stinking whore's son of a *coyote*."

"Hermano, come sit. You're tired and need to rest," Concepción urged, gently taking hold of Luis's arm and attempting to guide him over to the riverbank while the others looked on in glazed-eyed exhaustion. But the poor man was no longer in his right mind by then, and he shook her hand off as if it had been a fly.

"Diablo!" he hissed at her, his bloodshot eyes staring through her at something—or someone—only he could see. His battered straw hat sat atilt on his head, wisps of white hair poking from underneath it like ticking from a featherbed. He swung around to jab a finger in the direction of his fellow travelers, squatting on their heels in the dust. "You'll all burn in hell!"

Edgardo Estevez, a heavyset man whose large belly had shrunk over the course of their journey until it now resembled a deflated balloon drooping over his belt, let out a harsh, cracked laugh. "We're already there, my friend, in case you haven't noticed."

Hours later, Luis was dead.

Unlike poor Elena, he had a decent burial, at least. They scraped a shallow grave for him out of the parched soil and fashioned a cross out of small rocks laid side by side.

Natividad Vargas was the next to go. After three days in the savage sun, the plump little berry of a woman withered like a raisin and grew so listless that she was unable to keep up. When she and her husband, Ernesto, fell behind, Concepción despaired of ever seeing them again.

But on the afternoon of the following day, a lone figure appeared on the horizon from the direction in which they'd come, wavering in and out of view amid the heat that rose from the desert floor in shimmering waves. When it drew closer, she saw that it was Ernesto. He was alone.

After he caught up to them, Concepción listened with a heavy heart to his sad but all too predictable tale. "She begged me to go on without her. She didn't want me to die, too." Ernesto's eyes were red-rimmed but dry—he was too dehydrated even for tears. "But I told her I wouldn't leave her, not ever, not for anything. I told her we would go on together as soon as she was strong enough to continue. But she never . . . she—" A big, stalwart bear of a man, Ernesto buried his head in his hands, breaking into dry, hacking sobs.

Concepción, close to the breaking point herself, took him in her arms and held him as he wept like a child. She offered no words of comfort, for she knew there were no words for such grief.

Now, five days into it, all she could think about was water. Water, in all its many forms. Deep, cold lakes ringed with snowcapped mountains. Streams tumbling over rocks. Rainwater dripping from eaves. She dreamed of the slow-moving river where she used to swim as a child, and she'd have traded her soul for a dipper of cool, sweet water from the well in her village back home. Her thirst was an entity unto itself, a creature that raved and clawed inside her and would have killed for more than her meager ration had she unleashed it. Was she going mad, too?

Part of her would have welcomed it. For madness would soon be followed by death, which would reunite her with her daughter.

At times, she could have sworn she was there already. She would see her daughter skipping ahead of her, calling over her shoulder for Concepción to hurry up or they'd be late.

But late for what?

The past and the present became one, the visions dancing before her eyes no less real to her than the merciless landscape through which she trudged. She recalled the day of Milagros's birth and felt as if she were experiencing it all over again, her insides cramping with the pain. She could see the midwife at the foot of her bed, her withered brown hands, like the dried roots she used in brewing her potions, massaging the taut, rippling mound of Concepción's belly. And Gustavo peeking apprehensively into the room, hat in hand, looking not so much like an expectant father as like an errant schoolboy poking his head in where it didn't belong. She could hear the old midwife, Lupe, shooing him away, scolding that he had best behave himself now that he was about to become a father, and that if he didn't, she would come after him herself and beat some sense into him.

By then, his reputation was well-known among the villagers. But Concepción loved him despite his errant ways. How could she not? Even coming home late from bars stinking of liquor, he never walked in without a smile on his handsome gaucho's face, brimming with apologies and offering promises, no doubt heartfelt in that moment, that it was the last time, that he would never do this to her again. What did he need with all that when he had her? he'd say, pulling her into his arms. She was everything to him, the sun, the moon, and the stars all wrapped up into one. He would kiss her neck and whisper in her ear that he'd give her as many babies as she wanted, if only she would forgive him this one last time.

Each time Concepción would hate herself a little more for swallowing his lies. It wasn't until Milagros came that all that changed. In the instant that she first laid eyes on her daughter, the love she'd felt for her husband was transferred to the tiny, precious bundle with which she'd finally been blessed, after so much misfortune. Oh, she knew that Gustavo, in his own way, had tried to be the husband and father he'd always vowed to be. But the drink had had a hold on him as strong as the devil's. By the end, the only thing that had dried up had been his promises to quit drinking, until finally he stopped coming home altogether.

But now the daughter who'd filled that void inside her was gone, too. Which was why Concepción was so determined to make it through this ordeal. If she died out here in the desert, her soul would be in a state of eternal unrest, she feared. She had to stay alive long enough to accomplish what she'd set out to do. After that, she would willingly meet her maker.

Her thoughts were interrupted by Guadalupe Reyes wailing, "It's useless. We don't even know if we're going in the right direction. We're all going to die!" While the others had withered, she'd only grown more bloated. Her face, taut and shiny, was like a giant blister about to burst.

Concepción listened to as much of it as she could stand before she finally snapped, "If you're going to die, then hurry up and get on with it so you can leave the rest of us in peace!"

Guadalupe was shocked into silence.

Alberto Vargas spoke up in her defense. "She's right," he said wearily. "We could be going in circles, for all we know." The macho authority he'd bandied about earlier was nowhere in evidence now. His shoulders were slumped with exhaustion and defeat.

"We know that's west." Concepción pointed toward the distant hilltops, cast in the pinkish glow of the rising sun. "Which means if we keep going in that direction, we're bound to get to a road eventually." They were in California, that much she knew. A place where everyone owned their own car, two or three in some cases, she'd heard tell. And where there were cars, there were bound to be highways.

"Yes, but how much farther can we go without food or water?" asked the boy, Santos.

"We've come this far," she reminded him. "We'll make it the rest of the way, God willing."

"What about my wife? Was that God's will, too?" demanded Ernesto. "An innocent woman who'd have given her last drop of water to save someone else?" He glared at Concepción almost accusingly.

She thought once more of Milagros. Her innocent, good-hearted daughter, whose life had also been cut short. "I can't give you reasons." She spoke to Ernesto as a mother would to her child, firmly but not without compassion. "All I know is that we can't lose faith or we will die."

Somehow they summoned the strength to continue on. They trudged across the bare, scrubbed plain, passing through clumps of ocotillo and cholla that tore at their flesh and left them bleeding. After what seemed an eternity they crossed from the desert into scrublands, where the terrain was hillier and where they grew increasingly less mindful, while scrambling up boulder-strewn slopes, of the rattlesnakes that might be lurking in the crevices between rocks. So what if they were bitten? Death would only come sooner that way.

At midday, they stopped to rest beneath a rocky outcropping where there was some shade, at least. They passed around the last of the plastic jugs, in which only a scant inch or so of water remained, each taking a careful sip. When the sun had dipped below the horizon, they set out once more, Concepción urging them on despite her own exhaustion.

They were making their way up a steep ridge when she heard a sound that was like the rushing of a stream. The others heard it, too, and several people fell to their knees with cries of joy, while the more practical-minded, Concepción among them, were spurred on to scramble the rest of the way to the summit so as to more quickly reach the blessed body of water they imagined was on the other side.

But when she crested the ridge, there was no stream. It was something even better: a highway. The rushing sound they'd heard was that of cars whipping along it at high speed.

Concepción sank to her knees, sending up a heartfelt prayer of thanks. The boy, Santos, went charging down the slope, staggering in his delirium and crying out hoarsely. He might have succeeded in attracting the attention of a passing motorist if Alberto Muñoz, his good sense restored, hadn't run after him and tackled him to the ground.

"*Cuídate!*" warned the older man. "Don't you know what will happen if they catch us?"

It was at that moment that Concepción realized the journey, *her* journey, was far from over. Having emerged from the very fires of hell, she was now faced with another, seemingly insurmountable obstacle. How was she to locate her son-in-law, Eduardo, in this strange land, when she spoke no English and didn't know her way around? Where she would constantly be at risk of being apprehended by the authorities and sent back? She contemplated this as she stumbled along by the side of the road after having parted company with the others (at the suggestion of Alberto, who'd said that they would be too conspicuous traveling in a group).

She was near collapse when a battered yellow pickup pulled over onto the shoulder in a plume of dust and a pink-faced *gringo* in a battered straw hat stuck his head out the window. He called out to her in English, something she couldn't comprehend. It wasn't until he hooked a thumb toward the open bed of his pickup that she understood he was offering her a lift. She hesitated but an instant before climbing in. He might have been looking to turn her over to La Migra, he might even have been a murderer or a rapist, but at that moment she was too exhausted to care.

The *gringo* proved harmless, though. He dropped her off at the nearest filling station, in a sleepy little burg that didn't look to be much bigger than her village back home. She had a little bit of money—American dollars sewn into the hem of her dress—and, after quenching her thirst at the water fountain, she used some of it to buy a small carton of milk and some crackers and cheese in the convenience store. Luckily, the young man who waited on her was Hispanic. She asked him how to get to Los Angeles, and he pulled a road map from the rack by the counter. He was showing her which route to take when she stopped him, explaining that she was on foot. He gave her a peculiar look, taking note of her bedraggled appearance and perhaps guessing at the reason for it, before directing her to the nearest bus station. But by the time she reached it, it was closed. She was forced to spend the night on the hard wooden bench outside, which mattered little, as it turned out. She was so exhausted, she was asleep the instant she stretched out. The following morning, when the ticket counter opened, she purchased a one-way ticket to Los Angeles.

Four hours later, she arrived in LA, which she soon discovered wasn't so much a city as a loose sprawl of neighborhoods linked by freeways. It wasn't long before she was hopelessly lost. She would get off one bus only to board another that took her to some new, equally confusing location. Each neighborhood, she found, was like a separate nation unto itself, with its own set of inhabitants, its own culture: white, black, Asian, Hispanic. By the time she reached the one from which Eduardo's last letter had been sent, a Latino neighborhood called Echo Park, the sun had nearly set.

She spent the night on a park bench before resuming her search as soon as it was light out. Hours later, she finally arrived at the address on the envelope tucked in her pocket: a run-down apartment complex on a quiet, residential street. She didn't even know if Eduardo still lived there. There had been no word from him in some time. Had he even received her letter informing him of Milagros's death? For all she knew, he could have been caught and sent back. In one of his earlier letters to Milagros, he'd written about an incident in which INS agents had burst into the house he'd been living in at the time with a dozen of his *compadres,* and arrested everyone they could round up. Luckily, Eduardo hadn't been around when the raid had taken place or he, too, would have been put on a bus and sent back across the border.

She climbed the stairs to his apartment and knocked on the door. She was sweating, and her grumbling stomach reminded her that she'd had nothing to eat since the day before. There were no sounds of anyone stirring inside, but she waited even so, knocking again, harder this time, until her knuckles were bruised. The door, however, remained stubbornly closed. It was with a keen sense of disappointment that she finally turned away.

Still, she told herself that there was no cause for alarm just yet. It was half past eight, according to the clock outside the car wash across the street; Eduardo might have already left for work. In his last letter, he'd written excitedly to Milagros of having found a steady job as an automobile mechanic. In this country, he'd written, husbands and wives each had their own car, so there was always plenty of work at the garage where he was employed. He'd been hoping to finally be able to save enough money to send for Milagros. One day he would even buy her a house. Anything was possible in the land of the *gringos.*

Concepción cared nothing for houses or cars. All she needed right now was a place to stay until she could earn enough money to get to New York, where the Señora lived. That prospect seemed very distant at the moment, when she scarcely had enough money to pay for a decent meal.

She sank down on the patch of scruffy brown lawn that bordered the patio at the center of the apartment complex, under the shade of a palm tree that looked as if it, too, had seen better days. She would just have to wait until Eduardo returned, all day if need be.

She instantly fell into a deep sleep, waking hours later to find the sun high in the sky. It peeked through the palm fronds and cast long shadows over the grass where she lay. One of those shadows, she realized with a start, belonged to a man standing over her. She jerked upright, running her hands through her hair, which had begun to grow out and which was now sticking out all over her head like a tumbleweed, studded with burrs and foxtails and bits of grass. What a pathetic sight she must make! Like some common *vago*, sprawled there on the ground. She squinted up at the man, heart in throat, wondering what his intent was—was he planning on turning her in to the authorities . . . or robbing her of what little she had left?—but she couldn't make out his features with the sun's glare on his face.

It was a relief when he inquired politely, in Spanish, "Are you all right, *señora?*"

She nodded, finding it difficult to form words. Her mouth felt as if it were lined with cotton flannel. At last she was able to croak, "I'm looking for my son-in-law. Eduardo Sánchez. Do you know him?"

The man squatted down so that they were eye to eye, and now she could see that his was a kind face. Neither young nor old, handsome nor ugly. Just . . . kind. With a flattened nose above a wide, expressive mouth and thick, dark eyebrows that flared, as if in surprise or perhaps amusement, above a pair of eyes the color of strong coffee. She noted that he had good teeth, and that his curly hair was threaded with gray. Mainly, and most importantly, he was a fellow countryman. Even his clothes were different from the ones the *gringos* wore, with their fancy designs and garish logos displayed like bumper stickers on cars—plain jeans and a brown work shirt, a cap he held in one hand while he scratched his head, frowning as he struggled to recollect anyone by that name.

"There was a Sánchez who used to live in one of the apartments upstairs," he said, pointing toward the row of faded aqua doors along the walkway that wrapped around the second story of the complex. One was the door on which Concepción had knocked earlier. "I don't know if he was the same man you're looking for. It's a common name."

Her heart sank. "You say he *used* to live here?"

The man shrugged. "Was he an illegal? They don't stick around for very long." Her disheveled appearance and the fact that she'd been sleeping out in the open must have led him to believe that the man she sought probably didn't have a green card, either. "The ones who don't get caught eventually move on to wherever they can find work."

"Do they ever come back?" she asked hopefully.

He shrugged again, and she could see the answer written on his face, one she'd dreaded. "This Sánchez, you say he's your son-in-law?"

She nodded. Her disappointment was so keen that she could taste it on the back of her tongue, the salty-sweet taste of tears. Where would she go now? To whom would she turn?

"Do you know where I might find him?" she asked, struggling to keep the desperation from her voice.

The man shook his head, regarding her with sympathy. "I'm sorry, *señora*."

"There must be someone who would know. He said he had a job, a good one. Wait, I have the name of his employer." She pulled the letter from her pocket, smoothing it over her knees.

But before she could go any further, the kind-faced man informed her that even if she knew where Eduardo had worked, it wouldn't do her any good. "They pay the illegals in cash," he explained. "That way, there's no record in case the INS comes around. Though usually the only ones who get caught are the *campesinos* breaking their backs for a few dollars a day."

A new fear crept in. "What happens when they get caught?" She'd heard horror stories about beatings, and worse.

"Nothing much. Usually they're just bused back across the border. At least, that's what I've heard."

"You know a lot for a man who's never been caught himself," she said, growing suspicious all of a sudden. For all she knew, he could work for La Migra.

He broke into a grin, revealing a gap between his front teeth. "Not all of us are in this country illegally, *señora*. I myself am a citizen." In fact, he'd been born in this country, he told her. Concepción remained wary, nonetheless. Suppose he was only trying to gain her confidence in order to turn her in? As if sensing her reluctance to trust him, he was quick to reassure her, "You have nothing to fear from me, *señora*. I don't know if I can help you find your son-in-law, but if you need a place to stay, that I can easily arrange. In the meantime, will you allow me the pleasure of buying you breakfast?" Still smiling, he rose to his full height and put out a hand to help her to her feet.

He seemed sincere, but she hesitated even so. Concepción had never needed a helping hand more than she did now. Plus, she was ravenous. Still . . .

"I don't even know your name," she said.

"Ramírez. Jesús Ramírez. *Y usted?*"

She looked up into his smiling face, in which nothing appeared to be hidden—where would there have been room to hide in all that openness? Finally the last of her resistance gave way. With a sigh, she put out her hand, allowing him to help her to her feet. His hand was big, like the rest of him, its palm ridged with calluses, making her think of seasoned oak.

"Concepción," she told him. He didn't need to know her last name.

"Like the Virgin Sagrada," he observed.

"*Exactamente.*" She gave him a stern look, letting him know that, although she might be long past the age of guarding her virginity, she wasn't going to be had for the price of a meal, either.

Jesús Ramírez got the message and quickly let go of her hand.

Soon after, she was tucking into an enormous plate of *huevos rancheros*, refried beans, and yellow rice at a cantina down the street. When she'd had her fill, she pushed her plate away, groaning, "I don't know when I've eaten so much." She eyed the bill that their waitress had left on the table. "Won't you at least let me pay my share?" She still had a few dollars left. She wasn't completely indigent.

"*Claro que no.* You're my guest." Jesús withdrew a battered cowhide wallet from his back pocket, from which he extracted a few equally battered bills. He hesitated before slipping the wallet back into his pocket. "Do you need money? I could lend you some until you find work."

Concepción shook her head, too proud to admit that she *did* need money. "Do you know of any jobs?" she asked.

"There are always jobs cleaning houses or looking after children," he said. "How's your English?"

"I know a little," she said. She'd been practicing, using a phrase book.

"Don't worry, you'll learn. And there are always classes you can take."

She took another sip of her coffee, savoring its milky sweetness. "I won't be around that long," she told him. "I just need to earn enough money to get to New York."

"New York? That's a long way from here." He eyed her curiously. "Do you have family there?"

"No, no one."

"A job, then?" She shook her head. Jesús looked confused. "*Perdóname, señora,* but why would you want to go to a place where you know no one and you have no work?"

She deliberated for a moment, wondering how much she ought to tell him. They'd only just met, and they might never see each other again. Besides, she didn't know that it was any of his business. Concepción, thinking not of Jesús but of her daughter's restless soul up in heaven, replied simply, "I made a promise. A promise I intend to keep."

9

"What are we going to do about a Christmas tree?"

Lila lifted her head from the crossword puzzle she was working on to look at Neal. "I don't know, sweetie. I hadn't really thought about it."

In the past, she'd always gone all out at Christmastime—the tree decked in the ornaments she'd collected through the years, holiday gatherings of family and friends, tickets to *The Nutcracker Suite*, Christmas dinner with all the trimmings—but this year, her heart just wasn't in it. It would be their first year without Gordon, and their first one away from home. The most she'd been able to muster in terms of Christmas spirit had been to put out a scented candle and hang a pine wreath on the door to their little apartment over the garage.

Neal, seated on the sofa that doubled as his bed, paused in the midst of pulling on his snow boots to give her a reproachful look. In the week since he'd arrived home from school, she had yet to see his old, ready grin. He hadn't been himself, in fact, since his father's death. His initial attempts to put on a brave face, efforts that had bordered on manic at times, had given way to a sullen moroseness. She recalled how he'd looked, walking toward her across the platform, when she'd gone to pick him up at the train station, as if he'd been steeling himself somehow. He'd greeted her not with his usual rib-cracking hug but with a cool kiss on the cheek, saying with a queer formality, "Thanks for coming to get me. You didn't have to."

Reeling a bit, she'd attempted to make light of it. "Don't be silly. Your first day here, you think I'd let you ride home in a taxi?"

He'd shrugged. "I could've hitchhiked."

The glint in his eye had told her that it hadn't been an offhand response. Neal had meant to unsettle her. The question was, why? Did he hold her responsible for their current predicament?

Since then, it seemed that she'd done nothing but disappoint him. Like this business with the tree . . .

"Christmas is less than two weeks away," Neal said pointedly.

"Like I need you to remind me. I can't walk into a store these days without being bombarded by Christmas displays. And if I have to listen one more time to Mel Torme singing 'Chestnuts Roasting on an Open Fire,' I think I'll lose my mind."

But if she hoped Neal would cut her some slack, it wasn't working. He didn't even appear to be listening. He sat gazing out the window, wearing a faraway look. "Remember when I was little, how you and me and Dad used to drive around on Christmas Eve and look at all the department store windows?"

She smiled at the memory. "I always brought a thermos of hot chocolate for the car," she recalled. "And a blanket in case you got sleepy. But you never did. You were always wide awake." It would be long past Neal's bedtime by the time they set out to make the rounds in their hired car—Saks Fifth Avenue, Macy's, Bloomingdale's, and Lord & Taylor—an hour when the sidewalks were generally deserted and they could get out and enjoy the displays without being jostled or hurried along by the crowds.

"The best were the times it was snowing," he mused aloud. "It was fun seeing the streets all white like that. I used to pretend it was the North Pole." Neal, wearing a small, wistful smile, went on staring out at the snowy landscape, one that was far removed, in more than just distance, from those of his more untroubled past. She waited with pent-up breath for him to say something more, something she could use to bridge the gap that had lately opened between them, but then he roused himself and went back to lacing up his boots.

I'm a bad mother, Lila thought. Maybe she'd always been a bad mother and it was only just now becoming apparent, without Gordon to balance the equation. But that didn't mean she had to give up. "Listen, sweetie, if it means that much to you, of course we can get a tree. Though I'm not quite sure where we'd put it," she said. Her gaze traveled around the living room, which was less than a quarter the size of the one in their old Park Avenue penthouse. Maybe if they rearranged some of the furniture, they could squeeze it in.

"Never mind." His tone became brusque. "What's the point, if you're not into it?"

"The point is that it matters to you. And *that's* important to me."

"Forget it, okay? It's no big deal." From the tight jerkiness of his movements as he sat bent over, tying his shoelaces, it was obvious he was none too pleased with her.

If only she could find a way to get through to him! "I'm sorry if I've disappointed you," she said gently. "But, sweetie, it hasn't been easy for me, either. This isn't exactly my dream job."

"You didn't have to take it."

"I didn't have a choice. You don't think I tried everything?" An injured tone crept into her voice.

"Yeah? Well, I guess you must have, or we wouldn't be living in this shithole," he said with a sarcasm that went through her like a knife.

Lila felt a headache coming on, and she squeezed her eyes shut, willing it to subside. "Neal, please. Don't take it out on me. I'm just trying to get by here."

"In case you haven't noticed, you're not the only one." He shot her a dark look.

"I know that. I was only saying—"

Abruptly he catapulted off the sofa. "Look, can we talk about this another time? I don't want to be late for work." Neal had found a job at a deli downtown. Full-time for now, but the owner had agreed to let him switch to half days once he started classes at the community college in nearby Hudson-on-Croton.

Lila watched him cross the room in two long strides and reach into the bifold closet for his parka. She got up to peer out the window at the fat, wind-driven flakes swirling through the air like goose down from an Olympian pillow fight. "Drive carefully," she cautioned. "The roads might not be plowed yet." She worried about her son more than she knew was normal. But didn't she have good reason? The unthinkable had occurred with Gordon. What was to prevent something equally horrific from happening to Neal?

The old Neal surfaced briefly in that instant, and he teased, "Don't worry, Mom. It's not the Indy 500. I promise to take it slow."

Moments later, she sat watching from the window as he made his way down the snow-crusted steps and across the driveway to where her Taurus was parked. From behind at this distance, he might have been a youthful Gordon, with his long, lean torso and quick, impatient stride. Snowflakes caught in his hair, which was still damp from the shower, a mass of curls that would settle into soft waves once it dried. She remembered how he'd looked as a toddler fresh from the bath, pink and squirming, with his hair standing up in wet tufts all over his head. She had to remind herself that he was a grown-up now—well, almost—and capable of looking after himself. Hadn't he done just that while away at school? And he'd be leaving her again soon, next time to go off into the world.

She felt a deep tug inside at the thought.

For a long time after he drove off, she remained where she was, perched on an arm of the sofa with her coffee gone cold in its mug and her crossword puzzle lying forgotten on the table. Sundays, when she had the whole day to herself, were the hardest. The one advantage to housework was that it was mindless and repetitive, which had an oddly calming effect on her. Scrubbing toilets or mopping floors, ironing clothes or chopping vegetables, she would become lost in the rhythm of it, in much the way she imagined yogis did while meditating. It was only on days like today that her mind wandered, often down dark alleys where it was likely to get mugged by thoughts she normally sought to avoid.

Mostly what she thought about was Gordon—she fluctuated between longing for him and wanting to kick his dead body from here to Tuscaloosa—and what the future might hold for her and Neal. She thought about her brother, too, who was fighting for his life. And Abigail, who had her constantly on edge, never knowing quite what to expect.

Lately Abigail had been making an effort to be nicer to her, which had Lila confused and a little wary. The other day, she'd actually gone so far as to praise Lila for a meal she'd cooked, commenting, "I don't know when I've had pot roast this tasty. What kind of seasoning did you use?"

"Just regular old Lipton soup," Lila told her, getting a perverse pleasure out of the surprised look this elicited.

But Abigail, instead of reacting with disdain, merely smiled. "My mother used to make it that way. I haven't had it in years."

Lila smiled back. "Where do you think I got the recipe?"

It had been a nice moment, but Lila couldn't lose sight of the fact that she worked for Abigail. At times, the sense of despair she felt was so overwhelming that a kind of paralysis would overtake her, and on her days off, she'd be unable to do much more than drag herself out of bed.

Today was different, though. She felt so restless she thought she might jump out of her skin if she had to stay inside a moment longer. She got up and fetched her parka, tugging on her hat and gloves. Screw the weather.

It wasn't until she stepped outside that she had cause to regret the impulse. The cold hit her like a slap in the face, and she shrank into her parka like a turtle into its shell. It was the kind of cold she associated with Eskimos and ice floes, mountain climbers with frostbitten toes, entire blocks of red states buried under eight or nine feet of snow. Even though Rose Hill wasn't exactly off the grid—in good weather it was an hour's drive from Manhattan, just as Abigail had said—it was like a different world. The icy wind, without high-rises to block it, cut cruelly across the open stretches of pasture and howled down off the mountain. And the snow, which on city streets and sidewalks would have been plowed or shoveled away by now, accumulated at an unbridled rate: It was already well on its way to obliterating the tire tracks in the driveway, and it lay thick as the frosting on one of Abigail's cakes along the fence rails and the branches of the fir trees overhead.

Downtown Stone Harbor might be a relative hub of activity, with its shops and restaurants, and the bed-and-breakfasts that filled with tourists on weekends, but out here it was as desolate in the wintertime as the arctic tundra. The isolation was so complete that it could lead to cabin fever . . . or worse. She'd heard on the local news the other day about an elderly farmer who'd lived alone and who'd taken a fall out in his barn that had left him with a broken hip. Unable to crawl inside where it was warm, much less reach a phone to call for help, he'd frozen to death. With no one nearby to check on him, it had been days before his body had been discovered. The tragic story had left Lila feeling vaguely unsettled the rest of the day.

She was picking her way along the snowy drive, following the quickly disappearing tire tracks left by her car, when she spotted a lone figure walking toward her, bundled in a knit cap and parka. Karim. He'd become a familiar sight over the past couple of weeks, and a welcome one, she had to admit. Whenever there was something too heavy for her to lift or a repair that she couldn't manage herself—a leaky pipe, a stuck door, a kitchen appliance gone kaput—he materialized like a genie out of a bottle. The other day, when her car wouldn't start, he'd quickly determined the cause, and after a trip to the automotive store for a new fan belt, he'd had it running again in no time. Today was no different. He was carrying a bag of rock salt in one hand and a snow shovel in the other. Never mind that it was supposed to be his day off.

"For me? Really, you shouldn't have," she called out in jest.

His brown eyes sparkled, and his breath formed frosty plumes that funneled up into the chill air. "Never let it be said that I abandoned a damsel in distress." His smile alone was enough to melt the snow away, she thought.

However gray her mood was, Karim always had a way of lightening it. Partly it was because he was always so upbeat. He hadn't let the tragedy he'd known eclipse his natural optimism. It was almost enough to make Lila believe that she might get through her own season in hell.

Even so, she feared she was becoming too dependent on him. "So you've come to dig me out, have you? Well, as you can see, I got out just fine without your help," she replied with a laugh, stamping against the snowy pavement to knock loose the clots of snow stuck to her boots.

"Good, then you can give me a hand." Karim plunked down the bag of salt at her feet and went to work shoveling the walk.

"How much more of this do you think we'll get?" Lila asked after she'd finished salting the drive. She squinted up at the fat, wind-driven snowflakes swirling down ever more rapidly from a sky the color of the dust bunnies that she had become adept at ferreting out from under beds.

"Not much. Maybe another inch or so." He paused in the midst of his shoveling to look over at her, appearing barely winded from his exertions. "Why? Were you planning on going somewhere?"

"I was thinking of taking a walk."

"In this weather?" He pointedly eyed her boots, an old pair that had served her well when she'd lived in the city but weren't really suited to extremes like this. But she'd long since given away all her old snow gear, from her family's ski vacations, and she couldn't afford to buy new, sturdier boots, so these would have to do.

"I wasn't planning on going very far, just a little way up into the woods." She gestured toward the snow-covered hillside that lay beyond the cultivated grounds of Rose Hill. It comprised the northernmost end of Abigail and Kent's property—a forested tract that stretched for more than a mile. Lila had gone hiking there once before, though admittedly the weather hadn't been so inclement then.

Karim wore a dubious look. "It's easy to get lost up in there, especially when the trails are covered in snow."

"I'll sprinkle bread crumbs then, so I'll be able to find my way back," she said facetiously. It wasn't that she was dying to trudge through the snow on such a cold day; it had become a point of pride.

"The birds would only eat them," he replied, a twinkle in his eye.

"Well, then, I'll just have to take my chances. Besides, there's something I have to do." The idea had come to her as she'd been salting the drive. "I was going to buy a Christmas tree, but it occurred to me that the woods are full of them. You don't think Kent and Abby would mind, do you?"

He smiled and shook his head. "I'm certain they wouldn't. In fact, why don't I help you find one? You'll need help cutting it down."

"I can't ask you to work on your day off."

"Who said it would be work? Consider it a favor. Just wait until after I've finished here. I should be done in another hour or so. The snow is supposed to let up by then."

"Really, I can manage," she protested.

"Do you know how to operate a chain saw?"

"Well, no. But—"

He nodded, as if to say, *I thought not*. "In that case, I'll meet you back here in an hour." He was gone before she could offer any further protest.

As predicted, the storm had let up by the time they set out, and as they made their way up the wooded slope behind Abigail's house, just a few stray snowflakes drifted down through the cake-frosted branches overhead. The only sound besides the twittering of birds and the soft breath of the wind in the trees was that of her and Karim's boots punching through the thick crust of snow that covered the nearly obliterated trail. It was so peaceful, they might have been the only two people on the planet.

Lila was the first to break the silence. "This will be a nice surprise for Neal. He was asking about a tree, just this morning as a matter of fact." She felt the need to remind Karim that this outing wasn't strictly recreational. She didn't want him reading any more into this, which was a distinct possibility, as she'd sensed that his interest in her was more than friendly. Not that she didn't find him attractive, but in her current state, she wasn't remotely equipped to handle anything beyond this. Even so, at the thought of something more intimate developing between them, she felt herself grow warm inside the cocoon of her jacket.

"He's a good boy, your son," Karim observed, walking just ahead of her along the path, toting his chain saw. In his parka and knit cap, from which tight black coils of hair escaped, he might have been a Sherpa leading the way through an icy Himalayan pass.

"Yes, he is." Lila was happy to know that there was enough of the old Neal left for others to see.

"And you," Karim paused, turning to give her a searching look, "are a good mother."

He seemed to be reassuring her somehow. Had he picked up on the strain between her and Neal?

"I'm not so sure," she said.

"Why do you say that?" They'd reached a small clearing, and he slowed his steps so that they were walking side by side.

"It's just that I can't seem to give him what he needs right now," she said with a sigh. It was easy to confide in Karim; he was such a good listener, she found herself telling him things that until now she'd confided only to Vaughn. "I know he's grieving, but he won't talk to me about it. It's like he's lost sight of the fact that we're in this together, and now I've become part of the problem somehow. And who knows? Maybe he's right. Maybe I *am* part of the problem. If I'd made a career for myself instead of relying on my husband to support me, we wouldn't be in this predicament. I'd be an executive in some firm, not scrubbing toilets and mopping floors for other people."

Karim gave a thoughtful nod, suggesting, "Perhaps this is just Neal's way of coping with his grief."

"By reminding me of what a failure I am?"

He went on to explain, "In my country, the eldest son becomes head of the household when a father dies. This can be a heavy burden for one as young as your son. And even if it's only in his mind, perhaps it's more than he can handle right now and that's why he's attempting to distance himself."

"Maybe. But how would I know what he's feeling if he won't talk to me?"

"Give it time," Karim advised. "Perhaps something good will come of all this eventually."

"Like what? Right now, I can't think of anything remotely positive about this experience."

He turned to smile at her. "The Koran instructs us to be patient when studying the word of Allah, as the revelation is only gradually presented to us. The same is true in life. However hard one's circumstances, there's always something to be learned from them, something which reveals itself slowly over time and which will illuminate the path to the future."

"That all sounds pretty mystical," she said. "Right now, I'd settle for a kind word and a good-night kiss now and then." It wasn't that Neal didn't give her those things on occasion, but these days when he did, it seemed more force of habit than anything.

"When I first arrived in this country, I, like you, was filled with doubt and despair," he told her. "I didn't know if I would ever again see my family or my homeland, or if I would be able to teach again. I saw little purpose in life. Then my sister Soraya wrote in one of her letters that I'd given them all hope. I realized then what my purpose was: to shine a light where there had been only darkness. It wasn't a great, fiery revelation, but it was enough to keep me going until I could find reasons of my own for continuing on."

Lila mulled over his words as they made their way through the clearing. At one point, she wobbled a bit where the deeper snow made her progress less steady, and when he offered her his arm, she clung to it, acutely aware of his corded muscles even beneath several layers of heavy clothing. As soon as they reached the edge of the clearing, she let go of his arm.

"I don't know if there's a purpose to all this," she reflected aloud, "but if there is, it might have something to do with Abby and me."

He slowed his steps, eyeing her curiously. "How so?"

"We were friends growing up. Did she ever tell you that?"

Karim shook his head. He had to be the one person in the country, Lila thought, who hadn't either watched or read about the *A.M. America* segment in which Abigail had been cornered into defending her. Knowing him, he probably didn't even own a TV.

"Years ago, we had a falling-out," she explained. "I did something for which Abby's never really forgiven me. That's why she gave me this job, as a form of punishment. So, yes, maybe this is my destiny. I don't get to pass Go or collect my two hundred dollars until it's resolved."

If the news that she and Abigail had a history together came as a surprise, it didn't show on his face. His expression was more that of someone for whom a missing piece of the puzzle had fallen into place. Clearly it hadn't escaped his attention how tense things were with her and Abigail.

"Some say that friends and enemies are flip sides of the same coin," he commented.

She sighed. "In that case, I guess we're stuck with each other."

It wasn't all bad, she had to admit to herself. They were on the same side in one sense: They both cared deeply about Vaughn. Once Lila had gotten over her reluctance to let Abigail know his whereabouts, she'd had to concede, albeit grudgingly, that having Abigail back in his life was a good thing for Vaughn. The last time Lila had gone to visit him, he'd been more upbeat than usual. When she'd asked him why he was in such a good mood, he'd smiled secretively and said, "If I told you, you'd only accuse me of being a traitor." Instead, Lila had been left feeling petty and vindictive for having tried to stand in the way. If being around Abigail could perk him up this much, who was she to object?

"So what was this unforgivable crime you committed?" Karim asked, in the tone of someone who found it hard to believe she was capable of anything more malicious than a catty remark.

She hesitated before answering, "Do you know the story of Judas Iscariot?"

He nodded. *"Have not I chosen you twelve; and one of you is a devil?"* he quoted from the Gospel of St. John. Lila must have looked surprised that he knew so much about Christianity, for he explained with a smile, "I may be a Muslim, but I'm also a scholar. I've studied other religions. So, yes, I know about Judas Iscariot. He was the disciple who betrayed Jesus."

"That's how it was with Abby and me," she told him. "Her mother worked for us all the years I was growing up. She and Abby were part of the family—Abby was like the sister I never had. Then one day out of the blue, my mom accused Rosie of stealing and, just like that, they were gone. My crime was that I didn't know who to believe until it was too late."

"How old were you at the time?"

"Old enough to know better." Lila experienced a knife twist of the old guilt. "I was so ashamed, I couldn't even write to Abby to tell her how sorry I was. And the more time went by, the more difficult it became to pick up that pen. Now it's much too late."

"To tell her you're sorry? Or for her to forgive you?"

"Both." Lila heaved a deep sigh. "It's hard to say you're sorry when you know your apology won't be accepted. I've tried. Let's just say it didn't go very well."

He fell silent for a moment. There was only the plume of his breath trailing in the frosty air. "Forgiveness can be difficult," he said at last. "It requires a belief in the other party's sincerity, I suppose."

Lila was left pondering his words. Had she truly given Abigail an opportunity to forgive her? The one time she'd offered an apology, it couldn't have sounded too sincere, especially since it had come at a time when, as Vaughn had so aptly put it, it must have seemed self-serving. On the other hand, Abigail hadn't exactly made it easy for her. Given how beaten down Lila was already, would it have hurt Abigail to show her a little sympathy? Hadn't she suffered enough already?

The cathedral-like hush of the woods was broken when a laden branch released its load onto the path just ahead of them with a muffled thud that startled a flock of starlings into a cacophony of scolding. Karim tramped through the clotted snow to clear a path for her, and they continued on their way.

They were cresting the hill when she spotted it: the perfect tree. A Douglas fir, not too big and not too small, its branches densely packed and graduated to form an even, conical shape. Minutes later, the woods were echoing with the buzz of the chain saw. It was a young tree, hardly more than a sapling, so it came down easily. Karim bundled its branches with a length of twine and together, each holding one end, they carried it down the slope.

Back at the house, he found an old tree stand in the garage and helped her set it up. When the tree was finally in place, squeezed into a corner of her living room, they stood back to admire it.

"It's a fine tree," he remarked.

"It is, isn't it?" With the scent of evergreen filling the room, Lila felt her nascent holiday spirit stir back to life. She turned to Karim with a smile, saying, "I feel a little funny thanking a Muslim for giving me back my Christmas spirit, so let's just say I owe you one."

"Not at all. It was my pleasure." He laid a hand on her arm, as if in emphasis, and though his touch was light and in no way suggestive, a shiver went through her. It might have been her bare skin he was touching. She shifted her body so that she was facing away from him, and brought her gaze back to the tree.

"Now all it needs is ornaments. I'm thinking fairy lights and maybe some of those transparent glass bulbs," she said. "I just wish I still had my old decorations. But I'm afraid they got lost in the shuffle when we moved."

"The drugstore on Main Street stays open on Sundays," he informed her. "The last time I was in there, they had decorations for sale. I could drive you into town, if you like."

She was tempted to accept but decided against it. Hadn't he done enough already? Besides, she knew she would need some time alone to digest these new and unwanted feelings he'd awakened in her before she could risk going off with him again so soon. "Thanks. I appreciate it. But I have some stuff to do around here," she lied.

After he had left, she collapsed onto the sofa with a groan. Her Christmas spirit had returned, yes, and with it emotions that she had thought she'd buried along with Gordon: the desire to be made love to, the need to feel wanted. And what, pray tell, was she supposed to *do* with these emotions when they were about as welcome as mistletoe at a wake? Especially since it had become obvious to her that it wasn't one-sided.

Neal slid the hot panini onto a paper plate. Without looking up, he asked the next customer in line, "What'll it be?"

"A small Diet Coke."

The voice was familiar, and when Neal brought his head up to hand over the panini, he saw that it belonged to Phoebe Whittaker. His next-door neighbor, so to speak. Since their brief introduction, he'd only caught glimpses of her as she was heading off to school in her dad's vintage Mercedes coupe, with Dr. Whittaker at the wheel, or going somewhere in her own little red Jetta. (Not that he'd been spying on her, but living over the garage, it was hard not to notice the family's comings and goings.) Now he took note of her appearance. Up close, he could see how thin she was—a sliver of a girl who looked as if she hadn't had a decent meal in months and who dressed as if she'd just come from picking up trash along the highway. He never would have guessed her parents were wealthy if his mother hadn't worked for them.

At the thought, Neal experienced the little inner jolt he always did when reminded that he was no longer a child of privilege himself. But he flashed Phoebe a smile, acutely aware of the fact that her parents were the only reason he and his mom had a roof over their heads.

"Hey," he greeted her. "I didn't know you ate here." *Lame*, he thought. But he hadn't been able to think of anything more clever.

"I didn't know you worked here," she said, eyeing him across the counter with a flat, unsmiling gaze.

Neal bristled. So that was how little Miss Snot-Nose was going to play it? Fine. It was no skin off him. "You want anything with that Coke?" he asked in a more businesslike tone.

"What have you got?"

"The panini special is good if you like gorgonzola."

"I hate gorgonzola."

"You can have it with any kind of cheese."

"Just the Coke, please," she said in a snippy tone.

Neal grew even angrier. Who the hell was she to act so high and mighty? The fact that his mom worked for hers didn't mean she was better than he. It was a mere accident of fate, a throw of the dice. "Coming right up." He grabbed a cup and filled it under the spigot. "That'll be a dollar eighty." He shoved the cup across the counter as if he couldn't get rid of it—and her—fast enough.

She looked a little startled by this sudden show of hostility, and she fumbled a bit as she was digging the change from her purse. The coins slipped from her fingers, scattering over the counter, a few of them rolling onto the floor. As she bent to retrieve them, he saw that her cheeks were flushed.

Suddenly he felt bad for taking his anger out on her. She might be a snot-nosed brat, but it wasn't her fault that his life sucked.

"Sorry," she muttered when he came out from behind the counter to lend her a hand. "I'm not usually this clumsy."

He smiled at her as he bent to fish a quarter from under the coffee station. "Happens all the time. How do you think I make all my tips?"

This elicited a small smile in return. Emboldened by it, he carried her drink over to a table by the window, lingering after she'd sat down. There were no other customers in the deli at the moment—the guy with the panini had taken it to go, and traffic at the Earl of Sandwich was generally slow on Sundays, when a lot of the businesses downtown were closed—so he was in no particular rush to get back to his station. "Can I get you anything else, a napkin or a straw?"

"Are you always this helpful?" she asked.

He shrugged. "Only with people I know."

"Oh, so you think you know me?"

She tilted her head to give him a haughty look, but he sensed that it was just an act. There was something vulnerable about her under that brittle exterior.

"I know you don't eat much," he countered, his gaze dropping to the cup in her hand. He might have thought twice before getting so personal had they been on her turf, but this was *his*, and here the only ass he had to kiss was his boss's. "You on a diet or something?"

"None of your damn business."

He threw his hands up in self-defense. "Don't look at me. I don't give a shit. It's my mom. She's worried that you'll starve to death or something. But that's what moms do, right? It's their job to worry."

"Yeah, I guess." Phoebe relaxed a bit, taking a small sip of her soda. "Not that I'd know from personal experience. In case you haven't noticed, mine isn't exactly the motherly type. She spends more time at work than she does at home." After a moment, when he still hadn't made any move to leave, she asked pointedly, "Don't you have stuff to do?"

"Is that a hint?"

"No."

"If you want me to leave you alone, just say so."

She shrugged. "Suit yourself."

"Are you always this rude?" he asked.

They stared at each other for several seconds without speaking, as if challenging each other in some way. Then her gaze cut away, and he saw from the smile flickering at the corners of her mouth that, if it had been a showdown, he'd won. "Sorry if I was rude," she said. "Don't take it personally."

Taking her semiapology as an invitation, he dropped into the chair opposite hers, after first darting a look over his shoulder to make sure the owner, Earl Haber—the Earl in Earl of Sandwich—was nowhere in sight. "And here I thought it was just me," he said.

"Don't flatter yourself."

"Believe me, there's no danger of that. You haven't spoken more than two words to me since I got here. Did I say something to offend you, or is it just that you don't socialize with the hired help?"

Her cheeks reddened. "Why would you think that?"

"I don't know. You tell me."

"This has nothing to do with you, okay? So back off." For a worrisome moment, it looked as if she might start to cry.

Neal was quick to defuse the situation. "Look, maybe we just got off on the wrong foot. Why don't we start over?" He stuck out his hand, putting on a smile designed to show how harmless he was. "Hi, I'm Neal. I'm new here. If you're not doing anything later on, maybe you'd like to hang out or, I don't know . . . What do kids our age do for fun around here?"

Her face relaxed, and he saw that she was actually kind of pretty. "The short answer is, not much. Unless your idea of fun is bingo night at the Elks Lodge, it's pretty dead around here after dark."

"Is that why you're in such a bad mood?" he teased.

She looked as if she were about to get prickly again, but she must have decided that it wasn't worth the effort, for she merely said, "For your information, the reason I'm in such a sucky mood is because of this stupid dinner party my mom's throwing tomorrow night. How would you feel if you had to sit through a fake Christmas dinner, with cameras rolling, knowing that millions of people were going to be watching your every move?"

"Yeah, I heard about that," he said. It was for some TV special— "Christmas with Abigail Armstrong" or some such—that was going to be videotaped at the house. His mom had been working overtime to help get everything set up. "It sounds like it's a pretty big deal."

"Yeah. To my mom." Phoebe made a face.

"Hey, I can think of worse things," he said. *Like a holiday dinner looking at your dad's empty place at the table.* But he didn't dare let his thoughts go down that road. It was a road he'd been down too many times before, one he knew to be dark and treacherous, where each turn only took him farther off the path to some sort of understanding. He could easily get lost and never find his way back.

"Holidays are supposed to be about family, right? But with my mom, it's all about putting on a show." She spoke with barely contained contempt. "She doesn't care about my dad and me."

Neal felt a little uncomfortable with her telling him all this. But at least it meant that she'd decided he was an ally, rather than a member of her mother's supporting cast. Still, he felt obliged to point out, "I'm sure she does. But that doesn't mean she can't care about her job, too."

"Whose side are you on, anyway?" She glowered at him.

Neal shrugged. "I didn't know there were sides. Look, if it makes you feel any better, I get it. I've put in my share of command performances at my parents' parties. It's kind of a pain, I know, but think of it like a trip to the dentist. It's just something you've gotta do."

"At least with the dentist, they give you a shot to numb you."

Neal could see that he was getting nowhere with this line of reasoning, so he took another approach, swallowing his earlier reluctance to mention the subject he normally sought to avoid. "At least you have a family," he told her. "This'll be my first Christmas without my dad."

"Yeah, I heard about that." Her expression softened. "I'm sorry. I've never met anyone before whose father . . ." She didn't finish the sentence.

Grief and its evil twin, anger, inched their way out of the cave where Neal kept them penned. "Yeah, well, now you know that *I* know what it's like to have your life on display in front of millions of people," he said. "You want to know what sucks? Having your best friend call to offer his condolences after hearing about your dad on the six o'clock news."

Phoebe eyed him with new respect. "It must've been rough."

He shrugged.

"You don't like talking about it, do you?" she observed.

"Not especially."

"Okay, so we won't talk about it."

"Good."

"Hey, I just thought of something. If you're not busy tonight, do you feel like going to a concert?" she asked, brightening somewhat. "It's a benefit for some charity thing of my dad's, over at the community center. He got some of his musician friends to perform for free."

"Maybe you should check with your dad first," Neal replied tentatively, uncertain about his status in the Armstrong-Whittaker household.

"It's cool, don't worry. I'll have him set aside an extra ticket."

"Yeah, okay. Sounds like fun." So far, Neal's nightlife had consisted of playing Scrabble or watching TV with his mom. This would be a nice change of pace.

"Your mom can come, too, if she wants."

Neal considered the ramifications of this for a moment before replying less than honestly, "I think she has other plans." He felt a little bad for nixing the idea without even running it by her—she might have enjoyed an evening out—but the truth was, he could use a break from his mom. He decided he wasn't going to worry about anyone but himself from now on. For all the worrying he'd done over his dad, look how much good it had done.

"It doesn't start until eight-thirty, but Dad wants to get there early, so we'll meet you out front at half past seven," Phoebe told him. "We can all go in his car. It's just the three of us, so we should be able to fit."

"Your mom's not coming?" It wasn't any of his business, but it struck him as odd. He and his parents had always done things as a family.

Phoebe rolled her eyes. "She says she's too busy getting ready for the party tomorrow. I guess even a fake one is a lot of work." Her gaze drifted toward the window, and for a long moment, she sat staring out at the holiday shoppers hurrying along the snowy sidewalk, bundled up in their coats, laden with shopping bags. When she finally brought her gaze back to Neal, the angry look was gone, in its place one of deep melancholy. She pushed aside her half-finished soda. "I should probably get going. I have some stuff to do," she told him, though she appeared in no hurry to leave.

"Okay," he said. "So I guess I'll see you back at the house?"

"You bet." She pointed a finger at him. "Half past seven. Don't forget."

"Don't worry, I'll be there."

For a brief, shining instant Neal felt almost as if he were back in his old life, when hooking up with a friend on the spur of the moment and having no other responsibility in life but making decent grades had been things he'd taken for granted, like the air he breathed.

Then his boss, Mr. Haber, stuck his big, hairy gray head out from the kitchen to bellow at Neal, "What, I pay you to sit around schmoozing with the customers?"

The spell was broken.

With a sigh, Neal stood up, muttering to Phoebe, "Listen, I'd better get back to work. Later, okay?"

10

The table was set for eight, a nice, even number that struck a note of much-needed harmony in what was shaping up to be a messy situation on the home front. Even as Abigail stepped back to admire the fruits of her labor—the place settings gleaming with her Herend china and Tiffany silver, Waterford goblets and wineglasses; the starched linen napkin tucked into each of the filigreed sterling napkin rings; the braided evergreen boughs at the center studded with dried persimmons and pomegranates, with candles at either end—thoughts of Kent and Phoebe nagged at her. They'd made it clear to her how they felt about participating in tonight's event, a special that would invite millions of viewers into their home when it was televised. Kent not so jokingly referred to it as her "dog-and-pony show," and Phoebe was on the verge of mutiny.

Abigail felt the anger that was never far below the surface gain a foothold. Damn it. Why should she need to remind them that this was what she did for a *living?* One that provided them with many of the luxuries they enjoyed. And where did Phoebe imagine the money for her college education was coming from? With all the patients Kent treated for free, his earnings weren't enough to put her through four years of a top school, not without their feeling the pinch.

Nevertheless, what had seemed like a brilliant idea when the executive producer of the Home and Garden network had first floated it—a holiday special showing Abigail and her family and a few close friends enjoying a quiet "Christmas" dinner at Rose Hill, which would not only boost her visibility but help regain some of the credibility she'd lost with Tag—now seemed like just another excuse for Abigail's husband and daughter to hate her. This whole day, preparing for the event, all she could think about was Joan Crawford after she'd become known to the world as Mommie Dearest.

Well, it was too late to back out now, even if she'd wanted to. The film crew would be here any minute. The stage was set. The champagne was chilling and the food prepped. In the living room, the Christmas tree was aglow, the logs stacked in the fireplace, and candles placed strategically. All that was missing, she thought, was Tiny Tim piping, "God bless us, every one!"

What does any of it matter, she thought, *with my marriage on the rocks and my daughter barely speaking to me?*

And what would Kent think if he knew about Vaughn? If it was all so innocent, why hadn't she told him where she'd been going on her lunch hour these days? She'd been back to see Vaughn several more times since that first visit. And she could no longer use the excuse that she was merely paying a call on a sick friend. Earlier this week, Vaughn had felt well enough to go on an outing. She suggested something indoors, a movie or a museum, but he insisted on their going to the Central Park Zoo, which she confessed she hadn't visited since Phoebe was little. She wasn't thinking about Kent then; she merely felt guilty about taking the time off work. But despite that, and despite the weather's being brisk and windy and many of the zoo animals in hiding, it was one of the most pleasant, relaxing days in recent memory. Afterward they went to the Boathouse for lunch, where they lingered until well into the afternoon, reminiscing about old times.

They were strolling through the park on their way to catch a cab, wind-driven leaves dervish-dancing at their feet, when Vaughn asked out of the blue, "What is it you want out of life, Abby?"

She was momentarily at a loss. Wasn't it obvious? She already had everything a person could possibly want. Then she realized that wasn't what he'd meant, and she smiled and tucked her arm through his. "This," she said. At that moment, she wanted nothing more than to be strolling along arm in arm with Vaughn. The fact that he was walking more slowly than usual, due to his illness, only made their time together more precious. With the sun shining overhead and the air crisp as a new apple, her family and business woes seemed far away.

He smiled back at her, the light in his eyes undiminished, though the rest of him had begun to show the effects of the chemo—he was thinner, little more than skin and bones, his body like some magnificent, if fragile, rock formation sculpted by the elements. A man beset by illness, stripped to the barest essentials, with no home of his own. And yet . . .

He's complete, she thought.

Now she wondered what it was that he saw in *her*, when to Kent she was nothing more than a career-obsessed workaholic and to Phoebe an inattentive mother. At work, she was the boss and, at the most basic level, a brand. Where was Abigail Armstrong the *person* in all this?

As she looked around at the carefully set stage of her dining room, it seemed to Abigail that it was almost *too* perfect. She found herself recalling holiday dinners past: Kent playing the avuncular host to their guests, her rushing to get everything on the table while it was still hot, and Phoebe smiling and happy, the picture of health. Those meals had been spontaneous, full of laughter, everyone talking at once, not carefully staged productions as genuine as a facade on a Hollywood back lot.

"Where would you like me to put these?"

At the sound of Lila's voice, she turned around. Lila had spent the better part of the afternoon polishing every piece of silver in the house, and now she stood in the doorway holding a pair of gleaming candlesticks.

"Those can go over on the buffet." Abigail gestured toward the sideboard, where an array of serving utensils had been laid out with the precision of surgical instruments. "Thanks," she remembered to add as Lila set down the candlesticks.

She'd been making more of an effort to be nice lately, though Lila didn't always make it easy for her. Lila saved her smiles for Kent and Phoebe. Kent, in particular. It hadn't escaped Abigail's notice, the way Lila lit up whenever he walked into the room.

"Is there anything else you need me to do?" The expression on Lila's face was pleasant but neutral.

"Why don't you see if Brenda needs any help in the kitchen?" Brenda Allerton, a former neighbor from Greenwich who'd been with Abigail since the beginning and who now ran her catering business, was personally overseeing tonight's production.

"Certainly." Lila gave a deferential nod.

She was about to walk away when, on impulse, Abigail volunteered, "I saw Vaughn the other day."

This sparked Lila's interest. "Oh?"

"We went to the zoo."

Lila arched a brow. "I'm surprised he was feeling up to it."

"He did get a little tired toward the end," Abigail admitted.

"Knowing him, he probably refused to let it slow him down."

"Something like that."

They exchanged a small, knowing smile, then Lila's expression turned anxious. "I worry about him. Underneath it all, he still thinks he's invincible. I'm afraid he'll push himself too far."

Abigail worried, too, but she didn't dare let on. "Lucky for Vaughn, he's got the three of us to look after him," she said. Gillian might not have been her favorite person, but she was heaven-sent as far as Vaughn was concerned. Gillian made certain he didn't stray too far and that he stayed hydrated and got plenty of rest. "He'll be fine," she assured Lila. "He's also got the world's best doctors. Not to mention a constitution of iron."

Lila seemed to relax a bit, some of the tightness going out of her face. She seemed on the verge of saying something more, but just then the doorbell rang. In that instant, the spark of easy familiarity between them was extinguished, and Lila's face closed over once more.

"I'll get it," she said, her tone coolly professional.

Moments later, Lila was ushering in the film crew, a pair of cameramen and the female producer, collectively lugging what had to be about three hundred pounds of equipment. All were seasoned veterans, and they immediately went to work. The younger of the two cameramen, a lanky Irishman named Seamus with reddish hair cropped close to his head, erected standing lights in strategic spots around the living room and dining room while Glenn, his swarthy, mustached partner, shot a B-roll of the exterior and interiors. Meanwhile, the producer, an attractive, light-skinned black woman by the name of Holly Dawson, met with Abigail in the kitchen, where they went over the timeline and mapped out everything in advance.

By the time Abigail was done shooting both her intro and demo, she had just enough time to dash upstairs and change into her evening finery. But when she came back down a short while later, there was still no sign of Kent or Phoebe. She glanced at her watch, frowning. It was half past six. Hadn't she told them to be ready by six o'clock on the dot? What on earth could be keeping them?

She was picking up the phone to call Kent on his cell when he came breezing in through the front door, as if from a round of golf. "Sorry, darling, I got waylaid." He delivered a cool kiss to her cheek. "Sylvia—you remember Sylvia Shine? We're on the committee together. Well, she called to ask if I'd help her go over the box-office receipts from last night. Do you know, we raised over twenty thousand dollars?"

"That's wonderful, dear," Abigail said distractedly. "But our guests will be here any minute, so you need to get dressed."

He groaned. "Am I that late? Well, it'll only take me a minute."

He'd started up the stairs when Abigail called after him, "You haven't told me what you think of my dress." She was a little hurt that Kent hadn't commented on it. She'd gone to a great deal of trouble and expense to have the dress made especially for the occasion by a designer friend of hers. Panne velvet, in a shade of deep emerald that complemented her coloring, it fit her like a glove, ending at her knees in a subtle flounce. Setting it off were the pair of emerald earrings Kent had given her for their tenth anniversary.

He stopped to look her up and down before giving a low wolf whistle. "Nice. Though I don't know that anyone's going to be looking at the food with you dressed like that."

"They'd better, after all the trouble I went to." She smiled, though she'd have appreciated the compliment more if she hadn't had to solicit it. "Do you know where Phoebe is?" she asked. "I thought she was in her room, but she wasn't there when I checked."

"The last time I saw her, she was heading out with Neal. They were going to the store to pick up some supplies she said she needed for a school project," he told her. "She said they wouldn't be long."

"How long ago was that?"

He frowned, as if trying to recollect. "Oh, I don't know, about an hour or so. Have you tried her cell?"

"Twice. All I got was her voice mail."

"Well, I'm sure she'll show up soon," Kent said breezily as he bounded up the stairs.

Watching him go, Abigail felt the tension that had been building in her all day tip over into fury. How could he be so cavalier? And Phoebe . . . Hadn't Abigail put her own needs on hold, time and again, to be able to give her everything *she* hadn't had growing up? All she asked in return was that her husband and daughter show her a little support now and then, instead of constantly undermining her.

Her fury boiling over, she stalked upstairs. She sailed into their bedroom just as Kent was pulling on a clean shirt. The rest of his outfit, the suit and tie she'd chosen for him, were laid out on the bed. "How could you have let her go off like that?" she demanded. "You *knew* how important this was to me."

He paused in the midst of buttoning his shirt to give her a coolly dispassionate look. "Since when is it my job to keep track of her? If it was so important to you, you should have kept track of her yourself." Gone was the animation he'd shown when sharing the good news about the benefit. Abigail might have been looking into the eyes of a stranger.

"As you can see, I've been busy," she replied frostily.

"Fair enough. Just don't make me the fall guy if you need someone to blame for the fact that our daughter doesn't seem to want to participate in your little dog-and-pony show."

"Is that what this is to you? Just some vanity production?"

He finished buttoning his shirt and reached for his tie. Really, the man was infuriating. "You're the one who said it, not me."

"You act like I'm doing this for fun! It's *work*, you know. Do I say anything when you're late getting home from an emergency call?" It wasn't the same thing, she knew; matters of life and death were always going to trump those of commerce, but at the moment, she was too mad to care.

"How would you even know? You're almost never around."

"Oh, no!" she cried. "You're not going to pin *that* on me again. Why should I feel guilty just because I want my business to succeed? Which, may I remind you, you and Phoebe benefit from as well."

"I'm not saying you shouldn't care about your business, or that you don't have a right to your success," he argued with calm, clear-headed reason, peering into the mirror as he knotted his Hermès tie. "But there's a fine line between wanting success and having it never be enough."

"If I've worked hard, it's because nobody ever handed me anything on a silver platter," she shot back.

"Unlike Lila, you mean?" He didn't raise his voice, but she caught the flash of disdain in his eyes. Clearly he'd noticed her coldness toward Lila and had come to the wrong conclusion about it. He must have thought she was heartlessly kicking Lila when she was down for no other reason than because Lila had been born with a silver spoon in her mouth.

But how would he know any different? a voice whispered in her head.

"I can see this discussion is going nowhere," she said. "I'll be downstairs when you're ready to join me." She was turning to go when she caught her husband's reflection in the full-length mirror and saw his rainy-day eyes flash with unaccustomed fire.

"Yes, dear," he replied in a voice thick with sarcasm.

Out in the hallway, she leaned against the wall and closed her eyes, taking slow, deep breaths and feeling her anger fade. Why couldn't she learn to just put a lid on it? It had been unfair, taking her frustration out on Kent. He wasn't to blame for Phoebe's failure to show up on time. And hadn't he always gamely risen to the occasion whenever it was required of him?

She found herself recalling the night they'd met. She'd been catering a party for a doctor and his wife, in Greenwich, to which Kent had been invited (she found out later that Dr. Sorensen was chief of surgery at the hospital where Kent had been doing his internship at the time). Toward the end of the evening, Kent wandered into the kitchen as she was cleaning up to thank her—the only one of the guests considerate enough to do so.

"That was the best meal I've had in ages," he told her, adding with a rueful chuckle, "Though, come to think of it, it's probably the *first* real meal I've had in I don't know how long." He explained that, as an intern, his hours were such that he usually had to eat on the run.

"I know what you mean," Abigail commiserated. "Even though I'm around food all day, it seems like I never get to sit down to eat."

"In that case, if you have a free evening sometime in the next couple of weeks, why don't you let me take you out to dinner? That way we'll both have a chance to sit down."

She was a little taken aback by his boldness, but intrigued nonetheless. "You sure don't waste any time," she said with a laugh. "Couldn't you have just asked for my phone number?"

"Already taken care of." His gray eyes twinkling, he pulled her business card from his pocket. "I told our hostess that I needed a caterer for a party I was throwing. She was only too happy to oblige."

"Did you just make that up, or is there really going to be a party?" she asked, though from his impish expression she already knew the answer.

Kent shrugged, reaching across the counter to snag one of the crudités she was packing away in a Tupperware container. "A party? No, I don't think I could swing that right now. Now, dinner, on the other hand . . ."

Abigail had been charmed into accepting. She remembered being struck not only by his clean-cut good looks but by his quick wit and intelligence (both his parents were professors, she later learned). Abigail had thought, *I could fall in love with this guy.* She'd dated her share of men since living on her own, but no one had come close to making her feel what she had with Vaughn. Kent had been the first one with whom she could imagine making a life.

Now, all these years later, she wondered where that life she'd envisioned had gone.

But she didn't have time to wonder for long because just then the doorbell rang downstairs.

It was showtime.

The St. Clairs were the first to arrive—blond, bearded Ted St. Clair, the curator of medieval armature at the Metropolitan Museum, and his glamorous, Argentinean-born wife, Eva, a much-sought-after opera singer. They were soon followed by Hoppy and Deirdre Covington, the husband-and-wife publishers of *Cook's Companion* (a magazine to which Abigail frequently contributed), looking like a pair of Russian nesting dolls in their festive holiday attire, both plump and round, with Hoppy only an inch or so taller than his wife. Last to arrive was Jay Silverstein, Kent's partner in his medical practice, a distinguished-looking older gentleman who'd been recently widowed after fifty years of marriage.

Jay handed Abigail a bottle of merlot and a bouquet of slightly wilted freesias, saying a bit apologetically, "Coals to Newcastle, I know, but I'm a little out of practice at this sort of thing." His wife had always taken care of such matters, Abigail knew, and she was uncomfortably reminded by the faintly forlorn look he wore of what a tightly knit union was like.

She thanked him warmly, never mind that the wine she was serving with dinner had been as carefully selected, with the help of her friend Anton, the chief sommelier at Le Bernadin, as if this were a White House affair. "If we don't get around to drinking it tonight, I'm sure we'll enjoy it another time," she told Jay.

It was her job as hostess to make everyone feel special, pampered, part of the inner circle, and there was no one better at it than Abigail. She didn't have to ask what anyone wanted to drink; that information was stored away in some mental filing cabinet, and as her guests were ushered into the living room, each found the preferred cocktail appearing like magic at his or her elbow: a Grey Goose martini with a twist of lemon for Hoppy; Dewar's on the rocks for Jay; pinot grigio for Eva; Lillet for Deirdre; and a plain club soda with lime for Ted, who was on the wagon.

She gave each one a turn on center stage as well by encouraging the retelling of amusing anecdotes they'd shared with her on previous occasions. Conversation never lagged. She'd taken the trouble to familiarize herself with this season's lineup at the Metropolitan Opera so she could discuss it intelligently with Eva St. Clair. With the Covingtons, she talked about the Aspen Food Festival, at which they'd be hosting a cook-off next year. She was equally adept at steering the conversation *away* from politics, religion, and any topic of which she was ignorant. When it came time to sit down to dinner, everyone was so relaxed that any self-consciousness they might have felt at wearing the wireless mikes with which they'd been fitted had long since faded. They seemed scarcely aware of the cameramen hovering at the fringes of their jolly little group, recording their every move.

The only one who wasn't able to relax was Abigail herself. All she could think about, as she passed around platters and poured wine (the catering staff was staying out of sight, so as to make it look as if she were effort-lessly doing it all herself), was Phoebe's glaring absence, as achingly apparent to her as a pulled tooth despite the fact that her daughter's place setting had been removed when it had become clear that she wasn't going to show.

Underlying her fury was the fear nibbling at her that something might have happened to Phoebe. Suppose she'd been in an accident and was lying hurt by the side of the road?

By the time she brought out dessert—pumpkin crème brûlées with brandied whipped cream and homemade ginger biscuits—Abigail was exhausted from the effort of keeping her smile pasted in place. Not that anyone would have guessed. To her guests, she appeared to be having as wonderful a time as they were. Toward the end of the evening, Hoppy stood up to make a toast, his expansiveness matched by the ruddiness of his cheeks, from all the wine he'd drunk. He lifted his glass, saying heartily, "To Abigail, the queen of her domain. Long may she reign!"

But Abigail didn't feel like a queen. She felt like an imposter. They didn't know what a failure she was at what mattered most: being a wife and mother. She wasn't even a good person. Indirectly or not, she'd managed to get an innocent girl killed. Phoebe's disappearing act would seem like nothing compared to the blood on her hands, should her friends and fans ever get wind of *that*.

Even after the meal was over and the last of the coffee cups had been cleared away, the guests were reluctant to leave. When Abigail threw a party, no one ever left early. She was accustomed to people lingering, occasionally until long past midnight. When she finally closed the door on the last guest, she turned the film crew loose in the kitchen to devour what was left of the food.

"Good stuff," mumbled Holly around a mouthful of turkey roulade with cornbread-andouille stuffing. It wasn't until she gestured toward the stack of Beta cassettes on the table beside her that Abigail realized she hadn't been talking about the food. "It's way more than we need, but we'll edit it down to a tight half hour," she explained. "Too bad your daughter couldn't make it, though."

"Yes, I'm sure she'll be sorry she missed it." Abigail forced a smile. Her face *hurt* from smiling.

When the crew had finished eating and packed up their equipment, she saw them out. She was on her way back into the kitchen when she heard the sound of Kent's voice mingling with Lila's. The catering staff had packed up and left as well, and he was helping her wash up. A familiar domestic scene, one that had played out countless times before in that very spot—only then it had been Abigail sharing a private moment with Kent after their guests had gone. Now, listening to the soft sounds of their banter, Abigail felt as if she were walking in on something more intimate.

The worst of it was, they didn't even notice her. As she stood watching them from the doorway, she might have been invisible. Kent laughed at some lighthearted comment Lila had made, and Lila swatted him playfully on the arm with her dish towel. It was like a knife twisting in Abigail's heart.

Once more, with Lila, she was out in the cold.

Quickly retreating before they could spot her, she turned and fled down the hallway. Her face was hot, and she felt tears swelling behind her eyes. What she needed was some fresh air, she told herself, or she would *really* lose it. She headed for the coat closet, where she kicked off her high heels and grabbed a pair of boots, tugging them on. Snagging her parka from the hook on the inside of the door, where she'd left it when she'd come in earlier from walking the dog, she stepped out through the front door. She was making her way down the front path when she reached into the pocket for her gloves and felt the unmistakable bulge of her cell phone. She must have tucked it into her pocket earlier, then forgotten it.

She decided to try Phoebe again. This time, though, when she punched in her daughter's number, she heard its familiar ringtone—Avril Lavigne's "Sk8ter Boi"—coming from somewhere nearby as well as in her ear. She paused on the path and cocked her head. It seemed to be emanating from the direction of the garage.

Moments later, she rounded the privet hedge to find Phoebe and Neal, half hidden by the shadows of the garage overhang, locked in a passionate embrace.

Neal hadn't meant for it to get hot and heavy so fast. It was funny because Phoebe wasn't even his type. It hadn't been until the night before, at the concert, that he'd begun seeing her in a new light. It wasn't anything she'd said or done. It was just . . . well, a vibe.

After they'd gotten home from the concert, they'd hung out in her room, talking and listening to music, until long after her parents had retired for the night. That was when the suspicion that had been growing in him all evening was confirmed. He discovered that she wasn't just an ordinary, overindulged teenaged girl bitching about how her life sucked. There was something dark and twisted inside her.

It was the strangest thing. One minute they were sitting on the bed, his back propped against the headboard, Phoebe lying on her side at his feet while they debated the social significance of Foo Fighters' lyrics compared to Fall Out Boy's (he considered both bands far inferior to Nirvana in its day), when suddenly she sat up, hitched up her skirt, and moved in to straddle him. The next thing he knew, her mouth was covering his and her tongue was halfway down his throat.

It was their first kiss.

Somehow, despite his growing erection, he managed to disentangle himself long enough to croak, "Whoa. What brought that on?"

"You want me to stop?" Her face inches from his, she stared into his eyes as if challenging him somehow.

"I didn't say that."

"Okay. Then shut up and enjoy the ride." She kissed him again, with even more conviction this time, grinding her mouth against his almost as if she were punishing him.

Neal felt excited and strangely repulsed at the same time. He knew what his buddies would say, that he was one insane motherfucker for even *thinking* of turning this down, but he couldn't help feeling . . . well, the tiniest bit manipulated, somehow. Yet once they got into it, he found that he couldn't stop. Phoebe was everything his previous girlfriends hadn't been: rough, hot, and nasty. A *Penthouse Forum* fantasy fuck come to life.

She'd taken off her skirt and T-shirt, and he could see that she had a pretty nice body. Too thin, but not as scrawny as it had looked swimming around in all that clothing she'd had on. Not that it mattered. He was as lost in the moment as he had been in the music at the concert (which had been surprisingly good for a bunch of over-the-hill rockers).

It wasn't until Neal rolled off her minutes later, spent, that the ramifications of what they'd just done sank in. "Fuck. We didn't use a condom."

"Don't worry, I'm on the pill," she assured him with the world-weary air of an older woman. "And as far as STDs go, I've only been with one other guy, and he was married."

"Married?" Neal hadn't thought anything about Phoebe could shock him at this point, but that did. The thought of a potential case of the clap faded from his mind at this surprising bit of news.

"Don't look so shocked." Her expression was the same oddly defiant one she'd worn earlier in the day, at the deli, but in her eyes he thought he saw something broken and vulnerable. He recognized that look because he knew that place; he was as intimate with it as he had been with Phoebe just now. "Are you going to tell me you've never been with an older woman?"

"Actually, I haven't." He and his former girlfriend, Lauren, had joked about the fact that she was six months older than he. That was the closest he'd ever been to having sex with an older woman. "Do your parents know?" he asked as she was pulling on her T-shirt and panties.

"No, and they can't know about *us*, either." She paused to look him hard in the eye. Spots of color stood out on her cheeks, and her dark hair was a mass of corkscrew curls. She might have been a rebel in one sense, but it was obvious she cared very much about her parents' opinion of her.

Once again Neal had the jarring sense of the pieces of this picture not matching up. She was a paradox, this Phoebe. And the feelings she evoked in him were equally conflicting. She made him uneasy, yet at the same time he found her oddly compelling. Even endearing, in a way. It was weird, because he hardly knew her, but Neal had the strangest feeling, for the first time since his father's death, of being in a place where he wasn't alone in the dark, where he *fit*.

He was so lost in thought, it was a moment before he became aware of Phoebe's asking somewhat irritably, "So, do you have a problem with that?"

Her voice carried a hint of defiance, but when he brought his gaze back to her, he could see the vulnerability in her eyes: the deep-seated glint of whatever was broken inside her. Neal regarded her for a moment, taking in the sight of her as she knelt before him on the mattress, in her flowered panties and T-shirt, like a little girl waiting to be tucked into bed—or a penitent looking for absolution—before answering, "Not in the least."

11

Vaughn, traveling north along the Henry Hudson in his and Gillian's rented car, found himself recalling Christmases past. There had been the Christmas in Madagascar, when he and some of the other crew members had stayed up half the night drinking, serenaded by howler monkeys. And the Christmas he'd spent on a crab-fishing boat out on the Bering Sea, lashed to a boom and frozen to the bone, in danger of losing life or limb with each pitching roll of the sea. A close second in terms of holiday cheer had been the Christmas in Tanzania, where the accommodating hotel staff had gone out of their way to prepare, in place of the usual Sukuma fare, a "traditional" American feast: roast turkey tough as cowhide, a gelatinous glob of canned cranberry sauce, and some mushy cooked vegetable of uncertain origin.

A parade of memories, none too cozy, though certainly colorful. Yet, in all those years, he couldn't remember once feeling homesick. Maybe because for him, the ideal of family togetherness was just that: an ideal. Any fond memories he had of childhood were mainly due to Abigail's mother. With his parents either too distracted (or too drunk, in his mother's case) to give more than a cursory nod to the holidays, it had been Rosalie who had seen to it that the tree was properly trimmed, a wreath hung on the door, and the lights strung on the outside of the house. She'd always insisted, too, that the tree be a real one, not the artificial kind his mother said was more "practical." And if the presents brought by Santa Claus were always just what he and Lila had wanted, it had been because Rosalie had seen to that as well.

Christmas dinner in their house had always been a royal feast that was days in the making. What little family togetherness they'd had back then had been thin stuff, held together by the glue liberally applied at every turn by their housekeeper, but on those occasions it had seemed real enough. He recalled looking around the table at the faces of his parents and sister, shining in the candlelight, the magnificent bird Rosalie had roasted glistening at the head of the table, and feeling true contentment. The feeling never lasted long, though. Like the day itself, it quickly faded into oblivion. The following morning Mother would be laid up again with one of her "headaches" and Dad rushing to get back to the office like someone desperate to escape a burning building. Now, here Vaughn was on his way to his sister's to celebrate their first Christmas together in at least fifteen years.

And possibly their last.

But Lila didn't need to know that the results of his most recent tests had been less than encouraging—it seemed that his white-cell count wasn't responding as his doctor had hoped. It would only worry her. And she had enough worries of her own.

Not that the day wouldn't be fraught in other ways. For one thing, there would be Abigail, a stone's throw away in the big house. Leaving aside the tense situation between her and Lila, he knew it would be awkward, her being so close and yet so far away, in terms of what he thought of as her "other" life. By all rights, he should feel comfortable stopping in to wish his old friend a merry Christmas. But he knew that he'd only end up feeling as if he were intruding. Not only that, the cozy domestic scene he was likely to encounter was sure to depress him. For lately he'd become aware of a shift in his feelings toward Abigail: What had started out as a trip down memory lane had veered into territory more dangerous than any he'd encountered in any of his travels.

"You're awfully quiet. Feeling okay?"

Vaughn surfaced from the eddying currents of his thoughts and looked over at Gillian. She was so petite she might have been a child at the wheel: a determined little girl, with white-blond hair sticking up in furious, pink-tipped bristles and wide green eyes in a pixie's face, with a gaze as intense as a blowtorch.

"I'm fine," he said, keeping his voice light. Gillian tended to hover— she had the kind of kinetic energy that, when not channeled into creative endeavors, had a way of consuming everything in its path—and Vaughn had had about all the hovering he could take.

"You're sure?"

"Of course I'm sure. Relax, okay?" All right, so he was tired and felt a little sick to his stomach, but that was pretty much the norm these days. No need to drag everyone else down with him.

"I'll breathe a lot easier once we have the results from your next CT scan," she said. In a few more weeks he'd be done with this round of chemo and they would know if it had had the desired effect. He just wished that he felt as optimistic as Gillian clearly did. "What did Dr. Grossman say about the fevers?"

"I haven't told him. He's away for the holidays, so I thought I'd wait until my next appointment. Anyway, it's not that big a deal." Weren't the mild spikes in temperature he'd been experiencing part of the territory, along with other fun side effects, such as throwing up and having his hair fall out in clumps?

Gillian darted a stern look at him. "Vaughn, this isn't something to fool around with, you know. You have *cancer*. Even with all the stuff they're giving you, half the time I wonder if these doctors know what they're doing. You can't take any chances." She frowned, her small hands knotting around the wheel.

"I'm sure Dr. Grossman knows what he's doing."

She gave a snort of contempt. "Yeah, right. And if you were a friend or relative of his who was sick, he wouldn't be too busy off skiing in Aspen to take the call."

"This isn't exactly what I'd call an emergency. Let's not blow it out of proportion, okay?" Vaughn was doing his best to curb his impatience. Gillian meant well, he knew, and she'd been terrific about letting him crash at her place, not to mention tending to him on those days when he was too sick to crawl out of bed. It wasn't limited to home care, either. The one time Lila couldn't make it into the city for his regular Wednesday appointment, Gillian hadn't hesitated to drop everything to accompany him to the hospital, even though it had meant two hours of sitting around outside the infusion suite, killing time, while he'd undergone his chemo treatment. If she got a little extreme at times, he knew that her concern was to a large degree justified. "I promise I'll call Dr. Grossman the minute he gets back—before then if it gets any worse." In her face, he caught a glimpse of the fear she normally kept under wraps, and he felt himself soften toward her. "Look, Gil, I know I'd probably be dead by now if it weren't for you. Lying out in the desert with vultures picking at my bones. But you've gotta lighten up. Please. It's Christmas."

She gave a dry little laugh. "You're not going anywhere. You're too stubborn to die."

"Me, stubborn? Look who's talking."

Gillian was the most persistent person he knew. And like a limpet to a rock, she'd attached herself to him. Not that he was in any position to object. She'd taken him in, sick as he was, no questions asked and no time limit set. Not only that, she was a regular Florence Nightingale. She read to him when he was too ill to focus on the printed page; she gave him ice cubes to suck on when he was so dehydrated from vomiting he could scarcely lift his head off the pillow; she brought him chicken soup from Eisenberg's Deli and Rice Krispy treats from City Bakery to stimulate his appetite. He knew she'd fallen behind on her work as a result, though she didn't seem too bothered by it. In fact, she almost seemed to be . . . *enjoying herself.*

The thought slithered in like a snake to coil about his heart, a heart normally filled with charitable feelings toward his ex-girlfriend. The snake hissed, *Pretty convenient for her, don't you think, your being grounded like a trussed calf?* His itinerant lifestyle, after all, was the main reason they'd broken up. Gillian had gotten tired of waiting around for him to show up between gigs. She'd accused him of using his work as an excuse to avoid being in a real relationship. Now here he was, pinned down by an adversary even stronger than the love of a good woman, and while he didn't doubt that Gillian genuinely wished for him to get better, wasn't there a small part of her that was glad she had him right where she wanted him?

It was a discomfiting thought. Pushing it from his mind, he turned his attention to the MapQuest printout in his hand. "Make a right at the next light," he directed. "That should put us onto Main Street. According to this, we're only a few miles from Abby's."

"Does she know you're coming?" Gillian asked, meaning Abigail, of course. She'd taken an instant dislike to Abigail and wasn't shy about reminding him of it every chance she got. It wasn't anything Abigail had said or done, as far as he could tell; just, he suspected, that Gillian wanted him all to herself.

"I may have mentioned it to her. But I'm sure she'll be busy with her own family." Vaughn struck a casual tone, but his heart rate picked up at the mention of Abigail. Her visits had come to mean more to him than a chance to see a fresh face now and then—someone who wasn't part of his new, constricted orbit, which mainly comprised of Gillian, his sister, and the staff and fellow patients on the hematology floor at New York–Presbyterian, with whom he was now on a first-name basis.

Gillian made the turn onto a street lined with quaint shops and cafés decked in seasonal finery. "I wouldn't be so sure about that if I were you," she said, a caustic edge creeping into her voice. "I doubt she'll want to miss this chance to wish you a *very* merry, up-close-and-personal Christmas."

"Come on, Gil. We're just friends." Vaughn maintained a light tone, though the words sounded disingenuous to his ears.

Gillian must have thought so, too, because she gave a contemptuous snort. "Is that so? Well, someone ought to tell *her* that. She seems to have other ideas."

"You're imagining things."

But even as he dismissed the idea, Vaughn knew there was some truth to Gillian's words. He sensed that Abigail's feelings for him were more than platonic. Not that anything could come of it. She was married. And Vaughn—call it high moral ground or the legacy of his philandering dad, or simply the fact that the supply of single ladies had always been more than plentiful—had made it a rule never to get involved with married women.

Still, the power of that old connection wasn't easily denied. Never mind that everything about her lifestyle was antithetical to his: the showpiece house, the car and driver, the designer clothes, the expensive scents she trailed whenever she came walking through the door. There was Abigail's public persona as well, as airy and artful as the confections she spun. If he hadn't known the *real* Abigail—the part she kept concealed from others like a bruise on an otherwise perfect piece of fruit—he wouldn't have encouraged her visits. Where Gillian saw only a stuck up bitch and Lila a vengeful one, he saw a woman who, beneath all the trappings of her success and despite the wounds she'd suffered along the way, was good and decent and hungering for more out of life. It made her appealing to him in a way that none of her beauty or artifices, fame or money, ever could.

It was when she talked to him about her daughter that her vulnerable side came through the most. She worried about the fact that Phoebe was so withdrawn, and though her worry was occasionally accompanied by flashes of irritation—sometimes downright anger, as when Phoebe had stood her up on the night of her big event—he could see how hard she was trying. She wanted for her and Phoebe the kind of relationship she'd had with her own mother.

"Do you know, I was the same age as Phoebe when Mom died," she'd said to him the other day when she'd been confiding to him about her latest fight with Phoebe—something to do with Phoebe refusing to eat breakfast. "It hurts sometimes to think of all the years we could have had together. I just wish Phoebe could know that the people you love aren't necessarily going to be in your life forever."

She'd given him a look that had cut right through him, and he'd known then that she was thinking of him as well. It had occurred to him that, for her, these visits were more loaded than he'd realized—watching him battle cancer, as she had Rosalie, knowing that he might not make it. And yet, unlike Gillian, she never let on. She didn't pressure him for details of his symptoms or test results, always waiting until he was ready to share that information. She didn't burden him with her own fears; she allowed him to simply *be*. On the days he wasn't feeling up to going out or even offering much in the way of conversation, she would simply sit with him, reading a book or working on her laptop while he napped. Sometimes he would wake to find her gazing at him with a furrowed brow, a pained look in her eyes, and he would know that she was reliving the torment of seeing her mother die, but she was always quick to cover it up with a smile or a lighthearted remark. She seemed to understand that a restful presence was what he needed most.

Now Gillian broke in. "*Am* I imagining things? Or is it just that you don't want to admit I'm right?"

Finally he growled, "Cut me some slack, okay? Could you do that?"

Gillian darted an apprehensive look at him, as if realizing she'd gone too far this time. "All right. For you. And because it's Christmas," she allowed generously, though not generously enough to refrain from adding, "But that doesn't mean I'm changing my opinion."

Vaughn wished he didn't have to deal with her jealousy on top of everything else. Though they hadn't been intimate in years—otherwise he never would have taken her up on her offer—it had become apparent soon after he'd moved in that she still had feelings for him. He knew she wouldn't rebuff him if he were to suggest that, instead of his sleeping on the sofa, they share her bed. If she'd known that Abigail's interest in him wasn't one-sided, she'd have been hurt.

Attempting to throw her off the scent, he commented jokingly, "Abby might feel differently once she sees me without my hair."

It had begun falling out the week before, just a few strands at first, then noticeable clumps, so Vaughn had decided to spare himself the grief of watching it go bit by bit and had had it shaved off all at once. He still wasn't quite used to the new look. Each time he idly reached up to run a hand over his head in response to an odd sense of weightlessness on top or an overly cool breeze, it always came as a little shock to find it hairless.

This coaxed a smile out of Gillian. "I think you look sexy bald."

"The last time I had a buzz cut was back in the fourth grade," he told her. "And believe me, no one thought I was sexy then."

"You remind me of Bruce Willis."

"Yeah, and look what happened to him. His wife dumped him and married a guy half his age."

"I think it was the other way around. Bruce dumped her," she said on a more dyspeptic note. Male abandonment was a touchy subject with Gillian.

Vaughn was quick to move to a lighter subject. "Either way, I'm not going to sit here mourning my dear, departed hair. At least the rest of me is still here. That's something to celebrate."

"You're right." She loosened her grip on the steering wheel, her face relaxing in a smile. When Gillian smiled, *really* smiled, it was a wonder to behold: Her face lit up like a supernova. "And here we are dashing through the snow in a one-horse open sleigh . . . oops, make that a Chevrolet."

"Did you know that in the Netherlands they have a mythical figure called Black Pieter? He's to St. Nicholas what the elves are to Santa," Vaughn said, hoping to sustain this new, lighter mood. "The Dutch folks parading in the streets in blackface don't seem to realize how politically incorrect it's become."

"You've witnessed this firsthand, of course," she commented dryly.

He smiled, recalling the Christmas in Amsterdam, which had come on the heels of a weeklong assignment in the fjords of Greenland, filming a show on extreme skiing for the Discovery channel. It was during the time he and Gillian had been lovers, and he could have flown home to be with her, but instead he'd selfishly opted to spend the holiday hanging out with his fellow crew members, taking in the sights and drinking too much glogg. Now, feeling a stab of guilt, he reached over to pluck one of Gillian's hands from the wheel and cover it with his.

"Thanks, Gil," he said softly.

"For what?" she asked him somewhat warily.

"For everything. And for coming with me today."

This time her smile was more cautious, as if she suspected he was only softening her up before some sort of blow. "You're welcome. Anyway, it's not like I was planning on flying home for Christmas." Gillian's family all lived in Duluth, where she'd grown up, and she had about as much in common with them, she'd once told him, as a diehard agnostic with a Baptist preacher. "Besides, I like your sister."

"She likes you, too."

"It must be hard for her. This being her first Christmas without her husband," Gillian reflected aloud after a moment of silence.

"I'm sure it is." Vaughn sighed, thinking about his late brother-in-law. He'd liked Gordon, though he hadn't spent enough time around him to get to know him all that well. And although he'd lost all respect for Gordon over the Vertex scandal, he was still sorry for the way things had ended. Mostly because of the devastating effect it had had on his sister and nephew. "Thank God for Neal," he said. "I don't know what she'd do without him."

"In that case, let's hope he doesn't follow in your footsteps. Lila would never forgive you," Gillian said.

Vaughn laughed. "Knowing her, she'd probably spare me the agony of a slow death."

Gallows humor helped, he'd found. Joking about his cancer took his mind off the battle being waged inside his body and the havoc it was wreaking on him, in the form of a persistent, low-level nausea that occasionally flared into full-blown vomiting, strange rashes and night sweats, and, worst of all, this pervasive, bone-deep weariness that he couldn't seem to shake.

Mainly, though, what he felt was scared. Scared in a way that he hadn't felt standing four feet from a crocodile, during a shoot in Brazil's Pantanal wetlands, that had looked as if it were about to eat him for breakfast. Or that time in the Congo basin, when their camp had been attacked by guerrillas and they'd been marched at gunpoint to the bush headquarters of the commandant (who, by some bizarre twist of fate, had gone to Ohio State with one of the other cameramen—their ticket to freedom, as it had turned out). Those brushes with death had been as much an adrenaline rush as a reason to say his prayers. Part of the jazz of what he did for a living was that it was dangerous, even life-threatening at times. Because once the danger was past, that was when you truly felt alive.

This was different. This was a gun-toting thug in a ski mask creeping up on him from behind. A silent, faceless enemy against which the sappy pep talks he gave himself were a feeble defense. *Think positive! You can beat this with the right attitude!* Slogans borrowed from the brigade of cancer survivors, with their pink ribbons and their support groups and their marches to raise money for cancer research, into whose midst he'd been unwillingly thrust.

He wasn't even sure how much faith he placed in Western medicine. With all its high-tech gizmos and wonder drugs, did it offer any more of a guarantee than a traditional healer would? Was he any more safeguarded than the Balinese who painted symbols over their doorways to ward off evil spirits, or the Nepalese who relied on ayurvedic medicine?

It was late in the day by the time they reached his sister's. After a few wrong turns—the only signs along this stretch of road were the ones that read "Private Property" and "No Trespassers Allowed"—they came to the gated entrance of an estate. The gate was locked, but he had the combination, so he rolled his window down and punched in the numbers on the keypad by the intercom. Moments later, they were rolling along a well-tended gravel road lined with open pastures on either side, in which the melting snow from last week's snowstorm formed frozen archipelagos. The road ended a few minutes later in a wide, circular driveway, where the house, a magnificent example of late-nineteenth-century hubris, stood lit up against the purpling sky, twinkling with Christmas lights.

So this is where Abigail lives—the famous Rose Hill, he thought.

By contrast, Lila's accommodations were extremely modest. Stepping inside her small, simply furnished apartment over the garage, he couldn't help comparing it to her old Park Avenue digs. It was a palace compared to some of the places he'd shacked up in—a certain hotel in Botswana came to mind, where he'd had to keep his belongings locked up to prevent them from being pilfered by the monkeys—but a far cry from what Lila was used to.

"Merry Christmas, you two! Thank God you made it. I was beginning to think you'd gotten lost." Lila relieved Vaughn of the shopping bag full of presents he was carrying, then turned to flash Gillian a grateful smile. "You were a saint to drive all this way. Was the traffic awful?"

"Not too bad. And we only got lost once." Gillian's gaze swept the room, and he could see from her expression that she was a little taken aback as well. She'd been to Lila's Park Avenue apartment, so she had to be thinking the same thing as he. "Anything I can do to help?" she asked.

"Not at the moment. As you can see, I've got it covered." Lila gestured with a somewhat ironic flourish toward the kitchen at the other end of the room—or what passed for one. It consisted of a stove and an apartment-sized refrigerator, a pair of cupboards above a sink, and a narrow counter at either end, every square inch of which was jammed with pots and pans and bowls. "It's a bit of a challenge, but we manage," she said in response to the dubious look Gillian gave her. "The only thing that had me in a bit of a panic was wondering how we were all going to fit around the table. It was Neal's bright idea to put a piece of plywood over it." Proudly, she pointed out the table, covered in a flowered cloth that looked suspiciously like a bed sheet, against which the Christmas tree was crowded so close that pine needles were sprinkled over it at that end. Folding chairs provided the finishing touch. "Voilà—instant seating for five."

"Who's the extra guest?" Vaughn asked.

"You don't know him. His name's Karim." Lila became suddenly animated as she bustled about, stirring pots and peering under lids. Vaughn wondered if the color blooming in her cheeks was due to this sudden burst of activity . . . or to this Karim fellow.

"He from around here?"

"Yes. He works here, as a matter of fact."

"Ah." Vaughn nodded thoughtfully. "So you two must spend a lot of time together."

"Not really. I take care of the house. He takes care of the grounds."

"I see. So you were merely taking pity on him?"

Lila shot him a narrow glance. "Of course not. He doesn't even celebrate Christmas. I was just being nice."

"Nice, huh?" He chewed on this for a moment, keeping his eye on Lila.

At last she whirled to face him, hands on hips. "If there's a point to all this, why don't you just come out with it?"

He threw up his hands in self-defense. "What? Did I say something?"

"I know what you're driving at."

Vaughn gave a rueful grimace. "Okay, I'm being protective, but is that a crime? You're the only family I have left, Sis. I just want to be sure some sleazy guy isn't putting the moves on you."

"He's not sleazy, and no one's putting any moves on me," she said. "Anyway, he'll be here soon, so you can judge for yourself. In the meantime, if you don't mind, I have supper to get on the table."

Vaughn went over to Lila and put an arm around her shoulders. "Forget I said anything, okay? I'm sure he's as nice as you say, and I promise to be on my best behavior." After a moment, Lila's stiff posture relaxed, and she dropped her head onto his shoulder. Standing there, side by side with her, Vaughn had that feeling he often got with Lila, of a closeness that transcended their being brother and sister, a *twinness*, for lack of a better word, that made her seem less a separate being than an extension of himself.

"Sorry I snapped at you. It's just that I've been getting it at this end, too," she told him. "Neal's not happy about the fact that Karim and I have become friendly. Like it has to do with anything other than the fact that Karim's the only adult within fifty miles of here who says anything more to me than hello and good-bye. That is, if you don't count Abby's husband—he's nice." Vaughn grew instantly alert at the mention of Abigail's husband. He wondered what Kent was like. Abigail didn't talk about him much. "Neal seems to think . . . Never mind. It doesn't matter." She drew away, looking as if she thought she'd already said too much, and went back to her preparations.

Gillian and Vaughn exchanged a look.

"Speaking of the devil, where *is* my favorite nephew?" Vaughn inquired.

"With Phoebe, where else?" Lila gave a small sigh.

"Abby's Phoebe?"

Lila nodded. "They're practically joined at the hip these days."

"What does Abby think about all this?" Vaughn was surprised that Abigail hadn't mentioned it to him. Usually she told him everything that was going on with Phoebe.

"I wouldn't know. I'm not exactly her closest confidante." Lila's tone was sardonic, but Vaughn caught the faintly wistful look on her face as she bent to open the oven door, and he wondered if she were remembering when she and Abigail had confided in each other about everything.

"It's perfect! I love it!" Gillian clapped her hands together in glee. "She's probably shitting a brick right now."

Lila peered at the turkey, poking at it with a long fork—more savagely than necessary, it seemed. "Right now, the only thing that concerns me is that she might use this to get back at me. I don't want to see Neal get hurt because of it."

But Abigail wasn't like that, Vaughn knew. She wasn't the petty dictator Lila imagined her to be, nor was she vindictive. She was just someone muddling through, like the rest of them. He took advantage of the opportunity to point out, "It's not like you and Abby are at war."

"No, but the fact is, she doesn't like having me around any more than I like being here." Lila closed the oven door and straightened, going back to the pot she'd been stirring on the stove.

"Maybe if you tried talking to her . . ."

Instantly Lila was on the defensive. "Oh, so now it's *my* fault?"

Gillian chose that moment to jump in, no doubt in an attempt to forestall an argument. "What's she like, this Phoebe?" She dug an olive from the open jar on the counter and popped it into her mouth.

"She's okay once you get to know her," Lila said. "Actually, I feel kind of sorry for her."

"Why is that?" Vaughn was curious. All he knew was what Abigail had told him.

Lila pondered it a moment, frowning. "I don't know. She just seems so sad. Like something's eating at her. Which is kind of ironic, since *she* doesn't eat. Though it's been a little better since she and Neal started hanging out together. She used to just rearrange what was on her plate. Now she actually takes a few bites of whatever I fix."

"She doesn't exactly sound like Neal's type," he observed. His nephew usually went for the athletic, outdoorsy sort. Melanie Beck, his girlfriend at Riverdale, where he'd gone to high school, had been captain of the girls' soccer team.

"I know. It's funny how they took to each other. Like a couple of lost souls." Lila fell silent for a moment, wearing a troubled look, before she roused herself and said with resolute cheer, "Well, there's no point in getting worked up about it. It's not like they're engaged or anything. Besides, they're just kids. How long can it last? I remember when I was that age—one minute I'd be crazy about a boy, and the next I wouldn't even want to hear his name."

As if on cue, Neal came blowing in through the door just then. "Hi, Mom. Sorry I'm—" He came to a halt as his gaze fell on his uncle, and he broke into a huge grin. "Uncle Vaughn! When did you get here?"

"A few minutes ago. Merry Christmas, Neal." Vaughn enfolded his nephew in a fierce bear hug, drawing back to inquire, "So what's this I hear about you and this Phoebe chick? Don't tell me you're going Oprah on us?" he teased. Vaughn used to joke that you knew you were in deep with a girl when you switched from listening to hip-hop to Lite FM and started watching *Oprah*.

But Neal didn't find it amusing this time. He merely shrugged in response, obviously not wishing to enlighten his uncle on the subject. "You look different," he said, studying Vaughn with narrowed eyes.

"You mean no hair." With a chuckle, Vaughn ran a hand over his newly shaved head. In the old days, Neal would have cracked a joke about it, but now he merely looked uncomfortable, as if Vaughn's cancer were a verboten subject.

"So, are you feeling okay?" he asked tentatively.

Vaughn was quick to reassure him, saying with a heartiness that didn't match his present stamina, "Better than okay. I'll bet you a buck I can still beat you at arm wrestling."

"There'll be none of that, you two," Lila chided. "Sit down. Dinner's almost ready."

Vaughn turned to introduce Neal to his ex-girlfriend. "You remember Gillian?" he said.

Neal shook her hand. "Sure. Hi." From the look on his face, it was clear that he didn't have a clue who Gillian was.

"Your parents had us over for dinner once," she reminded him. "You were just a little kid then, so you probably don't remember."

Neal looked mildly panicked, as if fearing this would lead to a conversation about those days, one he wasn't prepared to have. Lila unintention-

ally threw him a lifeline when she called over, "Who wants wine?" Neal
seized the excuse to mutter, "I'll get it," before ducking back outside.

"We keep it in a cooler on the porch. No room in the fridge," Lila explained in a matter-of-fact tone, as if this jury-rigged setup were the norm.
Vaughn could scarcely contain his amazement. Was this the same sister
who'd once complained that she couldn't find an espresso machine that
made real, European espresso?

Lila's new friend, Karim, showed up as she was getting ready to carve
the turkey. Seeing him walk in, a muscularly built man of medium height
dressed in a navy blazer and corduroys, with dark, close-cropped curls
and black eyes alight with lively intelligence, Vaughn was immediately
struck by his air of self-possession. Karim may have been a stranger in
their midst, but he appeared perfectly at ease. As they shook hands,
Karim seemed to size him up just as quickly and, as if recognizing in
Vaughn a kindred spirit, instantly found him to his liking. Before long,
they were chatting like old friends.

"I was in Kabul once," Vaughn told him after learning that Karim
was from Afghanistan. "It was at the tail end of the Soviet war.
Nearly got my ass thrown in jail by the *mujahideen*, for reasons I never
could quite make out. I think it had something to do with my having
long hair."

"You're lucky you're an infidel, or you *would* have been arrested," Karim
said with a dry chuckle. He was seated on a folding chair borrowed from
the table, looking as relaxed as if he were used to making himself at
home here. "Under the Taliban, even to go beardless was a serious offense. I know. I had my own share of run-ins with them." Vaughn caught
a glimpse of something steely in the other man's eyes. As if Karim, however gentle he seemed, wouldn't have hesitated to slit the throat of anyone who'd threatened him or a loved one.

Vaughn shook his head in shared disgust. "I never thought being an
infidel would come in handy in that part of the world," he said.
"Though I wouldn't want to try my luck nowadays. Times have changed."

Karim nodded, wearing a somber look. "Not for the better, I'm afraid. These terrorists, they care nothing for the true spirit of the Koran. They look only at the strictest interpretations of Islamic law while ignoring its true, spiritual meaning. But this is nothing new. A hundred years ago, it was the followers of the Wahhabi movement seeking to cleanse Islam of all those who weren't 'true' believers. Much as we might like to blame modern-day forces for the current state of affairs in the Middle East—Israel, the war, political forces here and abroad—what it really boils down to is the age-old struggle between the fundamentalists and those who seek true wisdom and understanding."

"It's certainly not limited to Islam," Vaughn said, thinking of countries like North Korea and Myanmar. *And let's not forget the good old U.S. of A., where they blow up abortion clinics.* "Other religions have their share of fundamentalism taken to extremes. I once met a Hasid who explained why it was that he didn't eat meat. It seemed that one of the three rabbis who were in charge of inspections at the only triple-glatt kosher butcher shop within walking distance was known to tipple now and then, and he feared that this tippling rabbi would be too hungover to do his job properly. Mind you, this was a man who thought nothing of charging me double the going rate to replace a cracked lens on my camera."

"I count myself lucky just to have made it out of the Bible Belt with my mind and soul intact," interjected Gillian as she sipped her wine.

"As a Confederate son, I take offense at that," Vaughn protested lightly. "We're not all Bible-thumping bigots. And let's not forget that some of our country's greatest freethinkers were Southern Democrats. Thomas Jefferson, for one. Thurgood Marshall, for another."

"Politics and religion are two subjects that should never be discussed at dinner parties," Lila scolded playfully as she squeezed past them on her way to the table, carrying a steaming casserole. "And somehow you've managed to work them both into the same sentence."

"Isn't that why you invited me, Sis, to stir things up?" teased Vaughn. He felt better than he had all day. Or maybe it wasn't so much feeling better—the nausea was still there—as feeling *alive*. Discussing world affairs was a refreshing change from talking about his white-cell and ANC counts, how his platelets were clotting, and whether or not he was in danger of becoming anemic.

"Enough stirring," Lila said. "Time to sit down and eat."

They all squeezed in around the table, Neal seated next to Vaughn, with Karim wedged in between Gillian and Lila. It was a lively group, except for Neal. His efforts to join in seemed forced, and he all but shut down whenever Karim attempted to engage him in conversation.

"So have you decided which classes you're going to take?" Karim asked him at one point, in reference to the community college Neal had enrolled at.

"Not yet." Neal kept his head down as he shoveled a forkful of stuffing into his mouth.

Karim looked a bit puzzled. "Unless I'm mistaken, your mother told me the deadline for spring enrollment is one week away."

Neal shrugged, studiously avoiding Karim's gaze. "I'm keeping my options open."

"Well, if I can be of any help, please let me know. I was a teacher in my other life, so I'm familiar with curriculums," Karim offered.

Neal only grunted in response.

Lila flashed Karim an apologetic look, but Karim seemed to take it in stride. For the most part, he had eyes only for Lila. Throughout the meal, even while engaged in animated conversation with the others, he surreptitiously tracked her with his gaze. It was apparent to Vaughn, if not to Lila, that Karim was smitten with her. It must have been apparent to Neal, too, because more than once Vaughn caught him giving Karim the fish-eye.

Lila wasn't blind to it, either, and Vaughn could see that it had her rattled. In close proximity to Karim, she'd become flustered, talking more animatedly than usual and at one point almost choking on a bite of food when his elbow accidentally brushed against hers. Given her earlier denials,

Vaughn guessed it was she felt guilty for being attracted to him. Knowing Lila, she'd think it was far too soon to be so much as looking at another man, with her husband barely cold in his grave.

"That was a delicious meal," Karim complimented her after the last plate had been cleared away to make room for dessert. "You're a woman of many talents, Lila."

"I don't know about that," she said with a self-effacing laugh, "but I guess I can still pull it together in a pinch."

"A toast to the world's greatest hostess," said Vaughn, raising his glass of sparkling apple cider—he was off booze these days, due to the chemo.

"The second greatest, you mean." Lila cast him an arch look as she was setting out dessert plates. "I'm sure I can't compare to Abby."

Karim was quick to change the subject. He turned to Neal to say, "Your mother tells me you're looking to buy a car. I know of one that's for sale—a '98, but with low mileage and a recently overhauled engine. It belongs to a friend of mine. I could get him to give you a good price if you're interested."

"Thanks, but I already have something lined up," Neal replied none too graciously, his eyes studiously trained on the table in front of him.

"Really?" Lila seemed surprised; this was obviously the first she was hearing of it. "Weren't you just telling me there was nothing in your price range?"

"It's not definite yet." Neal kept his head down. "Just . . . well, there's this buddy of mine from school who's looking to upgrade, and he thought I might be interested in his old car."

"What kind of shape is it in?" she asked.

"I don't know. I haven't looked at it yet," he admitted.

"In that case, it wouldn't hurt to check out Karim's friend's. At least then you'd have something to compare it to." She grabbed a knife and began slicing wedges out of the pumpkin pie she'd just set down on the table, seemingly oblivious to Neal's discomfort.

He flicked her an irritated glance, saying, "I've got it covered, Mom. Okay?"

Lila wisely let it drop.

After dessert, everyone helped wash up, and then it was time to open presents. Lila apologized as she handed Vaughn his gift, saying, "It's not much, I'm afraid. My budget isn't what it used to be." He opened the box to find a knitted scarf and matching cap, obviously homemade, though not by Lila, he knew—she couldn't knit to save her life. Still, he was touched.

Neal gave him a collection of fisherman's flies that he'd scored at a garage sale. They swapped a few reminiscences about the times Vaughn had taken Neal fishing, and Neal seemed to lighten up a bit. Vaughn could only hope that eventually the happy memories his nephew had of growing up would come to outweigh the more recent, tragic ones.

Vaughn's gifts to his sister and nephew, while equally modest, had also been chosen with care. Lila expressed genuine delight at the hand-carved teak box he'd brought her from Namibia, similar to the one he'd given Gillian back at the loft. For Neal, there was a carved tribal mask and an African thumb piano, which made eerie music reminiscent of the plinking of raindrops on a tin roof.

Gillian presented Lila with a gift basket of soaps and bath oils. For Neal, there was an autographed CD put out by an edgy new rock group that one of Gillian's friends was in. In return, she received from them a vintage postcard of a covered bridge set in a rustic birch bark frame.

But it was Karim's gift to Lila that was perhaps the most thoughtful of all: a collection of poems by the thirteenth-century Afghani poet Jalal ad-Din Rumi, translated from the original Persian, in an ancient, leather-bound volume. "Rumi was our country's greatest poet," he told them, explaining that it hadn't been Afghanistan then but part of the Byzantine Empire. "Which is ironic, since he spent a large portion of his life in exile."

Lila was clearly touched, though she also appeared somewhat embarrassed—the book was obviously a rare edition that must have been

worth a lot. The necktie she'd given him must have seemed painfully prosaic in comparison. She opened the volume and read aloud at random.

In the ocean are many bright strands
and many dark strands like veins that are seen
when a wing is lifted up.
Your hidden self is blood in those, those veins
that are lute strings that make ocean music,
not the sad edge of surf, but the sound of no shore.

She stumbled over the last words, growing a little teary-eyed, and
Vaughn knew that she was as moved by the meaning contained in those
words as she had been by the gesture of the gift itself. For a long moment after she'd closed the book, she sat fingering its tooled binding,
gazing off into space, before she roused herself and bent to retrieve the
last remaining gift from under the tree: a slim white envelope with
Vaughn's name printed on it.

She handed it to him, saying in a neutral tone, "It's from Abby. She
asked me to give it to you."

Inside the envelope was a receipt for season tickets to Yankee Stadium.
For two. Box seats. Vaughn was so blown away he didn't react at first; he
just sat there, staring at it. Nobody gave season tickets to a dying man,
he thought. It was Abigail's way of letting him know that she had no
doubt he'd be well enough to use them when the time came. The note
clipped to the receipt was equally thoughtful. It read simply, *I hope Gillian
likes baseball.*

Gillian was equally dumbfounded when he showed it to her. All she
could say was, "Wow."

She passed it around so the others could see. Lila regarded it without
comment, wearing an odd look, and Karim nodded in appreciation. It
was Neal who broke the silence, saying jokingly to Gillian, "If you're not
a fan, I'd be more than happy to go in your place."

"Forget it, buster," she growled, wearing a look that said she'd sooner give up one of her kidneys.

At last Vaughn's sister roused herself to remark, "Well. That was certainly generous of her." He couldn't tell whether or not she was being sarcastic.

He rose to his feet. "I should go thank her."

Gillian darted him an anxious look. "You don't want to wait? Like you said, she's probably busy with her family."

Vaughn ignored her, grabbing his jacket and heading for the door. "I won't be long," he said.

Outside, he was met by a blast of wind that was bitter cold. The temperature had to have dropped a good ten degrees since they'd arrived. As Vaughn made his way through the shadowy darkness, guided by the glowing windows of the house, which cast their light across the wide strip of lawn separating it from the garage, a host of conflicting emotions arose in him. He imagined the cozy family scene behind those windows— Abigail with her husband and daughter, gathered before the fire, the smoky-woodsy smell from which wafted on the wind, a haunting reminder of a life he'd never known. Never before had he questioned his loner existence or envied those of his friends who'd taken the well-traveled road of marriage and fatherhood, many of whom he viewed as slaves to their nine-to-five jobs and mortgages. If anything, they had only reaffirmed his choice to remain single and unencumbered. It was only lately that a little worm of doubt had wriggled in. He'd begun to wonder if he might indeed be missing out, as his married friends were always insisting he was. Not so much on the life he might've had with a wife and children but on the comfort he'd have known in dying surrounded by loved ones.

He could always count on Lila, he knew. But she had her own life, her own problems to deal with. She couldn't be expected to always drop everything to be at his side. And Neal—the poor kid was in such a bad place himself, he wouldn't know what to do with a dying uncle. Right now, like it or not, the only constant in Vaughn's life was Gillian. She

would be there for him as long as he needed her. It was just that he wasn't
about to let her abdicate her life for a man who didn't love her in
return—it wouldn't be a fair trade-off. Gillian didn't know it yet, but
should the chemo prove no match against his disease, if palliative care
was all that was left, he planned to go somewhere far away—that little
village in Bali where he'd spent one gloriously indolent winter nursing
himself back to health after an attack of malaria . . . or the Marianas,
where smiling faces were as prevalent as the mangoes and bananas growing everywhere—so he could die in peace, without inflicting it on her.

The one person he would have wanted to have near him at the end, he
realized, was Abigail. She was close to his heart in a way that made him
reflect, as he approached her house, not just upon what might have been
but on what might still be—if he were lucky enough to live out his life,
and if she were ever to decide to divorce her husband and run away with
him. The latter notion brought a smile. Abigail would no sooner choose a
free-spirited (and, at the moment, income-less) vagabond over all *this* than
a kid who talked of running away to join the circus would actually do so.

The path he was on led through a side yard toward the back of the
house, ending in a patio bordered in ornamental shrubbery dramatically
lit from below. Stepping onto it, he caught a movement within the shadowy recesses of the cabana by the pool, and he moved in for a closer look.

There, seated on a bench, bundled in a fur coat, was Abigail.

With her body angled away from him, she didn't spot him at first.
"Abby?" he called softly. She jerked around in surprise, and he quickly
moved into the dim glow cast by one of the recessed uplights so she
could see him. "Sorry. I didn't mean to startle you. I just came over to—
hey, are you okay?" He caught the silvery gleam of tears on her upturned
face as he sank down beside her on the bench.

"It's nothing," she said, clearly embarrassed. "Just a touch of the holiday blues, I guess."

"Anything you'd like to talk about?" Holiday blues, he thought, didn't
have you sitting outside in subfreezing temperatures.

"Not especially. It would only bore you."

"Try me," he said.

For the longest time, she didn't say anything. There was only the ghostly vapor of her breath rising and falling in the chill night air. The breeze that had kicked up sent a handful of fallen leaves scuttling crablike over the patio tiles around them. From inside the house came the faint tinkling of piano music. Finally she spoke.

"That's Phoebe," she said. "She's been taking piano lessons since she was a little girl."

"She plays well." Vaughn recognized the tune from the musical *South Pacific* and thought, *This is some enchanted evening, all right. Abigail sitting out here crying while her husband and daughter are whooping it up inside.* Clearly, something was wrong with this picture.

"She does, doesn't she?" Abigail perked up a bit before her face collapsed once more into misery. "Not that she plays much when I'm around. She says I make her nervous. Of course, it's a different story when it's her dad putting in a request. There's nothing she won't do for him." Her voice was at once bitter and full of longing.

"Girls and their daddies," he said in an attempt to console her.

"No, it's more than that. I sometimes think she'd be happier if I were out of the picture altogether."

"I'm sure that's not true."

"What if it is?" She turned a pair of anguished eyes on him.

"She's sixteen. All teenagers are like that," he said, thinking of how moody his once happy-go-lucky nephew had been these past months. "She'll grow out of it."

"Spoken like someone with no children of his own," she said with a dry little laugh.

Seemingly oblivious to the cold, she sat with her hands curled loosely in her lap, palms facing upward. He brought his fingertips to rest against the inside of her wrist. She wasn't wearing gloves, and though her flesh was cool to the touch he could feel a pulse beating there. "Is that all that's bothering you?" he asked, sensing there was something more.

There was another long pause before Abigail confided in a low, tremulous voice, "It's my husband, too. We . . . we've been fighting a lot lately. No, that's too strong a word. We don't fight. It's more like a cold war. We're like coworkers who don't particularly like each other but who have to put on a good face for the sake of the company."

Vaughn felt tenderness well up in him—the same urge he'd felt earlier in wanting to protect Lila. Only Lila wasn't hurting at the moment. Struggling, yes, but not the basket case she'd been a few months ago. Abigail, on the other hand, despite all her outward success, was clearly in torment: this strong, capable woman who'd built up so many defenses around her that they had become a sort of trap. For all of his sister's resentment of her, he thought, it was Lila who was inside where it was warm, surrounded by family and friends, while Abigail was spending Christmas night out here alone in the dark.

"I used to think that if I spent more time at home, we could go back to the way it was when we were first married," she went on in the same sadly resigned tone. "And maybe that was true at one time. But I don't think it is anymore. He's moved on. I can sense it."

"Has he told you as much?"

"Not in so many words. But it's there, like an invisible wall between us."

"It might help if you talked to him about it." Vaughn knew he was about as qualified to offer marital advice—to a woman he'd fantasized about making love to, no less—as a quack doctor to perform heart surgery, but he thought it was worth a shot.

"I have," she said. "But all we do is go around in circles. Not that I blame Kent. It's mostly my fault."

"Don't be so hard on yourself." Vaughn might not have been the world's expert in such matters, but he knew it took two to tango.

"No? Then who's to blame?" Her eyes, illuminated by the light from the windows facing onto the patio, sparked with some of her old fire. "Kent's not the one who got his priorities screwed up. I was so hell-bent on making a name for myself, I lost sight of what it was all for. Now everything I do to make it better only seems to make it worse. Phoebe?

She barely speaks to me, and tonight she hardly touched the supper I went to so much trouble to make. And Kent? It's me he won't touch." Her mouth twisted in a pained smile. "See? Aren't you sorry you asked?"

"Not at all. I'm not exactly the guy to go to for advice on such matters, having never been married myself, but I'm a good listener." He threaded his fingers through hers.

She shot him a grateful look before saying in a contrite voice, "You're the last person I should be dumping on. You must think I'm the most self-centered person on the planet. What are my problems compared to yours?"

He smiled. "It's not a contest."

"Still. Look at you, you're shivering. What are you doing out in this cold, anyway? You'll catch your—" She broke off before she could say the verboten word.

Vaughn filled the awkward silence that ensued by withdrawing from his pocket the envelope containing the receipt for the Yankees tickets. "I came over to thank you," he said. "I don't know what to say. It was incredibly generous of you. It must have cost a fortune."

"I can afford it. Besides, I wanted you to have something you could really use."

"I just hope I get the chance," he said, his smile fading a bit.

"Don't talk that way." She frowned, tightening her fingers around his, as if he were in imminent danger of slipping away. "You're going to be around for a long, long time. I'm more worried about the Yankees than I am about you, with the losing streak they've been on," she added with a shaky laugh.

"I didn't get anything for you," he said abashedly.

"Don't be silly. You've just given me the best gift of all," she told him. "I was going a little crazy out here until you came along. Thanks for talking me off the ledge."

"My pleasure." He tipped an invisible hat. "I'm always available to lend an ear. Or a shoulder, if need be."

"In that case . . ." Smiling, she snuggled up to him and dropped her head onto his shoulder. He could feel the collar of her fur coat tickling his neck, and something softer and silkier that he realized was her hair. Her voice drifted up. "Merry Christmas, by the way. At least, I hope it's a merry one."

"Very." He thought of the cozy scene taking place in the little apartment over the garage, one that six months ago he never could have imagined.

"Good. That makes one of us, at least." There was a silence, then her voice drifted up again, softer this time. "Vaughn? Do you ever wonder what would've happened if my mother and I hadn't been sent away? With us, I mean. If you and I had . . . you know . . ." She let the sentence trail off, though he could tell from her tone that their little interlude out at the quarry on that long-ago night wasn't just a distant memory for her. She gave a sigh. "I suppose our parents would've put a stop to it if they'd found out."

"They were hardly in a position to judge," Vaughn replied in a harsher tone. "Your mom was sleeping with my dad, and *my* mom was drunk most of the time."

"Still, do you ever wonder?" She lifted her head, her eyes searching his face.

"The thought," he said slowly, choosing his words with care, not wanting to spoil what they had in the here and now, "has occurred to me from time to time."

"What do you think would've happened?"

Vaughn tried to recall how he'd felt at the time. He hadn't been just another horny teenaged boy looking to score, that much he knew. The truth was, he'd been in love with Abigail. He had been, secretly, for quite some time before he'd made his move.

"I think we would've been in over our heads," he replied honestly.

She gave a knowing laugh. They sat for a moment in silence before she said with an uncharacteristic shyness, "Would you do me a favor, Vaughn? Would you kiss me? For old times' sake."

Not stopping to think it through, Vaughn leaned in to gently kiss her on the lips. Her breath was sweet with wine and something faintly, deliciously spicy. Then, unexpectedly, the kiss deepened and he was wrapping his arms around her, forgetting everything else in that moment—the fact that he was ill and that she was a married woman—as he sought to re-capture more than just the memory of their teenaged selves. She surren-dered to the moment as well, her mouth opening to his, her body soft and pliant in his arms. He could feel her shivering—not just from the cold, he suspected. Something born of nostalgia—a sweet, almost ironic brushing together of lips—had become something far more than either of them had bargained on.

It took every ounce of Vaughn's willpower to draw back. "You should go inside," he whispered, releasing his hold on her.

"You're right," she said. "It's freezing out here." Even so, it was a mo-ment before she reluctantly rose to her feet.

"I was thinking more of your family," he said. "They're probably won-dering what's keeping you."

"I doubt that. But thanks for the thought. By the way, just for the record, you're right. We *would* have been in over our heads." She gave him a fleeting smile before turning to go, calling softly over her shoulder as she headed back inside, "Merry Christmas, Vaughn."

Watching her retreat into the house, the sweet taste of her lips still on his, Vaughn knew that they'd crossed over into a realm from which there would be no turning back. He thought, for the first time in a long while not in relation to his illness, *Man, you are so fucked.*

Sliding the patio door shut behind her, Abigail paused to lean against it for a moment with her forehead pressed to the cold glass. Through the closed louvered doors to the living room, she could hear her husband and daughter on the other side. Phoebe had segued from show tunes to more traditional holiday fare. She was playing "Winter Wonderland," Kent singing along in his somewhat rusty but still serviceable tenor.

Abigail shivered inside her mink coat. She might have been standing there naked, she felt so chilled. Chilled and shaken. *Like a martini*, she thought. Which she could use right now: a little liquid cheer to take the edge off. Lord knew nothing else seemed to be working.

Vaughn's kiss, however sweet, had only served to reinforce the knowledge that her marriage was on shaky ground. If she'd thought it would put an end to any nagging questions about what might have been, or provide what her former shrink would have called *closure* (a ridiculous concept, if there ever was one), it had had the opposite effect: She was more confused than ever. What did she feel for Vaughn? Was it love? Or was she merely seeking to recapture a more innocent time in her life? Something she could hold on to while the life she'd built for herself—out of substandard materials, it had turned out—teetered on the brink of collapse?

And it wasn't just her marriage that was in trouble. Perez had reported earlier in the week that the Delgado woman was indeed on her way here, presumably for some sort of showdown—it had been confirmed by a relative of hers. What did she want? More money? She'd rejected the money Perez had offered on Abigail's behalf, so maybe she was holding out for a larger sum and thought that a face-to-face with Abigail was the way to get it. Somehow, though, Abigail didn't think that was it.

What was she after, then—revenge? Was she going to go public with this? Make Abigail the new object of the media hounds' bloodlust? Whatever her intentions, one thing was for sure: Her being in this country spelled trouble.

Abigail regretted now more than ever having taken Perez's advice. She should have flown down to Mexico immediately after the fire and met with the Delgado woman herself, if only to let her know how truly sorry she was. Now it was too late; the damage was done.

Abigail straightened and drew in a breath. "Merry Christmas," she muttered grimly to herself.

The scene she encountered when she walked into the living room was straight out of a Hallmark commercial: Her husband and daughter, their songfest concluded, snuggled on the sofa in front of the crackling fire, with Brewster curled asleep at their feet. Kent was telling Phoebe one of his stories, which she never seemed to tire of—tales of the blue-blooded, Yankee Doodle Dandy Christmases he'd enjoyed as a boy at his parents' country house in Fairfield, Connecticut. Seeing them together like that, so perfectly at ease and attuned to each other, Abigail felt something catch in her chest. It was a mighty effort to put on a cheerful face.

"Who wants dessert?" she called out brightly. After they'd finished dinner, Kent and Phoebe had each proclaimed that they were too full to eat another bite, but Abigail was determined not to let the plum pudding she'd gone to so much trouble to make go to waste.

Kent glanced up at her, not seeming to notice that she was wearing her coat. "Will it keep? I'm still pretty full," he said, patting his stomach.

"Same here," Phoebe seconded.

"Well, I'm not going to eat alone, so I suppose it'll have to wait." Abigail kept her tone light, but inside she was burning, as if it were a personal rejection.

Finally one of them noticed that she had her coat on. Phoebe said, in a disinterested voice, "Are you going somewhere?"

Not that it would matter to either of you, Abigail answered silently. But all she said was, "I stepped out for some fresh air. What are you two up to?" She shrugged off her coat and tossed it over a chair. Years ago, she'd read in some magazine that a real lady treated a mink coat as if it were cloth and a cloth coat as if it were mink, and it was a habit she'd adhered to ever since.

"Not much," Phoebe said in her usual desultory tone. In the old days, she would at least have offered to help clean up, but now she only stared at the flames leaping in the fireplace. Abigail wondered if she was still sulking from the chewing-out she'd gotten after the disastrous video-taped Christmas dinner, a confrontation that had quickly escalated into a shouting match. When Abigail had accused her of being more interested in some boy she'd just met than in her own mother, Phoebe had hurled back at her, "At least with Neal, I don't feel like I'm invisible! With you, it's like I'm not even there. I'm surprised you even noticed I wasn't at your stupid party."

Hurtful words that had only served to make Abigail feel as if she were the invisible one.

Her thoughts flew back to Vaughn. In her mind, she replayed his kiss, the warmth of his lips against hers, contrasted with the delicious coolness of his fingers caressing her cheek. She wasn't invisible to *him*. To Vaughn, she was someone with feelings, desires, and needs. Someone who might have made her share of mistakes but who was doing her best to rectify them.

No sooner had she sat down than Phoebe rose languidly to her feet. "I'm going out. 'Bye, guys."

"And just where do you think you're going at this hour?" Abigail spoke more sternly than she'd intended.

Phoebe gave her a blank look. "What do you mean? It's only eight-thirty. Besides, Daddy already gave me permission."

"Permission for what?"

Phoebe sighed in the exaggerated manner of someone terribly put upon. "Neal and I are going for a drive," she answered grudgingly.

"You were with him most of the day," Abigail reminded her. "Besides, it's Christmas. This is the time to be with your family."

Phoebe turned to Kent with a look of mute appeal. "Daddy?"

"I don't see the harm in it," he said, sending Phoebe on her way with an indulgent wave. "Go on, baby, have fun. But, remember, I want you back before midnight."

As soon as Abigail and Kent were alone, she turned on him, saying angrily, "Why do you always do that?"

"Do what?" He played innocent.

"Undermine me like that."

"I did no such thing," he said mildly. "I'd already told her she could go. I don't see why you're making such a big fuss about it."

"So you don't think it's a big deal that our daughter is spending practically every waking minute with this boy?" Abigail retorted. "For all we know, they could be having sex."

"She's a sensible girl," Kent replied in the same maddeningly reasonable tone. "If we haven't raised her with the right values, it's too late to start preaching now."

"You don't seem very concerned about it."

He eyed her thoughtfully. "Is it the idea of her having sex, or is it specifically sex with Neal that you find so upsetting?" As usual, he'd cut to the quick with surgical precision.

"I don't have anything against Neal," she replied somewhat defensively. "He seems like a nice enough boy."

"Even if he happens to be related to Lila," Kent finished the sentence for her.

"Now you're putting words into my mouth. Honestly, I don't care who he's related to. He's older than Phoebe, which means he's more experienced."

"He's eighteen. Hardly what I'd call a man of the world."

"Still." Abigail didn't know what to say to that. It was true that Neal didn't seem all that worldly.

"Phoebe's always been her own person," Kent reminded her. "How do we know it's not the other way around, that she isn't exerting some sort of an influence over him?"

"That's ridiculous. She's sixteen!"

Kent went on eyeing her with his steady, implacable gaze. "She's also your daughter. Don't you remember what *you* were like at that age? Pretty single-minded, from what you've told me."

"Please don't make this about me," Abigail said in a tone that was more pleading than angry. "Everything can't always be my fault."

"Actually," he said, "I have a feeling this has more to do with you and me than with our daughter."

She narrowed her eyes at him. "What makes you think that?"

"You know. Don't make me spell it out."

She knew, of course she knew, but at the same time she wanted to refute it. He was her husband. She loved him and hoped he still loved her. All she could manage was a watered-down version of the truth. "Okay, since you brought it up, yes, I've noticed that you've been distant with me lately."

"Have I? I would've have said it was the other way around. You've been distant with me for years, Abby. Not," he held out a hand to keep her from interrupting, "that I'm suggesting you're cold or unloving. I don't think that. It's just . . . well, there's a part of you I've always felt I couldn't reach. It's like you don't trust me enough to share it with me."

A memory of her uncle unfurled in her head like the smoke curling up the chimney. For an instant, she could almost feel the hard pressure of his body against hers, the disgusting hair on his chest prickling against her bare skin. A memory that brought the taste of bile to the back of her throat.

Helplessly, she gazed at Kent, struggling to find the words. *You can tell him. He's your husband,* urged a voice in her head. But the words wouldn't come; she could only stand there, mute. In the early days of their marriage, she'd kept it from him because she hadn't wanted to spoil what they had. Such a thing would have been utterly alien to him, however hard he'd have tried to understand. He'd grown up in a household where there were no dirty little secrets, no fearful locking of the bedroom door at night; at the dinner table, there had been no one barking orders or spewing foul-mouthed diatribes—people were respectful of one another, and only lofty ideas were discussed.

It was only as time passed and she'd grown more trusting of Kent that she'd realized nothing would have changed how he felt about her, not even that. Several times she'd come close to confiding in him. What had held her back then was the fear that it would come between them—not that she'd been molested but that she'd kept it from him all those years.

Now it was simply too late.

"Well, if that's how you feel, I'm sure nothing I could say would change your mind at this late date," she said at last.

"Try me." She saw something flash in his eyes and knew it wasn't just idle words.

Once more, she was tempted to come clean, but in the end she couldn't do it. She merely sighed and said, "Not tonight. I'm much too tired for this discussion. I've been on my feet in the kitchen all day." She feigned a yawn, rising to her feet. "In fact, I think I'll head on up to bed."

"I'll join you in a bit."

She was crossing the room when something made her pause and turn around. "Kent, I—" She longed to bridge the gap between them. It had been weeks since they'd had sex. But pride prevented her from being the first to make a move, so she only said, "I'll wait up for you."

She didn't expect to see him again until morning—recently he'd fallen into the habit of staying up late, then slipping in under the covers after she'd gone to sleep—so she was surprised when minutes later, he appeared in the bedroom doorway. She'd been sitting up in bed, reading, and now she closed her book and set it down on the nightstand.

"You certainly took your time," she teased.

Smiling, he walked over to the bed and sat down. "I had to take Brewster out." A nightly ritual, she knew, that involved their dog's sniffing at every bush before peeing on it and that could sometimes take up to half an hour. The fact that Kent had cut it short said something in itself. Now he placed a hand on her leg. Even through the covers, she could feel its warmth. "That was a nice dinner you made. The whole day was nice, in fact."

"Thank you. I'm glad somebody noticed."

"Phoebe liked it, too."

"Really? That must have been why she was in such a hurry to get away."

"Don't take it personally. She's in love."

Their daughter hadn't used those words—she insisted that she and Neal were just friends—but it was a natural assumption. "Yes. I'd almost forgotten what that was like." Abigail's lips curled in an ironic smile.

"Would you like me to remind you?" Kent's hand moved farther up her leg.

"Oh, I don't know. It's been a while. I'm not sure I can remember that far back."

He stood up, wearing a sly grin. "Why don't I refresh your memory? Just let me get out of these clothes."

Minutes later, they lay naked together under the covers, her arms around her husband, her hands moving over his body, which she knew as intimately as her own. It felt good slipping back into their old routine. *This* was what she wanted, she told herself, striving to push any thought of Vaughn from her head. If tonight she'd kissed another man, it had only been to reassure herself that she was still desirable, that that part of her life wasn't over.

Kent's mouth traveled down her neck in a series of soft butterfly kisses. He ran his fingers through her hair. She was reminded of the first time they'd made love, of how gentle he'd been, as though he'd sensed her trepidation—not of him but of the act itself, which back then she'd still associated with her uncle—and hadn't wanted to scare her off. Now, all these years later, with the lights turned low, they might have been those young lovers embarking on a life together. She might almost have believed they could turn the clock back if she hadn't seen his face just then, illuminated by the wedge of light slanting from the door to the bathroom. Kent's eyes weren't on her. He was staring past her into the darkness at some imagined lover. Or so it seemed.

When he came, it seemed almost wrenched from him. His face twisted as if in pain, and a shudder went through him. Moments later she was climaxing, too, with an ease born of long practice with the same lover. Afterward, snuggled in his arms, pleasantly spent, Abigail allowed the thought that had briefly reared its ugly head to resurface. If her husband's mind hadn't been on her the whole time they'd been making love, whom *had* he been thinking of? The answer came to her like a bolt of lightning following a thunderclap.

Lila, she thought.

12

Concepción had gotten the job through a friend of Jesús. It was in an office building in Century City, where she cleaned after hours. The pay was decent, and if the work was hard, she nonetheless felt lucky to be employed. Also, it had been easy to fall into a routine, since each of the four floors to which she'd been assigned was divided up in the same way—executive offices around the perimeter and the center space taken up by a series of interconnected modules lit by banks of ceiling fluorescents. The one thing she still hadn't gotten used to was the solitude. At the factory, at least, she'd been working around other people. Here, the only people she came into contact with were the scattering of office employees finishing up at their desks when she arrived at the beginning of each night's shift, and they never spoke a word to her except the occasional mumbled greeting.

Nonetheless, she thought it likely that she knew more about those employees than they did about each other. She knew that the person whose desk was nearest to the largest of the executive offices on the sixteenth floor, and whose computer showed an image, presumably of himself—a fair-haired young man at the helm of a sailboat—yearned for something more out of life than the eternal high noon of his cubicle. She knew that the woman with the pink sweater draped over the back of her chair and the collection of porcelain cats covering nearly every spare inch of her desk was lonely, judging by the absence of any other, more personal, mementos . . . and that the female occupant of the cubicle across from the break room was a slacker, from the discarded crossword puzzles filling her wastebasket and the fashion magazines haphazardly tucked beneath the folders on her desk.

Concepción had become a voyeur of sorts. Each night, between the hours of five and midnight, she made her way through the labyrinth of cubicles, pushing her cart and inadvertently stealing glimpses of people's lives as she tidied up. From underneath chairs and desks, she retrieved bits and pieces of those lives: lost keys and earrings, carelessly discarded bottle caps and gum wrappers. From the partially filled mugs left on desktops, she knew who took their coffee black and who liked it with cream. And emptying the contents of wastebaskets, she could determine who was watching their waistline and who ought to be, and, from the occasional condom wrapper, if a male executive in one of the offices had had sex.

Her boss, a squat man by the name of Felix Salazar, with a face as weathered as a barn door, was from Taxco, not far from where she'd grown up—a *paisano*—so when Jesús had prevailed upon him to hire her, Salazar had taken pity on her, though he'd been reluctant at first, saying it wasn't his practice to employ illegals. Thus, they had an understanding: He always paid her in cash, and she took what was given without complaint. It was less than she would have made if she'd had a green card, she knew from asking around, but it took care of her modest needs, with enough left over to put away a little each week.

Jesús had also found her a place to live—a house in Echo Park, which she shared with nine other people, all of them Mexicans like herself. It was noisy, and there was no privacy. She slept in the bed next to that of a fat woman named Soledad, who snored loudly enough to wake the dead, and there was always a line for the one bathroom. Still, she was grateful for a roof over her head. Most of all, she was grateful for the kindness of Jesús. Since that first day, he'd been her guiding light, making sure she wanted for nothing and asking for nothing in return.

She thought back to the previous Sunday, when she'd gone over to his place, in the apartment complex where her son-in-law used to live, to cook him dinner. It was the least she could do after the many kindnesses he'd shown her, she'd told him, and Jesús had been only too pleased to take her up on her offer. After a trip to the market, they'd returned with several bags of groceries, which he'd insisted upon paying for, and Concepción had immediately gone to work in the small kitchen of his apartment.

Three hours later a feast emerged: *arroz con pollo*; tamales made with shredded goat's meat; black beans with chiles; and for dessert, a caramel flan. Jesús ate with relish, and when he finally pushed his plate away he declared it the best meal he'd had in years. He cast a meaningful glance her way, saying, "A man could get used to this."

Perhaps it was the beers they'd drunk with dinner that prompted her to reply, "So why is it you never married?"

Jesús didn't respond at first. He sat there a moment, sunk in his own thoughts, his face heavy with some private sorrow. Finally he seemed to come to a decision, and he rose from the table, disappearing into the next room. He returned carrying a photo, in an ornate pewter frame, of a pretty, plump woman with a young girl seated on her lap. "My wife and daughter," he said. "They were killed in a car accident shortly after this was taken. That was twelve years ago. Selena would have been a young woman by now."

His voice carried no trace of bitterness—whoever, or whatever, had killed his wife and daughter, he seemed to have made peace with it—but Concepción could see the pain etched on his face: For that there was no remedy. Her heart went out to him. She was intimately acquainted with that kind of loss and knew the heartache he must have endured.

"I lost my daughter, too," she confided. Until then, she had been vague about her reasons for coming to this country, preferring to keep the matter private. But after Jesús's revelation she felt comfortable opening up to him. "The man I was looking for? My son-in-law? He was her husband."

Jesús shook his head in sympathy, sinking heavily into his chair. "Was it recent?"

She nodded, her throat tightening. "She died in a fire."

"My sympathies, *mi amiga*." They weren't just words; she could see that he was genuinely sad for her. He took her hand, giving it a gentle squeeze. His eyes were overbright in the glow of the candles she'd lit to create a more festive mood. "Do you have other children?"

"No, she was my only one. Milagros—my miracle." Concepción said nothing of the babies who'd died at birth. That was for another day.

He nodded slowly, maintaining his grip on her hand. "It's hard, I know. I grieved for my wife, of course, but there is nothing like the loss of a child . . . knowing you will never see her grow up . . . never again hear her calling out your name." He gazed down at the photo. "I look at this and I wonder, 'What would she be like now? Would she be married with children of her own?' But whenever I try to picture her, all I can see is her face as it was on the day she was taken from me."

"My daughter's dream was to come to America." Concepción closed her eyes for a moment, summoning Milagros's sweet face. "She was wait-ing only for her husband to save up enough money so he could send for her. They had it all planned. One day they would even buy a house. She always used to say to me, 'In America, anything is possible.'" Concepción found that she could smile now at the memory, however painful it was.

She opened her eyes to find Jesús gazing at her solemnly. "She was right about that," he said.

Jesús was living proof. He'd told her the whole story that first day as they'd walked back to his apartment after breakfast. His parents had come to this country without a cent to their names and had worked their whole lives to make a better life for him and his brothers and sisters. Jesús, as the eldest, was the only one of his siblings who hadn't gone to college. He had gone to work right out of high school instead, to help with the family's finances. By the time he was twenty-one, he'd saved up enough money, even with the portion of his paycheck that he faithfully turned over to his parents each week, to buy a used truck and go into business for himself. A business maintaining the grounds of his wealthy Beverly Hills clients, which twenty-five years later was thriving. He now had two trucks and half-a-dozen employees.

"That might be true for some, yes," she acknowledged, thinking that it was all well and good for those, like Jesús, who aspired to greater things. But she hadn't come to this country to build a better life for herself in the land of the *gringos*. She had more pressing business at hand.

Jesús must have mistaken her meaning, for he replied, "Why shouldn't it be true for you as well? Salazar tells me he's never seen anyone who works as hard. And you wouldn't have to spend the rest of your life cleaning. There are classes you can take to learn the skills you'd need to get a better job, one that will pay more money."

She shook her head. "I still wouldn't have a green card. And even if I did, I won't be staying long enough to find another job. I have to get to New York."

His shoulders sagged. "I was hoping you might have changed your plans," he said, eyeing her forlornly.

"No," she replied firmly.

"And will you come back after that?"

She shook her head. "It was my daughter's dream to be in America, not mine," she said gently.

Jesús went on eyeing her unhappily. Seated at the table amid the ruins of their supper, he looked like a large, dejected bear. "I see. So your mind is made up?"

Unable to bear the thought of his taking it as some sort of personal rejection, she told him the whole story then, about the fire and its terrible aftermath, Perez's loathsome offer of money, and her decision to track down the Señora and confront her face-to-face. The plan sounded wild and improbable as she laid it out for Jesús, who appeared dubious even as he sat there listening respectfully.

"And just what is it that you hope to accomplish by confronting this woman?" he asked when she was done talking.

If she'd caught a single note of judgment in his voice, she would have put an end to the discussion then and there, but she could see that he was asking only out of curiosity and perhaps concern for her. "I'll know when the time comes," she told him.

"What will you know?"

"Whether or not she's truly sorry for what she's done."

"And if she's not?"

Concepción's expression hardened. "Then she will be."

Jesús grew pale. "You're not suggesting——?"

"That I'd harm her? No," she replied impatiently. "But there are other ways to make someone accountable."

"Such as?"

"I have an idea." It had come to her the other night when she'd been cleaning one of the offices. An article in a newspaper she'd found discarded in the trash had caught her eye, about an actress from a popular TV show who'd been charged with accidentally killing another motorist while driving drunk. Concepción's English had improved quite a bit since she'd arrived in this country—she'd been studying the language, using the tapes and tape deck Jesús had loaned her—so she'd been able to make out the gist of it. The article had gone on to say something about the actress having been dropped from her show as a result. Though she'd managed to avoid jail time, her career was in ruins and her future uncertain. "Señora Armstrong is well-known in this country," she reminded Jesús. "If I told my story to the newspapers . . ."

His expression remained dubious. "That would be one way. Another would be to simply walk away."

"Why would I do that?" she demanded.

"For one thing, from what you've told me, it's unclear that this Señora was even aware of the laxness in safety measures until after the fire."

"She had to know! Nothing got done without her say-so."

"Nevertheless, you say it was the manager, this Perez fellow, who implemented these measures."

"What difference does it make?" Concepción seized hold of Jesús's arm, once more the wild-eyed *bruja* of those nightmarish days just after Milagros's death, leaning in to hiss, *"She's the reason my daughter is dead!"*

Jesús made no move to free himself from her grip. He met her gaze with unflinching steadiness, saying calmly, "Yes, but you must ask yourself, is this what your daughter would have wanted?"

In the days since, she'd found herself mulling over his words. Had she, in her mindless grief, been too quick to blame the Señora? she wondered. Was it possible the Señora had been guilty of little more than being ill-informed? But in the end, Concepción had decided she wasn't wrong to pursue this. That was just what people like her had been told all their lives: that they, the poor who toiled to line the pockets of the rich, weren't smart or educated enough to understand how these things worked. They were expected to swallow whole every excuse that was made to cover up wrongdoings, and to smile while doing so.

Well, she wasn't going to stay silent. It was time for someone to speak out in the name of justice. Justice not only for her daughter but for all the voiceless workers. The only thing that nagged at her still, planted there by Jesús like the seed of a pesky weed that had taken root, was the growing suspicion that this might not be what Milagros would have wanted.

It was impossible to stay annoyed at Jesús, though, especially when Christmas Eve rolled around and she emerged from the office building at the end of her shift to find his familiar blue truck parked at the curb. Normally she took the bus home from work, so it was a pleasant surprise to find him waiting for her.

Still, she pretended to be cross with him. "What are you doing here?" she scolded as she climbed into the passenger side. "It's late. You should be home in bed like everyone else."

But he only sat there, grinning. "It's Christmas," he said. "No one should be alone on Christmas."

Christmas? Concepción glanced at the glowing clock on the dashboard and saw that it was indeed after midnight, officially Christmas

Day. She'd been delayed by the extra cleanup from an office party on one of her floors that had left the desktops strewn with paper plates and cups and the carpet with glittery confetti, which she'd had a devil of a time vacuuming up.

"In that case, you ought to be with your family," she told him, thinking of his nieces and nephews.

"There will be plenty of time later in the day for my brothers and sisters and their children."

He leaned over to kiss her on the cheek. A kiss that warmed her even as she frowned at him in disapproval, trying not to smile. It wouldn't do to encourage him, she thought. She wouldn't be around long enough for their friendship to deepen into something more, however tempting that prospect had come to be. In another five or six weeks, she'd have enough money saved for the plane fare to New York, and then it would be time for her to say good-bye. She felt an unexpected pang of regret at the thought.

"Well, I'm afraid you picked the wrong person to keep you company," she told him somewhat grumpily. "I'm too tired to celebrate, even if it is Christmas."

His face, pulled into an expression of mock seriousness, looked almost comical in the greenish glow of the dashboard, which emphasized its deep lines. "We'll see about that," he said mysteriously.

She wondered what he had planned. But Jesús said little on the way home, seeming content to leave her to her thoughts as he drove. Passing a billboard depicting a Santa Claus bizarrely outfitted in red, fur-lined swim trunks, riding the waves on a surfboard with a sack of toys slung over one shoulder—an advertisement for some department store—she found herself reflecting, as she often did, on the strange ways of the *gringos*. Where she was from, a child felt lucky if Christmas morning brought a small trinket and a few sweets, but in this country, children were forever pleading for more, it seemed, and parents lavishing large sums of money on spoiling them. She'd seen long lines at the cash registers in stores and had heard tell of fistfights breaking out over an especially popular item that was in limited supply. This she found to be the most peculiar thing of all. She'd heard of grown men fighting over honor and love, and, yes, money, but never a fuzzy, battery-operated toy.

She was roused from her reverie by the realization that the residential street they were on was an unfamiliar one. She turned to Jesús, asking irritably, "Why are we going this way?" It was late. She wanted to get home to bed.

"There's something I want to show you," he replied, with a wink.

"What?" she asked.

"If I tell you, it won't be a surprise." In the wash of headlights from an oncoming car, his face was briefly illuminated—a face as sturdy and economical as the square, work-hardened hands resting on the wheel. Not handsome, no, but comforting in the way that familiar landmarks were. In the short while they'd been acquainted, Concepción had come to know its lines the way she had known every crack and cranny of her house in Las Cruces: the deep grooves on either side of his wide mouth and the smaller ones, like arrows in a quiver, that fanned from the corners of his eyes and curved down to meet his temples when he was smiling, as he was now. "All I will say is that it's a gift, mine to you. If I'd bought you one in a store, you would only have scolded me for spending my hard-earned money, so this was the best I could do."

He made a turn onto another street lined with modest older homes that were interspersed with newly constructed or remodeled ones built on a much grander scale. This was the part of Echo Park that was changing, a result of *gringos* grabbing cheap real estate where they could, according to Jesús, who bemoaned the fact that soon there wouldn't be anything affordable left for their people.

And yet the more modest the home, it seemed, the more fanciful the holiday display. Electrified reindeer romped across rooftops. Huge blow-up Santas and snowmen bobbed on lawns, and giant plastic candy canes lined concrete walkways. And everywhere there were lights: colored lights, blinking lights, the tiny white ones called fairy lights. Every window and eave, every bush and tree and blade of grass, it seemed, was outlined in lights.

At last he pulled to a stop in front of a small, run-down house strung with so many lights it might have been midday for the glow they cast, a glow that spread to the opposite side of the street and halfway down the block on either side. In the center of it all, amid the strings of lights zigzagging everywhere like a mad science experiment gone awry, was a Nativity scene, dramatically lit from above and below. Not just any Nativity scene but one of such beauty and artistry that it took Concepción's breath away. Each life-sized figure was hand-carved from wood and painted in a style that was amazingly lifelike. There were Mary and Joseph, bent over the infant Jesus in his cradle, and the three wise men astride their donkeys, along with a host of other barnyard creatures—pigs, cows, goats, chickens. And hovering over it all, suspended from an overhanging branch, the angel Gabriel, his wings outspread.

"It's beautiful," she said in a hushed whisper. "Whose is it?"

"The owner of this house, a man named Ignacio Fuentes," Jesús answered. "It's taken him more than ten years to carve those figures. Each Christmas, he adds a new one. And each year, more and more people come to admire his work. At first it was just the people in this neighborhood. But now they come from all over the city. There was even a write-up about it in the paper."

They got out and walked over to the fence, where they stood in silence admiring the Nativity scene. When she finally turned to Jesús, her eyes were swimming with tears. "How did you know?"

"Know what?"

"That this would be the perfect gift."

Just moments before, she'd been so exhausted all she could think about was the warm bed waiting for her at home. Now, seeing this—this *miracle*—she felt, for the first time since her daughter's death, something akin to hope. Hope that she would one day find a way to get past her grief.

Jesús just smiled and slipped an arm around her waist. They stood that way for a little while longer, linked in companionable silence, seemingly the only living creatures out and about at this hour, except for a cat that streaked past before disappearing into the shrubbery.

Then, before she knew it, he was kissing her. Jesús's lips were soft against hers, as if he knew to tread gently where no man had gone in more years than she could count. It felt strange and yet at the same time strangely familiar. Not just as if they'd done this before but as if they'd been doing it for years.

He drew back to murmur in her ear, "You are *my* gift. From the very first moment I laid eyes on you, asleep underneath that palm tree, I knew you'd been sent to me from heaven."

She was moved but unable to respond in kind, so she only gave a little laugh and said, thinking of her ordeal in the desert, "More like the fires of hell."

He smiled. "All the more reason to cherish you."

She pulled away from him, shaking her head with regret. "If you're asking me to stay, I'm afraid I can't do that," she told him. But even as she spoke, a part of her wished she could remain here forever with Jesús. That she could put the past behind her and leave the dead to rest.

Even as he lowered his head in resignation, she saw a flicker of hope in his eyes. "Yes, but that doesn't mean you can't come back. Will you at least think about it?"

She gave a slow nod, careful to add, "I can't make any promises."

He pondered this for a moment, his eyes searching her face, before he heaved another sigh. *"Está bien,"* he said. "Just know that when all this is over, I'll be waiting for you."

A light chill danced through her at the thought. She realized that she would miss Jesús more than she would have thought possible, given the relatively short time she'd known him. A realization she recognized, in some deep part of her, as the first stirrings of love.

And Jesús felt the same way about her.

For a brief moment, she allowed that knowledge to shine through her in all its glory, like the lights casting their glow around her. Once more, she was tempted to let her journey end here, to remain in LA with Jesús, where she would be loved and cared for. But that was impossible, she knew.

She couldn't give up now, not when she'd come so far already.

13

Lila was walking down Main Street, on her way to pick up the dry cleaning, when a sign in the window of Tarkington's Travel—"HELP WANTED"—caused her to slow to a halt. She lingered on the sidewalk, her heart doing a little shuffle step. Dare she inquire inside? What would be the harm in that? But she hadn't forgotten the sting of all those previous rejections and didn't feel like subjecting herself to more disappointment, especially not on a day like today, when she was already suffering from the brutal weather and had a whole list of other things to do.

She was about to move on when she caught sight of a poster inside, showing a happy couple strolling along a secluded tropical beach. A memory surfaced—her and Gordon in Aruba, Gordon teasing her for being spooked by a large fish that she'd mistaken for a shark while out snorkeling—one that in the old days would have brought a smile but now only made her feel sad. Gordon was gone, and there would be no vacations from now on. The most she could hope for was the chance to make something of herself one day.

It was that thought that succeeded in nudging her in through the door.

Job or no, it was a relief just to be out of the cold, Lila thought as she deposited her umbrella in the bucket just inside the door. Though it was mid-March, winter showed no sign of loosening its grip anytime soon. Several more inches of snow had fallen overnight, and it was still coming down hard. Here in town, snow was clumped along the curbs where the plow had been through, and storm drains gurgled with melt from the salt pellets that had been strewn. Elsewhere, a freeze had settled in, hard-packing what was left over from previous snowfalls and turning the main drag into a virtual ghost town. The only other people she'd seen out and about were stalwart country folks, like old Mr. Gill, dressed in foul-weather gear down to the floppy brim of his sou'easter, and those like her who were running errands that couldn't wait.

Lila stamped on the doormat to dislodge the snow from her boots. When she looked up, she found the woman seated at the desk in front— fiftyish, on the plump side, wearing tweed slacks and a ribbed turtleneck— eyeing her with an expression of pleasant expectation, as if she thought Lila might be a potential customer. She appeared to be the only one in the office at the moment.

"Nasty out there, isn't it?" She rose to help Lila off with her coat. She had a nice face, with even features and a snub nose that made Lila think of the '40s actress Jane Wyman. Her short gray hair curled in wisps around her ears, and she smelled faintly of some grandmotherly perfume redolent of violets. "Barbara Huggins," she introduced herself. "But everyone calls me Barb."

Lila shook her hand. "Lila Meriwhether." Since moving here, she had gone back to using her maiden name; it was easier that way. "And, yes, I'm beginning to think global warming is just a rumor," she said with a smile.

"Don't I know it! As you can see, I'm the only one who made it in to work today. Kara and Janet both got snowed in." Barb gestured around the deserted office, where a pair of particle-board cubicles, each with its own desk, sat empty. "Can I get you some coffee? I just made a fresh pot."

"Thanks, no. Actually, I'm here about the job." If she was going to be told no, best to find out now and spare herself more grief.

Some of the wattage went out of the woman's smile, but she replied pleasantly enough, "Oh, that. I'm sorry, but it's been filled—as of this morning, as a matter of fact. I just haven't gotten around to taking down the sign yet. The phone's been ringing off the hook, and as I said, I'm here all by myself."

Lila's heart sank, but she kept up a cheerful front. "No problem. I just happened to be passing by and thought I'd ask."

"You should have stopped by yesterday. You probably would've been hired on the spot. It was a madhouse."

Glancing around her, Lila remarked, "Well, it seems quiet enough at the moment."

"Come back in an hour; it'll be back to bedlam. Right now everyone's out to lunch." Barb sighed and shook her head. "It's always like this around this time of year—seems everybody decides all at once that they've had it with the lousy weather and they want—no, *need*—to get away to someplace warm. I've booked three cruises just this morning." She studied Lila for a moment, taking in her bedraggled appearance. Lila didn't have to be standing in front of a mirror to know that she looked like one of those people in sore need of a vacation: her hair hanging in damp tatters and her pale skin speaking of serious sun deprivation. "You sure I couldn't interest you in one of our package deals? I could give you a great deal on seven nights at the Four Winds in Barbados," Barb offered, as though it were even a remote possibility for Lila. Clearly, Barb had pegged her as just another bored housewife looking to get out of the house and earn a few bucks at the same time, not someone whose interest in the job was driven by necessity.

"Believe me, I'd love nothing more." Lila had been working for Abigail going on five months now, with no break other than her regularly scheduled days off. "But I'm afraid I couldn't afford to take the time off work." A half truth was less embarrassing than having to admit that she couldn't afford it, period.

"Tell me about it." Barb made a sympathetic face. "Look, I really am sorry about the job. It's my boss's sister, you see. She's getting divorced and needs a place to put her life, so when she found out about the job opening . . ." Barb gave a philosophical shrug. "Between you and me, I think it's a mistake. Not that she isn't a hard worker, mind you, but the way she goes on and on about her husband. The woman is obsessed! And believe me, if you're looking to escape to a desert isle, the last thing you want to hear about is how Cheryl Lee got dumped by some two-timing jerk."

Lila nodded in understanding, as if she knew all about two-timing husbands. Well, at least she hadn't been turned away due to any failure on *her* part. And she could derive some satisfaction, from this woman's seeming to view her as a viable alternative to the husband-obsessed sister. "Well, if it doesn't work out, I hope you'll keep me in mind," she said. "Here, let me give you my number." She scribbled her cell number on the back of one of Barb's business cards.

"Thanks. I just may give you a shout. You never know." Barb cocked her wispy gray head, seeming to assess Lila with new interest. "Sure you wouldn't like that cup of coffee?"

This time Lila said, "What the heck. Why not?" It wasn't as if the world would come to an end if she didn't pick up Abigail's dry cleaning in the next ten minutes.

"Have you had any experience in the travel industry?" inquired Barb when they were seated at her desk with mugs of coffee. There was nothing idle about the question—Lila knew that she was being sized up for a potential job down the line. She gauged her response accordingly.

"Other than having organized a million trips? No." She brought her mug to her lips, blowing on it before taking a careful sip. "But I'm very detail-oriented. Also, I've *been* to a lot of the more popular destinations, so I could tell people what to expect in the way of hotels and sightseeing and such. My husband and I did a lot of traveling when he was alive, you see."

"Oh, I didn't realize. I thought . . ." Barb glanced at the wedding ring on Lila's finger, letting the rest of the sentence trail off.

Lila felt the old catch at the back of her throat. "He died about six months ago," she said, in answer to the question in Barb's eyes. "I moved here, with my son, to take a job that . . . well, frankly, isn't quite what I expected. I was hoping for something that would be more, um, in keeping with my abilities."

"Have you ever done office work?" Barb asked.

"Not really," Lila admitted. "But I can type. And I'm taking a computer class." She'd only just signed up, in fact—it was one of the classes offered by the adult ed program at the local high school—but Barb didn't have to know that. "I should be up to speed before too long. Or at least in the same universe as my son."

The older woman gave a knowing laugh. "You're not the only dinosaur, believe me. Each time we get a new piece of software, it takes me weeks to get the hang of it." Barb leaned back in her chair, sipping her coffee and regarding Lila thoughtfully. At last, she seemed to come to a decision. "Tell you what. We'll need someone to fill in for Kara in a few months, when she goes out on maternity leave. She's due at the end of May. Twins!" She smiled, shaking her head in wonderment. "Why don't I speak to my boss about it and get back to you?"

"That would be . . . I don't know what to . . . Thank you," Lila stammered, overwhelmed with emotion. She didn't dare say more, or the woman would think she was a complete lunatic, making a huge deal out of the mere possibility of a job offer.

She was getting up to leave when Barb said casually in passing, "You didn't say where you worked. Somewhere around here, I take it?"

Lila felt herself grow warm, the collar of her wool sweater, damp from the snow, itching against her neck. The news that the infamous Lila DeVries was alive and well and working for Abigail Armstrong had been the talk of the town after her current whereabouts had been revealed on *A.M. America*. She wouldn't have thought there was a single person in Stone Harbor who hadn't either seen or heard about the broadcast, so it had come as a bit of a surprise when Barb had failed to recognize her as soon as she'd walked in. Now Lila found herself growing panicky. If she were to 'fess up about her current situation, Barb would surely put two and two together, and that would be the end of her potential job offer.

But Lila also knew that if she were to make up some lie, she'd be caught at it eventually, so she had no choice but to give an honest answer. "I work up at Rose Hill," she said, tensing a bit in anticipation of Barb's response.

Barb's entire demeanor changed, and Lila could see that she was belatedly connecting the dots. Barb gaped at her, unable to mask her surprise. "Goodness. I had no idea it was *you*. I probably should have recognized you, but you look different than in your newspaper photos." She blushed, as if realizing too late that Lila might not want to be reminded of all that.

"I suppose I *have* changed." Lila gave a rueful grimace. "A lot's happened since then."

This is where I'll be shown the door, she thought. Wasn't that partly what had landed her in this backwater in the first place—the notoriety that had prevented her from getting a job elsewhere?

But Barb surprised her by replying kindly, "Well, I'm not one to judge. Half of what the newspapers print is nothing but a pack of lies, in my opinion. And you seem like a nice person, so I'll tell you what, the offer still stands. I'll talk to my boss as soon as she gets in tomorrow."

Lila swallowed against the lump in her throat. It probably wouldn't amount to anything, but she appreciated the gesture nonetheless. "Thank you. That's very kind of you."

"Don't mention it." Barb walked her to the door. "I suppose you'll be at the big do tomorrow night?" she asked as Lila was leaving.

Lila was momentarily at a loss; then she recalled the benefit at the yacht club on Saturday. Kent was one of the organizers, and he'd been nice enough to set aside tickets for her and Neal—tickets that would have cost her a hundred dollars a head had she had to pay for them. Not that she was exactly dying to go. This would be her first social event since moving to Stone Harbor, and she feared the reception wouldn't be as warm as the one Barb had given her.

"Of course. I'm looking forward to it," she lied.

Barb smiled as she handed Lila her coat. "Well, in that case, I guess I'll see you there. I had to twist my husband's arm—the only thing Joe hates more than spending money is dressing up to go out at night. But I told him we were going if I had to drag him kicking and screaming all the way."

Lila knew just how Barb's husband felt. This would be more like a trial by fire than the event of the social season for her. Already she was bracing herself for being stared at and whispered about. She'd have given it a pass if Kent hadn't talked her into going.

"Don't forget, you're flying under my flag," he'd said with a wink when she'd shared her fears with him. "Whatever anyone might think, they won't dare say a word."

On her way back to the house, after stopping at the dry cleaner's and at L'Epicerie to pick up the items on Abigail's shopping list, Lila's thoughts returned to Kent. It wasn't just that he treated her with respect. With him, she could forget for whole chunks of time that she was the household help; he always acted as though she were someone he'd have enjoyed spending time with under any circumstances. In the evenings before Abigail got home, he'd often sit and chat with her over a glass of wine while she cooked dinner. He would tell her about his day, usually managing to work in an amusing story about some patient—never referring to them by name, of course. He'd always remember to ask how Lila's day had gone, too. As if the only thing to break up the monotony of her routine on any given day weren't the UPS guy showing up at the door. And if something was on his mind, he'd often run it by her.

Just yesterday, he'd asked her, "So what do you make of this business with Phoebe and Neal? Do you think it's serious?"

Lila paused in the midst of chopping scallions to eye him across the kitchen counter. "I don't know. What's your take on it?"

Kent, seated on a bar stool at the counter, took a thoughtful sip of his wine. "I'm not sure, to be honest. They're certainly thick as thieves these days."

The way he said it made her wonder if it hadn't been just a poor choice of words. "Are you worried that they're having sex?" she asked, knowing she didn't have to tiptoe around Kent.

"Worried? No. I assume they're up to something." At the shocked expression she must have worn, he smiled. "Don't forget, I'm a doctor, so I've seen it all. I've had girls as young as thirteen coming to me for pregnancy tests. It's not so much whether or not my daughter is having sex that concerns me as whether it's *irresponsible* sex. I just hope whatever they're doing, they're being careful about it."

"Neal's always been responsible," she told him. A little too responsible at times. "I don't know anything about his sex life—he'd bite my head off if I ever stuck my nose in *there*—but I feel it's safe to say that he's not going to make me a grandparent anytime soon."

Kent chuckled. "Good. Because that would make me one, too."

"The main thing is, he and Phoebe seem to be making each other happy, so I don't see the harm in it."

She wondered if "happy" was the right word. Neal was still moody, and Phoebe, though perhaps a little less withdrawn these days, was hardly a ray of sunshine. It was more like whatever was eating at Neal, he'd found a kindred spirit in Phoebe, and vice versa.

Just as Lila had found one in Kent.

If only Abby were as easy! she thought. For a while, it had seemed as though Abigail were softening toward her. There had been moments when it had almost been like old times, the two of them in the kitchen together, Abigail instructing her in the intricacies of some recipe or, on occasion, helping her clean up after a meal, the two of them chatting while Abigail washed and Lila dried. And there had been that scary incident a few days after Christmas, when Gillian had phoned to say that Vaughn was on his way to the hospital with a fever of 105. Though it had been late at night, Abigail hadn't hesitated to jump into her car and drive Lila all the way into the city. In their shared concern over Vaughn, all grievances had been temporarily shelved. More than that, Lila had derived real comfort from Abigail's presence as they'd sat huddled together outside Vaughn's hospital room, waiting for the doctor to complete his examination.

"Do you think he'll be all right?" Lila asked anxiously at one point.

"Of course. He's survived far worse, hasn't he?" Abigail reminded her, sounding more confident than Lila suspected she felt. "What's something like this compared to a sniper's bullet?"

"He told you about that?"

Abigail nodded. "He even showed me the scar."

"Remember the time he broke his arm falling off the hay mower out at old Mr. Hutchins's farm?" Lila recalled, thinking of how reckless Vaughn had been as a boy—really, it was a wonder he'd made it this far in one piece. "I thought Mr. Hutchins was going to have a heart attack, but Vaughn kept insisting he wasn't hurt, that it was just a sprain. He was so mad when they put his arm in a cast because it meant he couldn't play ball for the entire summer."

"How could I forget? He spent the time coaching everyone else on the team on how to up their game."

Abigail and Lila shared a smile at the memory. And for a little while, Lila felt as close to Abigail as in the old days as they sat there, side by side. By the time the doctor emerged to report that Vaughn would be all right, that he was suffering from nothing worse than a touch of pneumonia and they'd already started him on a course of antibiotics, Lila had already known somehow that it was going to be okay.

But these past couple of months, the coolness Abigail had shown toward her in the beginning had returned. Lila had become uncomfortably aware, too, of Abigail's watching her more closely as she went about her tasks, the way she might have if she'd suspected that Lila were stealing from her. (What déjà vu *that* would have been!) Lila wondered what had prompted it—had she said or done something to make Abigail distrust her?—but when she'd asked Kent about it, he'd brushed aside her concerns, saying, "I wouldn't make too much of it if I were you. She's probably just keeping an eagle eye out for some spot or stray piece of lint that you might have missed."

If Abigail had been around more, it might have been intolerable, but these days she usually didn't get home from work until late, often not until well after Kent and Phoebe had gone to bed. On more than one occasion, Lila had been roused from sleep by the crunch of tires in the driveway and had peered out her window to see a lone female figure making a dash for the front door, shoulders hunched against the cold. Lila might have suspected Abigail of having an affair and wondered if her ungodly hours had more to do with late-night rendezvous than her brutal schedule, but she knew better. The "other man" was Vaughn, and he was too sick to lift his head off the pillow half the time, much less climb under the covers with Abigail. (Not that he would have under any circumstances, not with a married woman.) So that pretty much ruled out any hanky-panky. As for what else Abigail was up to, Lila thought it might have something do with a sticky situation at work—she'd overheard snatches of conversation the few times she'd been in the same room as Abigail while she'd been on the phone, something to do with her factory in Mexico, from what Lila could gather. Whatever it was, it had Abigail on edge. Maybe that was why she'd been behaving so strangely. Maybe it had nothing to do with *her*, Lila thought, hoping it was true.

She arrived back at the house to find the just-plowed drive dusted with another inch or so of new-fallen snow. As she climbed from her car, she waved to Karim, who was shoveling the walkway alongside the house. She was picking her way cautiously toward the back door, holding the bundle of dry cleaning high to keep its plastic shrouding from trailing on the ground, when she slipped on an icy patch of concrete and went sprawling backward onto her rear.

Before she could make a move, Karim was bending to help her to her feet. *My guardian angel!* she thought. He even looked like one—the photonegative of an angel, at any rate, with his dark eyes and dusky skin, wearing a navy parka and black watch cap, against the snowy backdrop.

"Are you all right?" he asked, peering at her with concern.

She brushed snow from her coat. "As much as anyone can be while looking like a complete fool," she said with a self-conscious laugh. "It's my fault. I should've watched where I was going."

"Here, let me help with that," he said as she bent to gather up the plastic-shrouded clothing lying in a heap on the ground. Together they sorted the tangle of hangers into an orderly bundle, which Karim, noticing that she was limping slightly from her fall, insisted on carrying inside for her. Lila was left with no choice but to follow meekly behind. He didn't relinquish the dry cleaning until they'd climbed the stairs to the master bedroom.

"You seem to have a habit of showing up when I'm at my most helpless," she observed as she emerged from the closet after hanging up the clothes. "I'm not always like this, I swear. I used to be fairly self-sufficient." If you didn't count the doorman and the super at her former residence, she added silently.

"In my country, a woman would be severely reprimanded for such ideas," he replied with mock seriousness. "But you've been punished enough for one day, so I shall let it go this time." He cast a glance at the sore hip she was rubbing, his brown eyes crinkling in amusement.

Lila was suddenly conscious of the fact that they were standing in the bedroom. No one else was home. Phoebe was at school, and both Abigail and Kent were at work. It was just she and Karim, alone up here, with the snow swirling down outside, making her feel as though they were inside a giant snow globe. She felt slightly dizzy, partly from her fall but also due to Karim's nearness: the kind of vertigo she associated with climbing tall ladders . . . and falling in love.

Not that she had any intention of falling in love. For one thing, it was too soon. Her husband hadn't even been gone a year. Besides, she wasn't sure she ever wanted to feel that vulnerable again. It was enough just having Neal to worry about, without another person in her life over whom she would surely fret each time he was late coming home, knowing better than most how abruptly a loved one could be taken from you—a sudden illness, a heart attack, a car sliding out of control on an icy stretch of road. A loaded gun.

"I should bring in the groceries," she said in a strange, high-pitched voice she hardly recognized as her own.

"Please, allow me," Karim said.

Neither of them made a move. They just stood there, side by side, gazing out the window at the snow coming down, stealing glances at each other out of the corners of their eyes every now and then. Karim had taken off his jacket, and she saw that he had on the same burgundy knit pullover that he'd been wearing the day she'd gone into the woods with him in search of a Christmas tree . . . and had found something more than she'd bargained for.

Karim was the first to break the silence. He cleared his throat, asking, "So, this benefit tomorrow night, are you going?"

"As far as I know," she said. She'd made plans to go into the city to visit her brother earlier in the day, but she would be back in plenty of time.

"In that case, I thought perhaps we could go together." From his posture, so still and erect it was like a held breath, she could tell that it was more than the offer of a ride.

"Are you asking me out on a date?" she asked, filled with a strange mixture of panic and pleasure at the thought.

"Yes, I suppose I am." He gave her a sheepish smile. "Forgive me if I'm going about it all wrong. I'm not very practiced at this. Where I come from, we don't 'date.' A man must first approach the woman's parents, and nothing can happen without their blessing."

"By that, I assume you mean marriage?" He nodded, to which she responded with an arch look, "Let me get this straight: We haven't even gone out on one date, and already you're talking marriage." It had the desired effect of defusing the tension somewhat. Karim laughed, and she added, smiling, "Besides, both my parents are dead, so you'd be out of luck. Anyway, why should it be up to them? Doesn't the woman get a say?"

"Yes, of course. In most cases, she is free to reject anyone she deems unsuitable."

"And after the wedding? Who's in charge then?"

"The man may rule his kingdom, but it's the woman who rules the household," Karim said with an enigmatic smile.

"Well, since I'm not exactly a whiz when it comes to running a household, I wouldn't last very long in your culture," she said with a self-effacing laugh.

"Yet you're very capable at running this one," he pointed out, gesturing around him.

"Only because I never forget who's boss." She thought once more of Abigail and how watchful she'd been, feeling a cold finger of apprehension trace its way up her spine.

Karim stood looking at her a moment before he said softly, "You still haven't given me an answer."

Lila felt herself tense slightly in response, even as a part of her—the gooey part at the center—shivered in delight at the prospect of an evening out with Karim . . . and possibly more. "I'm not sure I'm ready for this," she said, choosing her words carefully. "Maybe in another time or another place. But Karim, I just lost my husband. I don't want to get involved with *anyone*, not just you."

He kept his gaze leveled at her, eyeing her as if he knew something she didn't. "Then I shall just have to be patient."

"It may be a long wait. I don't know that I'll ever be ready." Reflecting on the complications of grieving for a husband whom she alternately missed and was furious at, she sank down heavily on the unmade bed. "Sometimes I think there are three of us buried in that grave. What you're looking at right now is a ghost. And ghosts don't get to live normal lives."

Karim sat down next to her, putting his arms around her. Before she could pull away, his mouth was closing over hers. Held captive by the warmth of his lips, the tip of his tongue gently teasing hers, she felt blood rush up into her head . . . and to her lower regions as well. Ghost, indeed! She felt dizzy, breathless, the snow sizzling against the windowpanes blending with the white noise inside her head. She was sixteen again, making out with Ben Caruso at the beach at St. Simon's, on fire with more than a sunburn, the sand in her bathing suit not the only thing making her itch. She was as delirious as when she'd gotten drunk for the first time, on champagne at her cousin Vicki's wedding. She'd made a fool of herself then, and she was going to make a fool of herself now.

She was helpless to resist when he tipped her back onto the bed and pushed her sweater up to kiss her naked belly. Karim might not have had much practice at "dating," however his culture defined it, but it was obvious he'd had his share of experience. Loose Western women, no doubt. Which she was in danger of becoming herself if she didn't put a stop to this.

But Lila found she couldn't stop. It all seemed so unreal as she lay there with her eyes closed, Karim's lips moving over her bare skin with kisses so feather-light they might have been mere breaths of air, that she half expected to open her eyes and find herself in her own bed, just woken from a sexy dream. She made no protest when his hand insinuated itself past the waistband of her jeans—*It's only a dream*, she told herself. The nether regions of her body, whose wants and needs she'd been doing her best to ignore these many months, as she would a pesky child's, sprang to life with the brush of his fingertips, and all the pent-up longing that she'd suppressed came rushing in like a tidal wave.

It wasn't until Karim started to unzip her jeans that she came to with a rude jolt. This was no dream. And she wasn't in her own bed. This was *Abigail's* bed, where she was lying half unzipped and in disarray, like some teenager up to no good while her parents were out.

Lila immediately bolted upright. "What are we doing?" she croaked.

Karim sat up, his face briefly registering disappointment. But there was no hint of apology or embarrassment in the smile he gave her. "I just wanted to know what it was I'm waiting for." He ran a fingertip over her exposed belly button, his voice low and husky.

She jerked her sweater down. "This is crazy."

"Is it?" he murmured.

"Anyone could have walked in."

"No one's home." He tilted his head to look at her. "Unless there's another reason you're afraid."

"I told you, I'm not ready for this," she said. The words sounded decidedly less convincing than when she'd first spoken them. "In fact, if you had any sense, you'd run from me like the plague. Look at me; I'm a mess. I'm also a lousy bet. If I'd been a better wife, maybe my husband wouldn't have—" She broke off, feeling a shudder pass through her.

"I promise you, Lila, I'm nothing like your husband."

Lila leaped off the bed. "Don't talk to me about my husband! You don't know anything about him!" She knew she was overreacting, but that did nothing to temper her emotions, which were running high. "You've only known me a few months. That's nothing. I was married to Gordon for almost twenty years. We had a *life* together."

"I meant no disrespect." Karim frowned as he rose to his feet, wearing a troubled look. "I'm sure he was a good man for you to have loved him. I only meant that I would never hurt you."

"He never meant to hurt us, either. Whatever his faults, he loved us. I never doubted that."

"Then wouldn't he have wanted you to be happy?"

She didn't have an answer for that. Karim was confusing her with his words. Lovely, sinuous, sensuous words, like in the book of poems he'd given her, which coiled like smoke from an opium pipe to cloud her reasoning. But she couldn't allow herself to be seduced by them. If she gave in to Karim, it would be for all the wrong reasons. And didn't she owe it to herself to be certain, if and when the time came, that it had nothing to do with her feeling lonely and vulnerable?

"I can't have this conversation right now," she told him. "I have work to do." She turned away and began stripping the bed—the bed to which she'd come so close to falling victim—her movements brisk as she tossed pillows onto the carpet and jerked sheets from their moorings.

Karim stood watching this furious burst of energy from the sidelines for a minute or so, his arms crossed over his chest, wearing a bemused look, before he said with a sigh of resignation, "All right, as you wish. Until you decide otherwise, we shall be as chaste as Layla and Manjun."

She straightened to look at him. She dimly recalled the famous story of frustrated lovers from a course in Middle Eastern literature that she'd taken in college. "Didn't they both die in the end?"

"Only after Manjun had been driven mad."

Lila couldn't help breaking into a smile at his scholarly way of driving his point home. Relenting the tiniest bit, she said, "Well, the only place I'll be driving you is to the benefit on Saturday night. That is, unless you'd rather we took your car." Seeing him brighten, she hastened to add, "I meant what I said before, but that doesn't mean we can't be friends."

He nodded respectfully. "Neal is welcome to come with us if he likes."

"Thanks, but I'm sure he'll want to ride with Phoebe."

Karim murmured something in response . . . or perhaps it was just the keening of the wind outside. She was bent over, gathering up the sheets off the floor, and when she straightened, he was gone. She stood there, holding the sheets bunched to her chest, listening to the muffled tread of his footsteps on the staircase. A minute later, she heard the sound of a car trunk slamming shut outside.

The groceries. She'd forgotten all about them.

She sank down on the mattress, her legs suddenly too weak to support her. Her heart was beating much too fast, and her breathing was coming in shallow little bursts.

I might be a ghost, she thought, *but I'm far from dead.*

Early the next morning, Lila took the train into the city to visit Vaughn. He was between rounds of chemo and feeling energetic enough to take a long walk, so they hoofed it all the way up to Rockefeller Center, despite the threat of another snowstorm. By the time they arrived, it was almost noon and the sun was peeking out from behind the clouds. It was just warm enough to sit outside, with all the layers of clothing they had on, so Vaughn bought some soft pretzels from a vendor and they sat down on a bench to eat them.

"Look at you. You look almost human," she said. She watched him break a piece off his pretzel and toss it to the pigeons that had gathered at their feet. Her brother's hair was starting to grow back; it looked like the pale fuzz Neal had sported as an infant. He'd put on some weight, too; he no longer looked as if he were drowning inside his clothes.

Vaughn turned to smile at her. "As opposed to what, a dead man walking?"

He spoke lightly, but she heard an edge in his voice that caused her to grow alert. Was there something he wasn't telling her?

"That reminds me—how did it go at the doctor's yesterday?" she asked in what she hoped was a normal tone of voice. She was eager to know the results of Friday's postchemo checkup and had only kept a lid on it until now because she knew how much he hated it when she hovered. But she couldn't take the suspense any longer. One way or another, she had to know.

"I start my next round of chemo in two weeks," he informed her. His tone was so dispassionate, he might have been reporting on the weather—*fair conditions, with a high-pressure system building to the north*—but she knew him too well. This was how he acted when he was scared.

"What does that mean?"

"The short answer is, I'm far from a lost cause . . . but I'm not out of the woods yet, either."

"Can you be a little more specific?"

Reacting to the trepidation in her voice, he reached for her mittened hand, squeezing it to reassure her. "See, this is why I wasn't in a hurry to tell you. I knew you'd jump to conclusions. And it's not bad news."

"It doesn't sound like good news, either. Vaughn, is there something I should know?"

He gave her a long look, no doubt wondering if there was a way to wriggle out of this one. But he must have known that Lila had his number and that she wasn't going to let up until he'd told her everything, so he surrendered at last with a sigh. "There's no reason to panic, okay? Just this one little area that lit up on my PET scan. Other than that, I'm clean as a whistle." He tossed the last of his pretzel to the pigeons and rose languidly to his feet. "And now, since it doesn't appear that I'm in any immediate danger of kicking the bucket, why don't we table this discussion and talk about something else instead?"

Lila longed to browbeat him into giving her every detail, but she knew that would only make him clam up tighter. He'd told her all he was going to for the time being. She would just have to sit tight until further word and trust that his doctors knew what they were doing.

"What do you want to talk about?" she asked, getting up to walk beside him.

He shrugged. "I don't know. You tell me."

Something in his voice made her say, "You say that like you think there's something *I'm* keeping from *you*."

"Is there?" He turned his head to give her a probing look.

"No. Why do you ask?"

"Just curious. You still seeing that Karim fellow? Nice guy, by the way. I really liked him."

She frowned. "I'm not *seeing* him. I told you, we're just friends."

"So there's no one else?"

"Of course not. Don't you think I would've told you if there were?"

"Not necessarily. Not if he was, say, a married man."

"Why on earth would I be seeing a—" She clapped a hand over her mouth, suddenly realizing what he was driving at. In fact, a lot of things she hadn't understood before were becoming clear to her now. "You've been talking to Abby, haven't you?" When Vaughn didn't deny it, she went on, "So *that's* why she's been following me around like she thinks I'm up to something. She suspects there's something going on between Kent and me? God, I can't believe it." She gave a harsh laugh. "What's even more unbelievable is that you actually bought into it. How could you think for one minute that I'd sink that low?"

He had the decency to look contrite. "I wasn't accusing you of anything, Sis. I just had to know for sure."

"Well, now you know." Truth to tell, her anger was directed more at Abigail than at Vaughn. Of all the mean things to accuse her of! "And as far as Abby goes, I suppose it's only the pot calling the kettle black. If anyone should be worried, it's Kent."

Vaughn shot her a narrow look. "What's that supposed to mean?"

"You know perfectly well. Are you going to pretend that the only reason you've been spending so much time with Abby is because you have nothing better to do?"

"I'm not sleeping with her, if that's what you're implying," Vaughn growled.

"I didn't say you were. But clearly you've thought about it, or you wouldn't have been so quick to deny it. And while we're on the subject, what exactly *is* going on with you and Abby?"

His eyes flashed her a warning. "I don't owe you an explanation."

"Maybe not. But I think you owe Gillian one."

"Why? It's none of her business, either."

"She's crazy about you, for one thing."

"If she is, I've done nothing to encourage it."

Despite his callous tone, Lila knew a man with a guilty conscience when she saw one. She'd obviously struck a nerve. She knew that, deep down, Vaughn felt bad about any suffering he was causing Gillian, especially since she'd been so good to him. Under any other circumstances, he'd have spared her the grief by checking into a hotel . . . or hitting the road . . . but that wasn't an option. Until he beat this thing, he wasn't in any shape to be on his own.

"Even if Gillian weren't in the picture, you're still playing with fire," she told him. "Abby's a beautiful woman. And you're like a bird with a broken wing who can't fly. It's a recipe for disaster, I'm telling you."

Vaughn cast her a furtive look as he strolled along, his hands shoved deep into the pockets of his ancient leather bomber jacket that was like a second skin. "What makes you so sure?"

"You think I don't know that something was going on between you and Abby that summer?" The long-ago summer, before Rosalie and Abigail had been sent away and the sun had gone down on their household.

"You never said anything. I didn't think you'd noticed."

"How could I not? You and me and Abby—we'd always been a threesome. When you two started sneaking off together, it was pretty obvious you had the hots for each other." They'd come to a stop at the Plexiglas barrier overlooking the ice rink, and now she gazed down at the skaters gliding and twirling below, her voice soft with regret. "Maybe that's why I didn't try harder to keep Mother from kicking her and Rosie out. Partly it was because I was too shocked to stand up to her, but maybe . . ." She pulled in a breath. "Maybe deep down, there was a small part of me that wanted you all to myself again." Lila felt ashamed to admit it, even after all these years. If Vaughn were to decide to hate her, too, she deserved it.

Her brother turned to face her. The muffler wrapped around his neck, the one she'd given him for Christmas, was covering his chin, and, with his knit cap pulled low, it made the exposed part of his face seem vulnerable somehow. Amid its rugged contours, with his tan faded to the mellow shade of an old Martin guitar he'd once owned, his eyes seemed to stand out even more. His gaze was so intense it was hard for her to meet it straight on—like looking into the sun.

"Look, nothing happened back then, and nothing's going to happen now. We fooled around a little one time, out at the quarry, that's it," he said. "Anyway, how come you never told me any of this before?"

"I don't know," she said. "I guess it's hard admitting something like that even to yourself."

"Have you told Abby?"

"God, no. Not that it would make any difference at this point."

His expression softened. "She's trying, Sis. I know it doesn't always show, but she *is* trying."

Lila narrowed her eyes at him. "How? By accusing me of sleeping with her husband?"

"She didn't accuse you. She just can't help worrying is all. You're an attractive woman who's around all day, and her husband . . . well, I guess it's no secret that they're having problems."

No one was more aware of that than Lila, with all of them living practically under the same roof. For one thing, Abigail and Kent almost never ate together. Also, in tidying up their room, she'd noticed that their bed covers seldom showed signs of anything more than peaceful slumber. When she and Gordon used to make love, it had been almost enough to turn the mattress inside out. But all she said was, "Well, if they are, it's certainly none of *my* concern."

"Tread lightly, that's all I'm saying."

"Is that supposed to be some kind of warning?"

"No, just a piece of brotherly advice. When tensions are high, you know how things can get blown out of proportion, and I'd hate to see anything you said or did get misinterpreted."

All the way back home on the train, Lila mulled over his words. She certainly had no designs on Kent, but what if the same wasn't true of him? It hadn't occurred to her until Vaughn had brought it up, but now the thought wormed its way in: Suppose Kent had his eye on her? Could she blame him? A husband starved for affection, even a good husband, might be tempted to stray.

That evening, standing in front of the full-length mirror in her bedroom as she dressed for the benefit, she assessed herself for the first time since Gordon's death as she imagined a man might—Kent or Karim. She'd regained a few much-needed pounds and, along with them, her curves. The hollows in her face were no longer so pronounced, and there was color in her cheeks. Her hair, which she'd recently had styled at a salon in town, fell in shining waves about her neck and shoulders. In short, she looked alive again, after so many months of looking out at the world through dull, dead eyes. So, yes, maybe there was a reason, besides her sparkling wit and recently acquired homemaking skills, why a man would find her attractive.

With that in mind, she discarded one outfit after another, wanting to look her best without looking as if she were trying to draw attention to herself. Not that she had much to choose from—she hadn't bought anything new in a while, and her old clothes were either too large or too dated. Finally she settled on a plain black skirt and a dressy sweater in a pale shade of lilac, which showed off her neckline without baring any cleavage. She added a string of imitation pearls—her real ones had been sold off long ago—and the diamond studs that were the one piece of signature jewelry she'd kept. After slipping on a pair of high heels, she was good to go.

"You look nice, Mom."

She turned around to find Neal poised in the doorway, wearing his favorite black jeans and a navy blazer over a button-down shirt.

"So do you," she said, warmed by the unexpected compliment. "I'm sure Phoebe will be suitably wowed."

His expression at once turned sullen. "It's not like that with us."

"I didn't mean anything by it," she told him. "It's just . . . well, you two *have* been seeing an awful lot of each other."

She spoke carefully, conscious of how prickly Neal was these days. The most innocent remark could set him off.

"What of it?" Neal said. "You and that Karim guy are always hanging out together. Do I make a big deal out of *that?*"

"You don't have to. You've made it perfectly clear how you feel about it."

Just then, a horn honked outside. Karim. They'd decided to go in his truck.

Neal drew the curtains back to peer out the window. "Looks like your *date* is here."

Lila hastened to correct him. "He's not my date."

"What should I call him then, your fuck buddy?"

Lila was shocked, as much by the contempt with which he'd spoken as by the coarse language coming out of her son's mouth. This was Neal, *her* Neal? But when she looked into her son's face, she saw a stranger looking back at her. An *angry* stranger. Dear God. Did he hate her that much?

She recalled Dr. Goldman's advice not to engage with Neal at his level when he was acting this way, and as soon as she'd regained her composure, she replied in a cool but nonconfrontational tone, "There's no call for you to speak to me that way. Nothing's going on with Karim and me. And even if there were, I should hope you'd respect my privacy."

"Privacy? Is that what you call it?" Neal shook his head in disgust. "Christ, Dad hasn't even been gone a year and already you're doing some other guy."

Lila was too stunned to be angry. She could see on his face the pain her son was in, and that hurt her more than any words he might hurl at her in an effort to dispel some of that pain. "Oh, honey. That's simply not the case. Besides, you know nothing could ever change the way I felt about your dad." Her eyes filled with tears, but when she reached out to put a hand on Neal's arm, he jerked away, as if he couldn't bear to have her touch him.

"Yeah, I know. You hated him."

If she'd been shocked by his earlier words, she was rendered momentarily speechless by this new revelation. "Why would you say a thing like that?" she gasped. "You know I loved your dad very much."

"Yeah? Then why'd he kill himself?"

Before she could respond, Neal spun on his heel and disappeared into the next room. A moment later, she heard the front door slam shut.

At the party, Lila drifted about, shaking hands and murmuring pleasantries, but her mind was elsewhere. She couldn't stop thinking about the argument with Neal. Had his outburst been just that of a boy blindly lashing out, or was it a sign of something more troubling? She'd assumed that Neal was still taking the antidepressants he'd been prescribed, but when was the last time she'd checked to make sure? Spying him across the crowded room, deep in conversation with Phoebe, Lila tried to draw reassurance from the fact that he appeared none the worse for their tiff, but she couldn't shake the feeling of dread that lay over her like a mushroom cloud.

Ironically, the person she most wanted to be with right now was Karim, but she'd let him know on the way over that she'd prefer it if they kept their distance from each other tonight. Respecting her wishes, he'd remained at her side only long enough to fetch a drink for her before moving off to mingle with the crowd. Now, spotting him at the other end of the yacht club's thronged dining hall, his dark, boldly ethnic features standing out amid the sea of mostly white faces, she was at once filled with regret, wishing they could have met at another time in her life. He'd said he would wait, but would he wait forever? There had to be other women who'd leap at the chance to be with him. Like Chrissy Elliot, who at the moment was hanging all over him. The elfin blond owner of the toy store on Main Street, called the Elephant's Trunk, who was always in jeans and sneakers whenever Lila saw her downtown, was tonight dressed to the nines and wearing killer heels, looking as if she wanted to jump Karim's bones. Watching her lay a hand on his arm, laughing too loudly in response to something he'd said, Lila felt a stab of jealousy. If Karim had remained unattached this long, she thought, it was only by choice. Also, unattached didn't necessarily mean celibate. After that steamy little scene in Abigail's bedroom the other day, she could well imagine him taking a lover. And if she wasn't available . . .

A stitch in her belly pulled taut at the thought.

As for her own popularity, she'd gone from being a social pariah in the city to something of a curiosity here in Stone Harbor. Once the buzz had died down, the townsfolk hadn't known quite what to make of her. Whenever she encountered them while out shopping or running errands, she could see the confusion in their eyes: Was this the same rich bitch who'd been so reviled by the press? Where were her furs and jewels, her fancy designer clothes? She could sense them wondering, too, why someone of her obvious pedigree would be employed as a housekeeper. And not just any housekeeper, but *Abigail Armstrong's* housekeeper. But those who had gotten to know her a bit—like Grace Stehosky from L'Epicerie and John Carmine from the fish store, both of whom had greeted her warmly when she'd arrived tonight—treated her no differently than they would anyone else. And Barb Huggins, whom she'd run into earlier, had gone out of her way to be friendly, promising to call as soon as her boss had decided what she wanted to do about filling the temporary position they'd spoken about.

Now, as Lila milled around, introducing herself to people whom she hadn't yet met and chatting with acquaintances, she felt as if she had as much right to be here as anyone. And she had to admit it felt good, flexing her near-atrophied social muscles while at the same time putting old ghosts to rest. She didn't have to pretend to be someone she wasn't . . . or apologize for her husband's bad behavior. She could just be herself: Take it or leave it.

It was also her first real evening out since she'd moved here, except for the occasional movie or bite to eat in town. The first time, too, that she'd been inside the yacht club. Wandering around, checking out its various public rooms, she found herself drawn to the view from the window that overlooked the harbor in one of the smaller sitting rooms off the dining hall. The club was situated on a point that jutted out into the river, so it was surrounded by water on three sides. From her vantage point, high above the snow-covered lawn that sloped to meet the marina, she could imagine that she was standing aboard a ship set to embark. Below, the marina looked deserted, the only movement that of the tall masts swaying in the breeze like so many trees in a defoliated forest. Farther out on the river, chunks of ice floated ghostlike along invisible black currents, and a tugboat chugged along, pulling its phosphorescent wake.

"Beautiful, isn't it?"

She swung around at the familiar sound of Kent's voice. The room had been deserted when she'd wandered into it. He must have slipped in while she'd been admiring the view. He stood before her now, drink in hand, looking more formal, in his suit and tie, than she was used to seeing him. Handsome, too, with his tweedy, silvering hair that perfectly complemented his gray eyes. She thought back to her brother's warning earlier in the day and felt herself grow warm.

"It's a lovely spot," she agreed.

"It's even nicer out on the water," he said. Kent was happiest, she knew, at the helm of his sailboat, not hanging around tony clubs or hobnobbing at parties.

"You must be looking forward to when the weather warms up," she said.

He tipped his tumbler of scotch, as if in a silent toast to the gods of good sailing weather. "I was thinking of heading south this year. Maybe sail along the Florida coast. Do some fishing."

"I didn't know you liked to fish," she said.

"I don't, but maybe it's time I took it up. On the other hand, you know the saying—you can't teach an old dog new tricks. I guess I'm pretty predictable that way. Some might say boring."

"You? Hardly," she scoffed.

"You should get out more. You're beginning to think like me." His mouth curved in a smile that didn't reach his eyes.

"You're right, I should. Unfortunately, my free time is pretty limited these days."

She spoke lightly so he wouldn't think she was complaining. The truth was that she wasn't entirely unhappy with her job. She found a kind of perverse pleasure in the aching of her muscles at the end of a hard day's work. She took pride, too, in how handy she'd become. The other day she'd fixed a toilet handle that was sticking, without any help from Karim. Knowing which canapés to serve at a party or the perfect gown to wear to a black-tie event wouldn't do her much good in the event of an actual Armageddon, but being resourceful just might.

"That will change," he said. "Mark my words, you'll be moving on to better things before too long." From the careful way he enunciated each word, Lila realized he was tipsy.

"Really? Do you know something I don't?" she said with a laugh.

Kent didn't answer. He didn't even appear to be listening. He stood gazing contemplatively out the window, taking slow sips of his drink. Briefly, she wondered where Abigail had gotten to. The last Lila had seen her, she'd been over by the tables where the items for the silent auction were on display (one of which was a dinner party for eight, to be catered by Abigail Armstrong Catering), a small crowd of adoring admirers gathered around her, hanging on her every word.

Abruptly, Kent turned to face her. "I'm going for a walk. Would you care to join me?"

It seemed more of an appeal than a request, so Lila said, "I'll get my coat."

Minutes later, they were slipping out through a side entrance. Outside, it was deserted. They walked along the path to the marina, Lila, in her high heels, holding on to Kent's arm to maintain her footing on the icy paving stones. When they reached the gated entrance to the dock, Kent punched in the code on the keypad, and soon they were wandering along the floating pontoons, where boats of all shapes and sizes were moored, the planks beneath them swaying and creaking with their weight. Kent pointed out his sailboat, not the largest or the fanciest but certainly the most elegant, with its sleek lines, its teak siding and deck. A biting wind blew off the river, and instinctively she huddled closer to him, thinking nothing of it when he slipped an arm around her shoulders to warm her.

"Well, I think it's safe to say your event's a success," she remarked, glancing over her shoulder at the clubhouse, from which the sounds of music and merriment drifted. "As a veteran of many fund-raisers, I can honestly say I've never seen one more well attended. It looks as if half the town showed up."

"Well, that's something, at least," Kent replied, but his tone was lackluster.

"You don't sound too happy about it," she observed.

"I'm pleased, of course. But happy? No, I'm not very happy at the moment."

He looked so troubled that Lila was prompted to ask, "Do you feel like talking about it?"

Kent gave a deep sigh. "Not particularly. But, as it seems I'm not very good at keeping secrets, I have to tell someone, so it might as well be you." He paused before going on. "I don't suppose it'll come as any surprise to you that Abby and I, despite our public image, aren't exactly the portrait of domestic bliss." He spoke with an air of deep regret, which surprised her—from the way he acted around his wife, Lila wouldn't have guessed that he felt anything more than a distant affection for her. "I suppose she and I could have gone on this way for years. Probably we would have, knowing how much we both hate change. Only, you see, I've met someone."

Lila thought once more of Vaughn's earlier warning. So Abigail's husband *was* in love with another woman. Only that woman wasn't her. She felt relief wash over her, followed closely by concern for Kent. If he was having an affair, it clearly wasn't all satin sheets and champagne.

"Is she someone you've known long?" she asked.

He nodded. "She's the mother of one of my patients—an eight-year-old boy with cystic fibrosis. Joey's in and out of the hospital all the time, as you might imagine, so she and I . . . well, we've gotten to know each other through the years. It was only recently, though, with this last crisis of Joey's, that . . ." He gave a small shrug. "We've been seeing each other a little over four months now."

"Is it serious?"

"Very."

"And I gather she feels the same way about you?"

"Oh, yes." His face lit up. "She's amazing, Lila. Beautiful. Smart. And so brave. She never lets on to Joey how scared she is of losing him. And she's handling it all alone. Her husband walked out on her not long after Joey was diagnosed. She's been divorced for the past seven years. If I weren't married myself . . ." He let the sentence trail off, the light fading from his eyes.

An image rose in Lila's mind of Abigail's tired, pinched face on the evenings she dragged home late from work. Lila felt an unexpected twinge of sympathy for her. "What are you going to do?" she asked with some trepidation.

"I suppose I'll have to tell Abby at some point, before she finds out on her own," he said. "Frankly, I'm more concerned about Phoebe. She's having a tough enough time as it is. She didn't get into Princeton, did I tell you? It was a big disappointment, to say the least. Something like this . . . it could cause her to become unglued." He heaved another sigh, gazing out over the water, which glittered with tiny knife points of reflected light. "God, what a mess."

"Phoebe has Neal, at least." Lila's tone was less than reassuring, for she felt a flutter of uneasiness at the thought of her son and Phoebe becoming even more entwined. Neal's recent behavior had made her wonder if they were only feeding off each other's misery. "Anyway, you shouldn't let that stop you. If you're this miserable, you're not going to be able to make anyone else happy, least of all Abby."

"You're right. It's just that I—oh, Christ." He gave a strangled sob, his arm dropping from her shoulder as he reached up to cover his face.

Lila, acting on instinct, put her arms around him to console him. She was holding Kent, stroking his back and murmuring words of comfort, when a familiar voice leaped out of the darkness.

"You! I should have known."

Lila jerked around to find Abigail poised at the other end of the dock, silhouetted against the moorings, the boats rocking gently as if with some unseen turbulence while she stood still as a stanchion. When she finally moved forward into the glow from the sodium arc lights that illuminated the marina's perimeter, Lila saw that she wasn't wearing her coat, just a thin pashmina shawl, which she clutched tightly about her shoulders as she shivered convulsively.

"Oh, I had my suspicions," she went on, her eyes narrowing as they fixed on Lila. "But I couldn't believe even *you* would go that far. You wouldn't steal my husband after you'd already stolen my *life*. Well, clearly I was wrong. You *are* the snake in the grass I always knew you to be."

"It's not what you think," Lila said, feeling the blood rush up into her face. "We were . . . I was only trying to . . ." She stopped herself before she could reveal Kent's secret.

But Kent murmured, "It's all right, Lila. She would have found out anyway." As he stepped forward, Lila was struck by the expression of eerie calm on his face, as if after all the agony of struggling to come to this decision, it was a relief to have had it made for him. She watched him walk over to where Abigail stood and take hold of her arm, not without tenderness. Abigail tried to tug it away, but he only tightened his grip, saying, "We need to talk, Abby. Alone."

14

Lila let herself in through the back door. The house was silent. Kent must have dropped Abigail off, then left—his Mercedes wasn't in the garage—and there was no sign of either Neal or Phoebe. Lila wasn't even sure what *she* was doing here. Instinct alone had caused her to seek Abigail out in the wake of the dreadful scene at the marina. Past hurts and present injuries had all faded into oblivion at the sight of her childhood friend's pale, stricken face. Whatever her sins, whatever Lila had done to her, Abigail was a woman whose husband had just confessed to an affair.

How could Lila *not* reach out to her?

She dropped her jacket and keys onto the bench in the mudroom before making her way into the kitchen. It was dark, the only illumination the glow from the outdoor lights, which were rigged to a motion detector that had been tripped when she'd walked up the path; that and the little red light blinking on the answering machine by the phone. The only sounds were the muted hum of the Sub-Zero and the ticking of the antique wall clock over the breakfast nook.

She moved into the hallway beyond, calling, "Abigail?"

No answer. The only response was a halfhearted bark from upstairs. She looked up to find Brewster on the landing above, ears pricked as he investigated the source of this intrusion on his nap. When he saw that it was only she, his tail began to wag, and he yawned and tottered back to his doggie bed.

Lila did a quick search of the downstairs before concluding that Abigail must be up in her room. Even so, she hesitated before starting up the staircase. Suppose Abigail was asleep? She didn't want to disturb her.

Lila was quick to dismiss the idea. Given Abigail's likely state of mind, what were the chances of that? Also, when had she ever seen Abigail so much as put her feet up? Even late at night, Lila was used to seeing the light burning in Abigail's second-floor study, often until well past midnight. And in the mornings, she was always the first one up, usually while it was still dark out. She was like some nocturnal creature in constant, restless motion.

As Lila mounted the stairs, she caught the faint scent of the furniture polish she used to polish the banister—once a week, like clockwork. For some reason, it only heightened her anxiety. Then she remembered: On the morning of the day that Gordon had taken his own life, she'd polished the woodwork throughout the apartment (partly because it had been something to keep her mind off her husband's looming incarceration and partly because she hadn't been able to bear the thought of the new owners' snidely remarking that, for all the money she'd squandered, she hadn't kept the place up), and the same lemony scent had been in the air then. The memory caused something to lurch inside her chest.

In the darkened hallway on the floor above, she could see a pale shaft of light angling from the open door to the master bedroom. "Abigail?" she called again, with trepidation this time.

No answer.

An image reared in her mind, like a spooky shadow on the wall of a haunted house, of her husband sprawled lifeless on the floor in his study, his head resting in a pool of congealing blood.

But Abigail would never—*would she?*

The mere thought was enough to make Lila's heart momentarily stutter to a standstill.

The first thing she noticed as she stepped into the master bedroom were the clothes scattered over the floor—the midnight-blue Elie Tahari sheath Abigail had worn tonight, a pair of smoke-colored pantyhose squiggled like graffiti over the cream carpet, a trail of lacy undergarments. And there, lying facedown on the king-sized bed that Lila so meticulously made each morning—with hand-embroidered Burano sheets, pale gold Pratesi coverlet and matching shams, the cashmere throw folded at the foot, and pillows in various shapes and sizes—lay the wreck formerly known as Abigail Armstrong, wrapped in an old tartan robe, with her head buried in a pillow.

"I suppose you've come to gloat." Her muffled voice rose from the depths of the pillow. One bare foot dangled off the edge of the mattress. The shoes she'd worn to the party, a pair of black Prada high heels, lay toppled on the floor beside the bed like evidence in a crime scene.

Lila sat down gingerly on the edge of the mattress. "Actually, I came to see if you were all right."

Abigail rolled onto her back to glare up at Lila with swollen, bloodshot eyes. "Do I *look* all right?"

"I've seen you look better," Lila had to admit.

Abigail sat up, propping herself against the padded headboard and pulling a small satin pillow onto her lap, like a small child reaching for a stuffed animal. Her hair was sticking out all over her head in messy clumps, as if she had repeatedly raked her fingers through it. Her face was puffy and blotched from crying. "Tell me, and I want an honest answer: Did you know all along?" she demanded, her red-rimmed eyes fixing on Lila like a pair of heat-seeking missiles.

Lila replied honestly, "No. I only found out tonight. That's what we were doing out on the dock. He needed someone to talk to . . . and I just happened to be available. It's not like we were in cahoots."

Abigail glared at her. "No?"

"I swear to you, Abby."

Abigail glared at her a moment longer, then sighed. "Either way, I suppose you're on *his* side."

"I'm not on anyone's side. As far as I can see, there *are* no sides. Just two unhappy people."

"One of whom is going to be a miserable son of a bitch once my lawyer gets through with him," Abigail growled, her face contorting in fury.

"Do you really want to go that route?" Lila spoke in a calm, reasoning tone, as if to a child having a tantrum. "If you don't care about Kent, think what that would do to Phoebe."

Abigail's face crumpled in misery, and a tear rolled down one cheek. "I just wish I knew what went wrong. I mean, I've known for a while that things haven't been right between us, but I never thought . . ." She gave a small, tremulous smile. "It wasn't always like this, you know. Believe it or not, there was a time we were crazy about each other. I always thought we could get back to the way it was when we were first married, if only I could—" She broke off, as if suddenly becoming aware of who it was to whom she was baring her soul, and her expression hardened. "I don't know why I'm telling you this. You probably think it's all *my* fault. That I'm the bitch who got what she deserved."

"I don't think anyone deserves to be hurt like this," Lila told her.

"You didn't always feel that way."

Lila was once more reminded of what Abigail had suffered all those years ago, partly, because of her. Now she seized the opportunity to make long-overdue amends. "I never meant to hurt you back then," she said softly. "I realize that's a pretty piss-poor excuse, so I don't expect you to forgive me. I know I wasn't a very good friend, and I'm sorry for that—truly I am." She averted her gaze, unable to bear the hot accusation in Abigail's eyes, looking down at the coverlet instead as she traced its stitched pattern with her fingertip, as if it were the hands of a clock that she could turn back. "I was a kid faced with a situation I didn't know how to handle. And the reason I never wrote to you was because I was so ashamed of letting you down, I didn't know where to begin." Lila's shoulders lifted and fell in a helpless shrug. "I know it's not much of an apology, but it's all I have to offer."

She brought up her head to find Abigail staring at her, but not with the pitiless eyes of before. "I thought you didn't care," she said in a small, cracked voice. "I thought our friendship had meant nothing to you.

Then when my mom died . . ." Her face convulsed as if in physical pain. "I had no one but my aunt and uncle, and believe me, they were worse than if I'd been living on my own. My uncle—" She broke off, and Lila saw that she was squeezing the pillow in her lap so tightly that, had it been a small creature, she'd have choked the life out of it. "You can't imagine what it was like for me."

"Actually, I can," Lila said. "I don't think I fully realized it until after I'd lost everything of my own, but now I know just how awful it must have been for you." She felt her throat tighten, and she had to swallow hard before she could continue. "I know I can never make it up to you, Abby, but won't you at least let me try? Not," she added with a dry note of remonstrance, "by cleaning up after you. But by being your friend. I think we could both use a friend, don't you?"

Abigail's eyes narrowed. "Give me one good reason why I should trust you."

"For one thing, don't you think I've been punished enough?"

"Actually, I think I've been remarkably fair, all things considered." Abigail's haughty tone was back. "Remember, you came to me. I could just as easily have turned you out into the cold."

"The only reason you didn't was because you wanted to see me grovel. Not that I blame you," Lila was quick to add. "You had every right after what I did to you. But at least have the guts to admit it. Don't tell me you didn't enjoy seeing me on my hands and knees."

Abigail gave a small, grudging smile. "Actually, I thought I'd enjoy it more than I did. The truth is, I was getting a little tired of your Cinderella routine. Also, I won't deny that it bugged me, the fact that you and Kent got along so well. Even Phoebe likes you better than she does me."

"No one likes their mother at that age." Lila thought once more of her fight with Neal, how awful it had felt to be the focus of her son's rage, even if he'd only been lashing out blindly. "You can't take it personally."

"I suppose you're right," Abigail conceded with a sigh. "But that doesn't make it any easier. And just wait until she finds out that her father and I are getting divorced—she'll hate me even more."

"Do you really think it'll come to that?"

Abigail's expression hardened once more. "Ask Kent. He seems to be the one with all the answers."

"I would, except it doesn't look as if he's around at the moment," Lila said, glancing about her.

"That's because he packed his bags and cut out as soon as we got home from the party."

Lila's gaze was drawn to the walk-in closet, which stood open. Inside, dresser drawers gaped, and there was an empty space on the rod where Kent's suits and blazers had hung.

"Where did he go?" she asked, although she had a pretty good guess.

Abigail gave a bitter laugh. "He didn't say, but I'm sure he's with her. In which case, I doubt he'll be coming back anytime soon."

"Would it be the worst thing in the world if he didn't?" Lila ventured, not wanting to overstep her bounds. "After the smoke clears, you might be happier on your own."

"Happy?" Abigail snorted in derision. "I don't even know what that is anymore. It's all a crapshoot, whichever way you look at it. You, of all people, should know that—look what happened to you. Your brother's the one with the right idea. He was too smart to fall into that trap."

Lila wanted to ask what role Vaughn would be playing in Abigail's new life as a divorcée, but now wasn't the time. Besides, she wasn't sure she wanted to know the answer.

"So what now?" she asked.

Abigail sighed once more. "You tell me."

An idea popped into Lila's head, and she smiled. "There's a bottle of champagne in the fridge. What do you say we crack it open? I think we could both use a drink. Maybe more than one."

Abigail rolled her eyes. "Please. I'm still recovering from the last time we got drunk together."

Lila had forgotten all about it, and now the memory came rushing in: the night they'd gotten plastered on Boone's Farm apple wine (purchased for them by an older brother of Lila's friend Missy Stanislaus). They'd been fourteen at the time, and Lila's parents had been away for the weekend. Rosalie had given Abigail permission to stay over at the big house, and Vaughn had been away, too, on an overnight camping trip with his Scout troop. It had been just Lila and Abigail, and they'd stayed up until all hours, getting sillier with each pull off the bottle and singing along in their underwear to Duran Duran.

Now, all these years later, she laughed and said, "Come on, it'll do you good."

Abigail closed her eyes, as if to shut Lila out. She remained motionless for so long that Lila thought she must have drifted off to sleep. Then her eyes opened and she abruptly swung her legs off the mattress. "This doesn't mean we're back to being friends," she said as she rose to her feet. She scowled at Lila, drawing herself up to her full height and tightening the sash on her robe.

Lila struggled to keep a straight face. "No, of course not. You can tell everyone I took advantage of you while you were drunk."

"Just as long as it's not Boone's Farm apple wine. God, do you remember how we were up half the night throwing up? The bathroom smelled like rotten apples. Do you know it was years before I could even look at an apple?" Abigail paused as they were making their way down the staircase, smiling faintly. "We had some good times back then, didn't we?"

"Yeah," Lila said. "We did."

"You're not thinking of backing out, are you?"

Phoebe was eyeing him as if he'd said something, when he hadn't spoken a word. She must have read his mind. "No," he replied glumly. She gave him a look that prompted him to add, "What, you think I'm just saying it to make you feel better?"

"I didn't say that. It's just, you know, it's a big deal."

"No turning back. I get it."

"Why are you so mad? You're not mad at me, are you?"

"No, I'm not mad at you," he said through gritted teeth.

"Then what the fuck's your problem?"

"Why do you keep asking me that? Maybe you're the one with the problem."

"Yeah, I have a problem all right—you," she shot back, furious at him all of a sudden. As if she hadn't just blown him. As if they weren't sitting in the front seat of his mom's car, Neal with his jeans unzipped and Phoebe with her lipstick all smeared. "If you're going to back out, do it now so I'll know not to count on you. Anyway, it's not like I need you. Don't forget, it was my idea to begin with. You're just along for the ride."

They were parked out by Miller's Pond, a favorite make-out spot for the local high school kids. There was a sign posted at the entrance to the dirt road leading up to it that read "Private Property," but everyone knew that the owner lived out of state, so they pretty much came and went as they pleased. Now, in the moonlight that shone through the winter-blown trees, Neal could see the trash scattered about. Beer bottles and soda cans, the charred remains of a campfire. The last time they'd been out here, during the day, he'd even spotted a few used condoms. He remembered thinking at the time, At least someone's having fun.

The fun had long since gone out of his and Phoebe's fucking. Not that he ever would have used the word "fun" to describe what they did. It was more like a fever that had settled into his brain, an itch from a heat rash that he couldn't keep from scratching. There had been times, with Phoebe bucking beneath him, hissing in his ear, Harder . . . harder, while grinding her hips into his, that it had almost seemed as if she were punishing him . . . or maybe herself. In the end, after he'd come, he would always feel a little dirty. Not because of any stupid moralistic reasons but because he felt beside the point somehow.

He was aware that guys weren't supposed to feel that way, that it was mainly the province of "nice" girls. But with Phoebe, nothing was ever like it was with other people. At times, it felt as if they were like two magnets repulsing each other; at other times, as if she were the magnet pulling him in, a pull he was helpless to resist. When that happened, it was like the high from having pounded one too many beers kicking in:

that part-sickening, part-exhilarating realization that it was too late to undo what was done, so he might as well hang tight and enjoy the ride, even knowing that he might end up doing something really stupid—no, would almost surely do something stupid—while blasted out of his mind, and that he would have a wicked hangover in the morning.

But the really great thing about Phoebe was that he didn't have to fake it with her. With everyone else, he merely went through the motions, playing the role of dutiful son, hardworking employee, straight-A student. He'd fooled everyone—Dr. Goldman, his boss at work, his teachers at school, even some of his closest friends. Everyone, that is, except his mom.

He knew she was on to him because earlier tonight, when he'd let his guise slip, he'd seen the look on her face. She hadn't even been mad; more like alarmed—the way she might have looked if she'd found a loaded gun in one of his drawers.

What made it so tough was that he knew she probably would have understood if he could have found a way to tell her what was going on inside his head. She'd been there that day. She'd seen it with her own eyes, just as Neal had: his father lying there on the floor in his own blood. So, yeah, she'd have understood, and she would undoubtedly have sympathized. At the same time, she would have insisted on sending him back to Dr. Goldman, or to some new shrink. As if paying a fortune for fifty minutes' worth of some lame doctor pretending to give a shit about him was going to do any good.

Even the antidepressants Dr. Goldman had prescribed were a joke. All they'd done was mess with his head even more. After dutifully taking them for the better part of a month, thinking that eventually the effects would kick in, he'd realized that wasn't going to happen and had tossed the remaining pills. Now there was no hope. No series of commands, like on his computer, with which to erase the memory of that horrible day. No miracle that was going to bring his father back to life. Whenever he thought back to when he'd been a kid, when he and his dad used to hang out and do guy stuff together—like going to auto shows or watching movies at the IMAX theater on West 69th, where his dad had always let him have all the junk food and candy that his mom wouldn't let him eat—that kid always seemed to him like some other person, like someone he'd been friends with a long time ago who'd moved away.

No, there was only one way out, he thought: the solution Phoebe was offering. The exit strategy to end all exit strategies.

What was weird was that, as soon as he'd made the decision, a strange euphoria had overtaken him. A feeling that was a little like—he cast another look at Phoebe, huddled in her seat staring out the window—well, like falling in love. He wouldn't have to tear himself to shreds trying to dig himself out of the collapsed mine shaft that was his life.

He could just let go.

There was only one thing nagging at him: He couldn't stop thinking about his mom. This would destroy her. And despite his having lashed out at her tonight, which had been stupid, he knew—getting all hot under the collar about that Karim guy when, really, why the fuck should he care? Especially since Neal wasn't going to be around much longer—he still cared about her. She was still his mom; nothing could ever change that.

But on the other side of the equation, there was Phoebe . . . and the promise of sweet release she held out to him.

He reached over and took hold of her hand. "Hey, what are we fighting about? I told you, everything's fine. I've already talked to Chas about getting the stuff we'll need."

"You're sure?" Phoebe turned to him, her eyes glittering in the moonlight.

Neal hesitated only an instant before answering, "Yeah, I'm sure."

Phoebe seemed to take his word for it, and in the silence that followed, Neal gazed out at the pond, its frozen surface a ghostly glimmer in the darkness. He'd heard that some kid had drowned in it years ago, and he pictured the body trapped beneath the ice, locked in eternal limbo. He began to shiver. His mom had gotten the car heater fixed, but he still felt cold, even with it going full blast.

"I was just thinking . . . Do you ever wonder about your parents? Like what it'll do to them," he asked cautiously.

Phoebe leaned into the door on her side, resting her head against the window. "My dad, yeah. I know it'll be hard for him. Not my mom, though—she probably won't even notice I'm gone." Phoebe looked so forlorn in that moment, like a scared little girl lost in the woods, that Neal's heart went out to her.

"What about him?" he asked.

Something in his tone must have told her that he wasn't referring to her dad, for he could see the muscles in her jaw tighten even as she replied in a bored voice, "Who cares what he thinks?"

Neal knew it'd be best to let it drop, but some perverse impulse wouldn't let him. They'd never talked about it in any depth. When she'd finally told him the whole story of her so-called affair with the married guy, she'd glossed it over, making it sound as if it were just one of those things, something you do that you later regret but that's no real skin off you—like having too much to drink at a party . . . or getting into a minor car accident.

"You don't care that he'll never have to pay for what he did?"

"He didn't do anything," she said, sounding irritated. "I was into it, too. Why are you making such a big deal out of it? I'm sorry I even told you. Anyway, it was just a stupid mistake."

"A grown man with a wife and kids? That's no mistake. In this country, they call it statutory rape."

"And your point is?"

"My point is that guys like him belong in jail."

"Yeah, right. Like that would ever happen." She tried to shrug it off, but he could see that he'd hit a nerve. She was picking at a thumbnail, the way she always did when she was tweaked about something.

"All you'd have to do is go to the police," he said.

"Yeah, Mr. Know-It-All, and what then? He's not the only one people would be pointing the finger at. They'd all be saying it was my fault, that I led him on. You don't know him. He's the most popular teacher in our school. I'm just the school weirdo. They'd crucify me before they'd ever lay a finger on him. Besides," a note of uncertainty crept in, "it's not like he forced me or anything."

Neal found himself growing angry. It pissed him off to think of a lowlife like that getting off scot-free after ruining a girl's life, while his dad had been socked with ten years just for making some bad decisions. "You don't have to rape a girl at knifepoint for it to be against the law," he said. "You were only fifteen. He's, what, in his forties? Also, you probably weren't his first."

Phoebe shook her head, but her voice when it emerged was small and ragged. "He said he loved me."

"If he'd really loved you, he wouldn't have wanted to see you get hurt."

"It's not like he broke up with me or anything. I'm the one who ended it," Phoebe informed him loftily.

"Yeah, but not before he did a number on you. Look at you. You don't eat. Your grades are in the toilet." A recent fact that her parents were unaware of. "Sometimes I get the feeling you don't even like sex that much. And now you're planning to—" He stopped before he could utter the words.

Phoebe twisted around suddenly, leaning toward him. "Go on, say it," she hissed.

"I don't have to say it. Isn't it enough that you're doing it?" *We're doing it,* he silently amended.

"But not because of him. I just want that made clear."

"Still . . ."

"Still what?" She glared at him.

"Nothing." He slumped back against his seat.

"I'm not some head case, if that's what you're thinking. I don't need to be psychoanalyzed. Certainly not by you. I'm perfectly capable of making a rational decision. And I'm assuming you are, too. So are you in, or not? If you're not, don't waste any more of my time."

Phoebe would be horrified to know, he thought, how much she'd sounded like her mother just then.

Neal waited a second, taking a deep breath and slowly releasing it before he said, "All right, then. Let's go over the plan one more time."

15

Concepción stepped off the plane at JFK into a world filled with brown faces. Not just those of *paisanos* but blacks, Asians, tea-skinned *indios* from the East, and Latinos chattering away in unfamiliar accents. There were *gringos*, too, lots of them, rushing past her, pulling their wheeled suitcases, and talking into their cell phones, but what she was most struck by was the sheer number of foreigners like herself. In LA, when you saw someone with a brown face, chances were that it was a *compadre*. In some ways, Echo Park had been like Las Cruces writ large and mysteriously transported to the North, the only difference being that the majority of its people spoke English as well as Spanish. Here she was just one of many in a vast, polymorphous sea. Unless she found someone Spanish-speaking who looked as if they knew their way around, she wouldn't even be able to ask for directions if she were to get lost—her English had improved considerably, but not enough for her to comprehend the stream of words that invariably rushed at her in response to an inquiry.

She thought of Jesús and felt a sudden, sharp tug of longing. He would have known what to do, where to go. He would have understood what the *gringos* jabbering in their incomprehensible English were saying. His presence alone would have been a comfort.

But if he wasn't at her side, she had only herself to blame. In the days before she'd embarked on this journey, he'd begged her to allow him to accompany her. He'd warned her of the dangers that she would face, a woman alone on the streets of New York City. "People will try to take advantage of you," he'd said. In New York City, there were *gabachos* even more unscrupulous than those in LA. Men who would as soon kill you as rob you, and many others who weren't above trying to cheat you out of your money.

But she'd remained firm. This was her journey, and hers alone. In some ways, it reminded her of the pilgrimage to the shrine of Guadalupe that her *abuelita* had gone on many years ago, when Concepción had been a child. She recalled her grandmother telling her what it was like, how she, and the other devout pilgrims, had crawled on their knees, clutching their rosaries, until the stones lining the path to the shrine were red with their blood. How she'd kissed the feet of the Virgin and prayed that her husband, who was sick with kidney disease, would be healed.

Concepción wished for an end to suffering, too—her own. She didn't know if this would be the answer. Would she find any respite from her grief by forcing the Señora to admit her guilt? Maybe not. Maybe Jesús was right, and her coming here was as senseless as her daughter's death. But if there was a chance that she would gain some consolation, either in a show of true contrition on the Señora's part or in seeing her punished, then she had to see this through to the end. She would never be able to live with herself otherwise.

Concepción made her way through the confusing maze of signs toward the baggage claim, where she was nearly plowed down by a big, yellow-haired *gringo* pushing a cart piled high with suitcases. *"Perdóname,"* she murmured politely, though it hadn't been her fault. But the man barreled past her without a word of apology, not even glancing her way. She might have been invisible, which in a way she was—just another brown face, another immigrant spilling into the teeming reservoir of humanity that was New York City.

Good. That meant she stood a better chance of blending in. The last thing she needed was to attract the attention of La Migra. That she'd made it this far was a feat in itself. For even after she'd saved up enough money for the airfare, she'd still lacked the proper identification she needed to board the plane. Once again, Jesús had come to her rescue. He'd known someone who had been able to supply her with a fake driver's license (a pardonable offense, in her view, given the fact that she was already in this country illegally). The rest had gone smoothly, though the hardest part, she knew, still lay ahead.

She collected her suitcase and pushed her way through the revolving door onto the curb, where she was met with a blast of bitter cold. Cold such as she had never known before, not even on those nights in the desert after the heat of the day had evaporated like the waters of a flash flood from an *arroyo*, leaving them all huddled around their meager campfire, shivering in their insubstantial clothing. The thin wool overcoat that she'd purchased at a secondhand store in LA, where winters were never this brutal, was scant protection against it, and she found herself wishing that she'd thought to buy a scarf and gloves as well.

She boarded the shuttle bus to which a skycap had directed her, and soon she was on her way into the city. Originally, she had intended to head straight to the Señora's, but she'd quickly discarded that plan. First she would need to get her bearings. Tomorrow morning, after a night's rest, she would take a bus or a train to this place called Stone Harbor, where the Señora lived. (Jesús had gotten the address off the Internet.) She'd rejected Jesús's suggestion that she go instead to the Señora's place of business in the city, arguing that it was too risky. Important people like the Señora were always surrounded by layers of functionaries, any one of whom could alert the authorities before Concepción got anywhere near her. Most likely, she would never make it past the reception desk. Besides, she was far more likely to catch the Señora alone, with her guard down, at home.

Lulled by the rocking motion of the bus, Concepción closed her eyes and let her head fall back against her seat. Her thoughts drifted back to the night before. Jesús's truck had been waiting at the curb when she'd come out of the building after her last day of work. And, as on the previous occasion he'd come to pick her up, he hadn't taken her straight home. With the firmness of a man who would brook no argument, he'd said, "Tonight, you will stay with me."

It had been late, and she'd been on her feet for the better part of the past eight hours, nor had she slept well the night before, due to anxiety over her forthcoming trip, but all her weariness had been swept away by her pleasure at seeing him and by the stirrings of something she hadn't experienced in so long she'd almost forgotten what it was like—a feeling like butterfly wings brushing against the insides of her belly . . . and below.

Once they arrived back at his place, though, he grew less sure of himself. As if to give her the opportunity to back out, he offered more timidly, "We could sit and talk, if you'd prefer." He gestured toward the sofa, with its painting of the Virgin on the wall above it. "Would you like some coffee?"

Her response was unequivocal. "Thank you, no—I never drink coffee this late. And we can talk just as easily lying down as sitting up." She spoke the last part with a hint of seduction in her voice.

Jesús's whole face lit up. He needed no further encouragement. And if he'd expected any shyness from her in the bedroom, he was in for another surprise. For although Concepción hadn't lain with a man in years—not since the widowed pharmacist whose company she had briefly enjoyed back in the days when Milagros was still in school—she hadn't forgotten the feel and taste of it, the urges that took hold of you like some *bruja's* spell. She took her clothes off with no coaxing from Jesús. And when at last she stood naked before him, it was without shame. She didn't apologize with her stance for her belly that was marked with creases from all the babies she'd borne, creases like the dried-up tributaries of a once mighty river, or for her full breasts that were no longer taut. *Take me as I am, or not at all*, was the message she delivered with her eyes.

"I'm not as young as I once was," she said in a tone that was almost defiant.

"Nor am I." Jesús cast a rueful glance down at his thickening belly.

"I only wish . . ."

"What do you wish, *mi corazón?*" he asked, drawing her into his arms.

"That you could have seen me before I cut off all my hair." She smiled, self-consciously fingering the neatly trimmed ends. Her hair had grown out to below her ears, but she missed the long braid that used to swing at her waist—the last vestige of her youth.

Slowly he shook his head. "You're beautiful to me just as you are," he whispered.

At first his kisses were almost reverent, as if Jesús half feared that she would vanish into thin air with but the gentlest of touches, like some figment of his imagination, but as she coaxed him along, with murmured words and caresses, he became bolder. Even then, he acted as if she were bestowing a great favor on him. She could see herself mirrored in his eyes, like some precious gift of which he wasn't entirely sure he was worthy.

But if anyone was unworthy, it was she. *Who am I to be placed on a pedestal?* she thought. She, whose hands were as rough as a man's, whose face was marked by life's passages. It was she who ought to be thanking Jesús, on whose broad shoulders rested her burdens as well as his.

As they lay together on the bed, wrapped in each other's arms, she marveled at the sturdiness of his body—his arms and legs roped with muscle and all the places that were hard where she was soft. No, he wasn't handsome, but that somehow made him all the more desirable. Her husband, in his youth, had been the handsomest man in their village (and hadn't he known it, too, with all his preening?) but he'd only disappointed her in the end. Jesús, she knew, would never abandon her as Gustavo had. Instead, it was *she* who was leaving him.

But not on that night. That night, she was his fully and completely. As they moved together, joined in body and in spirit, there was no thought in her head of what the future would hold. No thought of the suitcase packed in readiness back at her place. There was only Jesús's warm breath against her neck . . . his hands touching her in places that would have made a virgin blush . . . his body moving against hers like a slow-swelling tide. And then that tide was carrying her out to sea, only to toss her ashore moments later, limp and sweating and gasping for breath.

Afterward, lying blissfully spent in his arms, she was struck by a profound realization: All this time, until now, she'd been dead and simply hadn't known it. Content to exist in that state only because she hadn't known what she was missing out on. And the terrible irony was that it had taken Milagros's death to free her from that self-imposed prison. It was difficult for Concepción to admit that some good had come of that tragedy, but it was no use denying it. From the ashes of the fire that had killed her daughter, she, Concepción, had emerged as a woman capable of feats that she never would have imagined before this. A woman who wasn't afraid of anything or anyone. She felt a moment of sadness then, knowing there would be no returning to the shallow level of contentment she'd known and that, having tasted life, she'd be doomed to forever thirst for it.

Now, as she rode the bus toward her destiny, whatever that might be, she was turning the steel galvanized in that fire to a flintier purpose. She pictured the Señora as she'd looked in the magazine photo Concepción had seen. In it, the Señora had been shown picnicking out on the lawn with her husband and pretty young daughter, the three of them seated around a lavish repast that she'd presumably prepared. Her lovely face had appeared relaxed and content, and there had been nothing to spoil the perfect family portrait. But suppose it had been *her* daughter who had been killed? Would she have been smiling then?

The bus deposited Concepción at the Port Authority terminal, another vast and teeming place, from which she emerged onto an equally busy street. Pedestrians bustled past her on the sidewalk and vehicles rushed by on the street, honking their horns: yellow taxicabs, trucks and buses, shiny new *gringo* cars. A man whom she took to be a beggar, from his raggedy clothes and the black plastic garbage bag tied about his shoulders like a cape, eyed her hopefully as she hurried past clutching her purse in one hand and her suitcase in the other. But she had no coins to spare.

In her pocket was a slip of paper with the address of a hotel written on it in Jesús's neat hand. It was the least expensive hotel he could find within walking distance of the terminal, but even so, she'd balked at the price. Forty dollars! Nearly a quarter of her savings just for one night. Still, it was that or sleep out on the sidewalk. If her only concern had been being out in the elements, she wouldn't have let that stop her—hadn't she endured far worse than cold weather?—but there was also the risk of those who would rob and possibly kill her. To have come this far only to meet her end as some nameless *indigente* on the street? No, it was unthinkable. She might have been poor, but she had her dignity.

But the hotel that on the street map had looked to be close by turned out to be a long distance for someone traveling on foot, lugging a suitcase. By the time she reached it, her feet hurt and she was chilled to the bone. She made her way past a group of boys on the sidewalk talking loudly to one another, dressed in what she'd come to think of as the uniform of young black men from poor neighborhoods—baggy pants that hung from their hips seemingly in defiance of gravity, hooded sweatshirts large enough for someone three times their size, and expensive-looking sneakers that showed no trace of dirt, despite how grimy the streets were. They paid her no notice as she walked past them and climbed the steps to the entrance.

As she entered the lobby, its harsh fluorescent lighting greeted her like a polar sunrise. A heavyset *gringo* with thinning hair and pouches under his eyes sat behind the reception desk, smoking a cigarette, despite the sign prominently displayed on the wall above his head that read, "NO SMOKING."

"Yeah, we got rooms," he informed her none too politely. "You gotta pay in advance, though. Cash," he added, his eyes flicking over her as she stood there in her cheap shoes and secondhand coat, looking very much like someone who'd arrived on foot.

"I have money," she said, quickly reaching into her purse.

Minutes later, she was climbing the staircase, then making her way down a dingy hallway. Her room turned out to be even more cramped than the one she'd shared with Soledad and her two sisters back in LA. The only furniture was a twin bed, a small dresser, and a nightstand ringed with watermarks. The carpet was worn threadbare in spots, and in place of a closet there was a metal bar fixed to the wall, with a handful of wire hangers that tinkled forlornly in the gust of air that blew into the room as she shut the door behind her. In a corner of the room was a small sink with a folded towel on its rim. The toilet, she had been informed by the *gringo* at the front desk, was down at the end of the hall.

Nevertheless, after her long trip and the even longer-seeming walk in the cold, Concepción thought, *A palace.* She pried her shoes from her swollen, aching feet and stretched out on the bed, not even bothering to take off her coat. Tomorrow, she knew, she would rise with a keen sense of purpose. But right now, all she could think of was sleep. The need to sleep was so overpowering, it took precedence over the grumbling of her belly, her need to urinate, even thoughts of the Señora.

Concepción's eyes drifted shut, and in the half-awake state just before her conscious mind set sail, she saw, like a full moon rising in the velvety darkness behind her closed eyelids, the smiling face of her daughter. Milagros. Beaming down at her like the Virgin of Guadalupe herself.

Phoebe appeared to take the news in stride.

"Like you're telling me something I don't already know?" she said upon her parents' announcement that they were getting divorced. She looked as bored as she would have been by the rerun of an episode of *The OC.*

"I suppose we should have discussed it with you earlier," Abigail replied apologetically. "But your father and I weren't sure if this," meaning the separation, "was going to be temporary or not." It had become clear to her as soon as Kent had moved out that he wasn't coming back, but she wanted to soften the blow to Phoebe.

But Phoebe was no dummy. "Dad's shacking up with some other woman, and I'm supposed to think it's just a temporary thing? Yeah, right." She rolled her eyes. "God, you guys are so pathetic."

The three of them were gathered in the living room, the setting for so many cozy domestic scenes through the years, a fire crackling in the hearth and Brewster sacked out on the rug, but the mood was anything but cheery. And judging by the dark circles under Phoebe's eyes, it was obvious, despite her pretense at being bored by all this, that it was weighing on her.

Abigail bit her tongue before she could scold Phoebe for her rudeness. "We know it hasn't been easy for you, sweetie. But we—*I*—" She caught herself, thinking there was no "we"; it was just going to be her from now on, "think it'll be better for all of us this way."

"The one thing your mom and I agree on," Kent interjected, "is that you come first. We both love you very much, and we don't want to see you get caught in the middle."

But Phoebe only sat there shaking her head, as if she couldn't believe they thought she was that stupid. "Seriously, like you're not gonna expect me to choose sides? Get real."

"Baby, I know this is hard for you." Kent wore a deeply pained look. "But your mom and I are going to do our best to make sure this doesn't get ugly. And nothing's changed as far as you and I are concerned. We'll still see each other every chance we get. In fact, there's a spare bedroom at Sheila's, and she suggested making it *your* room for when you stay over. We could even go shopping together to pick out stuff for it. How does that sound?"

Phoebe gave him a withering look. "Honestly, Dad? No offense, but I'm not going to be staying with you and what's-her-name. Ever."

The look of contempt she wore was one that Abigail had never expected to see directed at Kent. She might have derived a sliver of satisfaction from his getting the medicine he deserved, and from his finally being given a taste of what *she'd* been putting up with for so long, if she hadn't felt so bad for Phoebe. She knew how close Phoebe was to her dad; his moving in with another woman had to seem as much a betrayal to her, in some ways, as it did to Abigail.

Kent, slumped in the wing chair by the fireplace, cast a helpless look at Abigail. But she wasn't going to bail him out of this one. *He's the one who got us into this mess*, she reminded herself. At the same time, she knew that pitting herself against him would only prove Phoebe's point.

Abigail gritted her teeth as she turned to her daughter, saying sweetly, "You feel that way now, honey, but I'm sure that once you get used to the idea, it won't seem so bad."

Phoebe gave a harsh laugh. "You guys *so* don't get it."

She stood up and sauntered out of the room, leaving Abigail and Kent to puzzle over what it was, exactly, that they didn't get.

The following day, Abigail learned that her family life wasn't all that was in ruins. She was in her office at work, tackling the paperwork on her desk, when Hank Weintraub, CFO of Abigail Armstrong Incorporated, poked his head in to ask if he could have a word with her. She waved him in, even though she was swamped at the moment. From the somber expression on Hank's face, she had the uneasy feeling that this couldn't wait.

He sank into the Barcelona chair opposite her desk. "I was up half the night going over the figures," he began without preamble. "Abigail, we can't keep on ignoring the facts. Net revenues have slipped five percent since our last quarterly report. Unless we do some serious damage control, I don't want to even think about what the next quarter will look like."

The normally unflappable CFO was noticeably worried, and from the way he was compulsively picking at a cuticle on his thumb—a nervous habit of his when he was under more than the usual amount of stress, like around tax time—it was obvious that he wasn't overstating the crisis.

"What are you saying, Hank? That we're going to have to file for Chapter Eleven?" Abigail spoke in a mild tone despite her mounting anxiety. It wouldn't do for Hank to see the boss sweat.

"No . . . no. It's not *that* dire. Not yet," he added ominously. "But if we don't get our numbers up, it's not something we can rule out down the line. I just got off the phone with Citibank." Hank had been in talks with the bank about restructuring their current loan. "They're balking, for some reason. They won't say why, but I have a bad feeling they're going to call the loan."

"That's insane! They can't do that." Abigail momentarily lost her cool.

"They most certainly can, and they will if we don't come up with either the cash or an alternative plan." Hank was shaking his balding head, looking every inch the accountant he'd been, before she'd plucked him out of obscurity and elevated him to CFO, in his brown suit and Oxfords, his Yale rep tie. He wasn't flashy, but he was always the sanest of voices in any given crisis. She was counting on him to be that now.

"You told them the only reason the numbers look bad is because we fell behind on those orders? Once we're back on track . . ."

"They're not interested in projected figures. They only want hard ones."

She leveled her gaze at Hank, wearing a small, grim smile. "Go on, say it. I know you're dying to. You advised against us taking on the manufacturing ourselves." He'd warned that the high risk factor would outweigh the greater profit margin. "And I insisted on going my own way."

He shook his head. "There's nothing to be gained from saying I told you so. What's done is done. All I'll say is that we'd better get that factory rebuilt and up to speed before too long or we're cooked. If there are any further delays . . ." He didn't have to finish the sentence. His dour expression said it all.

"All right." Abigail took a deep breath. "Let's talk about what we can do in the meantime . . ."

Her voice was businesslike as she consulted with Hank on a plan for cutbacks, but inside her mind juddered and spun like a wheel about to come loose from its axle. She thought about the dead girl's grieving mother. She hadn't heard anything new from Perez in a while, but if the woman was in this country, presumably she was on her way here. She could show up at any time. And what then? Would she be satisfied by more money or an explanation that seemed lame even to Abigail? Or would she hold Abigail's feet to the fire?

She might even go to the press. It would be no more than Abigail deserved, but she would hate to see the company and all its employees suffer, too, for the hit she would take. Because, for all of Hank's dry facts and figures, she knew that a business was made up not of numbers but of people, people who'd become important to her and who depended on her for their livelihoods. What would happen to *them* if her company should go under?

Yes, Hank had warned about the perils of manufacturing. But she'd pigheadedly ignored his advice. And look what had come of it! That poor girl would be alive today if not for her.

To add to her troubles, the rebuilding of the factory in Las Cruces was taking longer than anticipated. There had been one delay after another, both with the insurance company here and with the authorities in Mexico—the usual maddening bureaucratic roadblocks and red tape. And as Hank had so pointedly reminded her, these setbacks were coming at a time when the company could least afford them.

Now Abigail forced herself to confront the very real possibility that she could lose everything. If so, would she be able to start over? Anything was possible, she told herself, struggling to suppress her apprehension. She'd survived Kent's leaving her. And look at Lila. She'd had to start all over from scratch, and it hadn't killed her. Just the opposite; it had made her stronger and more resourceful—a person whom Abigail was actually beginning to like again.

She hadn't fully forgiven Lila. But they'd made peace with one another. They'd been talking more lately, not just civil exchanges but actually *talking*. Also, Lila had been surprisingly evenhanded about the domestic upheaval in the wake of Kent's moving out. She had studiously avoided taking sides while at the same time making it clear to Abigail that she was there for her if Abigail needed her. So far—except for that one night when they'd polished off a bottle of Dom Perignon and had stayed up until long past midnight alternately cursing and bemoaning not just their men but the entire male species—that need hadn't arisen, but it was reassuring to know that Lila had her back.

As Abigail discussed various belt-tightening measures with her CFO, she felt her anxiety start to ebb. She wasn't powerless. And even if the company went belly-up, she would still have her own, very marketable name. Starting over wouldn't be the end of the world. She'd done it once;

she could do it again. Perhaps, as with the ending of her marriage—which, however difficult, was proving to be a relief in some ways—she would even find a silver lining in it somewhere. Even if it was only a lightening of the yoke—a yoke that, though fashioned by her own hand, weighed on her heavily at times. Where had it gotten her, that ambition, except to a pinnacle where she was not only alone but in danger of falling into the abyss?

Somehow she managed to respond intelligently to Hank's suggestions. By the end, she felt she had a handle on it. She told him, "This all sounds good. Why don't I give it some thought over the weekend, and we'll talk again on Monday? In the meantime, I'll make some calls." First on the list was Perez. She would also reach out to Mr. Henry, her former employer from Greenwich, who was retired now but who still had ties to the banking world—he might be able to help her line up another bank to take over the loan. "Good work, Hank." She gripped his hand as he was heading out the door. "I want you to know how much I appreciate all your hard work. We'd be in a lot worse shape if it weren't for you."

He reddened, looking ridiculously pleased, which left her wondering if she had been overly stingy with her praise in the past.

Alone at last, she contemplated the long list of names on the call sheet in front of her, ordered in terms of priority, all of them people with whom she had business of varying degrees of importance to discuss. But there was only one person she *wanted* to talk to . . .

Before she knew it, she was punching in Vaughn's number.

"Are you doing anything right now?" she asked when she had him on the line.

"Other than reading up on the various methods of mosquito extermination in east Africa? No, why?" he replied with a wry chuckle.

He'd been working his way through Gillian's collection of *Time-Life* books as a way to pass the time while he recuperated. She hesitated before answering, "I was thinking of playing hooky." The last thing she wanted to do was tax him with a visit if he wasn't up to it.

"Intense day?"

"You don't know the half of it." She sighed. It was irresponsible of her, she knew, to cut out in the middle of the day, especially with so much at stake, but if she didn't take a break, she wouldn't be of much use to anyone, least of all herself. "Are you going to be home for a little while?"

"Where else would I be?"

"I don't know, out wrestling alligators in Central Park?" She kept it light, knowing he hated being reminded of the reason for his forced captivity.

He laughed. "No such luck. In fact, I could use the company. How soon can you get here?"

She felt a spark catch in her chest and flare as she reached under the desk for her handbag. "I'm on my way."

You're out of breath. Did you run the whole way?" Vaughn grinned at Abigail as she stepped through the door. It wasn't often that she dropped by on a moment's notice—usually her visits were planned a day or two in advance—and he seemed delighted to see her.

She kissed him on the cheek. "No, but try getting a cab in this weather."

"What happened to your driver?"

"I gave him the day off. Some sort of family crisis—he had to be in Hoboken."

Vaughn's eyebrows went up, but he offered no comment. She knew what he was thinking, though: Since when did she give an employee the day off because of a family crisis?

Since I found you. The words hovered on her lips, unspoken.

She glanced around her as she shrugged off her coat. "Where's Gillian?" Vaughn's ex-girlfriend usually made her presence known when Abigail visited. Even when she had work to do, she found excuses to putter around the loft rather than hole up in her studio. It was a surprise—a pleasant one, Abigail had to admit—to find Vaughn alone for a change.

"Bryn Mawr," he replied. "Her show opens in a few weeks. She's meeting with the curator this afternoon, then having dinner with some of the patrons who're sponsoring the show. She won't be back until tomorrow."

Abigail recalled now Gillian's having mentioned that she was having a show at a small museum associated with Bryn Mawr College, just outside Philly. "Sounds like a great gig. I'm sure it'll be a success," she said. Abigail always bent over backward to be generous toward Gillian, despite Vaughn's ex-girlfriend having little use for her. It was more gratitude than anything else. Not only was Abigail grateful that Gillian took such good care of Vaughn, she knew that if it hadn't been for Gillian, he wouldn't have had a place to stay in the city and might have had to seek treatment in some foreign hospital where he wouldn't have received the same level of care. And where would he be now, if that had been the case?

Where would *she* be?

If at one time Abigail had cast herself in the role of helpmate to a seriously ill friend, the tables had been turned: Now it was just as often Vaughn ministering to her as the other way around.

"Can I offer you a glass of wine?" he asked, padding into the kitchen.

She noticed that he wasn't wearing any shoes, just a pair of gray wool socks. It made her think of an old snapshot that she'd seen of him recently. The other day, she'd been helping Lila carry a piece of furniture over to her place—a small bookcase out of Kent's old study, which Abigail was turning into a sewing room—and they'd been lugging it into the bedroom when she'd happened to spy a framed photo on the dresser. A photo of a much younger Vaughn—the Vaughn she remembered from her youth. She'd picked it up to examine it more closely. In it, he'd been posed barefoot and bare-chested on some tropical beach, brown as a native, wearing only a pair of baggy swim trunks, his longish, sun-bleached hair blowing in the breeze. He might have been on the cover of a romance novel for how heat-struck Abigail had been as she'd stood there gazing at it. He looked that way now, in his oldest jeans and a checked flannel shirt the same deep shade of blue as his eyes, unbuttoned over a faded Greenpeace T-shirt—only slightly older and without the long hair.

"I'd better not," she said. "I haven't had anything to eat all day. It would only go to my head."

"In that case, how about a sandwich?"

"That would be nice, if it's not too much trouble."

"No trouble at all. Have a seat."

She sat down at the table, watching as he fetched a loaf of bread and a Saran-wrapped bowl of tuna salad from the fridge. She'd had her secretary cancel her lunch at the Four Seasons with Bernice Goodman, from *Country Living*, and now she smiled at the irony of her dining out on a tuna sandwich instead of Dover sole and finding it vastly preferable.

When he'd finished making the sandwich, he carried it over to the table, along with a pitcher of sweet iced tea, which he was never without—the last vestige of his southern heritage—and sat down across from her, pouring them each a glass of tea. "Aren't you having anything to eat?" she asked, noting that he hadn't brought a plate for himself.

"Nah, you go ahead. My appetite's a little off these days," he told her, a reminder that he'd started his second round of chemo earlier in the week.

That was all he said on the subject. Abigail didn't press him on it. When Vaughn felt like discussing his health, he did. The rest of the time, he kept quiet about it, as if he wanted their time together to be a retreat from all that. Usually when she was with him, she was able to tuck all of that into the back of her mind, too. It was only every so often—like just now—that the thought would hit her like a blow to the solar plexus: He—they—might not have all the time in the world.

She was encouraged, though, by the fact that he'd fleshed out some even since her last visit. He'd managed to get some sun as well. Leave it to Vaughn to find the one ray of sunshine in the gray doldrums of winter. With his hair already in need of a trim, he looked less like a cancer patient than a rangy explorer emerging from the wilderness after weeks of living off what he could forage.

After she was finished eating, they moved into the living room, where they settled on the sofa. Abigail gazed out the floor-to-ceiling windows spanning that end of the loft. "Looks like there's a storm brewing," she said, taking note of the dark clouds massing above the roof of the Flat-iron Building off to the east. A moment later, it was confirmed by the rumble of thunder. "I should have brought an umbrella. You wouldn't happen to have one I could borrow?"

"Leaving already?" he teased. "You just got here."

"You know me, always thinking ahead."

"I thought that's why you liked coming here, to take a rest from all that."

"Right you are," she acknowledged with a laugh, kicking off her high heels and pulling her legs up under her. "Well, in any event, you're stuck with me until this blows over."

"Have you listened to the weather report? They're saying it could go on all night. In which case, you're welcome to stay over." He didn't have to remind her that Gillian wouldn't be around.

"Don't tempt me," she said.

Was it her imagination, the meaningful look he gave her? Lately she'd become aware of a new tension between them. Ever since Kent had moved out, she'd been fantasizing more and more about what it would be like with Vaughn. Vaughn must have been wondering the same thing because every so often she'd catch him looking at her a certain way: the way a man looks at a woman when he has more on his mind than the weather.

"How are things on the home front?" he asked now.

She felt a familiar pang, thinking of Kent. "Oh, you know . . . I have my good days and my bad days. Nights are the worst. It's not easy to get to sleep when you're used to having someone next to you in bed."

He nodded in sympathy. "You were married a long time."

"*Too* long, according to Kent." A note of bitterness crept into her voice.

Vaughn reminded her gently, "People fall out of love all the time. It's not a deliberate choice."

She sighed. "I keep telling myself that, but it's hard sometimes."

"Have you ever considered the possibility that he's doing you a favor?" She must have looked taken aback, for he hastened to add, "I don't mean to sound heartless. But usually these things work out for the best. Divorce can be a catalyst for change."

"Like you would know. You've never even been married, much less divorced," she replied, giving him an affectionate cuff on the arm. "Though I'm sure there have been plenty of women who've tried to corral you into it."

He didn't respond to that. He only gave his usual enigmatic smile. "All I'm saying is, once the smoke clears you might get a fresh perspective on all this."

She nodded thoughtfully. She'd already begun to see glimmers of the better life that awaited her. Right now, though, it was hard to see past the wreckage. "I suppose you're right," she said grudgingly. "At least I've stopped imagining all the ways I'd like to see him suffer. That's progress, I guess. One of these days I might even get around to remembering why it was I married him." She smiled at Vaughn. "What about you? How come you never got married? Seriously. You never told me."

He shrugged. "There was never anyone I loved enough to marry."

"Not even Gillian?" He shook his head, a fleeting look of remorse crossing his face. Or was it regret? "She's still in love with you, you know," Abigail went on. She hadn't meant to blurt it out like that. But she wasn't sorry it was out in the open. Vaughn's ex-girlfriend was the proverbial eight-hundred-pound gorilla they'd been tiptoeing around, and Abigail was curious to know where things stood between Gillian and Vaughn. Not that it was any of her business, as Vaughn had let her know the only other time she'd brought it up, and not that Abigail had ever seen him show anything more than affection toward Gillian, but men went to bed with women for all kinds of reasons, most of which had nothing to do with love. Why should Vaughn be any different?

But while Vaughn didn't deny that Gillian was in love with him, he didn't seem happy about it. "I suppose I should feel flattered that she still finds me attractive," he said morosely. "In my present condition, I'd have thought I'd be about as appealing as a blind, three-legged dog."

"So there's no chance of you two picking up where you left off?" Abigail tried to sound as if she were asking only out of casual interest, but she was aware of her heart rate picking up.

"No." His voice was soft with regret, but there was no equivocation in it.

Abigail was more relieved than she should have been. "Does Gillian know that?" she asked.

"I think she's gotten the message by now."

"Maybe, but hope springs eternal. Look how long I waited for you." She struck a lighthearted tone, but the remark was wrapped around a kernel of truth. She remembered when she used to fantasize about him swooping in to rescue her. She would imagine him showing up at her aunt and uncle's house and the two of them roaring off into the sunset in his shiny red truck. Practical concerns like where they would live and how they would support themselves never entered into the picture. But what was hope if not an absence of reason?

"Did you? Poor Abby. And all you had were those dopey letters I sent." Smiling, he scooted over to loop an arm around her shoulders, as he had so many times when they were growing up. Only this time it was different. She felt her breath grow short and her heart start to pound.

"They weren't dopey," she said. "They were . . ." *the only thing that kept me going.* "They gave me something to look forward to. And believe me, I didn't have much to look forward to in those days. I know it sounds crazy, but I always felt that you somehow *knew*, and that you were doing what you could to make it better."

"I didn't write because I felt sorry for you."

"Why did you then?"

"I *was* in love with you." His tone was so matter-of-fact that it took a moment for the words to register; then a delicious shock wave coursed through her. "I couldn't put *that* in a letter. I was afraid it would come across as sappy. So I wrote about all the mundane stuff instead."

"It was probably for the best. It would only have made it worse for me if I'd known how you felt." It would have been torture, in fact, since there was nothing either of them could have done about it. "Let's face it, for one reason or another, the timing's never been right. One of us is always leaving."

"I'm not going anywhere," he said, looking into her eyes.

"For now."

He smiled. "For now."

But she refused to think about that, about whether next time it would be distance or death that separated them.

Outside, there was another, louder crack of thunder, followed by a strobe flash of lightning. The storm broke and rain began sluicing down, pelting the windows with a sound like hurled gravel. She snuggled in closer to Vaughn, resting her head against his shoulder. He smelled of buttered toast and the old flannel shirt he had on, warmed by his skin.

Glancing down at his lap, she noticed the unmistakable bulge of an erection. It sent a pulse of excitement through her, and she was flooded with memories of that night out at the quarry. At the same time, it left her feeling more than a little panicky. Should she comment on it or pretend she hadn't noticed? What was the protocol for a newly separated woman and an old boyfriend who'd just confessed to having been in love with her?

In the end, listening to the rain, she only commented, "It's coming down pretty hard," while thinking, *That's not the only thing that's hard.*

"The invitation's still open if you want to stay over," he said. Was he serious? she wondered. He seemed to sense her uncertainty, for he put his hand under her chin and tipped her head up to meet his gaze. "What are you afraid of, Abby?" His eyes searched her face. Eyes like the clear waters of the quarry into which she'd dived on that long-ago night.

She didn't know what to tell him. What *was* she afraid of? Falling in love again so soon after her husband's leaving her? Or falling in love with a man who might leave her, too?

"Who says I'm afraid?" She aimed for a flippant tone, but with her breath short, it came out sounding more like a nervous whimper.

Smiling, he ran a finger down one cheek, igniting a trail of fire. In his eyes, she saw the same spark of challenge as on the night that he'd urged her to go swimming out at the quarry. "All right, then, let's put it to the test. Kiss me."

She didn't protest or pull away, which he must have taken as acquiescence. Holding her face gently cupped in his hands, he brought his lips to hers. It wasn't like when he'd kissed her out on the patio on that otherwise miserable Christmas night; there was nothing tentative or nostalgic about it this time. And if she'd felt any ambivalence then, there was no trace of it now. She twined her arms around his neck, kissing him back as uninhibitedly as she had the first time, as a teenager. She ran her fingers through the bristles of his newly grown-out hair, as soft as the worn flannel of his shirt. Curled against him, her body's curves and angles dovetailing perfectly with his, she felt as if she were coming home in a sense. Any fear she might have felt that they were starting down a road that could only lead to more heartbreak melted way, and with rain pelting down outside and lightning splitting open the sky, she opened herself to Vaughn as she hadn't to another human being in more than twenty-five years. Not even her husband.

Wordlessly they undressed and stretched out on the deep-piled rug in front of the sofa. The sight of Vaughn naked came as both a shock and a revelation. He was no longer the smooth-skinned youth with whom she'd lain at the quarry. She could see the toll that his illness had taken on him in the jutting angles of his frame and in the vivid scar from his biopsy under one arm, where they'd removed one of his lymph nodes. There were old scars, too, from some of his more colorful adventures overseas. Yet somehow all of it, the whole damaged package, only made him more beautiful in her eyes. He was like a wild, battle-scarred beast.

"Where did you get that?" she asked, pausing as she was caressing his thigh to run a finger over a puckered, purplish scar.

"In the Gobi desert, from a puff adder. Let's just say we didn't exactly see eye to eye." His tone was as matter-of-fact as if the bite had been nothing more than a bee sting. "By the time I made it to the nearest clinic, my leg was so swollen they had to cut me out of my pants."

"But you didn't let it stop you from going back. You didn't stop doing what you did because you were afraid," she said, thinking they were alike that way—neither of them was a quitter.

He caught her hand and brought it to his mouth, kissing her upturned palm. "No, I didn't. The only thing I've ever been afraid of is dying without having lived." For Vaughn, she knew, not to have lived to the fullest would have been a fate far worse than death.

In response, she drew him to her so that he was lying on top of her. Locked in an intimate embrace, they moved together as one. In a way, it felt strange making love to another man after so many years of being with just her husband, but in another way, strangely right. As if Vaughn and she were two pieces of a whole that had been torn apart and were now being joined.

"I'm not hurting you, am I?" he whispered in her ear.

"No, why?"

"You're crying." With his thumb, he brushed a tear from her cheek.

She gave a self-conscious laugh. "Trust me, it's a good thing."

Then she was holding on to him, holding on as if for dear life. A flicker of the old fear rose in her, and in that instant she felt herself sliding downward, sliding toward that old, dark place . . . only it wasn't dark anymore; it was warm and inviting. Moments later, she was coming with an abandon that took her by surprise. With other men, even Kent, it had always required a certain degree of conscious effort, but with Vaughn, it felt as natural as taking the next breath. It rolled through her, wave after wave of delicious, mindless sensation, leaving her literally tingling all over, from the top of her head all the way down to her toes.

Afterward, it was several minutes before she could speak or even breathe normally again. She was afraid that if she said anything, anything at all, she would betray her emotions. "I get it," she said at last. "So all this time you were just pretending to be sick."

He propped himself up on one elbow, smiling down at her. "That was good for you, was it?"

"Good doesn't begin to cover it."

He grinned. "For me, too. It's been a while."

"Well, I can see that you've had lots of practice."

"I've had my share," he replied casually.

"Are we talking a cast of thousands here?"

He shrugged, wearing the same enigmatic smile as when she'd previously asked about the women he'd known.

"So what now? Where do we go from here?" She attempted to strike a casual note, but the question was anything but casual.

Vaughn didn't answer. *Not a good sign*, she thought, her heart sinking. Finally, wearing a faintly apologetic look, he replied, "I'll be honest with you, Abby. I've never been very good at this part. The part where you snuggle in bed afterward and whisper sweet nothings in each other's ears. So don't be upset if I'm not telling you what you want to hear."

"Well, since technically we're not in bed, it looks as if you're off the hook." She spoke lightly, but she couldn't help feeling let down. She'd hoped for—what? Words of love? It was too soon for that.

Or maybe too late.

"Don't take it personally. It's a guy thing. And, for the record, I meant what I said—that was amazing." He leaned in to run the tip of his tongue lightly over her lips, as if to capture any lingering sweetness.

Abigail knew she should let it go at that, but something made her ask, "So, was it different than with those other women?"

"Different? Yes, I'd say so."

"In what way?"

"With you, I feel . . ." He paused, frowning a little, as if searching for the right words. "I feel like I'm home. Only not the one I grew up in. The kind of home I'd want to be in if I were ever to settle down. Does that make sense?"

She smiled, feeling herself relax. "Perfectly." Didn't she feel the same way about him?

"So you're not upset with me?"

"No. Why should I be?"

"I don't know. With most women, it seems I only end up disappointing them."

"I'm not like most women, in case you haven't noticed."

"Oh, I've noticed, all right." He ran a hand down the length of her throat and over the curve of one breast, causing her to break out in goose bumps.

Then they were kissing again. Kissing with a hunger that made it seem as if their appetites hadn't been sated just minutes before. After they were done making love for the second time, she drifted off to sleep, along with Vaughn, their entwined bodies keeping them warm. When they awoke, it was almost dark, and rain was still pouring down outside.

Abigail peered at her watch and groaned. "Lord in heaven, how did it get to be this late? Phoebe will be wondering what's keeping me." Though it was probably wishful thinking on Abigail's part—most of the time her daughter went out of her way to avoid her.

"I wish you could stay the night," he said, nuzzling her ear.

"I wish I could, too." She was sorely tempted, but duty called. It was with the greatest reluctance even so that she rose to retrieve her clothes, which were scattered over the sofa and floor. They dressed in silence, neither wanting to break the spell that would send them catapulting back into the real world, with all its attendant concerns and commitments.

"Thanks," she said when they were saying good-bye at the door.

"For what?" he asked, putting his arms around her and pulling her close.

"For showing me that life doesn't end with divorce."

"You didn't need me for that. You'd have figured it out eventually."

They stood that way a minute longer, swaying gently from side to side, as if to music that only they could hear. Then she was out the door, plunging into the wind-whipped rain, holding on to her borrowed umbrella as if for dear life.

It was well after dark by the time Abigail arrived home. The rain had tapered off some, but it was still coming down in fitful bursts. Cruising along the drive in the taxi she'd caught at the train station, she was relieved to see that the damage from the storm was minimal—some flooded areas and a few tree limbs knocked down here and there. Also, it looked as if the power was out. The house was dark. She didn't even have the porch light, normally on at this hour, to guide her way as she started up the front walk. Otherwise, she would have noticed the bedraggled figure huddled on the stoop.

When she finally spotted it, she came to an abrupt halt, her heart jumping up into her throat. The moon that had been playing hide-and-seek with the clouds broke through just then, revealing the figure to be that of a woman. A woman now rising to her feet and stepping out from the shadows of the portico.

"Señora Armstrong?" She was Hispanic, around Abigail's age, and soaked to the skin from the looks of it. Only her eyes were dry; they burned like hot coals. Her head held high, speaking in slow, careful English, she said, "I am Concepción Delgado."

16

At first Abigail couldn't move. Finally she unlocked her frozen limbs and, in a remarkably calm voice that betrayed none of her heart's fevered palpitations, said, "Señora Delgado. I've been expecting you. Why don't you come inside?"

The woman hesitated before inclining her head in a stiff-necked nod. By the pale light of the moon edging its way through the fraying cloud cover, Abigail could see that she was shivering, her jaw clenched with the effort to keep her teeth from chattering. Abigail had never seen anyone more pitiful-looking . . . or more proud. From the look on Señora Delgado's face, it was clear that she wasn't going to be intimidated by Abigail or her fancy house. Nor was she going to be seduced by them.

Abigail's hand shook as she let herself in with her key. She flipped on the light switch just inside the door before remembering that the power was out. No one was home, either. Only Brewster bounded out of the shadows to greet her, barking to let her know he hadn't appreciated being left alone in the dark. She wondered briefly where Phoebe was—she should have been home long before now—before her mind was jerked back to the situation at hand. She led the way down the darkened hallway into the kitchen, where she fumbled in the top drawer of the pine hutch for the box of matches stored there. She found them and lit the candle in the glass holder on the hutch.

The dead girl's mother flared into view. A woman who under ordinary circumstances would have been called handsome but who right now looked like death, pale and shivering, with her short dark hair plastered against her head. Standing in the archway to the kitchen, her wet clothing dripping onto the tile floor, she might have been Persephone poised at the gateway to the underworld.

"Please, sit down. I'll make some cocoa. You look as though you could use some." Abigail gestured toward the kitchen table, but the woman made no move to sit down. She merely advanced a few steps until she was standing before Abigail, who had to fight the urge to shrink back. It was an effort to maintain her polite, forced smile. "Do you speak English?" she asked, though something told her the problem wasn't a language barrier.

"A little," Concepción replied in her heavily accented English. From her tone, Abigail got the feeling that "a little" would be more than enough.

"I understand you've come a long way," Abigail said, in an attempt to make conversation.

The woman nodded once more. "Yes."

"Perez told me you were coming."

"Perez," the woman spat in disgust.

"He also told me what happened." Abigail forced herself to look the woman squarely in the face, resisting the urge to retreat behind a diffusion of corporate-spun evasions. "I'm so sorry, Señora Delgado. Not just about your daughter, but about . . . well, you see, I didn't know. It wasn't until afterward that I learned . . ." Her hands fluttered in a helpless gesture.

The woman was silent, her flat, black-eyed gaze unwavering. Abigail gamely plowed on. "I felt awful about it, of course. I wanted to phone right away, but . . ." She faltered once more, realizing that she was already making excuses, when really there was no excuse. The plain fact was that she shouldn't have taken Perez's advice. She should have followed her own gut instinct. Now she grasped at the chance to make amends, even knowing it was probably too late. "Is there anything you need? Money? A place to stay?" Concepción shook her head, still wearing that haughty, scornful look. "Shall I call you a cab, then? You really shouldn't be out in this weather. Don't worry about the cost. I'll take care of it. In fact, I'd be happy to cover all your ex—"

Concepción cut her off before she could go any further. "There is nothing I want from you." Her dark eyes flashed.

Abigail eyed the woman in confusion. "I'm sorry. Then I don't know how I can help."

"There is no help. That is not why I am here." The dead girl's mother drew herself up to her full height. "I come to see for my own eyes the woman who took *mi hija* from me." She leveled an accusing finger at Abigail. "The blood of my daughter is on *you*, Señora."

Abigail flinched as if from a blow. She realized that the full impact of the girl's death hadn't hit her until now. The name Milagros Sánchez had been just that—a name, an unfortunate casualty. Now, looking into the face of the girl's grieving mother, Abigail wished desperately for something . . . anything . . . to help make up for this woman's loss. But what explanation could she offer? What words of comfort? Neither would bring any solace.

If she'd been at the office, there would have been staff to deal with this, but here, there was no escape. She was trapped, nowhere to run, pinned down by those terrible, hot eyes. The eyes of an avenging angel. Concepción had said or done nothing to threaten her, yet Abigail felt as frightened as if she were being held at gunpoint.

She managed to reply at last, in a low, shaken voice, "If I'd known . . . if I could've prevented it, believe me, I would have. You don't know how sorry I am."

Concepción shook her head in disgust. "Sorry? You are not sorry, Señora. You are only sorry because I am here. Now you cannot hide."

"Please, I know you're upset, but—"

The woman advanced another step. "You have a daughter, no?"

Abigail's back went up. "Let's leave my daughter out of this, shall we?" How did she know this woman wouldn't try to get back at her by hurting Phoebe in some way? She felt herself go cold at the thought. If only Kent were here! He was good in situations like these. Hysterical patients who came to him bleeding or with broken bones and whom he always managed to calm down.

"My Milagros, she was a good person. A good girl," Concepción Delgado went on in that same implacable tone. "She work hard for to make money to come to America and be with her husband. That is her dream. Now there is no more dream. Now my child is gone. But you no care. For you, she is nothing." Her pinched lips, blue with cold, were in stark contrast to the lancing heat of her gaze. Abruptly, she reached into her coat pocket and pulled out a photo, which she thrust into Abigail's face: a snapshot of a smiling, dark-haired woman who looked like a younger version of Concepción. "*Mirá*. See her face. Know what it is you have take from me." Tears stood in her eyes, but they were hard tears—black ice on the roadway over which Abigail now felt herself skidding. "You have your daughter. What do *I* have? Tell me that, Señora."

The shadows cast by the candle's flickering light loomed on the walls, seeming to close in on Abigail. The kitchen, fragrant with the scents of cinnamon and cloves and filled with beloved objects—the blue Spatterware bread bowl that had belonged to her mother, the sampler stitched by her great-grandmother and passed down through the generations, the lumpy clay dish made by Phoebe when she was in the first grade—suddenly seemed a cold and unwelcoming place.

"I know there's nothing I can say that will ever make up for your loss," she began, speaking slowly and carefully so that Concepción would comprehend . . . and so that she could maintain her grip on the control that she felt slipping away. "And I won't deny that I bear at least some responsibility for what happened. But when I gave the order to increase production, I had no idea that Señor Perez would put everyone at risk by taking certain . . . shortcuts." She'd been horrified when she had learned of it, in fact, and her first instinct had been to fire Perez. But he knew too much, and she didn't doubt that he'd use that to his advantage if need be. Now she realized how weak an excuse it must sound to Concepción, even as she struggled to make her see reason. "It was a terrible tragedy, yes. But there are times, in situations such as this, when no one is to blame. Sometimes it's just a series of bad decisions. People make mistakes. That's what this was, a mistake."

Concepción may not have understood every word, but she'd understood enough. She sucked in a breath, her eyes glittering and twin dots of color appearing on her pale cheeks, like bloodstains on snow. "*Mistake?* You would say the same if it was *your* daughter?" she demanded, cutting to the heart of the matter with that one simple sentence.

The truth was that if it had been Phoebe, Abigail not only would have fired Perez, she'd have seen to it that he never worked again—in fact, she would have made his life a living hell. In that unguarded moment, she regarded the woman standing before her, a woman who was a stranger to her but with whom Abigail had one important thing in common: They both knew what it was to be a mother. She said ruefully, "It's always different when it's your own child, isn't it?"

Their eyes locked: two mothers acknowledging the truth in that statement. Concepción said, "Then you will know what I have come for to do. Why I am here. There can be no rest for me, for Milagros, otherwise."

Something in her voice caused Abigail to stiffen. "Is that a threat?"

Concepción bared her teeth in a smile of triumph. "You are afraid? Good. You should be afraid, Señora."

The dead girl's mother carried no weapon. In her present, bedraggled state, she didn't look as if she posed much of a physical threat, either. But appearances could be deceiving, and Abigail knew firsthand what that kind of grief could do to a person. The day after her mother had died, when her uncle had slipped into her room under the guise of consoling her, she'd said, "You ever lay a hand on me again, old man, you'd better be prepared to stay awake for a long, long time. Because the minute you fall asleep, I'll take that ax out back and chop you into little bits."

Uncle Ray must have seen something in her eyes that had made him wonder if it wasn't an idle threat, for he'd backed away at once and had never come near her again. Abigail didn't know what she would have done if he hadn't. She doubted that she would have gone so far as to chop him into little bits, but one thing she knew for certain: He wouldn't have emerged unscathed.

Before she knew it, she was reaching for the phone on the wall. She'd punched in 911 before she realized there was no dial tone. Whatever had brought the power lines down had most likely taken the telephone lines with it. And her cell phone was still in her purse, which she'd dropped on the table in the front hall when she'd let herself in—a distance that suddenly seemed like miles. And what would she have told the dispatcher, anyway? *A woman I invited into my house refused my hospitality and is now threatening to*—what? Concepción had issued no specific threat. She'd done nothing violent.

It was partly her own guilty conscience at work, Abigail realized. Still, she couldn't shake the fear that crawled up into her throat.

"I think you'd better leave," she said.

Concepción gave her a long look—a look that burned straight down into Abigail's soul. "Don't worry, I will go, Señora, but remember this— I will be here, always, in you." She tapped her forehead. "You will no forget the name of Milagros Sánchez."

At that moment, Concepción Delgado seemed to represent everything that had gone wrong with Abigail's life. All the mistakes she'd made. Everything she'd lost and stood to lose. The woman was a pillar carved from granite, a monolith of a finger pointed at her in accusation. The puddle of water at her feet, glistening dark in the faint, guttering candlelight, might have been blood.

Her legs trembling, Abigail gripped the edge of the counter for support. "Go. Please. Just go." It came out sounding less of an order than an appeal.

From the damp folds of her coat, Concepción pulled a dignity befitting a queen. With a look more eloquent than any words, she turned and

majestically retreated into the shadowy recesses of the hallway, so noise-
lessly that Abigail might have believed she had been an apparition if not
for the puddle of water on the floor and the trail of glistening footprints
leading away from it.

Concepción stumbled along the drive, only vaguely aware of the direction
in which she was headed. When she'd arrived at the Señora's house, after
the seemingly endless walk from the train station in the pouring rain,
which had left her soaked to the skin, it had still been light out. Now it
was pitch black. She was dizzy as well—she hadn't eaten since breakfast—
and despite the rain, nearly as thirsty as when she'd been wandering in the
desert. An awful sense of futility closed over her like a fist. What had she
accomplished, other than to half kill herself in getting here? What colos-
sal punishment had she brought crashing down on the Señora?

Perdóname, mi hija. She turned her face to the sodden black belly of the
sky. Suddenly she knew the answer to Jesús's question: No, this was not
what her daughter would have wanted. Milagros would have wanted her
to forgive the Señora.

There was no justice to be had here, she realized. Even if a newspaper
would print her story, what good would it do? It wouldn't bring her
daughter back to life. Nor would it prevent something similar from happening to other poor, defenseless workers. There would be a brief outcry,
yes. But corruption would go on unabated; the rich would go on getting
richer off the backs of the poor; common decency would continue to be
sacrificed in the name of greed; and no one, except those who'd directly
suffered as a result, would even care.

As for the Señora, there might be some satisfaction in seeing her
brought down, but she wasn't the greed-driven monster Concepción had
imagined. Concepción had seen from the look on her face that she was
not without a conscience. And though whatever remorse the Señora
might feel was nothing compared to what Concepción had had to en-

dure, Concepción also had to admit there had been some truth to the Señora's words, when she'd said that it was different when it was one's own child. Would she, Concepción, have felt this towering sense of outrage had it been another woman's child who had died in that fire? Sylvia Ruiz's girl, who'd worked in the station next to hers? Or that fat, silly daughter of Mañuela Ortega?

She squinted, straining to make out in the darkness the even darker shape that had appeared ahead. The moon had disappeared behind the clouds, so she could scarcely see two feet in front of her. It wasn't until she drew nearer that the dark shape materialized into a small shed. She veered off the drive, squelching her way through the muddy grass alongside it, heedless of her already ruined shoes. She tried the door to the shed, expecting it to be locked, but it opened with a turn of the knob. Concepción offered up a silent little prayer of thanks as she ducked inside. It was only temporary shelter, but she would be dry, if not exactly warm. And she wouldn't have to stumble around in the dark. Tomorrow, as soon as it was light out, she would find her way back to the train station.

Instantly she was assailed by the strong, earthy scent of cow dung. She fished in her pocket for the book of matches she'd picked up at the diner where she'd had breakfast—a cup of coffee and a plate of buttered toast, the thought of which now caused her belly to rumble. But they were damp from the rain, and she had to strike several before one caught and flared.

Looking around her in the flickering light of the match pinched between her thumb and forefinger, she saw an array of gardening tools—some hanging from pegs, others propped against the walls—a wheelbarrow, bundled stakes, a coiled hose, a mower under a plastic cover. The scent of cow dung, she saw, came from the sacks of fertilizer stacked at one end.

Quickly, before the match burned down, she located a stack of folded canvas tarps. She spread them over the concrete floor, sinking onto her makeshift bed as gratefully as if onto a mattress. Curled into a ball in an effort to warm herself, she felt closer to Jesús somehow amid these tools of his trade. But even the thought of his arms around her did little to ease her discomfort. Behind her closed eyelids rose an image of the Señora, the look on her face when Concepción had threatened to expose her, as if Concepción were some filthy *vago* attempting to rob her. An invisible band tightened around her rib cage, making it hard for her to breathe. She took in small sips of air between clenched teeth, pleading silently, *Díme, Dios.* What do I do now; where do I go from here?

Abigail rummaged around in the kitchen drawers until her hand closed around a flashlight. She switched it on, the beam bouncing about in her unsteady grip, leaping up walls and skittering over surfaces. Phoebe. She had to find Phoebe. The encounter with the dead girl's mother had left her nerves shattered and filled her with a sense of foreboding. It was probably unfounded, but nonetheless, she wouldn't rest until she'd made certain that her daughter was safe and sound.

Brewster picked up on her mood and began to whine, following closely at her heels as she headed upstairs to check Phoebe's room, grabbing her cell phone from her purse on the way up. But the room was empty. There was no one home over at Lila's, either; she peered out the window to find the place dark. The power was likely out over there, too, but she would have expected to see the flicker of candles or a flashlight. She remembered then Lila's having mentioned something about going out tonight. Neal must be out as well, for the Taurus wasn't in its usual spot alongside the garage. He and Phoebe had probably gone off somewhere together and simply lost track of the time, she told herself.

The thought did nothing to calm her nerves.

After trying Phoebe's cell and getting only her voice mail, she decided to phone Kent. It was unlikely that Phoebe would be with him, since their daughter had made it clear that she wanted nothing to do with either him or his girlfriend, but it wouldn't hurt to check.

"It's me," she said when he picked up. "I just got home and Phoebe's not here. Is she with you?"

"No. Was she planning on coming over?" Abigail pictured him frowning in puzzlement. He had to be thinking the same thing she was—that if Phoebe was on her way over to see him, their real daughter had been kidnapped by aliens and the one headed his way was merely a clone.

"I don't know. She didn't say."

"Is something wrong? You sound worried."

"I'm sure I'm overreacting," Abigail hedged, not wanting him to think she was turning into one of those abandoned wives who cling to their kids as a means of coping. "It's just that it's getting late and she hasn't phoned. I thought she might have gone over to your place."

Your place. How strange it felt to say that about somewhere other than this house.

Kent sighed. "I wish. But I'm afraid I'm radioactive right now as far as she's concerned." He spoke ruefully but didn't sound overly concerned. His tone was that of a father confident enough in his relationship with his daughter to know she'd come around eventually. "I wouldn't worry, though. She's probably out with Neal or one of her friends."

His calm demeanor that used to drive Abigail crazy was balm to her ragged nerves now. "You'll let me know if you hear from her?" In the background, she could hear the clinking of dishes and a light female voice over the sound of running water. She must have caught them in the midst of making supper. Abigail pictured them seated around the table chattering away as they ate—Kent and Sheila and her son—and felt something tighten inside her.

"Sure thing," he promised. "You do the same. Call me when she gets in so I know she's okay."

As soon as she hung up, Abigail headed back downstairs, grabbing her purse and keys on her way out the door. Brewster tried to follow, no doubt thinking it was time for his evening constitutional, but she shooed him back inside. "No, boy, not now. I have to find Phoebe."

Crossing the side yard on her way to the garage, she made a mental list of all the places that her daughter might be if she wasn't with Neal. The public library? The Beanery, where she often met her friends for coffee? The school—some event that had slipped her neglectful mother's mind? She began to feel a little foolish for being such a worry-wart, telling herself there was nothing more going on here than a case of shattered nerves.

Still . . .

Something scratched at the back of her mind, like the dog whining to be let out. Something Phoebe had said to her the other day. Shouted, rather. *Don't worry, Mom; I won't be around much longer to make your life miserable.* Abigail had assumed it'd had to do with her going away to college. But now she wondered if there had been a darker meaning. Suppose Phoebe was planning to do something stupid like skip college to bum around the world, as she'd once threatened to do? She could well afford to. She had some money saved up, and when she turned eighteen next year, she'd come into the trust fund that Kent's parents had set up for her.

Abigail felt her heart lurch at the thought. Phoebe could be on her way to the airport at this very minute, for all she knew.

Something else occurred to Abigail, far worse than her daughter's heading off into parts unknown. What if the Delgado woman had had something to do with Phoebe's absence? Abigail wouldn't soon forget those burning eyes. There had been Concepción's vaguely threatening words as well. And God only knew how long she'd been lurking about before Abigail had shown up.

Abigail jumped into her BMW, thinking the woman couldn't have gotten far on foot. If she was on her way to the train station, Abigail would soon catch up to her. Moments later, she was shooting down the drive in a spray of mud and gravel, her foot pressing down hard on the accelerator. *What have you done with my daughter?* she mouthed silently.

The answer came to her in a sickening flash: *An eye for an eye, a tooth for a tooth.*

"So, *are we* good to go?" Phoebe, seated on the bed in her room, her hands folded demurely in her lap, gazed up at Neal with an expression of calm resolve.

She looked amazingly serene, he thought, for someone about to kill herself.

He gave a tight nod as he stood there holding the glass of water he'd fetched from the bathroom. Then he set the glass down on the nightstand and lowered himself onto the bed. It wasn't just talk anymore. They had the means now: several vials of prescription drugs purchased from a guy he worked with at the deli who moonlighted as a drug dealer—they'd just come from Chas's house on the other side of town. They also had the opportunity: His mom was out, and so was Phoebe's.

It would be several more hours before his mom returned—she was having dinner with Karim—but he didn't know how long Phoebe's would be gone. She kept late hours, so presumably she was still at work, though he was less certain of that than he'd like to be, despite Phoebe's reassuring him that the coast was clear. He'd seen a black BMW the same model as Abigail's flash by, headed in the opposite direction, as he and Phoebe had been making the turn onto Swann's Road on their way here. Also, when they'd gotten to the house, he'd noticed mud tracked across the kitchen floor. Nervous about it, he'd suggested to Phoebe that they postpone their plans, thinking that her mom had merely stepped out and would be returning soon, but she'd brushed off his fears, insisting that the BMW he'd seen could have been anyone's—half the people around here drove black Beamers, she'd said—and that the muddy tracks on the floor were no doubt Brewster's.

Now Neal sat contemplating the enormity of what they were about to do. *It's the only way*, he told himself. He'd examined every other route, and they all led back to this one: the one his father had taken. Some might have seen it as the coward's way out, he knew, but to Neal it was more like the answer to a tricky equation in algebra that, once arrived at, seemed so simple you wondered why you hadn't seen it all along. And, as with algebra, for every problem there was only one solution.

Still . . . the thought of his mother kept snagging at his resolution, like a burr on a freshly honed blade. He knew how devastated she'd be, especially after having lost his dad the same way. Was it fair to put her through all that again? Just when she was starting to make a new life for herself?

Then Neal reminded himself bitterly that she'd still have her new best friend, Karim. His mother had billed tonight's date as just "a couple of friends getting together for dinner," but Neal didn't buy that. He'd have to be blind not to notice the way they looked at each other, like they wanted to rip each other's clothes off. However disgusting the thought, it was only a matter of time before they did just that, if they hadn't already. If anything was holding his mom back, he thought, it was her problem son. *Who won't be a problem much longer.*

He and Phoebe had weighed the various methods before deciding on this one. It seemed the most painless. Also the least messy. No blood or blasted bits of brain tissue; no bloated bodies to be fished out of the river. They'd researched it online so there wouldn't be any fuckups. It was amazing what you could find on the Internet. If he were a terrorist, he'd have all the information he needed to build a bomb, or if he were a serial killer, all the ways to off someone. Figuring out the best way to commit suicide had seemed almost ridiculously prosaic in comparison, like logging on to MapQuest for directions. Except there was no map for where they were going.

"What are you waiting for?"

Phoebe's voice broke into his thoughts. He looked over at her, noting the tiny crease between her brows. She was impatient to get on with it. He envied her, in a way. He wished that he could be as crystal-clear about this as she was, with no troubling thoughts to muddy the waters.

"What's the rush?" he said. "It's not like we have to be somewhere."

When they'd arrived home to find the power out, it had seemed the perfect metaphor for what they were about to do. As though observing some sort of pagan ritual, they'd lit candles and placed them throughout the house. Now, as he gazed fixedly at the fat, scented candle flickering

on the nightstand, which was making an eerie but beautiful phantas-
magoric display of the tumbler of water beside it, it had a strangely hyp-
notic effect.

From the flapped pocket of his army jacket, he withdrew the vials of
pills and dumped their contents onto the bedspread. Carefully, he
counted them out, dividing them evenly into two piles. Phoebe was
scooping one of the piles into her palm when the dog began scratching
at the door, whining to be let in. Neal saw her hesitate, frowning. The
only real emotion she'd shown tonight had been when they'd first walked
in and Brewster had come running to greet her, tail wagging. She'd knelt
down and put her arms around him, burying her face in his shaggy ruff.
When she'd brought her head up, there had been tears in her eyes.

Neal stared down at his pile of pills—half of them pink, the other
half white—which looked so innocuous scattered over the flowered bedspread. He thought of his uncle Vaughn, fighting for his life. It seemed
unfair somehow that his uncle had to suffer so while *he* was taking the
easy way out, like getting a free ticket instead of having to pay. But life
wasn't fair. Hadn't that been made abundantly clear to him already?

He reached for the glass of water on the nightstand. The pills were
like a lover's kiss as they left his palm, lingering for an instant on his
tongue before sliding down his throat. He watched closely as Phoebe
swallowed hers, looking for any signs of uncertainty. There were none.
She might have been downing a handful of vitamins. It wasn't until afterward that she acknowledged the seriousness of what they were doing by
saying, with a funny little smile, "No turning back now."

In the candlelight, her eyes were bottomless pools in which he could
see twin points of flame reflected. He wondered what kind of life she
would have had if she'd lived into old age. But when he tried to picture
her with wrinkles and gray hair, it was as strange and improbable as trying to imagine his mother married to someone other than his dad.

They lay down together on the bed, fingers entwined. The drugs were
starting to take effect. Neal's limbs felt heavy, and his head had somehow
become unhitched from his body.

"*Romeo and Juliet.* That's what they'll think when they find us," Phoebe murmured thickly.

"We should take our clothes off to make it look more convincing." Neal was feeling loopy, like when he'd had too much to drink at parties.

She giggled. "You want to see my tits again, DeVries, you'll have to wait until we get to wherever it is we're going."

Neal fell silent, pondering that. "You believe in heaven and hell?" he asked after a bit.

"Yeah, I guess."

"Any chance we'll get into heaven, you think?"

"We'll know soon enough, won't we?" she said. He frowned at her in annoyance, and she added more philosophically, "Look, if there's such a thing as heaven, it's only because life here on earth sucks. Anything would look good in comparison."

"Thanks for the lesson in theology." He felt angry at her for some reason. But it was a once-removed feeling, like listening to muffled shouting in another room. Mainly what he felt was . . . high. Pleasantly so. Like an astronaut at zero gravity, weightless, suspended in space.

Phoebe was quiet for so long that he thought she must have drifted off to sleep, but when he looked over at her, he saw her staring up at the ceiling with a look of such fixed concentration that it gave him a jolt: He might have been looking into the sightless eyes of a dead person.

A thick fog rolled into his brain, and he surrendered to it, losing himself in its velvety gray folds. Soon his eyes were drifting shut. *This isn't so hard,* he thought. *All you have to do is . . .*

. . . let go.

Minutes later—or was it hours?—he was roused by the acrid smell of smoke. In his foggy state, he was only distantly aware of it, like when he was asleep and had to pee. But, like the pressing of a full bladder, it grew increasingly insistent until at last it forced his eyelids open.

He could see it now, in the moonlight slanting in through the blinds: thin, pale rafts of smoke floating up near the ceiling. He felt a pulse of alarm, but it was muted, like the sirens he'd grown so used to, living in the city, that they'd been little more than white noise. It wasn't until he drew in a lungful of smoke and began to cough that it hit him: The house was on fire!

Christ. If they didn't get out, they'd be burned alive. It didn't occur to Neal, in his drugged state, that they would have died anyway. Apparently the will to live, which unbeknownst to him had been humming away in some remote sector of his brain, superseded all else.

He struggled into an upright position. "Phoebe!" He shook her, but her head only lolled on the pillow, her eyelids fluttering without opening all the way. "Phoebe!" he croaked again. "Come on . . . wake up. We gotta get out of here." His tongue felt thick and foreign in his mouth, like when he'd been to the dentist, making it hard to get the words out.

No response.

He tried hoisting her into a sitting position, but she only flopped back down again. With rising panic, he realized he had no choice but to leave her while he went in search of help. But even that seemed an impossible feat. He didn't see how he was going to propel himself past the bedroom door, much less down the stairs. And even if he could manage that, it might be too late by then. The smoke was thickening, making it harder to breathe with each passing second—not pleasant-smelling smoke like that from a wood fire but the smoke of burning refuse, oily and choking. He coughed again, violently this time, and somehow the act served to catapult him off the bed and onto the floor, where he landed with a thud.

On his hands and knees, he crawled toward the door, the way he'd been taught to do in school fire drills. But it was like an optical illusion: The closer he got to the door, the farther away it seemed. Downstairs, he could hear the dog's frenzied barking. Brewster was trapped inside, too, just like him and Phoebe, he realized with a sickening lurch of his belly.

With a mighty effort, Neal pushed himself the last few feet. Unthinkingly, he reached up to grab hold of the doorknob, and a searing bolt of pain shot through his hand and up his arm, causing him to cry out. But the pain had a galvanizing effect. The clogged pipe in his head opened another centimeter to allow a trickle of adrenaline into his bloodstream.

He had the presence of mind to pull off his shirt and wrap it around his throbbing hand, forming a sort of mitt, before he reached up to grab hold of the doorknob again. Then he was in the hallway, still on his hands and knees, battling his way toward the landing through onrushing waves of heat and roiling smoke. Downstairs, the dog went on barking in high, frantic yips. The only other sound was the crackling of flames from below. A comber of panic rose and crested in some unmuddled part of Neal's brain. This wasn't the city, where firemen would be crawling all over the place by now. They were out in the middle of fucking nowhere. No one was coming to rescue them. Even if he made it out alive, it would be too late for Phoebe by the time help arrived.

Dinner was an unexpectedly lively affair. Karim had taken Lila to a Turkish restaurant, where along with their meal had come entertainment in the form of belly dancing and a live trio playing traditional Turkish music. If she'd feared that their first real evening out would take place in an intimate restaurant where he'd try to seduce her over a romantic, candlelit dinner, she'd fallen victim instead to something far more insidious: a good time.

"I can't remember the last time I had this much fun," she said when the check finally arrived.

Karim smiled at her across the low table at which they sat, or rather reclined, on the plump tapestry cushions piled on the floor around it. He looked perfectly at home, like a Bedouin entertaining her in his tent. "You sound as if you weren't expecting it," he replied with a laugh.

"No, I can't say that I was." Lila, realizing how it must have sounded, was quick to say, "I'm sorry. That came out all wrong. It's just that since my husband . . ." She paused, waiting for the little catch in her chest that always accompanied any reminder of Gordon. But it didn't come. Another surprise on this evening full of surprises. "It hasn't been easy for me to kick back and relax. Nothing's ever the same after something like that. It's always there, in the back of your mind."

"Yes, I know." Karim nodded in sympathy. It wasn't just words—he *did* know. "Which is why I must thank you."

She smiled at him, perplexed. "Thank me? Why?"

"For allowing me to accompany you on this journey."

She knew what he meant, but she made light of it, feeling herself on shaky ground all of a sudden. "What, are we going somewhere I don't know about?"

He reached across the table to place a hand over hers. His eyes were black in the candle's mellow glow, and his mouth curled in a smile that sent a flood of warmth through her, as if she'd just tossed back a shot of vodka. "That's for you to decide," he said.

At the coat check, he helped her on with her raincoat. He paused to say a few words in Turkish to the owner, a courtly older man with a luxurious head of silver hair, as they were on their way out. The owner said something back to him, grinning as he clapped Karim on the shoulder while casting a meaningful glance at Lila, which she didn't have to speak Turkish to catch the drift of. She was blushing as they stepped through the door.

Any pleasant fuzziness from the wine they'd drunk with dinner ended with the gust of wind that came at them like a rude shove: the tail end of the storm that had broken earlier in the evening. Lila held tightly to Karim's arm as they made their way toward the parking lot. She felt a bit precarious, and not just from the wine. His presence, as always, had her off balance. The man ought to come with a warning label, she thought: *Beware! Can cause side effects such as dizziness, uneven heart rate, and loss of equilibrium.*

"You're very quiet," Karim observed when they reached his truck.

"I was just thinking about Neal," she said. It was partly true. She'd been thinking about her son on and off, all evening. "I was expecting him to give me a hard time when I told him you were taking me to dinner, but he acted like he couldn't care less. It was the weirdest thing." As if Neal had been a million miles away looking down at her from outer space. "Like he'd forgotten he even had a mother."

"He's in love," Karim observed with a chuckle as they climbed into the truck. "When I was his age, I once drove a donkey cart off the road into a ditch while in a similar state of mind."

She tried to picture the scene and found herself wondering briefly who the girl was that Karim had been so enamored of before her mind was drawn back to Neal. "Maybe that was it. . . . But I can't help wondering, if he's so in love, why is he miserable all the time?" It would make sense if Phoebe were giving him the cold shoulder, but she seemed just as crazy about him. "Isn't love supposed to make you feel like the world is your oyster? That's how it was with Gordon and me." *And the way it was tonight with you,* she added silently.

"Perhaps it's not love as we define it," Karim speculated. "Perhaps it's only that he and Phoebe give each other what they need."

"That's part of it, I'm sure," she said. "It's just that, with them, I always get the feeling that they belong to some secret society, like Skull and Bones, only it's a membership of two."

Karim switched on the engine, but made no move to put the truck into gear. He just sat there, staring straight ahead. The only sound was the spattering of rain against the windshield. "I've observed this, too," he said after giving it some thought. He turned to her. "But is it not typical adolescent behavior? It's the same in my country, young people rebelling against their parents. Though perhaps not quite so dramatically as here," he added, smiling.

"Neal's never been the rebellious type."

"Nor was I. But when I was his age, I had a battle with my parents that was so epic, my mother insists she still hasn't fully recovered from it."

She tilted her head to eye him curiously. "What about?"

"They wanted me to marry a girl they'd chosen for me—the daughter of close friends of ours—and I had my heart set on going to Cambridge, where I'd been granted a scholarship."

She smiled. "I don't have to ask who won." Karim nodded, though he didn't look happy about having been the cause of such parental displeasure. "But I don't think it's like that with Neal," she went on. "Something tells me this has more to do with his dad than with me."

"I'm sure that part of his unhappiness has to do with the fact that his mother is spending so much time with a man who isn't his father," Karim ventured more cautiously.

"No doubt. I told him we were just friends, but he's not buying it." Lila spoke briskly to counteract the flurries of emotion buffeting her like the gusts of wind rocking Karim's truck.

Karim rephrased it more accurately: "In other words, he has eyes in his head."

Lila felt herself grow warm, but she maintained her no-nonsense tone as she replied, "Okay, you've got me there. I won't deny it. But that doesn't mean I have to give in to those feelings." She might have been in a doctor's office, describing symptoms of an ailment. "I'm an adult. And adults are supposed to be able to control their impulses."

"They can, yes. But does that mean they should?"

He reached across the shadowy void that separated them and gently traced the outline of her jaw with his fingertips, his feather touch bringing an answering tug below her waist. He might have been running his hand between her thighs, so electric was the sensation. She was paralyzed by it, unable to pull away as those same fingertips traveled, light and sure as a safecracker's, down her neck to locate the curve of her collarbone— a part of her anatomy to which she seldom paid any attention but of which she was now acutely aware.

Still a little tipsy from the wine, she ignored all caution and leaned in to kiss him. She parted her lips and let his tongue play over hers. He tasted faintly of some exotic spice. She ran her fingers through the tight coils of his hair, which were unexpectedly soft, like lamb's wool. The only thing standing between them now, she noted with irony, was the rather awkwardly placed gearshift. But no matter. The newly liberated and somewhat inebriated Lila simply hitched up her skirt and climbed over it, plunking herself down without ceremony into Karim's lap.

Kissing him and letting him kiss her back, she refused to listen to the voice of reason in her head whispering that this wasn't just about sex. That there would be consequences far more serious than an attack of morning-after regrets. She could fall in love with this man. She could end up wanting more than this—his hands reacquainting her with her body, his lips moving light as a hummingbird's wings over her skin, his desire making its presence known through several layers of clothing— only to have her life shattered once again. Perhaps irreparably this time.

But it was too late to stop, even if she'd been in the mood to listen to that voice. When he reached under her sweater and unhooked her bra to cup her bare breasts, she moaned with pleasure, pressing against him to relieve the deliciously mounting pressure between her thighs. Oh, God. It had been so long. How had she managed to go this long without sex? She needed no further excuse, when he slipped a hand under her skirt, to wriggle out of her pantyhose. She hadn't made out in a parked car since high school, only now there was no feigned modesty, no murmured protestations when a hand climbed too high or too low.

She knew what she wanted. She wanted *this*. She wanted Karim.

It was the sound of a car engine firing nearby that brought her to her senses. She shrank down, flooded with embarrassment as the car swung past them, its headlights momentarily spotlighting them in its glare. The effect was that of a bucket of cold water dashed over her: She instantly sobered. God, what could she have been thinking? A grown woman with a grown son making out in a parking lot like some hormone-crazed teen- ager, especially a parking lot where they could easily be spotted— perhaps even by someone who would recognize her from her pictures in the paper. Someone who'd tell the story to a reporter, give it a titillating new angle. The press would dub her the "Merry Widow DeVries."

When the coast was clear, she crawled back over to her seat, mutter- ing, "Let's just get going, okay?"

Karim looked as though he was about to say something, but whatever it was, he thought better of it. Without comment, he put the truck into reverse and backed out. It wasn't until they were well on their way that she looked over and saw that he was smiling.

"What are you looking so damned pleased about?" she demanded.

"You," he said. "You're a woman of hidden depths, Lila."

"Depths, maybe. I don't know about hidden." Not after tonight.

"You shouldn't feel ashamed. You've done nothing wrong."

"I'm not ashamed," she said. "But don't expect an encore performance. Tonight was . . ." *unexpected, magical, thrilling.* "Well, let's just say I've had a little too much to drink."

"Oh, so now it's the evil demon alcohol that's to blame?" His smile widened into a grin.

"Just drive," she ordered gruffly. This kind of talk was only going to lead to more trouble.

They were a mile or so from home when she spotted the smoke rising above the treetops ahead—a charnel smear against the paler clouds from the dissipating storm. It looked as if it were coming from the direction of the house. Lila, her brain permanently rewired by her husband's suicide to always think the worst, felt her heart bump up into her throat. *Could it be . . . ?*

No, she told herself. Abigail's house couldn't possibly be on fire.

Concepción was awakened by the smell of smoke. For a disoriented instant, she thought it was a result of the nightmare she'd been having, the same one she often had, from which she always woke with a lump in her throat and tears streaming down her cheeks.

She dragged herself upright, wincing in pain. Every part of her ached from the cold concrete floor on which she'd lain and from her long walk earlier in the day. Her mouth tasted like the inside of an old boot. Her head throbbed. And though she was shivering, she felt hot, as if with fever. Struggling to her feet, she cracked open the door, peering out. It was still dark outside, but the landscape was queerly illuminated.

That was when she saw that the Señora's house was on fire.

Instantly she was transported back that terrible day when she'd been crawling about in blind terror, calling out her daughter's name as the factory in Las Cruces went up in flames.

It wasn't a conscious decision that sent her pitching out into the open and racing in the direction of the house.

The unfamiliar drive down which she'd stumbled a short while ago proved no obstacle to her now. The house was lit up like a giant torch, its flames casting a sulfurous glow over the surrounding grass and trees, guiding her way. She flew down the drive, splashing through puddles, ignoring the sharp bits of gravel that dug into the flimsy soles of her shoes. Up ahead, she saw someone emerge from the shimmering heat of the inferno: a tall figure weaving drunkenly, like her husband when he used to come staggering home after a night at the bar. She watched the figure lurch a few more feet before collapsing onto the grass in front of the house. A boy, she saw, as she drew near.

When she got to him, he was on his hands and knees, coughing so hard that he was retching. He lifted his head to look up at her, a string of saliva hanging from his lower lip, scarcely appearing human, his face was so blackened by soot. He looked frightened, too—the white-ringed orbs of his eyes like those of a calf being led to slaughter. He managed to gasp, "She's . . . she's still in there. . . . I couldn't get her to wake up. . . ."

Someone was still inside!

Milagros, she thought, in her fevered state. Somehow time had reversed itself, and it was her daughter who was inside that burning building. *"Dónde está?"* she cried, forgetting her English.

The boy pointed toward the upper story, where the flames hadn't yet reached, his arm jerking and twitching like an epileptic's, it was trembling so. He muttered thickly, "Please. Help."

Concepción took off like a shot and ran, her coattails flapping. As she plunged into the burning house, there was no thought in her head of her own personal safety. Her fevered brain was consumed with a single objective: to rescue Milagros. It was only after she'd gone a few feet and the heat and smoke came rushing at her like a locomotive that she was momentarily repelled. She hung back, coughing, her throat and lungs feeling as though they'd been soaked in kerosene and set on fire. Then she was shedding her coat, still damp from the rain, and throwing it over her head. Holding its hem over her mouth, like an Arab woman's veil, to filter out the worst of the smoke, she stumbled toward the staircase.

Upstairs, it was even hotter than below, unbearable almost. *Dios!* Was it possible for anyone to survive this? Nevertheless, she forged on. Her eyes were watering so badly that she wouldn't have been able to see where she was going if she hadn't kept a hand on the wall, using it to guide her along the smoke-filled corridor. What spurred her on was the mental image of her daughter.

"*Milagros, mi hija!*" she cried in a voice so hoarse, it was scarcely recognizable as her own. "*Estoy aquí! Tu madre!*"

No reply. The only sound was the devilish cackling of the flames as they tore through the lower part of the house, where the fire appeared to be contained for the time being. Finally she came to an open doorway. Inside, she could dimly make out the figure of a girl lying sprawled on a bed. For a terrible instant, she thought she might have arrived too late. Then she saw one of the girl's legs twitch. With a choked cry, Concepción rushed to her side, her heart swelling with relief.

But it wasn't Milagros, she saw.

The dark hair, the slender limbs, belonged to someone other than her daughter. In that moment of recognition, Concepción felt as though she'd been rudely awakened from a nightmare into another, even worse nightmare. But there was no time for despair. She couldn't leave the girl to die.

Concepción seized hold of her and shook her. But the girl's only response was to mutter something unintelligible, her eyes briefly fluttering open. Even when Concepción grabbed her by the wrists and managed to haul her upright, the girl only sat there swaying for an instant before she toppled backward onto the mattress. *"Ayúdame!"* Concepción cried . . . to God . . . to the spirit of her daughter . . . to anyone who would listen. She couldn't do this alone.

Yet somehow, she found the strength to hoist the girl off the bed and onto her shoulder. Carrying her to safety would be another matter, for however small and slender, the girl was dead weight. But Concepción didn't pause long enough to give it much consideration before she began staggering back the way she'd come, using the coat draped over her head and shoulders to cover what she could of the girl as well. It would provide scant protection against the inferno below, but she couldn't stop to think about that now.

As she painstakingly descended the stairs, the girl slung over her shoulder might have been a sack of concrete. Concepción's legs wobbled with each precarious step. One wrong move and she and the girl would go tumbling down the rest of the way. And that wasn't the only threat. When she looked down, she saw flames licking at the banister on the ground floor below. Moments later, there was a tremendous crash, and part of the wall along the corridor to the kitchen—a corridor she had traversed what seemed like an eternity ago—collapsed in a shower of sparks. Sparks that crackled about her like a swarm of biting insects, stinging the exposed skin of her cheeks and forehead wherever they landed.

A strange calm descended on her. *Dios, take me if you must, but spare this girl,* she prayed.

As if in response, the girl stirred suddenly to life, limbs jerking and flailing like those of a marionette. Concepción was thrown off balance and would have been pitched into the well of flames below, taking the girl with her, if she hadn't steadied herself just in time. Oddly enough, it hadn't seemed as if *she* were in control in that moment, but more as if an invisible presence had taken over her body, a force that was protecting her—them—from harm.

God might have deserted her once, but He would not fail her this time.

She was nearing the foot of the staircase when she saw, with a shock, that the greedy mouths of the flames had consumed the bottom two steps. She hesitated, engulfed by fear—more for the girl than for her—but she knew that if she didn't act quickly and fearlessly, she would have no choice but to turn back, and there would be no escape from this inferno.

Concepción lunged the last few feet. She heard a crack and felt something give way underfoot a split second before she landed, miraculously on both feet and even more miraculously without having dropped her precious cargo. But her sense of relief was short-lived. When she glanced down, she saw that the hem of her coat was on fire. And not just the coat. The doorway to the house was consumed by flames. It was like peering through the gates of hell itself.

They were trapped.

Abigail had searched everywhere, but Phoebe wasn't in any of her usual hangouts. Nor was she at any of her friends' houses; all of them had expressed surprise, in fact, when Abigail had phoned, that she would think Phoebe might be there. Phoebe's best friend, Brittney Clausen, had reported that it'd been months since she'd last seen Phoebe outside school. (*And why am I only just learning this?* Abigail wondered.) But she hadn't grown truly alarmed until the owner of the deli where Neal worked, a heavyset, middle-aged man named Mr. Haber, had informed her in a disgruntled voice, as he'd been locking up for the night, that he hadn't seen Neal's girlfriend—or Neal, for that matter—since yesterday. It seemed that Neal hadn't shown up for work that day.

For some reason, Abigail had found this bit of news more disturbing than the fact that her daughter was missing. Neal seemed like such a responsible kid. It wasn't like him to not show up for work. Had something happened? Something involving Phoebe? Suppose they had run off together?

But however worrisome the idea, it was preferable to what Abigail been dreading until that point. At first, when she'd failed to spot Concepción Delgado along the road into town (she must have taken a shortcut through the woods), her fears had run rampant. Now she could console herself with the thought that, if Phoebe had run off with Neal, at least she wasn't in any physical danger.

Briefly, she considered alerting the police, but they'd only tell her to check back in forty-eight hours if her daughter still wasn't home. It occurred to her then that Phoebe might have returned home by now, and with that in mind, she turned her car around and headed back.

She was nearing the turnoff to Rose Hill when she heard the distant wail of sirens. A sound rarely heard in this sleepy backwater, where crime was limited to the occasional break-in and car wrecks generally occurred out on the interstate. An instant later, she caught the smell of smoke. Not the pleasant smoke of firewood curling from a chimney or a pile of brush being incinerated in someone's backyard but that of an uncontrolled burn. A forest fire? Unlikely, after all that rain. It must be someone's house on fire. It didn't occur to her that it might be hers. When seconds later the thought did enter her mind, it brought a jolt of panic.

Oh, God. What if it *was?*

She pressed down harder on the gas pedal.

As soon as she turned onto her drive, she could see it in full, vivid Technicolor, her second-to-worst nightmare after that of an accident befalling Phoebe: her house going up in flames. She picked up speed, her mind spinning like the tires seeking traction on the muddy road. An accident? Or had someone purposely set fire to her house? If so, who in God's name would do such a thing?

A clear image rose amid the whirling chaos in her brain: the dark look Concepción Delgado had given her just before she'd taken off into the night. Suddenly it all made sense. Of course. *This* was the eye for an eye. Not the kidnapping of her daughter but the torching of her house.

The BMW had barely skidded to a stop before Abigail was leaping out. The fire engines hadn't arrived yet, but Karim's Dodge pickup was parked in front of the garage. There was no sign of Karim, but amid the smoke billowing from the house, she caught sight of Lila, kneeling beside a prone figure on the grass out front, silhouetted against the backdrop of flames. It wasn't until Abigail drew closer that she saw that the prone figure was Neal.

"What happened? Is he hurt?" Abigail cried in alarm.

Lila leaped to her feet at Abigail's approach. She was dressed as though for a night out, in a dressy black skirt and sweater, but she was a mess, her hair and clothing disheveled and smudges of soot on her face and hands. "He's a little out of it, but I think he'll be okay. Thank God he made it out in time," she informed Abigail in a shaken voice.

"Where's Phoebe? Was she with him?" Abigail glanced wildly about her.

Lila took hold of her shoulders as if to steady her. "It's going to be all right, Abby. The fire department is on its way. They should be here any minute. In the meantime, try not to panic." She spoke in the low, soothing voice that Abigail had heard her use in the past with spooked horses.

But Lila hadn't answered her question, and now panic kicked in with a vengeance. "I don't give a shit about the house! Where's my daughter?" Abigail's voice rose on a hysterical note.

Lila eyed her steadily, as if she could calm Abigail's fears simply by holding her gaze. "We think she's still in the house, but we don't know for sure. Karim's looking for her now."

"Oh, my God. Oh, Jesus." Abigail sank to her knees, a hand over her mouth to muffle the cry that rose. At first she couldn't think straight, her mind was whirling so, then she was on her feet again, shouting, "Don't just stand there! *Do something!* If we don't get her out of there, she'll *die!*"

Abigail dashed off in the direction of the house, but Lila was quick to intercept her, grabbing hold of her elbow and jerking her back with such force, it brought Abigail spinning around. When Abigail attempted to free herself, Lila clamped both arms around her to hold her in place. "You can't go in there, or *you'll* die," she managed to gasp between breaths as Abigail struggled wildly against her.

"Try and stop me," Abigail hissed through gritted teeth.

Lila's only response was to tighten her hold. Who would have imagined she'd be so strong? "I can and I will," she insisted. "Do you think I'm going to stand by and let you kill yourself?"

"Let go, you bitch!" Abigail managed to jerk one arm free, with which she began whacking at Lila's head and shoulders in an effort to get her to release her hold. Lila did her best to duck the blows, but even then, she didn't let go. She held on as if her own life depended on it.

"You'll thank me later on," she said, grunting when one of the blows connected.

"Fuck you! I'll kick your ass!" Abigail screamed, continuing to flail.

"You can kick my ass all you want, but I'm not letting go."

"That's my daughter in there!"

"I know, which is why I can't let you do this. She needs you, Abby, and you won't be much good to her if you die trying to save her."

"If I don't, *she* could die!"

Lila stood firm. "You don't know that. We don't even know if she's in there for sure."

"And if she is? Oh, God, I can't . . . I can't . . ." All at once the resistance went out of Abigail, and she crumpled to the ground. Huddled bonelessly on the muddy lawn, she began to weep hysterically.

"I know . . . I know . . . hush, now." Lila knelt down before Abigail, cradling her and stroking her hair, her arms gentle now. "It's going to be all right, you'll see," Lila murmured in reassurance. "If she's in there, they'll get her out. You have to believe that, Abby."

Abigail moaned, "Please tell me this isn't happening."

"Don't think the worst. We don't know anything yet."

Abigail clung to her, and they rocked from side to side. When Abigail's sobs had subsided somewhat, she drew back to choke, "Was . . . was Neal able to tell you anything?"

"A little, but, like I said, he's pretty out of it. He's not making much sense."

"What happened, do you know?"

Lila's face took on an even more somber cast. "Not the whole story, no. All I know is that they took some pills. Neal said something about trying to wake her, but I'm not sure if he knew what he was saying." She cast a worried glance at her son, still prone on the grass.

"Jesus."

In horrified disbelief, Abigail stared into the blazing inferno, thinking it wasn't just her house but her whole life going up in flames. Her marriage, the daughter she'd once thought she'd known better than Phoebe knew herself, her career, even. If Concepción Delgado had done this, maybe it wasn't so much revenge as divine retribution by the hand of His messenger. Punishment for the life that had been taken in the name of ambition. *If anyone is responsible for this,* she thought, *it's me.*

Consumed by her dire thoughts, it was a moment before Abigail noticed a stir of movement within the thick smoke pouring from the doorway to the house. Someone was in there. Karim? Had he gone in after Phoebe and managed to rescue her? Abigail's heart leaped at the thought.

That hope was dashed when Karim came running around the side of the house, shouting something that she couldn't quite make out. Oh, God. She'd only been hallucinating, willing a miracle where there was none. . . .

But all was not lost, it seemed. An instant later a figure materialized out of the thick gray haze. A woman holding a coat over her head. She had something—no, *someone*—slung over one shoulder.

Phoebe.

In the next instant, Abigail was on her feet and running.

The woman sank to the ground, still holding tight to Phoebe, just as Abigail reached her. The coat covering them was on fire, and Abigail ripped off her jacket and began beating at the flames. Karim and Lila joined her, and within seconds they'd managed to put the fire out.

Both the woman and Phoebe were alive, she saw to her immense relief. Abigail, tears streaming down her face, sank to her knees before them. Who was this woman? And how had she come to be here? Was she even human . . . or was she an angel from heaven?

The woman lifted her head, and Abigail saw with a shock that it was Concepción Delgado. She let out a gasp. Concepción's face and hands were blackened with soot, and her hair stood out in singed wisps all over her head, like wires from a blown transformer. When her gaze met Abigail's, Abigail found herself looking into the bloodshot eyes of someone who'd been to hell and back. Eyes that weren't so much looking at Abigail as looking *through* her, as if at some unimaginable horror that only Concepción could see.

Abigail laid a hand on her shoulder. "Bless you." It was all she could manage in her current state.

Concepción's eyes locked onto Abigail's then, and in that moment Abigail felt something pass between them before Concepción brought her gaze back to Phoebe. She gently stroked Phoebe's hair, gazing at her with a tenderness that was almost unbearable to behold. While behind her the blaze roared out of control and the wail of sirens grew louder—Abigail could now see the flashing of a bubble light through the distant trees—Concepción Delgado whispered to the girl cradled, semiconscious, in her arms, "You are safe now, *mi hija.*"

17

As Lila made her way along the hospital corridor, she could see them all assembled in the visitors' lounge—her brother, seated next to Gillian (who'd taken the train back from Philly as soon she'd gotten the news); Abigail, sitting hunched on the sofa beside her estranged husband, chewing on a manicured thumbnail; and Karim, standing tall and straight in their midst, sturdy and dependable as the hub of a wheel—and she had the queer sense that she was looking at a doctored photo in which the various people in her life had been cut and pasted to form a bizarre family portrait.

Vaughn jumped to his feet at her approach. "How is he?"

"The same," she replied wearily. She'd been assured by the resident on call that, physically, Neal was in fairly good shape, all things considered. They'd pumped his stomach to remove the residue of the pills, and Dr. Roantree didn't seem to think that Neal would suffer any long-term effects from the smoke inhalation, though he was on oxygen at the moment. Yet in other ways, her son was a long way from being out of the woods, she knew. The fire that had nearly cost him his life was the same fire that had ultimately saved it.

"What did the doctor say?" Gillian asked. With her spiky, bleached-blond, pink-tipped hair, wearing a short kelly-green coat with a hot pink knitted scarf, black tights, and black lace-up Doc Martens, she looked like an elf on leave from the North Pole.

"They're keeping him overnight. They want to do a psych evaluation." Lila's tone was matter-of-fact, but just saying the words made her feel sick to her stomach.

At the same time, a voice in her head protested that the only thing crazy here was that they were *talking* about Neal as if he were crazy. He'd been a little depressed, sure. Who wouldn't be, after all he'd been through? After what he'd witnessed with his dad? Really, it was a wonder he was functioning at all. But suicidal? No way.

She ignored that voice. She had to face the fact, however painful, that her son was in crisis. She couldn't keep pretending that time alone would heal his wounds. For if she refused to believe that he might not try it again, that it wasn't still a real threat, he could end up like his father.

Her gaze fell on Abigail, who looked as strung out as she. For once, they were in the same boat, except that Phoebe was in far worse shape than Neal. She was in the ICU, still unconscious and suffering from second-degree burns as well as smoke inhalation, not to mention the pills that were still in her system. No one was allowed in to see her for more than ten minutes at a time—not even her parents, which was the only reason Abigail and Kent were sitting out here when anyone could see they were desperate to be with their child.

It's going to be a long night, Lila thought.

Vaughn walked over to put an arm around Lila's shoulders. "You don't look so hot yourself, Sis. Why don't you go to the hotel and get some rest?" He'd booked rooms for them at the Marriott across the street. "I'll call you if there's any change."

Lila shook her head. "No. I want to be here when he wakes up."

"At least you know he *will* wake up." Abigail's voice seemed to rise from the bottom of a well, hollow and disembodied. Lila looked over to find Abigail staring at the wall in front of her, wearing a look of fierce concentration, the muscles in her face working in an effort to keep from crying.

Vaughn flicked a worried glance at her, but Abigail seemed oblivious to everyone and everything but her own anguish.

Kent gave his wife an awkward pat on the shoulder. "You can't think that way, Abby. She's young. She'll pull through. And I know the staff here—they're all excellent. Trust me, she's in good hands," he said, with a conviction that seemed forced. Tonight he wasn't the self-assured doctor in command of the situation; he was just another distraught parent struggling with his own fears.

"This time, maybe. But what about the next time? What if she tries it again?" Abigail swung around to face him, her voice rising on a shrill, frayed note. "There won't always be someone around to rescue her."

Lila thought then about the stranger who had come to Phoebe's rescue tonight. A Hispanic woman she'd never seen before but whom Abigail seemed to know. She was in intensive care at the moment, along with Phoebe. Abigail had offered to take care of all her expenses after it had become clear that the woman was uninsured. It was what anyone with means would have done for the person who'd saved their child's life, yet Lila couldn't help feeling that there was something more to it than that, some story she had yet to hear.

Kent attempted to reassure his wife. "We'll cross that bridge when we get to it. Let's just get through this, okay? Once she's back on her feet, we'll see that she gets all the help she needs."

"I just want her *home*." Abigail's voice struck a plaintive note. Lila couldn't help thinking that, if there had been any Abigail Armstrong fans around to witness the scene, they wouldn't have recognized this woman as the unflappable doyenne of domesticity who could whip up the perfect soufflé with one hand while getting a red wine stain out of a tablecloth with the other.

"Maybe it would be best if she stayed with me for a little while. Just until you find another place to live," Kent suggested tentatively.

It occurred to Lila that Abigail was now homeless. They were both homeless. Abigail could easily find another place to live. But what would *she* do? She felt mildly panicky at the thought.

"That's not an option," Abigail said tersely, clearly not in a frame of mind to be reasoned with. "She needs her mother right now. What difference does it make where we live? We can stay in a hotel, for all I care. All that matters is Phoebe. If I were to lose her . . ." Convulsively, she pulled into herself, making a tight fist of her body, her shoulders hunched and her arms wrapped around her middle. As she sat there shivering, despite the room's near-stifling warmth, it was clear that she needed her daughter as much as her daughter needed her.

"We're not going to lose her." Kent made another attempt to reassure her, but when Abigail refused to even look at him, he fell silent. Seeing him slumped over with his elbows resting on his knees, his hair rumpled, and his necktie askew, Lila thought that he looked sorely in need of comforting himself.

"I know what you're thinking," Abigail said in that same hollow, bottom-of-the-well voice. "You're thinking it's my fault. Well, you're right—it *is*. What does it say that something was so drastically wrong that our daughter wanted to kill herself, and she couldn't come to me, her own mother?"

Kent just sat there, shaking his head, wearing a forlorn look. He had to be thinking the same thing: that Phoebe could have come to him, too, and she hadn't. He had to be feeling the same guilt.

Gillian broke the tension by piping, "Anyone want coffee? I could use some myself." She looked around expectantly, but when no one took her up on her offer, she trudged off in the direction of the cafeteria, looking strangely bereft.

Vaughn went over to Abigail and lowered himself onto his haunches so that they were at eye level. He was wearing gray corduroys and a navy turtleneck sweater that made his eyes look even more startlingly blue than usual. Over the past few weeks, the bristle on his head had turned to dark blond waves that, here and there, had given way to errant curls. He looked almost like his old self—though Lila had to remind herself that appearances could be deceiving; he wasn't out of the woods yet, either.

"It's not your fault, Abby." He spoke gently. "This could have happened to anyone."

Abigail met his gaze, and something in the intimacy of the look they exchanged confirmed Lila's suspicions: They were lovers. She didn't know what to make of *that*. So she decided to tuck the realization away for a future date, when she could process it with a clear head.

"He's right. It's not your fault. It's no one's fault." All heads turned to Lila as she spoke. She was thinking about Gordon and how she'd held herself partly responsible for what he'd done. But how could she have prevented it? What could she have done differently? She'd stood by his side throughout it all; she'd even vowed to wait for him until he got out of prison. Maybe it was the same with Neal and Phoebe; maybe nothing either she or Abigail could have said or done would have altered the course of events. Lila stepped around her brother and held a hand out to her oldest and once dearest friend, saying, "Come on, Abby. Let's you and me take a walk."

Abigail nodded wordlessly and rose to her feet.

Slowly, like a pair of old ladies who'd known each other for so long that they matched each other's strides, they made their way together down the corridor. They ended up in a small atrium tucked off to one side of the elevators, which was deserted at this hour. There were only their ghostly reflections looking back at them from the darkened glass.

"You look like hell," Abigail said.

Lila gave a wan smile. "So do you."

"It's been some night, hasn't it?"

"You can say that again."

"I'm sorry I yelled at you, at the house. I wasn't myself."

Lila smiled. "I know."

"Thanks for keeping me from going in there. I probably wouldn't be here if you hadn't."

"I'm just glad I was around to stop you. If Karim hadn't gotten me home when he did . . ." Lila felt a chill go through her at the thought, and she added with an ironic laugh, "Nice, huh? I finally decide to let my guard down and go out on a date, and look how it turned out."

Abigail eyed her with mild curiosity. "I didn't know you and Karim were seeing each other."

"I didn't know we were, either." *Until tonight.* But that was a conversation for another time. The only thing that mattered right now was their kids. "Look, you can't beat yourself up for what happened with Phoebe," Lila said when they were seated. "I went through the same thing with Gordon. I kept thinking that if only I'd read the signals, if I'd been paying more attention, I could have stopped him from doing what he did. But I'm not a mind reader. And neither are you. We're just ordinary people who don't always get to play hero."

Abigail remained unconvinced. "Still, I should have seen it coming. If I'd been a better mother . . ."

"*We* should have seen it coming. It wasn't just Phoebe," Lila reminded her.

"So what now? What do we do?" For the first time in all these months, Abigail sat stripped of her armor. For the first time, she was admitting that she didn't have all the answers. She was asking for help.

It was almost more than Lila could absorb. *I don't have all the answers, either,* she answered silently. *I wish I did.* But Abigail didn't need to know that, so she said simply, "We do the best we can."

"What if our best isn't good enough?"

"It will be. It *has* to be."

"I'll do whatever it takes, I'll sacrifice anything for one more chance to make things right with her. But what if she doesn't pull through?" Abigail's voice cracked. "I honestly don't know if I could survive that."

"She'll pull through."

But Abigail wasn't in a mood to be reassured. "It might be easier to believe that if I didn't feel so alone."

"You're not alone. You have me."

Abigail gave her a dubious look. But when Lila put an arm around her, she didn't pull away. They sat that way for the longest time, joined in a silent solidarity, breathing in the smoke their hair and clothing were steeped in. When at last they drew apart, both women's eyes were wet.

"There's just one thing," Lila said.

"What's that?"

"I may not be around so much now that I'm out of a job."

Abigail blinked at her in confusion. Clearly, it had been the last thing on her mind, as it had been for Lila until just now. But the plain fact was that without a house, there was no need for a housekeeper.

"Are you sure you even want to go on working for me?" Abigail said when the ramifications of their situation sank in. "I can be a real bitch at times. Not to mention demanding."

Lila gave a dry laugh. "I won't argue that."

"Well, don't worry about it. We'll figure something out."

They were silent for a moment, staring out at the courtyard below, then Lila remembered to ask, "The woman who rescued Phoebe. How did she even happen to be there? You still haven't told me."

"It's a long story." Abigail hesitated before continuing. "It started when my factory burned down last year. One of the workers died in that fire, a nineteen-year-old girl named Milagros Sánchez." Lila must have looked surprised, for she added, "If you didn't hear about it, it's because I pay a fortune to keep things like that out of the press. Which I've managed to do a pretty good job of until now." Her mouth twisted in an ironic smile, and Lila knew that she was referring to her divorce, the news of which even her team of highly paid publicists hadn't been able to keep under wraps—it had been all over the tabloids. "Well, the woman who saved Phoebe's life tonight is the mother of that girl."

Lila struggled to make sense of it. "That still doesn't explain what she was doing there."

"She'd come by the house earlier. She was waiting for me when I got home from work tonight."

"Why? Do you know her?"

Abigail shook her head. "We'd never even met."

"So what happened?"

"I tried to tell her how sorry I was. I even offered her money, but she refused to take it. She said that wasn't why she'd come all this way to see me."

"What did she want, then?"

"To have me look into her face and see the suffering I'd caused. That's what she told me, in so many words. Her English isn't very good, but she managed to get her message across." Abigail stared sightlessly ahead, looking deeply distraught. "And she's right. I *am* responsible, in a way. That's what makes it damn complicated."

"I don't understand." Lila frowned in confusion. "How is it your fault?"

"It was an accident that never should've happened. You see, I was in such a rush to beef up production, I wasn't as vigilant about safety measures as I should've been. And now someone's dead because of it." She turned toward Lila, wearing a look of self-recrimination; Abigail didn't need anyone to condemn her—she was doing a thorough job of it herself. "So I guess I only got what I deserved. What goes around comes around, right?"

"Are you saying this woman might have had something to do with tonight's fire?" Lila was shocked to think that the blaze might have been intentionally set.

Abigail shrugged. "Who knows? Does it really matter, in the end? The important thing is, she was there when it counted. She risked her life. If she hadn't, Phoebe would never have made it out of there alive." She shuddered at the thought, crossing her arms over her chest.

"If she *did* set the fire, she couldn't have known that Phoebe and Neal were in the house."

"No, and I have no proof that she had anything to do with it. She may not be guilty of anything more than trespassing. Oh, I admit I had my suspicions at first. Who wouldn't? She'd all but accused me of being the archangel of death. You should've been there—it was quite the scene." A tremor passed through Abigail as she recounted the incident. "But it could be that she only came back to get the last word. Or maybe she'd decided to take the money after all. Either way, her timing couldn't have been more perfect."

"What will happen to her once she gets released?"

"She'll probably be deported unless I can pull a few strings. I know someone in the State Department. I'll see what I can do." Abigail's old determination surfaced briefly. "That is, if she even *wants* to stay in this country. God only knows what it took for her to get here, and I didn't exactly roll out the welcome mat."

"It's not too late."

"Don't worry, I have every intention of making it up to her. Even if she does hate me."

From the way she spoke, Lila doubted that anyone could hate Abigail as much as she hated herself right now. She touched Abigail's arm. "You're not a bad person, Abby. Don't think that."

Abigail gave a bitter laugh. "No? What am I, then?"

"You're human, like the rest of us."

Abigail managed a small smile. Gone was the Abigail who used to pace in front of the door, cursing, when her driver was late picking her up for work, the Abigail who'd been too preoccupied to notice that her husband was having an affair or that her daughter was suicidal. In her place was someone vulnerable, someone with depth, who was taking responsibility for her actions.

Someone Lila very much wanted to get to know.

"I've been so busy playing Wonder Woman, I'd forgotten what it feels like to be human," Abigail said with a sigh.

Lila smiled at her. "I'm afraid it's the one club you can't resign from."

"I've been pretty hard on you, haven't I?"

"Yeah, but it only made me realize that I'm a lot tougher than I thought."

Abigail startled her by confessing, "I've missed you." As she looked at Lila, the years seemed to fall away. "Oh, I know we see each other every day. But it's not the same, is it? I miss how it was in the old days. If I've been hard on you, it was only because I wasn't ready to forgive you."

Lila was so moved, it was a moment before she could trust herself to speak. "You had a lot to forgive."

"Maybe. But it's time we moved on, don't you think?"

Lila nodded, swallowing against the lump in her throat.

"Good," Abigail said. "Because I could use you in my lifeboat. I have a feeling it's going to be a long haul to shore."

"I have a feeling you're right." Lila's thoughts returned to her son, who would soon need the kind of care this hospital couldn't provide . . . and Phoebe, who would be in similar straits.

"I just hope you know what you're doing, because I sure as hell don't."

Lila smiled and hooked an arm through Abigail's, as they headed back to rejoin the others. "Me? I don't have a clue. But I'm sure between the two of us, we'll figure something out."

When it was time to look in on Phoebe again, Abigail turned to Kent and asked, "Would you mind sitting this one out?"

He looked a little taken aback, but then he nodded, seeming to understand that it didn't have to do with him, just that she needed to be alone with their daughter for a little while.

She rose to her feet, glancing over at Vaughn as she crossed the lounge on her way to the ICU. Their eyes met briefly, and she felt a current of electricity pass between them, but it was a low-voltage one—their lovemaking earlier in the day might have taken place in another lifetime. At the same time, she knew that the bond between them, which had sustained her in some of her darkest hours in the past, would continue to do so in the dark hours and days to come.

As she made her way down the corridor and past the nurse's station, where one of the nurses, a light-skinned black woman, glanced up at her in startled recognition, it occurred to Abigail that, aside from Phoebe, Vaughn and Lila, for all practical purposes, were the only family she had. True, they'd been apart for more years than they'd been together, but the connection ran deep. It had been there all along without her knowing it—in Lila's case, the underside of the chip Abigail had carried on her shoulder for so long. With Vaughn, it had been easy falling back into the old rhythms, but she and Lila couldn't just pick up where they'd left off all those years ago. Nor could they start over with a clean slate; they would have to cobble together a new friendship out of the spare parts from the old one. It wouldn't be easy, but the hardest part was behind them. And Abigail was grateful for Lila's presence; she would need the support of someone who was going through the same thing as she. One thing she knew: There was no going back. Her old life and the old Abigail were like her house that now lay in charred ruins: uninhabitable.

She braced herself as she entered the ICU. It always came as a little shock when she first stepped inside, seeing all those machines beeping and blurping away, half hidden by the curtains not quite enclosing the beds; the thick electrical cords and clear plastic tubing snaking everywhere—as if this were more a place of industry than of healing. The patients almost seemed beside the point.

Her gaze fell on Phoebe. Her daughter was still out like a light, which was a blessing in some ways, she supposed. Swathed in bandages, tubes running in and out of her, and an oxygen mask covering the lower half of her face, Phoebe looked like she would be in a great deal of pain were she conscious. But, of course, that was the reason she was here. Her beautiful daughter had been in so much pain that she'd wanted to kill herself.

At the thought, Abigail was engulfed by a wave of sorrow. If only she could go back in time, she'd do it differently. She would spend less time at work and more time doing the things that really mattered. She wouldn't take a single thing for granted. She would know that people—children, especially—can't be put on hold.

She placed a hand over Phoebe's heart. Her daughter's thin chest felt fragile, almost breakable; she could feel every bone. *Don't give up, my darling. I know you think life isn't worth living. But it gets better, I promise, even if it never gets any easier. And it is worth it. However much pain you're in right now, life is always worth it. You'll realize that someday, if you'll only give it a chance.*

As if sensing her presence, Phoebe stirred, her eyelids fluttering open for an instant, but she remained unconscious. Abigail leaned down and gently kissed her cheek, whispering to her as she had when Phoebe was a child, "Sleep, my precious girl. Mommy will be here when you wake up."

A low groan emanated from the next bed—the bed in which Concepción Delgado lay. Abigail peeked behind the privacy curtain and found the woman who had saved her daughter's life struggling to pull herself upright, grimacing with the effort.

Abigail approached the bed, asking, "Are you in pain? Should I get the nurse?"

The resident on call had informed her earlier that Señora Delgado was suffering from smoke inhalation as well as second-degree burns, primarily on her face and hands. But the prognosis was good. The doctor expected her to make a full recovery. Not that you'd know it to look at her. With her hands swaddled in gauze and the exposed areas of her face—a face so red, it looked boiled—smeared with salve, Concepción was a pitiable sight.

"No, *gracias*." Concepción's voice was a hoarse rasp.

"Is there anything I can get you? An extra blanket, some water?"

Concepción shook her head wearily, as if even the effort to speak were too much.

Abigail lingered at her bedside nonetheless, torn between the desire to respect the woman's obvious wish to be alone and her own need to say what was on her mind. Finally, she ventured, "Señora Delgado . . . I don't know what to say. There are no words to express my gratitude."

The woman who just hours ago had looked upon her with such hatred now appeared too exhausted to feel much emotion. "She is all right, your daughter?" she inquired in her halting but serviceable English.

Abigail cleared her throat against the knot forming. "I think so. I hope so."

"*Gracias a Dios.*" Concepción closed her eyes a moment.

Abigail felt a fresh pang of remorse. Having come so close to losing her own child, she now knew, at a visceral level, what Concepción had suffered in losing hers. How could she have turned her away? Why hadn't she tried harder to get through to her, to show more compassion?

"In fact, I owe you a lot more than thanks," she said. "What you did . . . after what happened with *your* daughter . . ." She felt herself choke up. "It took more than courage. It took a big heart. And I'd like to repay you. There must be something you want or need."

Concepción eyed her in confusion. At first Abigail wondered whether she'd comprehended. Then Concepción replied in her hoarse croak, "Is no for me, this." She held up her bandaged hands. "Is for your *hija*."

"Well, you're a better person than I. All I did was hide behind excuses."

Concepción blinked up at her, and said with a sigh, *"Ahora tú sabes."*

Abigail had taken Spanish in high school, language skills that had grown rusty with disuse, but she understood that much. What Concepción had said was: *Now you know.*

Yes, she thought, *now I know.* She knew what it was to lose a daughter, for she'd come close to it tonight, and Phoebe still wasn't out of the woods. But how could she ever repay Concepción? Would anything ever make up for the anguish of this woman's loss?

"If it's a public apology you want, just say the word. You deserve that much."

Tears rolled unchecked down Abigail's cheeks. She couldn't recall the last time she'd wept except in private, and here she was crying openly in front of a woman who was a virtual stranger. Not only that, she was offering to make a public apology, which would destroy everything she'd worked so hard to build. Had the world turned upside down? Or just *her* world?

For a long moment, Concepción regarded her in silence: the physical embodiment of Abigail's guilt. The guilt she felt not just for her role in Concepción's daughter's death but for all the smaller sins that had paved the path to her own personal hell.

At last Concepción Delgado spoke.

Concepción recalled little of the aftermath of the fire. All she remembered was being whisked away in an ambulance, concerned faces hovering over her, then being trundled down a hospital corridor on a gurney, banks of fluorescent lights glaring down at her like a cold sun, every inch of her body on fire despite the shot they'd given her for the pain.

After that, she'd slept—she didn't know for how long—awakening to the whoosh and beeps of machines, to find a plastic mask clamped over her nose and mouth. In her disorientation, she'd forgotten where she was and pulled the mask from her face in order to climb out of bed. She was prevented from doing so by the tube attached to her wrist at one end and to a bag of clear fluid hanging from a pole next to her bed at the other. Her fevered brain spun. *What place is this?* she wondered. Even her body, swathed in bandages, didn't feel like her own. It was swollen and throbbing, and it hurt to breathe.

When her head cleared, she remembered that she was in a hospital. From behind the curtain around her bed, voices floated toward her from time to time, and every so often, a nurse came to check on her. She drifted in and out of consciousness over the next hour or so until she was summoned from her sleep by a woman's voice—the voice of the Señora—murmuring to someone in the next bed, presumably her daughter. Then it all came rushing back, and the knowledge that the girl was alive brought grateful tears to her eyes. There had been enough tragedy already, she thought. She couldn't have endured another death, even one that would have evened the score.

And now here was the Señora standing over her, tears running down her face, asking for forgiveness. A display of remorse that had more to do with her own child than with Concepción's? Most likely. But either way, it no longer seemed to matter. Concepción was so tired. Not just bone-weary but tired of being on the move, of sneaking around like a criminal. Worn out, too, by the fire of righteousness that had burned within her. *Bastante.* She wanted an end to this madness. She wanted peace. She wanted . . .

. . . *Jesús.*

She remembered how he had looked when they were saying good-bye at the airport—the lines of worry in his face, the unspoken love in his eyes. Hadn't he rescued her, just as she had rescued the Señora's daughter tonight? He'd pulled her from the ashes of her despair; he'd given her hope. She wished he were here now to witness the end to her journey. For there was no doubt in her mind that it *had* come to an end. She could almost hear the voice of her *abuelita*, saying the same thing that she had when Concepción was a child who had gotten into a fight with her sister and was angrily threatening to get back at Christina: *The full heart has no room for revenge*, mi hija.

"I want nothing from you, Señora," she replied in her hoarse rasp. The very words she had used before, only now there was no rancor in them. All her anger was spent. "Tonight you have see for your own eyes how a life can be taken so quick, like that." She made a clumsy attempt to snap her fingers with her bandaged hand. "Never forget this."

"I won't," said the Señora, clearly meaning it.

"You are blessed to still have your daughter. I am happy for that."

"But you—"

Concepción put a hand out to stop her from going any further. "I am at peace," she said in perfect English—as if in that moment of clarity, she'd been granted fluency of the language as well. And it was true. In that moment, Milagros's presence was so strong, it was like a physical embodiment of her spirit.

"I promise you things will be different from now on," the Señora vowed.

Concepción regarded her from the dubious throne of her hospital bed, wondering whether the Señora would keep her promise. But who was she to sit in judgment? Hadn't she made her own share of mistakes? Hadn't she also known her share of mercy? Finally she let out a breath and eased back against the pillows. "*Claro,*" she said. Of course things would be different from now on. How could they not be? Too much had changed, too much had been lost, for it not to have altered the shape of things to come.

An awkward moment passed during which neither of them spoke. There was only the rhythmic whooshing of a pump somewhere in the room and the clattering of a cart as it rolled past in the corridor. Finally the Señora said, "Are you sure there's nothing I can get you?"

Shyly, Concepción answered, "*Sí.* There is one thing."

"Anything—you name it." The Señora looked relieved to be of some use.

She pictured Jesús once more. His mouth that always seemed on the verge of breaking into a smile; his eyes that showed every shading of emotion, whether happy or sad, angry or disappointed—anything but indifference, he was incapable of that—his sandpapery cheek that had been pressed against hers on the night they had lain together, nestled together like two spoons in a drawer.

The ghost of a smile touched her lips. "I would like to make a call, long distance, *por favor.*"

"Is there a rule that says hospital coffee has to be terrible?" Lila screwed up her face as she took another sip from the steaming Styrofoam cup in her hand.

She and Karim were in the cafeteria, seated at a table by the row of windows that overlooked the parking lot. Vaughn and Gillian had gone back to the hotel, at Lila's insistence. The last thing she needed was for *his* health to suffer, she'd told her brother after noticing how beat he looked.

She didn't know where Abigail and Kent had gotten to. The last she'd seen of them, they'd been headed outside, presumably to get some fresh air or maybe to talk in private. They seemed to have arrived at some sort of understanding. With this new crisis, it looked as if they were prepared to put their grievances aside in order to join forces in helping Phoebe.

Lila knew that she would need to apply the same focus to Neal. She mustn't let anything . . . or anyone . . . distract her from doing whatever was required to keep him safe and to help him along the road to recovery. Tragedy had been averted tonight, but a very real crisis loomed still. And it was her responsibility—hers alone, with his father gone—to see her son through this. Which meant that from now on, she would be putting Neal's needs above any selfish desires she might have. With that firmly in mind, she sat sipping her foul-tasting coffee, her eyes roaming about the room, alighting on the Band Aid–colored walls, the people hunched over trays at the other tables, the view from the window, anywhere but on Karim.

She couldn't allow her resolve to waver.

"I don't think their business depends on repeat customers," observed Karim with his usual dry wit.

Lila sighed. "You'd think I'd be used to it by now. God knows I've spent enough time in hospitals. But it was different with my mom because I knew she was going to die. And with my brother, I know he's going to survive. When it's your son and he's just tried to kill himself—" She broke off with a small, choked sound, dropping her head and bringing her fisted hand to her mouth.

"There was a reason he was spared." Karim's voice was low and soothing. "It wasn't God's plan that he should die in this manner."

She looked up at him, her eyes searching his face. "You still believe in God? After everything that's happened to you?"

He nodded. "In the Koran, it is written that the term of each life is fixed. Only Allah has power over such matters. If it were not destined so, I wouldn't be here. Nor would your son."

She arched a brow. "So we humans have little say in the matter?"

"Only in what we choose to do with the time that is allotted to us."

Lila had a feeling they weren't just talking about Neal anymore. "I used to believe in God," she said. "But it's pretty hard to believe in a divine being after seeing your husband on the floor with a bullet through his head." She hadn't set foot inside a church since Gordon's funeral.

Karim's mouth hooked up in a small, ironic smile. "And yet here you are. Surviving. Flourishing, some might say."

She thought back to what had happened between them earlier in the evening. "So I thought. Until this."

"You're not to blame for what happened to Neal," he said, his voice firm.

She shrugged. "I'm a mother. It goes with the territory."

"So what you said to Abigail, those were just words?"

"No. I meant what I said. I don't believe our kids tried to kill themselves because of anything we did or didn't do. But that doesn't mean we can go on as if it never happened. I have to do everything in my power to make sure Neal doesn't try something like that again. Even if it means putting my own life on hold for the time being." She averted her gaze, fearful of what it would reveal: that part of her wanted only for Karim to take her in his arms, whatever the cost down the line.

"You mean us," he translated with his usual incisiveness.

"There *is* no us. Don't you see?" Lila spoke harshly, knowing that if she didn't distance herself now, while she still had the power to do so, while the decision was still clear-cut in her mind, it would only become harder with time. "What happened with us tonight was just two people enjoying each other's company, one of whom had had too much to drink. Okay, so we enjoyed each other a little *too* much. But whatever you might think, it didn't mean anything. I like you, Karim. And I hope we can stay friends. But that's all I have to offer right now."

"I see. So your mind is made up?" He spoke calmly, but she could see from the ridge of muscle along his clenched jaw that he was fighting to keep his emotions in check.

"I'm afraid so."

"Then there's nothing more to discuss."

Lila felt relieved and at the same time oddly let down. She'd expected him to put up more of a fight. The fact that he hadn't only proved that she had been right to call it off, she told herself.

"I'm glad you understand," she said.

"You're wrong about that." His dark eyes blazed to life. He wasn't taking this lying down; she could see that now—far from it. "I think you're making a mistake, Lila *jan*," he said, sending a light chill through her with the Afghani endearment she'd only heard him use before when speaking on the phone with his mother and sister. "We've each been given a second chance, you and I. And such chances are rare. Do you really wish to squander it? Do you honestly believe that in doing so, you'll be helping your son? Have you considered that you might be doing him a grave dis-service instead?"

She gasped at his audacity. "How can you even *think* that?"

"Like Neal, I know what it is to lose a father," he went on in a voice as forthright as it was unapologetic. "When I tell you that the last thing your son needs right now is to feel that he is keeping his mother from her own happiness, I speak from experience."

"What are you suggesting I do, just abandon him?" she demanded.

"No, but there's a difference between walking away and knowing when it's time to let go," he told her. "I'm not suggesting you let go of Neal, not now. I understand that he needs you, and I fully support that. But perhaps what he needs most of all is for you to live your own life."

"I can't." She shook her head. "Not the way you mean. It would only cause more hurt, and he's been hurt so much already."

"You think that by denying yourself, you'll be giving Neal what he needs?"

"Who said I was denying myself? You're putting words in my mouth. If I gave you the wrong impression tonight, I'm sorry. I didn't mean—" She broke off as Karim, in a lightning move, seized her by the wrist. It wasn't a forcible grip, yet she felt powerless against it. He would respect her wishes, his eyes told her, but he wouldn't play this game of pretend: He knew she wanted him as much as he wanted her. Lila became aware of the rapid beating of her pulse where his fingers circled her wrist, and she almost confessed it then; she almost voiced what was in her heart. But she couldn't. It would only have reopened the door she was desperately attempting to nail shut. "I have to go." She slipped her hand from his grasp and rose to her feet. "I have to check on Neal."

18

For Abigail, the ensuing days were a blur. Between her work, overseeing cleanup from the fire, and moving into her new place, she managed most of the time to stay one step ahead of the inner demon that was in constant pursuit: the awful realization that her daughter had tried to kill herself. Whenever the thought did surface, it was like accidentally grasping hold of a hot pan handle. Then she would remind herself that Phoebe had come out of it alive and that she was in a safe place—she'd regained consciousness the morning after the fire and a week later had been released into the care of Dr. Hugo Ernst of the Dewhurst Psychiatric Facility.

Dr. Ernst had cautioned them not to expect immediate results, likening it to an onion's being peeled one layer at a time. But Abigail was impatient. She wanted to know *why.* What had been so horribly wrong with Phoebe's life that she'd wanted to end it? Until she had answers, there would be no helping Phoebe and certainly no peace of mind for *her.*

In the meantime, she was working on putting her own life together. The place she'd moved into, a furnished townhouse in a new waterfront development near the yacht club, suited her, in an odd way, for precisely the reasons she'd have hated it prior to all this. Its bland anonymity required nothing of her. She didn't have to think (or obsess) about details of decor or lighting. She didn't have to set the stage for her life; it had been set for her, and all she had was a walk-on part. As such, she'd scaled back her public appearances for the time being and had left the day-to-day running of her business to her very capable executive director, Ellen Tsao. Her days were spent, for the most part, dealing with the aftermath of the fire. Filling out forms and meeting with insurance people. Consulting with the architect she'd retained with an eye toward possibly rebuilding Rose Hill. All of it sandwiched between visits with Phoebe, her private sessions with Dr. Ernst, and meetings with Kent and their respective attorneys to hash out the terms of their divorce. (Like having a baby, there was never a good time for a divorce, she'd found.)

And at the center of it all, like a warm pulse, keeping her sane . . . keeping her from having to be carted off to Dewhurst herself . . . was Vaughn. They met whenever they could, usually on the fly, with Abigail being consumed by so many other things. Sensitive to his living situation, she no longer visited him at the loft now that they were lovers. Usually Vaughn took the train out to see her when he was feeling up to it. His first visit was two weeks after the fire. She took him to lunch at the yacht club, and afterward they went back to her place, where they ended up, as they usually did, in bed.

"What's the latest on the house?" he asked as they were getting up to take a shower after making love. "You haven't said a word about it all afternoon."

"I didn't want to bore you," she told him, padding after him into the bathroom, feeling deliciously languorous after having spent the past hour in his arms trying to forget about all that. "You're probably sick of hearing about it." Sometimes she bored herself talking about it.

He leaned over to kiss her shoulder. "I always want to know what's going on with you, babe. You know that."

"Okay, then. I got the final report from the fire marshal yesterday. The cause of the fire was officially determined accidental. Most likely a candle that got knocked over during the power outage."

"What could have caused it, I wonder?" Vaughn turned on the faucet in the shower, and when the water was hot enough, he stepped in. A moment later, she joined him.

"We think Brewster was the culprit. He always gets spooked during thunderstorms. He probably knocked over a candle trying to squeeze himself into a tight space. And Phoebe and Neal were upstairs. . . ." *So out of it they didn't notice until the place was going up in flames.*

Reaching past him for the soap, she felt the tension, for which their lovemaking was never more than a temporary remedy, start to creep back in. Vaughn, as if sensing the direction her thoughts had taken, reassured her: "You know it's going to be all right, don't you?" He took the bar of soap from her and began soaping her down, his big hands moving over her body with long, sure strokes.

"Do I?" The only happy ending so far was Brewster. After the fire had been put out, they'd found him in the woods behind the house, unharmed and running in crazed circles, barking his head off.

"Things generally have a way of working themselves out. Sometimes it takes a while, but eventually you get there." Vaughn worked his way up her neck, his soapy fingers finding the tight spot at the base of her skull and massaging. She closed her eyes and relaxed against him, savoring the feel of his warm, slippery body against hers amid the billowing steam.

Would the same hold true of Vaughn? she wondered. Would he survive *his* ordeal? Worrying about him, on top of everything else, was taking its toll. As tired as she was at the end of each day, she had trouble sleeping. Often she would lie awake for hours before finally giving up and turning on the TV or reaching for a book. They hadn't talked about it. They seldom did. But . . . she worried.

She straightened, saying with a sigh, "The only place I seem to be going these days is in circles."

"Circles can be good, too." He slowly spun her around to kiss her on the mouth, and she felt him start to stir below the waist.

They didn't stay in the shower very long.

But the question nagged at her even as they lay in bed after having made love a second time. *Is that what I'm doing—with Vaughn? Going in circles?* she asked herself. Abigail had no answer for that one, either. She was simply taking it day by day. Neither of them spoke of the future except in the most general terms. It was as if Vaughn's life, the life he'd had before this, were on hold. He'd never said, *I love you.* Nor had she said it to him. It would carry too much weight, and right now what they had was so precious . . . and precarious . . . she didn't want to upset the cart.

"I can't believe I'm saying this, but I think it's time for a haircut," she noted with a laugh, running her fingers through his hair, still wet and tangled from the shower. It had grown past his ears.

"What, you don't like the untamed me? I thought I was your walk on the wild side," he teased.

"Would that be a long walk . . . or just a stroll?" It was the closest she dared get to nailing down specifics.

"That's up to you." Smiling, he cupped one of her breasts and bent to kiss it.

Is it? Is it really up to me? she wondered. Or would fate dictate, as it had once before? Was it their destiny to be forever torn apart by circumstances beyond their control? She supposed it *was* up to her in a way. She could choose to stand on the brink, teetering at the edge of the unknown, or she could take a step back; she could guard against the opening of new wounds by maintaining a safe distance, if only an emotional one.

It was the opposite with Lila. These days, whenever they saw each other or talked on the phone, Abigail came away feeling safe and rooted. The soil from which their friendship had sprung was rich and deep, allowing it to flourish once more. They talked every other day, though they didn't get to see each other as often as before. Lila and Neal had moved into an apartment on the outskirts of town, and Lila was busy with her new job at Tarkington's Travel (having turned down Abigail's offer of a job in her company, saying she'd rather have Abigail as a friend than a boss). It was the middle of April, more than a month after the fire, before they were finally able to carve out time from their busy schedules to meet for lunch.

Driving into town, Abigail noticed that the forsythia were in bloom—spatters of bright gold against the backdrop of winter-brown trees. She spotted wild narcissi along the road as well, poking up from the fallen leaves that covered the ground like tiny periscopes scouting for other signs of spring. She smiled to herself. After the winter they'd had, she'd begun to wonder if she would ever see spring again, and here it was—a small miracle in itself.

She'd booked a table at Gabriella's, her favorite restaurant in Stone Harbor, where she found Lila waiting for her when she arrived. "Am I late?" Abigail asked with a glance at her watch.

"No. I got here a few minutes early." Lila added with a smile, "You trained me well."

Abigail commented on how well she looked. This was the Lila she remembered from their youth, healthy and clear-eyed, wearing a rosy glow. Her outfit, a cropped suede jacket and aubergine silk tank top, with black jeans, wasn't the haute couture of her days as reigning queen of society, but it was stylish, and it suited her better in some ways than the almost too perfectly assembled outfits Abigail recalled from those old society-page photos. But it wasn't just Lila's new look; she seemed more at ease with herself. Even saying jokingly, at one point, when Abigail had asked about her new job, "I think I'm finally getting the hang of the phone system, at least. I only accidentally hung up on one person this week."

"That's progress," Abigail agreed.

"I love it, though." Lila's eyes were lit up in a way they hadn't been in all the time she'd worked for Abigail. "In a way, it's like I'm getting to relive the best part of my past. All those trips Gordon and I used to go on—Rome, Paris, London, the Caribbean islands in winter." She gave a wistful sigh. "It's a daily reminder that, yes, I once actually had a life."

"And you don't now?"

"Oh, don't get me wrong. I'm not complaining," Lila replied with an ease that conveyed more than any words. "The job is great. In a lot of ways, my life is great, too. For one thing, six months ago, who would have thought you and I would be sitting here having lunch together?" She glanced about—they were seated at a table out on the patio, which was glassed in so they could enjoy the sunshine without becoming chilled—

before bringing her gaze back to Abigail, smiling. "I know it sounds clichéd, but it took losing everything to make me see what really mattered."

Abigail smiled back at her, dangerously close to echoing the sentiment. "How's Neal?" she asked. It had been several days since they'd last spoken, and she was eager, as always, to hear about the progress he was making—anything to give her hope.

"Good," Lila replied cautiously. Neal was seeing a therapist twice a week and responding to the antidepressants he was on—a different medication from the one he'd been taking originally—and according to Lila, the difference was like night and day. But she remained only guardedly optimistic, not wanting to burden Neal, or herself, with too many expectations. "We had a minibreakthrough the other day—a session with his therapist where a lot came out. It seems that Neal's been harboring a lot of anger not just at his dad but at me."

"Why? What have you done?"

Lila's sparkle faded and she grew a little pale. "I left Gordon alone that day."

No further explanation was needed. "I guess there's nothing rational about these things," commiserated Abigail with a sigh.

"It's not just me—Neal's been beating up on himself. He thinks that if he'd been a better son, Gordon would still be alive. It makes no sense, I know, but the feelings are real." Familiar furrows of worry showed briefly on her forehead before her face smoothed again. "But I'm glad he told me, even if it was hard to hear. At least I know what's on his mind. I'd rather have the real Neal, warts and all, than the perfect son who maybe isn't so perfect."

Abigail thought about Phoebe, who was still so closed off. *If only I could get her to talk to me. . . .*

Their food arrived at the table just then. A shrimp-and-avocado salad for Lila and the poached sea bass for Abigail, along with the house specialty—homemade focaccia stuffed with Taleggio cheese.

"How's it going with Phoebe?" Lila asked as she tucked into her salad.

"We're having our first family session tomorrow." Abigail felt her stomach dip at the thought. "Dr. Ernst says she's ready for it, and I assume he knows what he's doing—he keeps reassuring us that she's making progress. But honestly? We haven't seen much evidence of it. With Kent and me, I always get the feeling she's just going through the motions." Only with Lila could Abigail admit this. With other people, she always put on a smiling face when someone inquired after her daughter's health, giving them the official version: that Phoebe was staying with relatives out of town while she recuperated from her injuries.

"Neal gets that way, too, sometimes," Lila said. "We still have our bumps."

Abigail leaned in to ask in a low, urgent voice, "Has he said anything to you about, you know, what might have led Phoebe to . . ." She couldn't finish the sentence. It was still too raw.

"Not to me he hasn't." Lila appeared at a similar loss. "His exact words, the one time I asked him about it, were, 'If Phoebe has anything to say, it should come from her.'"

"Do you think he knows something he's not telling?"

"Maybe. But he's right—whatever it is, it should come from Phoebe."

Abigail sighed and put down her fork. Her appetite seemed to have vanished along with the relaxed mood. "The trouble is, we're not getting anywhere with her. It's like trying to break through a brick wall. I just wish I knew what was behind that wall."

"Usually it's not just one thing. With Neal, it's easy to blame everything on what happened with Gordon, but the truth is, he's got his own problems." Lila reached over to lay a hand on Abigail's. "If there *is* something Phoebe's keeping from you, it'll come out eventually. And remember, it's not so much about what happened as what happens from now on."

A yawning pit opened in Abigail's stomach at the thought. "That's what worries me. Sure, I want her home, but at the same time I'm terrified as hell. Do I lock up all the knives? Do I clean out the medicine chest? And even if I do all that, I can't keep an eye on her every minute of the day."

Lila eyed her in knowing sympathy. "It's not just you. I feel that way sometimes. But you'll get through this. We both will."

"How can you be so sure?"

Lila gave her a half-cocked smile. "I'm not. But I figure if I say it enough times, one of these days I'll start to believe it."

While they ate, they caught up on other things. Lila told Abigail more about her job and the various dramas of the ladies she worked with. And Abigail brought Lila up-to-date on her divorce—a subject that just a few short months ago would have had her cursing Kent but that now, to her surprise, she found herself taking in stride. "I never thought I'd hear myself say this," she shook her head in wonderment, "but in a way, I kind of admire him for what he did. I may not have realized it at the time, but our marriage was over long before he cheated on me. At least he had the guts to do something about it."

"What about you? You and Vaughn still going hot and heavy?" Lila asked.

Abigail had confided in her about Vaughn once the smoke from the fire had cleared—in more ways than one. How could she keep something like that from her? How could Vaughn? And what would have been the point? The only thing Lila didn't know was that Abigail had been feeling ambivalent about the direction—if any—this was taking.

Abigail put her fork down. "Yes, but it's . . . complicated."

"How so?" Lila arched a brow.

Abigail sighed. "Things are kind of up in the air right now."

"With everything, or with just you and Vaughn?"

"Both."

"Does that mean it's not serious with him?"

"Let's just say we're enjoying each other's company for the time being," Abigail hedged. She cast about for an excuse for her reluctance to commit. "Remember, I'm not even officially divorced."

But Lila wasn't buying it. "If you aren't, you will be soon enough. Come on, Abby, what's the *real* reason? Is it because he has cancer?" Her eyes locked on to Abigail's.

"No, of course not," Abigail was quick to reply. Perhaps too quick.

Lila gave her an odd look, as if wondering whether to believe her. "So what's the problem? What's holding you back?"

"From what? It's not like we're ever going to get married. I can't even see us living together."

"Why not?"

"Well, for one thing, we want different things out of life. What's it going to be like when he goes back to work?" Abigail didn't want to think about the alternative and knew Lila didn't either. "From what you've told me, he spends most of his time on the road."

"So? Like you'd be waiting with his pipe and slippers whenever he comes home?" Lila said with a laugh, shaking her head. "Face it, Abby, you're two of a kind. You're made for each other."

Abigail wished she could believe that. But the fact that they were both driven—she in her career and Vaughn in satisfying his wanderlust—wasn't enough to build a relationship on. She wanted more than a minor role in his life. When it had been her and Kent and the shoe had been on the other foot, wasn't that what had come between them, the fact that she'd been so unavailable? She wanted it to be different the next time—if there was going to be a next time. And from Vaughn's history with women, it was clear he hadn't exactly been a model of attentiveness. Look at Gillian, still hoping for a crumb off the table.

And, no, she couldn't ignore that he had cancer. What if it didn't go into remission? What then? To be at his side watching him waste away bit by bit would break her.

But to tell all that to Lila would only be opening a can of worms, so she changed the subject. "I stopped at the house on my way over," she mentioned as the waiter cleared away their plates.

"How's the cleanup going?" Lila asked.

"Almost done. Karim and his crew even managed to salvage some things—mostly china and silverware. Everything else is pretty much gone. Though I still have my great-grandmother's sampler—for some reason, that survived. Karim and I were joking that she probably had something to do with it. My mom always said she was a tough old gal."

"How is Karim, by the way?" Lila asked in a casual tone that didn't fool Abigail for a minute. She thought, *I'm not the only one with a tangled love life.*

"Fine. He asked after you."

"What did you tell him?" Lila's tone was one of only mild interest, but no one could have missed the color blooming in her cheeks.

"That you were well and working hard in your new job. He said to say hello." There had been no need for him to say more. Karim's unhappy face had told the whole story.

"That's it?"

"Was there something more you were hoping to hear?" Abigail asked with a hint of mischief in her voice.

"No, of course not. Don't be silly." Lila chose that moment to duck under the table to retrieve her napkin, which had conveniently fallen off her lap. There was no further discussion of Karim or any mention of their aborted relationship.

They lingered over coffee and dessert, in no hurry to get back to the pressures and concerns that awaited them in the outside world. It was almost three by the time they took their leave. As they were hugging good-bye on the sidewalk, Abigail was struck by the simple fact of them standing there like any two old friends who'd just broken bread together, as if there had never been a rift between them. Was it possible that just a few short months ago, she'd felt only bitterness toward Lila? That she'd suspected her and Kent of having an affair? That she and Lila had been able to resume their old friendship as if the only thing that had interrupted it was time and distance seemed nothing short of miraculous.

"Oh, I almost forgot," Abigail remembered to add as she was turning to go. "I got a postcard from Señora Delgado the other day. Remember, I asked her to keep in touch in case I needed to reach her?" Abigail had been looking into the possibility of getting her a green card.

"How's she doing?" Lila asked.

"Actually, it doesn't look as if she'll need that green card after all. It seems she up and got married—to that nice guy who picked her up from the hospital. It turns out he's a citizen."

Lila broke into a grin. "Really? That's great. Well, I hope it works out for her."

"I have a feeling it will. She strikes me as a lady who wouldn't marry for anything but love." Abigail decided to keep to herself for the time being the other reason she'd wanted to stay in touch with Concepción: the idea she'd been kicking around in her head of establishing a free clinic in Las Cruces in Milagros Sánchez's name. She didn't want to say anything, even to the girl's mother, until she knew whether she could pull it off. At this point, between her divorce and her current business woes, it was nothing more than a dream she hoped to one day realize.

"Love," Lila echoed somewhat wistfully. "If she's lucky, that'll be enough."

The dayroom at Dewhurst Psychiatric Facility was cheerfully furnished, with cushy armchairs and sofas upholstered in bold prints, round tables with chairs for craft projects, and framed Matisse and Chagall prints on the walls. A basket of toys sat in one corner for when young children came to visit, and in the built-in bookcase that spanned one wall, a collection of popular titles was arranged alphabetically by author. Even the view was cheerful—a wide vista of manicured lawn where patients could be seen strolling along the sunny, flower-lined walkways or relaxing on benches, some accompanied by family members, others enjoying a quiet moment of solitude.

Abigail had collectively spent so many hours in this room that she was quick to pick up on even the smallest of changes from one visit to the next—a throw pillow out of place or a picture hanging askew, a new notice tacked to the bulletin board. Today her gaze was drawn to the half-finished jigsaw puzzle on the table by the window, which seemed to symbolize what she hoped to accomplish with this family session: putting together the pieces that would help solve the mystery of why Phoebe had wanted to kill herself.

"Relax," Kent said, as she paced the floor, waiting for Phoebe and her therapist to appear. "You'll wear a hole in the carpet."

Abigail came to a halt, swiveling to face him. "What do you suppose is keeping them?"

Kent, seated on the sofa, glanced at his watch. "It's only two past the hour. I'm sure they'll be along any minute." Deeply tanned, wearing chinos and his brown corduroy blazer over a yellow Izod shirt (her best efforts through the years had failed to make a fashion horse out of him), he appeared relaxed, not just about the therapy session but about life in general. Specifically, life with Sheila. Abigail felt a tug of jealousy. It wasn't just that he was living happily with another woman. It was the apparent ease with which he'd moved on. Why couldn't it be that way for her? Why did everything always have to be so damn *hard?*

"I just hope it goes well," she fretted aloud.

"Dr. Ernst wouldn't have suggested it if he didn't think Phoebe was ready for it," Kent reasoned.

"Being ready to sit down with us doesn't mean she's ready to open up."

"It's a start, at least. Remember, Rome wasn't built in a day."

"How can you be so damned philosophical about it?" A note of impatience crept into her voice. "This is our *daughter* we're talking about, not one of your patients."

"I'm perfectly aware of that." He gave a small sigh, and she could see from his expression that he'd made up his mind not to allow her to provoke him just so she'd have someone to take out her frustration on. "I just don't happen to have the same expectations as you, is all. I'm not looking for answers. I just want Phoebe to know we're here for her."

Their conversation was interrupted by Phoebe's therapist striding into the room just then. Phoebe followed a few feet behind, walking at a slower pace with her head down and her arms folded over her chest. Dr. Ernst greeted them with his usual hearty handshake: a dry, firm clasp that always had the effect of instantly putting Abigail's fears to rest. *Don't despair. It gets better*, said those kind blue eyes behind the lenses of his wire-rim glasses. She found everything about him reassuring, in fact: his broad-shouldered athlete's build, his expertly cut hair the color of brushed stainless steel, the crispness of his French-cuffed shirt offset by the whimsical touch of a porpoise-patterned Hermès tie.

"Thanks for making the time," he said to them, as if they wouldn't have dropped everything to be here.

"What's more important than our daughter?" Kent directed an encouraging smile at Phoebe.

Phoebe didn't smile back.

"Not all our patients are lucky enough to have a family as involved as you two," replied Dr. Ernst with the air of someone who'd seen it all. "We've found it makes all the difference."

"Phoebe, honey, why don't you come sit by me?" said Kent, sinking back down on the plaid sofa and patting the cushion beside him. He was eyeing their daughter with a kind of eager hopefulness that Abigail found vaguely disturbing, for it meant that, despite his reassuring words of a moment ago, he was no more sure of Phoebe than she was. She watched as Phoebe lowered herself onto the sofa beside him—just far enough away to put some distance between them without its looking too obvious—and felt her anxiety creep up another notch.

The one heartening note was that Phoebe looked healthier than she had in a while. Still thin, but no longer like a model in a heroin-chic fashion spread. So at least she was eating. That was something. On one of their earlier visits, Abigail and Kent had discussed with Dr. Ernst the possibility of her having an eating disorder, but Dr. Ernst seemed to think that Phoebe's food issues were more a sign of emotional distress than of a psychological disorder.

"All right, then. Why don't we get started? Please, have a seat." Not until Dr. Ernst gestured toward Abigail did she realize she was still standing. He waited until she'd sat down before prompting, "Phoebe?"

Phoebe, her gaze fixed steadfastly on the carpet at her feet, didn't respond at first. She seemed nervous. There was a pimple on her chin that looked raw and irritated, as if she'd been picking at it, and her nails were bitten to the quick. It was all Abigail could do not to go to her and take her in her arms, the way she used to when Phoebe was little and had fallen down and hurt herself. But this wasn't some "boo-boo" that could be kissed away, she knew.

At last Phoebe brought her head up, her gaze skimming over her parents before lighting on a point just past Dr. Ernst's ear. "I don't know what I'm supposed to say." Her voice was soft, tentative.

"Just say whatever's on your mind," he coaxed patiently.

"Okay." She straightened her shoulders, putting on a game smile. "How are you, Mom? Dad?"

"We're fine," Abigail answered for them both, glancing over at Kent as she spoke. "Looking forward to having you home again. I have your room all ready at the new place. I think you'll like the way I fixed it up. All we have to do is buy you some new clothes."

Phoebe shrugged, looking disinterested. "Sure, whatever."

Kent cleared his throat. "We talked it over, and your mother and I agreed that it would be best if you lived with her for the time being," he said. "I'd like it if you could stay with me on weekends, though. It doesn't have to be every weekend, at least not right away. You can take it at your own pace. I know it's a lot for you to get used to," he added more tentatively, referring to his current living situation.

But Phoebe's mind clearly wasn't on her dad's new girlfriend. She glanced from Abigail to Kent. "So you two are, like, getting along now?" There was a note of distrust in her voice.

Kent cast a sidelong glance at Abigail, who replied evenly, "We're still your parents, no matter what. That's the main thing. We both love you and want what's best for you."

Phoebe didn't respond. She just sat there, the muscles in her jaw working as if she were engaged in some sort of internal struggle. At last she seemed to come to a resolution, and in a voice reminiscent of the old days, before she'd become sullen and belligerent and, more recently, politely disengaged, she said softly, "I know you do, Mom. And I'm sorry if I let you down. If it helps any, it wasn't anything against you or Dad."

Tears came to Abigail's eyes. She quickly blinked them back, determined not to let her emotions get the better of her. This was about Phoebe, not her. "I'm sorry, too," she said. "I know I haven't always been there for you. But I promise it'll be different from now on."

A corner of Phoebe's mouth hooked up in an oddly world-weary smile, that of a much older person who'd suffered too many disappointments in life to believe in fresh starts. "It's not just you, Mom. Or the divorce. It's . . . other stuff, too. Stuff that's got nothing to do with you guys." She paused, appearing hesitant to go on.

"It's okay, Phoebe. You're in a safe place," Dr. Ernst said gently.

Phoebe lowered her head, mottled blotches of color standing out on her cheeks as she sat twisting her hands in her lap. She said, in a low, unsteady voice, "I don't want you to hate me."

"Oh, baby." Kent started to put an arm around her, but when Phoebe stiffened in response, he quickly withdrew it, looking bewildered and more than a little hurt. "Don't you know there's nothing that would ever make us hate you?" he told her, his voice cracking with emotion.

"Whatever it is, you can tell us. It's okay," Abigail urged.

Phoebe's eyes remained downcast. Her words, when she was finally able to continue, were directed at the floor rather than to anyone in the room. "I . . . I didn't think anything of it at first. There was this extra-credit thing I was doing for his class, and he said he'd help me with it. He's always helping kids with stuff like that, so it didn't seem like any big deal, you know? I just thought he was being nice." She paused for a long moment, chewing on her lower lip.

"What happened then?" Dr. Ernst prompted.

But Abigail was already getting a funny feeling in the pit of her stomach. She knew where this was going. Hadn't the same thing happened to her? Oh, God. Why hadn't she recognized the signs?

"It was okay at first. I mean, I wasn't getting any weird vibes from him or anything," Phoebe went on. "Then one day he drove me over to his house after school so we could work on the project where it was quieter. His wife and kids were away, so he said we'd have the house all to ourselves." She shook her head, as if in disgust at her naïveté. "Yeah, I know. Like, how stupid can you get? I know stuff like that happens all the time, I've seen it on the news, but for some reason, I didn't think *he* was one of those guys. I mean, he's way older, for one thing, with a wife and kids and everything. How was I supposed to know?" Her voice broke, and she darted a panicky glance at Dr. Ernst, who nodded at her in encouragement, before she continued, "I didn't mean for anything to happen, I swear. Then after we . . ." She faltered, her cheeks growing redder. "I wanted to stop, but for some reason, I couldn't. It was like he had this control over me. Also, I felt like I was already this horrible person whose life was ruined, so what was the use?"

Kent stared at her in shocked disbelief. "Are you telling us this man had *sex* with you?" His voice trembled with outrage.

Phoebe brought her head up, her eyes pleading with him. "Don't be mad at me, Daddy. I know now that what I did was wrong. I wish I could take it back, but it's too late for that."

"You think I'm mad at *you?* Oh, Christ." Kent buried his face in his hands, letting out a small, choked cry. When he lifted his head, his eyes were wet. He turned a harrowed face to Phoebe. "Baby, I want you to hear me on this, because it's important." He spoke slowly and carefully, holding her gaze. *"It's not your fault.* Whatever you might think, that man, your teacher, he took advantage of you. And you can be sure it won't happen again to some other girl, because if I have my way, he'll be behind bars," he added through gritted teeth.

Phoebe looked faintly alarmed. "He's not a criminal. It wasn't like that," she protested tearfully.

"You're sixteen. He's a grown man. By God, if he were here now, I'd put him up against that wall. I'd—"

Dr. Ernst put out a hand to silence Kent. "Let Phoebe finish. This is about how *she* feels."

Abigail sat there in shock, too numb to speak or even move. At first she hadn't been able to process what Phoebe was telling them. Then it had sunk in: *My baby was raped.* Call it what you want—seduced, taken advantage of, sexually abused—in Abigail's mind, it was rape. It was also history repeating itself. For it seemed as if the rotten thing from her own past, the thing she'd done her utmost to bury, wasn't dead after all. It had risen from its grave to steal Phoebe's innocence, damaging her so badly in the process that she'd wanted to kill herself.

Listening to the whole ugly, and ultimately familiar, tale, Abigail wanted to die, too. At last she found her voice. "You should have come to us. Did you really think we'd blame *you?*"

Phoebe hung her head, her silence speaking for itself.

"Oh, sweetie." Abigail's control broke. For a long moment, all she could do was sit there, shaking her head as tears rolled down her cheeks. Finally she said hoarsely, "I'm so sorry."

"It wasn't *your* fault, Mom. You didn't do anything." Phoebe was eyeing her with a kind of panic. Clearly, she wasn't used to seeing her mother like this.

"It's not what I did, it's what I *didn't* do. I should have told you."

"About what? Mr. Guarneri? You couldn't have known."

"No, but I could have warned you."

"Abby, what are you saying? Did you *know* something about this?" Kent frowned at her, looking perplexed.

"I . . ." She was aware of everyone's eyes on her. They were all waiting for her to go on, but just as Phoebe had struggled to find the words to express the unspeakable, Abigail had been rendered momentarily mute by the demons that haunted her still, even after all these years. The room was slowly spinning as if she were on a carousel; she had to grip the arms of her chair to hold herself steady. "I . . . I don't know where to begin," she stammered.

"Why don't you start at the beginning?" Dr. Ernst's calm, reassuring voice floated toward her.

Abigail looked up to find him eyeing her encouragingly. Every particle of her being rebelled against the prospect of dredging up the past, *her* past, but she knew she had to, for Phoebe's sake. "Remember my telling you about how my mother and I went to live with relatives when I was your age?" she began, looking over at her daughter. Phoebe nodded, staring at her fixedly. "What I didn't tell you was that my uncle ... Uncle Ray ..." Just saying his name caused her to tremble. "He raped me." Her voice was so low it was nearly inaudible, but her words had the effect of a shot ringing out. Everyone grew very still, and Phoebe let out a little gasp. "He used to take me along on business trips, and we'd stay in roadside motels, where he ... he'd do things to me ... things I couldn't tell my mama about. She was dying, and I was afraid it would kill her even sooner if she found out. So I kept it to myself. I never told another living soul. Until now." She slumped back in her chair, as exhausted as if she'd just delivered a long speech.

"Oh, my God. *Mom.*" Phoebe gaped at her.

No one else spoke. Kent sat shaking his head, staring at Abigail with a dumbfounded look on his face, while Dr. Ernst regarded her with sharp interest.

"What I'm trying to tell you, sweetie, is that I *know,*" Abigail went on. "I felt ashamed, too. I thought it was my fault somehow." She glanced over at Kent. "I couldn't even bring myself to tell your dad."

"I wish you had," Kent said in a hollow voice that seemed to carry an edge of accusation.

"I wish I had, too." She eyed him with regret.

"What happened to him?" Phoebe wanted to know.

"Uncle Ray?" Abigail shook her head, the shame that she'd once felt so acutely draining from her like pus from a lanced wound. "I don't know. Needless to say, I didn't keep up with him and my aunt after I moved away. For all I know, they're both dead by now."

"I wish Mr. Guarneri was dead." Where minutes ago Phoebe had been slumped over staring at the floor, radiating waves of self-loathing, she now sat bolt upright, a fierce look in her eye. "Why am *I* the one stuck in this loony bin while he gets to go on with his life like nothing happened?"

"That's the attitude." Kent brightened a little.

"Don't worry. He's not going to get off so lightly," Abigail vowed.

At once Phoebe retreated back into her shell, asking fretfully, "You're not going to say anything to him, are you?" Abigail wondered if it was the public exposure she feared, or if it was her teacher whom she was protecting. Probably a little of both. Either way, it wasn't open to discussion.

"I won't have to," she said in a hard voice. "He can tell it to the judge."

After the session, Kent walked Abigail out to the parking lot. Floating along at his side, Abigail felt simultaneously jittery and drained, as if she'd put in a fourteen-hour day on no sleep with only caffeine to fuel her, while Kent merely looked spent, as if he'd aged ten years in the past hour, his shoulders stooped and his face creased with lines that hadn't been there before.

"I'd kill the bastard with my bare hands if I could," Kent growled as they made their way along the path. It had to be the first time he'd regretted having taken the Hippocratic oath, she thought.

"We'll have the satisfaction of seeing him ruined, at least," she reminded him. Dr. Ernst had saved them the trouble of calling the police. After the session, he'd taken her and Kent into his office and informed them that he'd alerted the authorities, as he was required to do by law in cases involving a minor. For all they knew, Phoebe's teacher could be facing an arrest warrant at that very moment.

"What about you? Are you going to be okay?" Kent shot her a concerned look.

"I'm a little shaky, but hanging in there," she told him.

"Good. Because I'd like to know what the hell just happened back there." He came to an abrupt halt, his eyes that had been dull and lifeless just moments before now ablaze with anger. "Christ, Abby, I can't believe you kept it from me all those years. Something that *huge*. Would you mind telling me why I'm only just now hearing about it?"

She looked into his eyes and saw the hurt there, behind the anger. The hurt she'd caused. She sighed. "I wish I had an answer for you."

"Did you think it would change how I felt about you?"

"No, it wasn't that. I wanted to tell you. It was just . . ." She gave a helpless shrug. How to explain the inexplicable?

"Jesus. When I think of all those years . . ." Kent shook his head before adding more gently, "You *could* have told me, you know. I wouldn't have loved you any less. If anything, it would have made me love you more."

Abigail cut her gaze away. She couldn't bear to look into his eyes and see the hurt and bewilderment she'd caused. She looked out over the lawn instead, where other people were out enjoying the sunshine. She spotted an older couple whom she'd noticed earlier on her way in, strolling hand in hand. A short distance away, a little tow headed boy was playing catch with a golden retriever, both reacting with the same unalloyed delight each time the ball was tossed and the dog went streaking across the lawn to fetch it. *Simple pleasures*, she thought, closing her eyes for a moment and trying to summon a time in her life when she hadn't been striving toward some goal, on fire with ambition. When she hadn't believed that the trademarked Abigail Armstrong created for public consumption was preferable to the real and very fallible woman, hiding like the Wizard of Oz behind his curtain.

"I know that now," she said, bringing her gaze back to Kent. "The problem wasn't you. It was me. I didn't love *myself* enough."

"Oh, Abby." He drew her into his arms.

"I guess a part of me will always be that girl, thinking it was my fault," she murmured into the hollow space between his neck and shoulder, the safe place into which she'd whispered her most intimate thoughts countless times through the years. "And now, knowing I might have been able to prevent the same thing from happening to our daughter, if I'd warned her about men like my uncle . . ." She was gripped by regret so profound that it was a moment before she could go on. "Instead, I fooled myself into thinking that if I gave her the kind of life *I* never had, she'd somehow be protected from harm. For *that*, I'll truly never forgive myself."

Kent drew back to look her in the eye. "We're not God, Abby. There was no way we could've protected her from *everything*," he reminded her.

"Remember when she was in the third grade and she broke her wrist falling off the monkey bars? We blamed ourselves for that, too."

"This isn't something that can be fixed like a broken bone."

He sighed. "I know that. So what are we supposed to do? You tell me." For the first time in all the years she'd known him, Kent seemed at a loss.

"We love her, that's what," she said, recalling Lila's words from yesterday. "We make sure she knows she can come to us with *anything*, even the stuff that's hard to hear."

"I thought that's what we were doing."

"Then we need to try even harder."

He nodded thoughtfully, his arms falling heavily to his sides. But his troubled look remained in place as they resumed walking along the path. After a bit, he ventured, "Abby? Do you think we should hold off on the divorce? I don't want to make this any tougher on Phoebe than it already is. Or on you." He darted her a glance, as if to gauge her reaction.

Abigail struggled to mask her surprise. Was Kent having second thoughts about all this? Maybe things weren't so hunky-dory with Sheila after all. She felt a heady surge of triumph at the thought, but it was short-lived. This wasn't a faltering business deal that could be brought back to the negotiating table. Nor was it simply about doing what might be best for Phoebe. What did *she* want? Was she even still in love with Kent? Was he in love with her?

She realized with a sinking regret that, while she did still love Kent, it wasn't the kind of love that could sustain a marriage. It really was over between them. They'd both moved on. Whatever they were feeling right now was merely shared concern for their daughter and perhaps the echo of what they'd once had.

Her thoughts turned once more to Vaughn. Something inside her rose, then dipped, like a bird taking wing. And with it came the realization, sneaking past the sentry guarding the border between her careful rationalizations and the lawless territory of her heart, that *he* was the person with whom she wanted to share her life—whatever form that would take. The feeling was so strong that she felt as if the wind had been knocked out of her. It was a moment before she could reply, "I appreciate your willingness, Kent, but I don't think you should put your plans on hold. I think we *can* agree to be civilized about it, though." She gave him a crooked smile. "You have my solemn vow that I won't have my lawyer tear yours a new one."

He nodded, looking more than a little relieved. His offer had clearly been guided more by a sense of duty than any lingering feelings for her. "Fair enough," he said.

They walked on in companionable silence, each wrapped in his or her own thoughts. Abigail, grateful for the continued presence of this kind, considerate man in her life. Kent, seemingly bewildered by the woman strolling alongside him who bore only a surface resemblance to his hard-charging wife. But each secure in the knowledge that, though they might not love each other as they once had, they'd still have each other to lean on from time to time.

There was only one thing left to resolve: Vaughn. She was being foolish, she realized, in letting her fear of losing him hold her back. He could die, sure. Or he could be released back into the wild, where he'd be just as lost to her. Either way, she couldn't let that stop her from telling him how she felt. He had to know that she loved him. That she wanted to find a way to make this work.

Unconsciously, Abigail reached into her coat pocket, idly fingering the smooth, metallic surface of her Nokia, into which she'd programmed the number for Gillian's loft.

19

While Abigail was contemplating phoning Vaughn, he was in his doctor's office contemplating the possibility that he might not live out the year.

He sat tensely, bracing himself for bad news, as Dr. Grossman closed the file that had lain open on his desk. Normally his nurse gave Vaughn the test results over the phone, but this time the doctor had asked him to come into the office. Now Vaughn studied the man's face as closely as a moment ago Grossman had been studying his chart. Short, rotund, with a mop of gingery curls shot with gray and an affinity for Oxfords and rumpled tweeds, Dr. Grossman brought to mind an aging vaudevillian doing a doctor routine, only there was nothing jocular about Vaughn's hematologist-oncologist, who had the bedside manner of a surgical-steel instrument. Nothing in the poker-faced expression he wore from which to draw encouragement. He could be gearing up to deliver a death sentence.

When at last the doctor's face relaxed in a smile, it was like a last-minute reprieve from the electric chair. "Well, Vaughn, I'm happy to report that these all look fine," he said, tapping the file in front of him with a stubby, ink-stained finger. "Your CBC readings are good. Your white count is thirteen point three—well within normal range. And nothing lit up on your PET scan this time. That's why I asked you to come in today, so I could give you the news in person—I think it's safe to say you're cancer-free." His smile widened into a grin. It was the first time in all these months that Vaughn had actually seen him grin.

Vaughn let out the breath he hadn't realized he was holding. The room seemed to rock a bit, like a boat listing at sea. "Wow. That's . . ." He paused to shake his head, unable to find the words to express what he was feeling.

"We'll need to continue monitoring you, of course," Dr. Grossman went on. "I want you back here in three months' time, and every three months after that for the next two years at least. But for now, I'd say you're good to go. Congratulations, Vaughn." He stood up to shake Vaughn's hand. "So what's next? You must be eager to get back to work."

"You don't know the half of it." Vaughn had simply been living day to day, trying not to think too far ahead, but now he realized that he was itching to get back into the field.

"I guess that means you'll soon be off to some remote corner of the globe."

"The farther away, the better. As long as I never have to set foot inside another doctor's office. For another three months, that is," Vaughn remembered to add. "No offense, Doc."

"None taken." Dr. Grossman smiled. "Just don't let it go any longer than that." He consulted the calendar on his desk, counting forward from April. "We'll see you the end of July, then?"

"You can count on it. Otherwise I'd have to rely on witch doctors, and believe me, as much as I'm open to new experiences, I don't want to go there," Vaughn joked. Reflexively, he ran a hand through his hair, gratified and a bit surprised, as always, by how long and thick it was. It had come back, and so had his life. Now all he had to do was figure out where to put that life.

Strolling west along East 68th Street on his way to the subway, he couldn't seem to stop smiling. He felt more lighthearted than he had in a very long while. In his mind, he saw the years spooling out ahead him like fresh blacktop on an open highway. He thought of all the places yet to explore and of the adventures yet to experience. He thought of . . .

Abigail.

Suddenly he realized what this would mean for them. Weeks snatched here and there between gigs. Phone calls and e-mails that were poor substitutes for the real thing. But what was the alternative? He wasn't about to retire, and he could hardly ask her to join him in the field. Even if she were willing, she had her daughter to think of, not to mention her business. Besides, when on assignment, he always flew solo, with the exception of his crew.

His mother's words came back to haunt him: *It's time you settled down and started a family.* Words spoken so often during her lifetime that they'd become almost a joke. As if she'd had anything but the remotest idea of what family was, her view had been so distorted from looking out at the world through the bottom of a wineglass. Not wanting to go with her into *all* the reasons he'd remained steadfastly single, Vaughn had always deflected the remark with some casual comment about not having met the right woman yet.

But now he *had* met the right woman. No, that wasn't quite accurate— Abigail had owned a piece of his heart all along. A heart that would be going back into cold storage before too long.

Two days ago, he'd gotten a call from Don Dempsey, a producer at the Discovery channel whom he'd worked with in the past. Don was putting together a crew—Denny Engstrom, Bif Harder, Judd Turnbull, and the gentle giant Olaf Lundgren, known to all as "Swede"—for a special on the creation of a newly designated wildlife preserve in the African nation of Gabon. Filming would start in two weeks' time. Did Vaughn think he'd be up to it? Don had wanted to know. Vaughn had expressed interest but left the door open, just in case. Now, with the green light from his doctor, he was already mentally booking his flight.

The only question that remained was where that left him and Abigail. They'd never spoken of a future together. He wasn't even sure if that was what she wanted. With all the complications in her life right now, why take on another one in the form of a (previously) cancer-ridden boyfriend with itchy feet and not much more to offer than the occasional roll in the hay between gigs? Oh, and let's not forget that he'd effectively be homeless. Still, he'd hoped that maybe . . .

It was a strange and not altogether comfortable feeling, this hope, after having spent his entire adult life chafing at such bonds. He'd never before questioned his priorities. Work had always come first, second, and third. Even if Abigail would have him, what the hell was he supposed to *do* with her?

He felt a little bad, too, about leaving his sister in the lurch. But Lila would be okay. She was doing better than he'd expected. His nephew was going to be fine, too. Neal was a good kid who'd temporarily lost his way but now he seemed to be on the right track.

And then there was Gillian. She'd known, of course, that it was only a matter of time before he moved out—either on his own steam or feet first. But he had the feeling the conversation he was about to have with her would be difficult nonetheless. She'd grown accustomed to having him around. They might not have been together in the sense that she would have wished, but they slept under the same roof and took most of their meals together, and when his laundry came out of the dryer, it was tangled up with hers.

He arrived back at the loft to find Gillian in her studio, in the process of welding a piece of metal onto a huge steel sculpture that she was doing for an office building in SoHo. The concrete-floored space, sectioned off from the living area by a solid wall of firebrick, was where his ex-girlfriend spent most of her time when she wasn't on site for an installation. She was as at home here as he was in airports and out in the field. Watching her in her painter's coveralls and protective shield, expertly wielding her propane torch, a fountain of sparks flying out around her, he felt a deep affection for her, thinking of how much she'd sacrificed for him.

She noticed him standing there and switched off her torch, lifting the plastic shield over her face to flash him a grin. "Hey, you. I didn't expect you back until later. How'd it go?"

He shrugged. "You know doctors—in and out."

Her eyes searched his face. "So? What did he say?" From her carefully subdued tone, it was obvious that she'd been on pins and needles all morning, awaiting word on his test results.

"You," he said, "are looking at a man who's cancer-free." She let out a whoop and dashed over to him, jumping up into his arms and wrapping her legs around his. She was so tiny, the full weight of her came as a shock. Gillian wasn't one to walk lightly through life. *Or let go easily*, he thought. He eased her back onto her feet. "The timing couldn't be better. Don Dempsey from the Discovery channel called the other day. He has a gig lined up, and he asked if I was ready to go back to work." Vaughn spoke casually, attempting to downplay it.

"And what did you tell him?"

"I haven't told him anything yet. I'm telling you first."

Gillian was standing so erect and taut, she was almost quivering: an aerial antenna picking up a distress signal. As the realization of what this meant sank in, she began to shake her head, slowly at first, then more vehemently. "No. You're not ready. It's too soon!"

"The doctor said it was okay for me to go back to work."

"He doesn't know you like I do. He doesn't know the kind of life you lead. What if you have a setback? How are you supposed to get proper medical care off in some godforsaken part of the world?"

"It's not like I'll be completely out of touch," he pointed out. "Nothing's ever more than a few days' jeep ride to the nearest outpost. And I can always catch a plane home, if need be. I'll be fine."

Her shoulders slumped in defeat. "Where to this time?" she asked wearily.

"Gabon."

"You'll have to excuse me. I flunked geography in school. I don't even know where the fuck Gabon is," she said.

"Nowhere you'd ever want to be," he assured her. "But it's what passes for civilization in that part of the world, so I should be all right in the event of an emergency."

"That's a comfort," she said sarcastically.

"Hey, don't be so gloomy. I should think I'd have pretty much worn out my welcome by now." He made an attempt at leavening the mood. "Just think, after I leave, you'll have the whole place to yourself again. No more wet towels on the shower rod. And you won't have to remind me to put the toilet seat down."

A small line appeared between her knitted brows, and her eyes shimmered with unshed tears. "Don't talk down to me. I'm not a kid," she growled. "You know why I don't want you to go."

He sighed. "Gil . . ."

"Oh, I know what you're thinking," she went on. "You think just because we're not sleeping together, you can waltz off, no strings attached. But that's not how it works, buster. *Everything* has strings attached. Just because you choose not to see them, it doesn't mean they're not there."

"I can't stay. You know that. Don't think I'm not grateful for everything you've done. But, Gil, we both knew this day would come."

"I never expected you to give up your career. That's not what I want."

"Then what *do* you want?" An edge of exasperation crept into his voice.

"Something other than a pat on the back would be nice." She studied him for a moment, wearing a faintly quizzical look, as if searching for something. But she must not have found what she was looking for because she abruptly threw up her hands and cried, "Go. Just go, will you? Go pack your frickin' bags. Maybe I *will* be glad to see you go. You're a pain in the ass sometimes, you know that, Vaughn? A real pain in the ass."

"I didn't say I was leaving this very second." Vaughn reached out to lay a hand on her shoulder, but she flinched and jerked back as if a spark from her propane torch had landed on her.

"All right, then, I'm *asking* you to go. Allow me that much, at least. I don't see why I should have you hang around just so I can have the fun of being tortured some more." She pulled a crumpled Kleenex from the front pocket of her overalls and blew her nose into it. "You can always stay with Abby. Why not? You're already sleeping with her."

Vaughn was momentarily taken aback. How had she known? He'd gone out of his way to be discreet.

She scoffed at the dumbfounded expression he must have worn. "Men. You're all alike. No, I didn't find a pair of panties under the bed that weren't mine, if that's what you're thinking. But I have eyes in my head, and I know what my gut tells me. You're fucking her, aren't you?" It wasn't a question.

Vaughn felt his back go up. It wasn't as if he owed Gillian an explanation. He'd always been up front with her, even when they were dating, never making any promises that he'd had no intention of keeping. "Whether we are or we aren't is beside the point," he replied coolly.

"The point," she jabbed a finger at him, "is that you love *her*, not me." All at once, having voiced the words that had lain between them all these months, unspoken, like some invisible Rubicon neither of them had dared cross, her pixie's face crumpled. "I get it. I'm not stupid. I knew you weren't in love with me, but I thought—" She broke off with a small, choked cry.

Vaughn gathered into his arms the tight, quivering knot of flesh that was his ex-girlfriend and soon-to-be ex-roommate. He felt like a rat. Whatever spin he might try to put on it, the bald truth was that he'd selfishly taken advantage of her while he'd needed her, only to discard her when he no longer had any use for her. She had every right to be angry at him. And she wasn't the first one to react like this—he'd been down this road with other women, too many to count.

Why should it be any different with Abigail?

"I'm sorry, Gil," he murmured into her hair, which smelled faintly of molten metal and the fruit-scented shampoo she used. "I wish it could've been the way you wanted. But I meant what I said before—I owe you my life. I'd probably be dead by now if it weren't for you."

"If you'd croaked, I'd have gotten to mourn you, at least." She lifted her head off his chest to give him a half-assed smile. Her eyes were wet, their thick black lashes clumped together like little starbursts. "It would have been one kick-ass funeral, too. I'd have worn a black dress and veil like Jackie Kennedy's, and everyone would have thought I was the love of your life. I'd have played it to the hilt."

"You look good in black." He smiled back at her.

"Good is for nice Catholic girls. I fucking *rock*."

"You do, at that."

Just then, the phone rang. Neither of them moved to pick it up. Three rings later, Vaughn heard the faint sound of Abigail's voice on the answering machine in the next room. His heart leaped, and he was torn between the desire to make a run for it before she hung up and a reluctance to rub salt into Gillian's wounds by doing so.

It was Gillian who made the decision for him. She jerked free of him, scowling. "Go on, answer it. You two deserve each other."

"I need to see you."

At the sound of Abigail's voice, like cool, sweet water to a parched throat after his confrontation with Gillian, Vaughn felt some of the tension go out of him. "Just name the time," he said.

"How about tomorrow afternoon?"

"Great. That little Italian place we went to the last time?"

She hesitated before answering, "I was thinking of somewhere a little more private."

"You could always meet me at my hotel," he said.

"You're moving out?" She sounded surprised.

He lowered his voice, casting a look in the direction of Gillian's studio to make sure the door was shut. "More like I'm getting thrown out."

"I see." Abigail didn't have to ask why. It must have been obvious. "Vaughn, I'm sorry."

"I'm sorry, too," he said, thinking of Gillian and feeling like a heel.

"I don't think meeting at your hotel is such a good idea, though," she told him. "We'd only end up in bed, and there's something I need to talk to you about."

He wondered what it could be. It sounded serious. "All right, then. Just tell me where to meet you."

They arranged to meet the following day at the Noguchi Museum. It was a little out of the way, she said, but it was the one public place where she was unlikely to be recognized and where they could talk in relative privacy. The museum, Noguchi's former studio, was on a grungy industrial block in Long Island City and thus not exactly over-run with tourists.

Vaughn arrived early the next day, well before the appointed hour, wanting to have a look around before Abigail got there. For one reason or another, he'd never gotten around to visiting the museum. Now, wan-dering from one vast, concrete-floored room, taking in Noguchi's sparely elegant sculptures, he found it a serene, Zenlike oasis. The mild appre-hension he'd been feeling since his phone conversation with Abigail the day before began to ebb.

After touring the exhibits, he exited into the walled courtyard out back. A slender woman, wearing dark glasses and a scarf over her head, was seated on a bench under a Japanese maple, gazing at a polished granite sculpture that made him think of a pair of entwined hands. It was an instant before he recognized her; then his heart leaped.

Abigail rose, walking toward him. Not the proud, confident Abigail he knew; this Abigail walked cautiously, holding herself as if she were a brimming glass that might spill over. Anyone who didn't know better, if asked which of them had been ill, would have picked Abigail.

"Have you been waiting long?" he asked.

She smiled at him. "Not at all. I only got here a few minutes ago." She slipped off her sunglasses and tucked them into her purse. Her eyes looked bruised, as if from lack of sleep. Clearly something was troubling her, and he wondered uneasily if it had to do with him.

They started down the graveled walkway, lined with trees and outdoor sculptures, that wound through the courtyard. The only sounds, other than that of distant traffic, were the rustling of leaves overhead and the pleasant gurgling of fountains. "So what was it you wanted to see me about?" he asked as they strolled along, hand in hand.

"I'll get to that in a minute. First tell me how it went with the doctor."

"Good. Better than good, actually. Dr. Grossman tells me I'm officially in remission. With any luck, I won't have to see him again for another three months."

"Oh, Vaughn. That's wonderful!" In an instant, her troubled look vanished, and she was grinning from ear to ear. "You don't know how happy that makes me. My God, what a relief." Her eyes shining, she paused to caress his cheek—the same light, almost reverential touch he'd used in smoothing his hand over one of the sculptures inside a minute ago when the guard's back had been turned.

The obvious next step would be for her to ask, *What now?* But he didn't want to get into that just yet. He wanted to hear what was on her mind first, find out what was troubling her.

"How about you? How'd it go yesterday?" he asked.

Abigail sighed. "Tougher than I expected. Something came out in the session. . . ." She paused before going on, wearing a deeply pained look. "It seems . . . well, it seems my daughter was sexually molested. By one of her teachers at school." Though the weather was sunny and mild, she began to shiver as if with a sudden drop in temperature. He understood then why she looked so bruised, and his heart went out to her.

"I'm so sorry, Abby. My God." He'd been to countries where it was legal for men like Phoebe's teacher to have sex with girls and boys as young as eleven and twelve. He'd witnessed it with his own eyes—older men trawling the side streets and alleys at night in search of young marks—and the sick depravity of it never got any easier for him to stomach.

"Kent and I have already spoken to the DA," she informed him. "As soon as Phoebe gives him her affidavit, he'll press charges."

Vaughn shook his head in disgust. "The sick bastard."

She stared past him, her mouth set in a grim line. "Believe me, I know all about sick bastards who prey on young girls. That's what makes it even worse. I should have recognized the signs."

"How could you? It's not something most people automatically suspect."

"I'm not most people."

"What do you mean?"

Abigail took a deep breath, as if to steady herself, and brought her gaze back to him. "I was sexually abused, too, when I was her age."

Vaughn stared at her in shock. "Jesus."

"It was my uncle," she said. "I was only sixteen. The only other person I'd been with until then was you. And we never . . ." She trailed off, her eyes welling with tears.

"Oh, Abby. My poor Abby." Vaughn wrapped his arms around her.

"When I told you your letters were a lifeline, I meant it," she whispered hoarsely.

He drew back to level his gaze at her. "If I'd known, I would have moved heaven and earth, if that's what it would have taken, to get you away from there. You believe that, don't you?"

She nodded, wearing a small smile. "I used to fantasize about it all the time. My knight in shining armor, riding to the rescue."

"I'd have done more than that. I'd have beaten the guy to a pulp. Why didn't you tell me?"

"I was too ashamed. I thought it was my fault, somehow. I never even told Kent. He didn't find out about it until yesterday, in the session."

"He must have been pretty taken aback."

"More like shocked. Angry, too. He couldn't understand why I'd kept it from him."

"Why did you?" Vaughn was curious.

She gave a small shrug. "I was good at keeping secrets. A little too good, as it turns out."

Suddenly a lot of things made sense to Vaughn. Mainly, why Lila's failure to get in touch with her had been even more hurtful to Abigail than it ordinarily would have been. How abandoned she must have felt! Stuck out there in the middle of nowhere, with her mother dying and her uncle . . .

But Vaughn couldn't think about that. If he did, he'd want to smash his fist through something.

He understood now the mountain she'd had to climb in order to forgive his sister, and that made him love her all the more.

"So is that what you wanted to talk to me about?" he said.

"Partly, yes." She gazed at him intently, looking more vulnerable than he was used to seeing her. "It made me realize something. I need to know where we stand, Vaughn. Not," she was quick to assure him, "that I'm trying to corral you in any way. Please don't think that. Right now, I'm in no shape to even make a date for next New Year's Eve, much less anything more long-range than that. I just need to know if this—*us*—is just for old times' sake or if there's really something there."

He took her in his arms and kissed her, a deep, lingering kiss that he hoped would put any doubts to rest. "Was that the answer you were looking for?" he murmured as he drew back.

"No, but you're definitely headed in the right direction." Her face lit up briefly, but her smile faded almost as soon as it took hold. "Seriously, Vaughn, where do you see this going? We're not kids anymore. Our lives are too complicated to just take this on a wing and a prayer."

She'd removed her scarf, and the sunlight filtering through the branches of the gingko tree under which they stood had brought out the natural red highlights in her hair, making them spark as if with electricity. Her face seemed pale in contrast. Vaughn longed to tell her everything she wanted to hear, but he'd only be painting a picture as false as the fantasy Abigail had had as a teenager, of them riding off into the sunset together. It would be unfair to let her think they could have a life together when the reality would be scattered visits and phone calls, so he bit the bullet and said, "I love you, Abby. But I'm afraid that's all I can offer you right now. I'm not even sure where I'll be on New Year's Eve."

"You're leaving?" It wasn't so much a question as a statement.

He nodded. "I got a gig with the Discovery channel. I'll be gone a couple of months, maybe longer."

"Then there'll be another gig. And another one after that." She gave a small, resigned smile that tugged at his heart. But unlike Gillian, she wasn't going to fall apart. She drew in a breath, as if to bolster herself, and said in a voice that was only a little ragged around the edges, "So. I guess this is good-bye."

"It doesn't have to be." Vaughn had been hoping against hope that she'd be willing to accept less than the full sum as a down payment on the life they could have one day, when they were both retired (though somehow he couldn't picture either of them retiring). "I'm not leaving until the end of next week. Why don't you stay over in the city this week-end? Seems a shame to let my hotel room go to waste." He aimed for a roguish smile that fell a little flat.

She shook her head. "I can't. I promised Kent we'd go over the finan-cial statements. We'll probably be at it all weekend." He sensed it was just an excuse. Was it just that she wasn't up for a long, drawn-out good-bye, or was there something else? The answer, when it came, rocked him. "Speaking of whom, my husband has very gallantly offered to move back in with me," she informed him.

Vaughn felt as if he'd been kicked in the stomach. "What did you tell him?"

"*Not* that I was in love with another man, you can be sure of that."

Vaughn felt some of the tension go out of him. "So you told him no?"

She nodded, putting him out of his misery. "He was only offering be-cause of Phoebe. I told him I didn't see what good it would do any of us if it was for all the wrong reasons."

"Wise choice."

Her expression grew serious again. "Which doesn't change the fact that the man I *am* in love with is leaving me." He heard a little quaver in her voice and knew she was struggling not to give in to tears, but there was no accusation in it, as there had been with Gillian.

"Not leaving *you*. Just leaving. For the time being. There's a difference."

He put his arms around her and pulled her to him, kissing her again. With abandon this time, the way you kiss a woman you love when you don't know when . . . or if . . . you'll be seeing her again. They could've been on a city sidewalk with people streaming past and he wouldn't have been any more aware of his surroundings than he was at that mo-ment, as they stood with their arms wrapped around each other, mouths and hearts joined.

When he finally drew back, it was to whisper, "I love you, Abby. I've always loved you." It felt good saying it, like when he'd finally been able to stretch his limbs and take in fresh air after those first few weeks of confinement. "It doesn't have to be the end."

"It does for me," she said with regret. "I'm not built the way you are, Vaughn. I don't live life on the fly. Don't get me wrong, I love who you are, but you're everything I'm not."

"That doesn't mean we have to cancel each other out."

"No, but it does mean we'd only end up making each other unhappy. Why not admit it now and save ourselves a lot of grief?"

"Abby . . ." He reached out to her, but she was already pulling away.

"I should get back to work," she said, adding somewhat ruefully, "I have a business to run."

There were many things Vaughn could have said just then. *I could travel the world over, and I still won't be able to leave you behind. I know, because I've tried. I may not have realized it then, but all that time, with those other women, there was only you.* But all he said was, "I'll write to you. Will you write back?"

Abigail seemed about to make some definitive statement about their future—or lack of one—but in the end, she only shrugged and said, "I'll write, sure. We've always been good at that."

Then she was gone, walking briskly back the way she'd come, as though fleeing some unseen assailant. Leaving Vaughn amid the beauty and serenity of this improbable setting, which all of a sudden seemed to mock him. She was right in one sense, he knew—they were polar opposites in nearly every respect—but wrong to think she could simply walk away. Neither of them would be able to walk away so easily. Memory was like evolution in that way, he thought, a process of natural selection—it took what it needed and discarded the rest—and for whatever reason, Abigail was encoded in his. It wasn't a matter of choice. It simply *was*. Like the earth revolving around the sun, his thoughts would revolve around Abigail.

He waited until he was sure she was gone; then with a sigh he turned and headed back inside.

20

"Mom? Can I talk to you?" Neal hovered just outside Lila's worksta-tion. His hair was windblown and his shirt untucked, as if he'd ridden over on his bike, which he probably had. The ten-year-old Hyundai he'd bought through a want ad hadn't left the garage since he'd brought it home and wouldn't until he'd earned enough money to pay for needed repairs.

"Sure." She punched the button on the phone that connected to her headset. She'd been on hold with one of the airlines, but it could wait. "What is it, sweetie?"

"Sorry to bother you at work." He appeared hesitant all of a sudden as his gaze swept her desk, which was cluttered with paperwork and brochures, itineraries to be faxed. Or maybe it was just that it always seemed to take him a moment or two to adjust to the sight of his mother with a headset on, wearing office attire—today's outfit an off-white linen suit and pale blue top and the new Kenneth Cole slingbacks she'd bought on sale. "If you're busy, I guess it could wait until later."

She flashed him a smile. "Never too busy for you. Anyway, I could use the break. I've been at my desk all morning. Why don't we step outside?" Whatever it was, she didn't want any of her coworkers listening in. Barb Huggins was a dear soul but somewhat of a busybody, as Lila had found in the months since she'd come to work at the agency—a temporary position that had become permanent, she'd proven so "indispensable," according to Barb.

Lila experienced a flutter of unease, wondering what was so urgent that it couldn't have waited until she'd gotten home. But she held her apprehension in check. Neal's therapist had warned against spinning worst-case scenarios. She could hear Dr. Frye's voice in her mind now: *Remember, you're not in control of Neal's decisions. You're not responsible for their outcome, either. Your only role is to guide him if he asks for your advice.*

They stepped outside, where they were met by a warm gust of air that filled the striped yellow awning overhead, causing it to luff like the sail of a schooner setting out to sea. They walked a little way along the sidewalk to the used bookstore a few doors down, where they settled onto the wrought-iron bench outside. They sat for a minute or two in companionable silence, watching the parade of pedestrians go by, locals and tourists alike, none of whom appeared in a hurry to get anywhere on this cloudless summer day. The store in front of which they sat, the Bell, Book & Candle, was owned by an older lady named May Crossley; in addition to used books, it sold greeting cards and such handicrafts as sand candles, wind chimes, and kitschy knick-knacks. At the moment, it was shuttered. The hand-lettered sign in the window read, "Closed for funeral." It wasn't the first time Lila had seen it hanging there. May had summed it up in saying bluntly to her the other day, "You get to be my age, all your friends are dropping like flies."

"So, what gives?" Lila was careful to strike a relaxed tone. No need to jump to dire conclusions just because her son had said he wanted to talk. Maybe it was good news. He'd been waiting to hear back from the law firm where he'd applied for an opening as tech support, and she said with a tentatively hopeful smile, "Don't tell me—you got the job."

He shook his head. "No. I mean, I don't know yet. I haven't heard." Clearly, that wasn't what he'd wanted to talk to her about. He tilted his head to peer up at her as he sat bent over with his elbows resting on his knees. "Anyway, I've decided not to take it even if they do offer it to me."

"Really? What made you change your mind?" She tried to sound only mildly concerned, though every nerve ending was on red alert. Dr. Frye had cautioned her about coming across as overly anxious.

"Something's come up." He shoved a hand through his hair, looking a little nervous. She noted that he was in need of a haircut; the dark curls spilling down his forehead were covering his eyebrows. "You remember John Kaplan from Riverdale?" he said. She nodded, recalling John as one of the boys Neal used to hang out with in high school. "Well, I ran into him the other day when I was in the city. Anyway, we got to talking, and it turns out that the guy he's sharing his place with is moving out. John asked if I'd be interested in taking over his roommate's share of the rent."

It took a moment for her to absorb the full impact of what he was saying: Neal wanted to leave home. Move away from her. Away from his safety net. It took a huge effort for Lila to reply in a neutral tone, "Do you think you can afford it?" As if her only concern were such practical matters. As if she weren't sick with fright at the prospect of her son's fending for himself, in New York City of all places, where he would face a thousand avenues of potential despair.

He shrugged, appearing unconcerned. "I'll get a job," he answered with the blithe optimism of youth. "I'm sure I won't have any trouble finding one. There are plenty of jobs in the city."

"What about school?"

"I can always take a year off."

What about me? she cried inwardly. *Am I supposed to sit home alone every night waiting for the phone to ring so I'll know if you're all right?* But all she said was, "Are you sure that's a good idea?" The real question, the one that had haunted her ever since the night of the fire, she kept to herself. It was one she never uttered aloud: *Will you try to hurt yourself again?*

Neal gave a derisive little laugh. "The only thing I'm sure about is that if I don't get out of this shitty little town, I'll go nuts."

"Is it really so awful?" She remembered when she'd felt as trapped as Neal. But it had been winter then, and the circumstances that had blown her here like an ill wind far from ideal. Now, as she looked about—at the people lingering outside the ice cream shop next door, licking their cones; the couples lunching at the sidewalk tables outside Gabriella's across the street; and farther off, the young girls in shorts and bikini tops sunning themselves on the grass along the river walk, no doubt hoping for some cute boy to notice—she couldn't think of another place she'd rather be.

"I can't believe you actually *like* it here." Neal shook his head in disbelief.

"Oh, I don't know—it kind of grows on you." She turned to smile at him. "Why don't you give it until the end of the year and see where you're at then? You might feel differently."

"I'm not asking for your permission, Mom." His firm tone made it clear that this subject wasn't open to discussion. He straightened to look her in the eye. "I already told John to count me in. I'm just giving you the heads-up. You know, in case you were making any kind of long-range plans."

She felt a familiar clutch in the pit of her stomach, and her resolve to keep her worries to herself crumbled a little. "Oh, Neal. Are you sure you're ready for this? Dr. Frye—"

He cut her off before she could finish. "Dr. Frye's the one who suggested it."

"He did?" Lila felt unreasonably hurt, as if the two had been colluding behind her back somehow.

"Yes, as a matter of fact. He thinks I'm ready for it."

"Still, couldn't you have at least talked it over with me first?"

"The only reason I didn't was because I knew you'd react this way," he said.

"Am I so predictable?"

"Yeah, you are." Neal spoke gently, as if to let her know that he wasn't going to hold it against her. "The way you look at me sometimes, it's like you don't trust me out of your sight. Not that I blame you. I'd probably feel the same way if it were my kid, after what happened. But, Mom, it can be a little hard to take, you know? I feel like I'm walking on eggshells half the time."

"Well, it hasn't exactly been easy for me, either." An injured note crept into her voice.

"I know it hasn't." The look her son gave her was almost tender. "And I'm sorry for what I put you through. But deep down, you know as well as I do that this will be the best thing for both of us."

"Speak for yourself," she said.

He shook his head, smiling at her in an oddly indulgent way, as if she were the child and he the parent, one whose patience was wearing thin. "Listen, Mom, don't take this the wrong way, but you need to get a life."

Get a life. Wasn't that what she'd been doing? Wasn't that what this job was all about? "I didn't realize I was holding you back," she said stiffly.

"Not me. You're holding *yourself* back," replied this new, strangely adult son of hers. "You never go out at night, unless it's with Abby or the ladies from work. And when was the last time you went into the city to see a play or go to a museum? You're hardly an old lady, Mom. You should be going out on dates. What happened to Karim? You two have a fight or something?"

"No, not exactly. Anyway, I thought you didn't approve of my seeing him."

She was glad they were sitting under the awning, where it was shady, or he might have seen that she was blushing. She'd thought she was past all that by now, but apparently not. Whenever she ran into Karim downtown, while out shopping or running errands, she felt that old quickening inside. She recalled what it had felt like to be wrapped in his arms. She missed the long talks they used to have and the feeling she'd had when she was with him that the world wasn't such a blighted place after all, that there was hope.

"Well, you shouldn't have paid any attention," Neal said. "I was being a selfish prick."

"I guess I've been a little selfish, too," she admitted. "It's just . . ." She reached out to smooth a stray curl from his forehead, the way she used to when he was a little boy, feeling herself start to choke up. "I was so afraid of losing you." She never took it for granted the way most mothers did, her son's being healthy and whole and on his way to manhood; she knew how lucky she was.

"You act as if I'm going away for good. I'll still come back for visits and stuff. And you'll visit me," he said. "It's not like I'm going off to the dark heart of Africa, like Uncle Vaughn."

"The less said about your uncle's whereabouts, the better," she replied. Lila didn't like the fact that her brother was so far away. Not after the scare he'd given them all last winter.

Neal rose to his feet. "Well, I should get going. I have to pack my stuff."

"So soon?" She cast him an anxious look.

"Relax, Mom. I'm not leaving until tomorrow. There's still plenty of time for you to sew up all the holes in my socks." He flashed her an irreverent grin as he leaned down to kiss her cheek.

That broke the tension, and they both laughed. She'd never in her life darned a sock; she didn't even know how. But she got the message: He was reminding her that she was still his mom.

Watching him head off, Lila found herself thinking back to his first day of kindergarten. She recalled how proud she'd felt—and, yes, a little bereft—watching her little boy eagerly rush up the steps of his new school, not hanging back or crying like some of the other kids. *Look at him, he's not afraid of anything!* she'd thought then, as she did now. *He'll manage just fine without me.*

For several minutes after he'd left, she remained seated on the bench, mulling things over. Neal had been right about one thing, she thought. She *had* been hanging on, and not solely out of motherly concern. As long as Neal was around, she didn't have to face the fact that she was essentially alone.

Sure, she was getting on with her life in other ways. There were days when she had to pinch herself because she could scarcely believe that she had a real job in a real office, where she was actually proving to be of some value. This month alone she'd booked five cruises, with several more pending. And her boss, Janet Munson, had even entrusted her to put together a wine-tasting tour of Burgundy for next summer, since Lila was the only one in the office who spoke French (albeit she was a little rusty in that area). If she didn't do anything to mess that up, there would be other tours down the line. This job had opened up a whole world of possibilities.

But her private life was another matter. Neal had struck a nerve when he'd accused her of being a stick-in-the-mud (no, he hadn't used those exact words, but that was what he'd meant). It was true that she seldom went out in the evenings, and then only with friends. She hadn't been out on a date since that one time with Karim, what seemed like eons ago. There had been a few male clients who'd asked her out, and Bob Kushner, who owned the insurance brokerage down the street, had once invited her to have coffee with him (she'd fended him off politely), but no one she'd been interested in. And the one man she *had* been interested in—more than that, to be honest—she'd run from as if from the plague.

She wondered if Karim was over her by now. Whenever she ran into him, he seemed fine, other than the inevitable awkwardness between them as they exchanged the requisite pleasantries. He could be seeing someone else, for all she knew. The only thing she knew for certain was that he was still working for Abigail, though it was unclear for how much longer. Abigail had mentioned to her the other day that Karim was thinking of moving out of state.

The quicksand feeling in her belly intensified at the thought. But wasn't he already long gone, as far as she was concerned? Hadn't she made certain of that?

She looked around her, once more taking in the sights and sounds and smells of the town she'd once viewed as a place of last resort. With the onset of the warm weather, the downtown area that had been bleak and gray all winter had come to life, blossoming like the begonias in their hanging peat baskets along Main Street. The shops were bustling and the sidewalk cafés thronged. There was a line now outside Rumson's Ice Cream, and on the sidewalk outside the gourmet store on the corner of Main and River, shoppers were clustered around a clerk offering free samples. Farther off in the distance, she could hear the pealing of carillon bells, no doubt in celebration of yet another wedding (she'd booked a number of honeymoon trips already this season), reminding her that everywhere around her, lives were being lived. Couples were taking leaps of faith. Futures were being mapped out. While she would be sitting home alone, night after night.

At last, she roused from her thoughts and glanced at her watch, surprised to find that she'd been sitting out here for nearly half an hour. With a sigh, she rose to her feet and headed back to work. Barb looked up from her desk as Lila walked in. "Everything okay?" she asked, in the tone of someone who was really asking, *Trouble at home?*

"Couldn't be better," Lila replied, smiling as if she hadn't a care in the world. Barb was a good person, but she was also an inveterate gossip, and Lila didn't want everyone in town knowing her business. She breezed past Barb on her way to her desk, where the lives of her clients—Nancy McCormick, for whom she was arranging a trip to Barcelona, which the newly liberated divorcée was calling her "consolation prize after thirty years with the same miserable man"; the husband who'd had her reserve a room at a resort in Cabo San Lucas for him and his mistress under the names "Mr. and Mrs. Clarren"; and eighty-year-old Mrs. Syms, who claimed to have found the fountain of youth on a Royal Norwegian cruise and who was eager for another go at it—would keep her from examining her own too closely.

The rest of the day flew quickly by, and when she glanced at her watch again, it was ten past five. Barb was getting ready to leave, and Janet and Cheryl Ann had already taken off for the day. Lila removed her headset and unplugged it from the phone. She turned off her computer and scribbled a note on a Post-it that she stuck to one of the pending files. When everything on her desk was tidied up, she sat back for a moment, staring off into space and absently rubbing her scalp where her headset had left a faint indentation. She was tired, but it was a mental exhaustion rather than the physical one she'd felt working for Abigail. And with it came the satisfaction of knowing that she was relying on her talents and wits rather than on sheer grit and determination.

The jingle of keys—Barb getting ready to lock up—brought her back into focus, and she stood up, retrieving her purse from under her desk. She thought about picking up something for supper on her way home, maybe some of that smoked turkey from the deli that Neal liked so much. But she immediately thought better of it. Neal could feed himself. He didn't need her to look after him. Hadn't he made that perfectly clear? She surprised herself by letting out a low chuckle, feeling strangely liberated.

She glanced up to find Barb giving her a coy, knowing look. "You look like the cat that got into the cream. Got something lined up for tonight?" Code for *Do you have a date?*

"No, nothing special," Lila replied.

But Barb must have thought she was merely being circumspect, for she coaxed, "Oh, come on, you can tell *me.*" The older woman's eyes shone in anticipation of a shared confidence, especially one that might involve a mystery lover.

Lila only shrugged and said cryptically (and a bit meanly), "You wouldn't believe it if I told you." *I have a hot date with a Stouffer's frozen lasagna and the new Tony Hillerman novel. I'm so boring I don't even flirt with men over the Internet. Old Mrs. Syms leads a more exciting life than I do. At least she has Bingo and shuffleboard.* Barb stood poised a moment longer, smiling expectantly, as if awaiting the punch line of a joke, but when Lila said no more, her face fell. Instead of chirping her usual sing-song good-bye as they headed out the door, she said with forced cheer, "Well, I'm sure you'll be having more fun than me. Joe's idea of a date is pizza and beer in front of the TV."

Lila turned as she was leaving to flash Barb an enigmatic smile. Let the poor woman have her fantasies.

An hour later, after stopping at the supermarket for groceries and then at the gas station to fill up her tank, she was in her car headed home when, on a whim, she found herself taking the turnoff to Rose Hill instead. She hadn't been back since the day after the fire, when she'd gone to see if there was anything worth salvaging of her possessions (there hadn't been—what little she'd had had gone up in smoke along with everything else when the garage had caught fire). What would have been the point? There was nothing there for her now. Nothing but . . .

Her thoughts turned to Karim, and she was forced to admit there was a part of her that was hoping she'd run into him.

She pulled into the drive to find that most of the debris had been cleared away. All that was left of the house was the foundation, with crumbling sections of wall sticking up here and there like broken, blackened teeth. She paused to reflect for a moment before getting out of the car. It made her sad, seeing Abigail's former pride and joy reduced to rubble. Not as sad as she'd felt in losing the Park Avenue penthouse where she'd enjoyed some of her best years, but as in the passing of an era. So much history here, all of it wiped away in an instant.

She noticed Karim's Dodge Ram parked off to one side of what used to be the garage, and her heart bucked up against her rib cage. A moment later she spotted him off in the distance, shirtless, prying at something in the dirt with a shovel. He waved to her as she climbed out of her car, then bent once more to his task. It wasn't until he'd finished that he set aside his shovel and started toward her. Even then, he appeared to be taking his time, walking at a leisurely pace that seemed to mock the wild beating of her heart.

When he finally reached her, he greeted her pleasantly enough. "Lila. What brings you here?" His expression registered neither delight nor annoyance at her unexpected visit.

"I happened to be driving by, and I thought I'd stop in and see how it was coming along. Aren't you working awfully late?" she asked, as if she hadn't been hoping to run into him.

He gestured toward the heap of rubble in the driveway—broken bricks and chunks of concrete, pieces of charred lumber, shards of glass. "I have a dump truck coming first thing Monday morning to haul all this off," he explained. "I wanted to make sure everything was ready."

The job had left him filthy. With his chambray shirt tied around his waist, she could see the tracks on his dusty arms and chest where rivulets of sweat had run down them, and noted that the bandana knotted around his forehead had done little to keep away the fine ash that had settled over his curls, turning them a premature gray. Yet Lila had never seen a more welcome sight.

"Were you able to salvage much?" she asked in an effort to make conversation. She already knew the answer from having talked to Abigail.

"Very little, I'm afraid," he told her. "What wasn't lost in the fire was too damaged to be of much use."

She glanced about in shared dismay. "It's hard to believe anyone actually lived here. It looks more like an archaeological dig." Her gaze took in patio and pool in back, now little more than a hole in the ground, and the piles of excavated dirt where the rosebushes and trellises had stood.

He nodded. "In some ways, it was. We had to sort through the ruins carefully so as not to destroy anything we dug up. But, as you can see, my work here is almost done."

"So what's next?"

He took a swipe at his sweaty brow with the back of his forearm. "I may head up north. My cousin Ahmed owns a restaurant in Providence, and he's looking for a manager."

She experienced a little inner jolt. "Providence, Rhode Island? I didn't know you had family there."

"Just my cousin. He came to this country many years ago, as a student, and stayed on after he graduated to go into the restaurant business. Now he and his wife are looking to open a second restaurant, which is why he needs someone to manage the one he currently owns."

"Providence is a long way off."

He shrugged, looking out over the ruins of Rose Hill. "There's not much to keep me here."

Had he forgotten so quickly? Had she meant so little to him? Lila wondered. Then she was quick to remind herself that *he* was the one who'd been spurned, not the other way around. Why shouldn't he move on? She certainly hadn't given him a reason not to. Nonetheless, she found herself pointing out, "I'm sure Abby will want you to stay on if she decides to rebuild. You'll have plenty of work to do around here, in that case." She looked around her at the once manicured grounds rutted with tire tracks from heavy earthmoving machinery, the trampled shrubs and flowerbeds once so lovingly maintained.

He nodded thoughtfully. "She has spoken to me about this, yes." He didn't volunteer any more than that.

Having reached the limits of polite conversation, Lila gave a little sigh and said, "Well, I suppose I ought to be heading home before my ice cream melts." She gestured toward her car, with its bags of groceries visible in the backseat. She felt keenly disappointed for some reason, though she couldn't think why. She hadn't come here for anything in particular.

Or had she?

Karim surprised her by asking, "Would you like to have a look around before you go?"

She gave one last, fleeting thought to her ice cream before deciding that if she was so pathetic that she'd choose Häagen-Dazs over a few more minutes with Karim, she might as well hang it up entirely.

"Maybe just a quick look. I can't stay long."

He took her on a tour of the once grand home, keeping a hand lightly cupped under her elbow as he guided her over piles of broken bricks and pieces of lumber. They made their way through what had been the living room, once filled with valuable antiques that she had come to know more intimately than any pieces of furniture she'd ever owned, of which only a few charred sticks remained. In the former kitchen, the blasted hulk of the stove stood like a relic from some ancient civilization, and broken floor tiles lay strewn over the exposed concrete subflooring like so many scattered playing cards. She peered up the tumble-down staircase, its remaining risers ascending into nothingness. It left her feeling more than a little sickened, thinking of the even greater tragedy that had been so narrowly averted.

"It's a shame, isn't it?" she remarked, pausing to take one last look over her shoulder as they were walking back to her car. "Whatever Abby decides, something will be put up here eventually, but it won't be the same."

"No, it won't," he agreed.

"If she does decide to sell, it'll be a financial decision more than anything. It's either that or buy out Kent's share, and I'm not sure she can afford to do that."

"It's a pity," he said, shaking his head. Lila assumed he was referring to Rose Hill until he observed, "Two good people. And yet two good people don't necessarily make a good marriage."

"No, but I think they're both happier this way." Lila was thinking of the other day when she'd bumped into Kent and his lady friend in the supermarket. They'd both been radiant with the flush of new love. "Or at least happier than if they'd stayed together."

"I suppose you're right." Karim's gaze drifted off, and she thought she caught a glint of sadness in his eyes.

Impulsively she asked, "Are *you* happy, Karim?"

He brought his gaze back to her. "Why do you ask?"

"I don't know. I guess seeing all this . . ." she gestured around her, "got me thinking. I mean, in traditional cultures, fires are used for cleansing or chasing away evil spirits. I wonder if any evil spirits got chased away here." She spoke with a lightness that belied her emotions.

With his shadow stretching over the debris-littered ground, he looked taller than his normal height, like a figure out of a mythic tale from one of those traditional cultures. "Have yours been chased away, Lila *jan?*" he asked softly.

The endearment, as much as the intimacy of his tone, caused her to go as warm as if the sun now setting had been directly overhead. She knew from the way he was looking at her that it wasn't an idle question, and she chose her words carefully. "I suppose so, in some ways. I've been so busy with my new job that I haven't had time to think about much else. But it's more than that—I feel like I'm starting to let go of some of that old stuff. It's amazing, really. I never thought there'd come a day when I wouldn't wake in the morning with a pit in my stomach."

"Then I'm happy for you," said Karim, sounding as if he meant it. "And your son? How is he doing?"

"Funny you should ask. He just announced that he's moving out."

Karim gazed at her intently, as if trying to read her thoughts. "And is this a good thing?"

"At first I wasn't so sure," she said. "But Neal seems to think it'll be the best thing for both of us, and I'm starting to think that maybe he's right. It's like you said—children move on, and if you don't make a life of your own, you're going to be in for some lonely days."

Karim gave a small smile. "I confess my advice was somewhat self-serving."

"Either way, you were right. I should have listened. Not that it matters anymore. It's obvious you've moved on."

If she'd been fishing to see what his reaction would be, she wasn't disappointed. "You're wrong about that as well, Lila *jan*," he said, wearing a serious expression. "As you can see, I'm still very much present."

"Does that mean . . . ?" Her heart was beating so hard, it felt as if it were going to knock a hole through her chest.

In response, he opened his arms. As she stepped into them, she caught the acrid smell of soot mixed with sweat, and thought she had never smelled anything sweeter. When he kissed her, there was no room for conscious thought or makeshift barriers. There was only the softness of his mouth and the gritty feel of his skin against hers. If their destinies were written, she thought, she didn't want to know how the story ended. All that mattered was that in this moment, she was happy. Happier than she could remember being in a long, long time. Maybe that was all she'd ever have. A series of moments like this one, strung together like a strand of pearls, one made all the more precious by the knowledge that it could break and scatter should she ever grow careless, as she had with Gordon in allowing herself to lose sight of her priorities. Maybe that was all anyone had a right to expect.

"I could get used to this," she murmured.

"Good, because I have every intention of spoiling you." He drew back to grin at her, his teeth startlingly white against his soot-dusted skin. "Why don't I start by taking you to dinner? Have you eaten yet?"

"No, but there's a frozen lasagna turning to mush in my car," she said.

He tipped her a wink. "I think we can do better than that."

"What did you have in mind?"

"I promised my cousin I would come see him before I decided whether or not to accept his job offer. I was planning to drive up tonight. If you would care to join me, we could stop for a bite to eat along the way, then have a proper dinner tomorrow night at Ahmed's restaurant. It's traditional Afghani food, not fancy—prepared the way our mothers used to make it. But if you haven't tried it, I think you'll like it. Have you ever had *pilau?* I promise you, it's a most excellent dish."

"You're talking food, and I'm still trying to wrap my brain around the idea of us driving all the way to Rhode Island," she said, smiling and shaking her head. "Are you seriously asking me to come with you?"

"Do you have other plans?" He eyed her questioningly.

"No, but . . ."

"In that case, I see no reason for you not to accompany me. You don't have to be back at work until Monday, which leaves us the whole weekend." He put a finger under her chin, tipping her head up to kiss her lightly on the lips. "I think it's the least you can do, since I'll be turning down my cousin's offer."

She felt her spirits soar briefly before coming back down to earth as her thoughts turned to Neal. Tonight was to have been their last night together. He was leaving in the morning. She'd tentatively planned on driving him into the city tomorrow and maybe taking him and his new roommate to lunch. But now she had a decision to make. Should she continue to play the devoted mother, even if it meant denying herself . . . or follow her heart and see where it led?

Any hesitation she felt vanished when she looked into Karim's warm brown eyes and saw the promise there. The promise of a life that would include, if not solely depend on, a man who loved and respected her. A man who would not necessarily make her complete—she'd already gotten a good head start on that herself—but would give her life a dimension it lacked.

With a full heart, she said, "When do we leave?"

21

"*This may come* as a shock to some of you . . ." Abigail, standing at the head of the conference table, paused to take a breath before continuing, "but I'm stepping down as CEO, effective immediately."

The initial moment of silence that greeted her announcement seemed louder than the collective gasps and exclamations that came from the assembled department heads in its wake. Smiling, she held up a hand to silence them. "I didn't say I was resigning! I'm well aware that this is about brand, and since we all know I *am* the brand—" She wasn't boasting, merely stating a fact—"there's no question about my maintaining an active role." She went on to explain that she'd still be involved in all creative decisions and that she'd be keeping up with her book and media appearances. "I'll do my best to make this as smooth a transition as possible. Now, I'm sure you have questions, so fire away." She waved a hand to open the floor.

Charlotte Rutledge, head of advertising, cut right to the chase. "Who's going to be the new CEO?" Slim-hipped and athletic, Charlotte ran marathons and was just as competitive in other ways. Clearly she was hoping a successor hadn't yet been appointed and there was still a chance that the job could be hers.

Abigail gestured toward her executive director, seated on her right. "Ellen will be taking my place at the helm. And, as you all know from when she was acting head during my leave of absence last year, she's more than up to it." Ellen had run things so well, in fact, that Abigail had been left wondering how she could ever have thought *she* was indispensable.

"How will this affect the bottom line?" asked Doug Mignorelli, who ran the book division. He always made Abigail think of a choirboy, with his apple cheeks and the swoosh of baby-fine brown hair he was forever raking off his forehead, as he was now, never mind he was closer to her age.

"I see no reason why it should have any effect, negative or positive." It was one of the advantages of the company being privately held, she went on to point out, grateful now that she'd made the decision not to go public. "As far as merchandising goes, the products will still have my name and face on them, so as far as the consumer knows or cares, it's business as usual."

"We're still recovering from the cutbacks in personnel," grumbled Fred Haines, head of human resources, his dour expression a match for the conservative gray suit he wore.

"Cutbacks that *had* to be made in order to keep us afloat," interjected her trusty CFO, Hank Weintraub, with his usual dry, no-nonsense delivery. "But if you take a look at our net gains for this last quarter, I think you'll find that the overall picture isn't so gloomy." He directed everyone's attention to the latest quarterly report, a copy of which sat on the table in front of each person's place in a clear plastic binder. As they began flipping through it, Hank provided the overview. The fire and subsequent rebuilding of the factory in Las Cruces had caused crucial delays, he said; delays that had resulted in a substantial loss of revenue, yes, but with Tag's successful launch of the Abigail Armstrong bed-and-bath-linen line in January—a launch timed to coincide with Tag's annual chainwide white sale—profits had nudged them back into the black. He expected a full recovery by this time next year.

After more questions and answers, mostly having to do with matters of protocol and job security, Abigail rose once more to conclude the meeting. "This wasn't an easy decision for me, as I'm sure you might imagine," she said in closing. "I don't have to remind you that a good deal of blood, sweat, and tears went into making this company what it is. Not all of it mine," she added with a self-effacing smile, to the accompaniment of knowing chuckles. "As a result, I've had to make certain sacrifices in other areas. Now I think it's high time that I answered the question, which I'm sure more than a few of you have wondered about yourselves, as to whether or not I have a life outside of work." More knowing chuckles. "For my sake, I sincerely hope I do."

It was a rare moment of candor for their boss, and the laughter that ensued carried a ripple of unease, as if those around her had just learned that there was some flaw in the infrastructure of the building itself. Even those of her employees to whom she was closest (with the possible exception of Hank Weintraub) had never before heard Abigail express doubts or show any kind of regret about the choices she'd made thus far. But if this new move was unprecedented, it wasn't entirely out of the blue. Most had noticed subtle changes in Abigail over the preceding months. She was more patient and less apt to become irritable. She was, in a word, *nicer*. If "nice" was a word that could be used to describe their CEO (now *former* CEO), who at times had played the evil twin to her cozy public persona.

"That went well, don't you think?" remarked Ellen after the meeting had adjourned and they were heading back to their respective offices. Abigail noted that she'd dressed down for the occasion, in a plain, almost drab black pantsuit and no jewelry except the small gold hoops in her ears. Knowing Ellen, she'd probably done so deliberately, so as not to upstage Abigail in her final hour at the helm or cause dissension among the ranks by calling too much attention to herself. Ellen's diminutive stature and the spray of freckles on her snub nose might have fooled some into not taking her seriously, but Abigail knew she was one smart cookie. She didn't doubt she'd chosen well and that the new CEO of Abigail Armstrong Incorporated would be a fitting successor.

"If you mean no one stood up and cheered, then yes, I suppose it went well," she replied with a small, ironic laugh. Ellen would never know how much she'd dreaded making that announcement. But now that it was over, Abigail felt a curious sense of relief. She wondered if she'd have felt the same way after having jumped off a cliff, knowing it was too late to change her mind.

Except this just might end up being her salvation. It had occurred to her not too long ago that after decades in the fast lane going ninety miles an hour, the horizon was no longer limitless. She was still young, but ten years from now she'd be fifty-two, officially middle-aged. And, seeing as how the last decade of her life had gone by in the blink of an eye, it no longer seemed like such a distant prospect. After that, how many more years of health and relative youth would she have left? She'd already missed the boat, to a large extent, where her daughter was concerned: The time for playing soccer mom was past; once Phoebe started at Vanderbilt in the fall, Abigail would see her only on school holidays. But what was still possible, still within reach, she'd decided, was a life for herself—a life outside work. If she even remembered what that was.

You'll figure it out, she told herself. Still, after decades of scaling the proverbial ladder, it felt strange and scary to be descending it, if only by a few rungs. "The truth is, it's been so long since I've had any free time to speak of, I'm not sure I'll know what to do with myself," she confessed.

"You won't sit idle, that much I know." Ellen shook her head, smiling. Chief among Ellen's responsibilities in the months to come would be making sure her former boss didn't worm her way back into the CEO's chair, in all but name. For Abigail didn't doubt that there would be times when she'd feel that old tug: the urge to be back in the roiling thick of it all. "You should take a trip," Ellen suggested. "When was the last time you went anywhere except on business?"

"I have the Mexico trip coming up," Abigail reminded her.

"Right. How's that going?"

Abigail brightened. "Believe it or not—and this has to be some kind of miracle, given all the hoops we had to jump through—it looks as if we're actually going to open on schedule."

She was talking about the free clinic in Las Cruces, funded in part by the sale of Rose Hill. (Kent had been generous enough to kick in a large portion of his share. How could he not? A cause as worthy as this was right up his alley.) Maybe the reason there had been fewer headaches in getting it off the ground than with the factory, she thought, was because it had been a true labor of love. More than that, some days it had been the only thing that had kept her from sinking into despair, during that period when she'd had the one-two punch of her divorce and the ordeal with Phoebe. Abigail felt a glow of satisfaction whenever she thought about what the clinic would mean to the people of Las Cruces. It wouldn't bring Concepción's daughter back, but it would hopefully save other lives down the line. It seemed fitting that it be named the Milagros Sánchez Clínica de Medicina.

Alone in her office, she sat idly gazing out the window instead of tackling the paperwork on her desk. She wasn't thinking about all the things she was going to do in the months to come that she'd never had time for in the past. She was thinking of the postcards tucked away in a desk drawer at home, from various exotic locales, the most recent from Iceland (a photo of a hotel lobby in Reykjavik, so sleekly modern it might have been situated in New York or LA), where Vaughn was currently on R & R with his crew after a month at sea filming a documentary on the remote islands of the North Atlantic.

He'd written, with his usual haiku-style brevity, *Don't know that I'll ever warm up again, but the sun is shining and I'm feeling good. The only thing missing is you. Love, V.*

All his messages were like that—brief and to the point, always ending on a breezily affectionate note. When he had access to a computer, he would e-mail her. Each time an entry from Vaughn popped up in her inbox, it was the highlight of her day. And each time, it brought a sharp pang of loss. She wondered now if she was only torturing herself by allowing even this minimal contact. It was like stitches being continually ripped from a wound, keeping it from healing.

Now she thought, *I miss you, too. I wish . . .*

But what did it matter what she wished for? She wasn't going to get it. Not with Vaughn. He was never going to settle down; that would be like trying to turn a cheetah into a house pet. Even if he could change, she wouldn't want him any different—he wouldn't be the man she loved.

She had to face facts. This was the most she'd ever have with him—e-mails and postcards, the occasional get-together when he was in town: visits she always anticipated with such pulse-fluttering eagerness that saying good-bye was almost a physical ache when the time came. Usually they met for drinks or dinner, and the previous season they'd gone to a few of the ballgames she'd gotten him tickets for. But though they'd slept together on more than one occasion, she'd never spent the night with him at his hotel room. Any extended contact, she knew, would be the death of her. Weren't her memories alone difficult enough to cope with? She'd replayed them so often, she was no longer sure what was real and what was embellished.

With a sigh, she turned her attention to her computer screen. The most recent e-mail from Vaughn was dated two days ago: *I'll be in town a week from Wednesday. Any chance of seeing you? V.* She hadn't responded to it yet. She didn't know what to tell him. Part of her wanted to throw all caution aside and spend his entire visit holed up in his hotel room. Only the thought of how depressed she would feel afterward kept her from leaping at the chance. She didn't need that in her life right now, not while she was still recovering from the events of the past year—primarily the trial of Phoebe's former teacher.

Predictably, he had denied the charges against him, publicly (and loudly) proclaiming his innocence. What had come as a shock was that the majority of Phoebe's classmates had taken his side. It was only in the courtroom that Mr. Guarneri's sheep's guise had begun to fray. A recent graduate had come forward to testify that he'd made advances to her, too, when she'd been his student. Phoebe's emotional and heart-wrenching testimony had been the final nail in the coffin. By the end of the second day, the tide had turned against Mr. Guarneri, and even his loyal band of supporters had deserted him. The only one at his side when the verdict had been read had been his wife. It had come as no surprise to anyone, except maybe Mr. Guarneri himself, when he was found guilty.

Not that there was anything to cheer about. Phoebe was still fragile emotionally, and she struggled with depression and issues of low self-esteem. After being all but ostracized at her old school, she'd made the difficult decision to drop out and enroll in the nearby Pelham Academy, in Westchester, for the remainder of her senior year. It was an adjustment that had proven tough, but with graduation behind her now, she seemed happier and more relaxed than she had in a while. At the moment, she was home packing for the trip to France she was going on with her dad—Kent's graduation gift to her. Abigail knew she was going to miss her: This was only the dress rehearsal for the real farewell in the fall, when Phoebe went away to college. And what made it even more bittersweet was that it had come at a time when they were beginning to grow closer.

On impulse, she reached for the phone. "Hi, sweetie," she said when Phoebe answered. "Just calling to see if there's anything you need me to pick up for you on my way home."

"Hmmm . . . let's see. Maybe a bottle of that shampoo?" She named a brand their local drugstore didn't always have in stock. "Other than that, I'm all set. By the way, Mom, you were right. I couldn't fit all that stuff in my suitcase. I had to take a lot of it out," she added somewhat sheepishly.

That morning on her way to work, Abigail had poked her head into Phoebe's room and commented that she was packing enough for a trip around the world. "Well, I'm sure whatever you run out of, they'll have it in Paris. They don't call it the fashion capital for nothing," she reminded her now.

"Can you just see me strutting around like a *Vogue* model? Dad would have a fit." Phoebe giggled at the idea.

"Not to mention he'd have to take out a second mortgage."

They gabbed for a minute or so longer before Phoebe, just as they were about to hang up, remembered to tell her, "Oh, I almost forgot. Lila phoned. She wants you to call her back."

"Did she say what it was about?"

"No. It sounded important, though."

Abigail was on her way home when she decided on impulse to stop in at the travel agency rather than call Lila. Lila was in her cubicle, on the phone with a client, when she walked in. She flashed Abigail a welcoming grin and motioned for her to have a seat, holding up her index and middle fingers to indicate that she wouldn't be more than two minutes.

"I'm not disturbing you, am I?" said Abigail after she'd hung up.

"Not at all." Lila pulled off her headset and settled back in her chair. The days of watching her go about her household tasks, dressed in drab clothing that did her figure no favors, seemed like another era. The woman seated before her now, wearing a midlength raw-silk skirt and whisper-thin cashmere tank accented by a chunky turquoise necklace, looked every inch the professional. "That was Mrs. Hendricks. Remember her? Little old lady lives up on Ridge Road? Well, last May I booked her on a Scandinavian cruise, and that's where she met the man she says is the love of her life. She just called to tell me they're engaged. Isn't that cute? They're both in their eighties. Proof that it's never too late, I guess."

"For some, maybe," Abigail commented dryly. "I'm sure I'll be spending my golden years with just my scrapbooks and memories to keep me company."

"If you're looking to meet someone, I could always book you on a cruise," Lila suggested teasingly, her eyes twinkling. "Of course, the median age of the men is sixty plus."

"No, thanks. I'm not that desperate." Abigail tried to keep a straight face, but it was hard with Lila smiling at her. "Speaking of romance, how's it going with you and Karim?"

"It's going." Lila was always low-key about it whenever Abigail asked, as though she didn't dare trust in happiness, knowing it could be snatched away at any moment. With a glance over her shoulder to make sure no one was eavesdropping, she leaned in to confide, "He wants me to move in with him."

"And?" Abigail raised a questioning brow.

"We've been looking at houses," she said with guarded enthusiasm. "Karim wants something with a garden so he can exercise his green thumb." After the sale of Rose Hill, Karim had found a dream job in the rare-books library of a small liberal arts college in nearby Harrington.

Nonetheless, something in Lila's demeanor made Abigail ask, "Are you sure you're ready for this?"

"Of course not," Lila replied with an airy laugh. "I'll probably never be ready. But if I waited until I was sure, then I'd be as old as Mrs. Hendricks. Sometimes you just have to take a flier."

"How does Neal feel about all this?"

"You mean my erstwhile son? Ever since he and Bettina moved in together, he barely notices I'm alive." Surprisingly, Lila seemed okay about it. Though Neal was still the light of her life, he was no longer the center of it. "Between his job and his love life, he doesn't have time to worry about dear old Mom." Neal had found work in the kitchen of a SoHo restaurant and taken to it like a duck to water. After just one year, he'd been promoted to line chef. He was starting classes at the Culinary Institute in the fall.

Abigail wondered if Lila felt it, too: that goose-stepped-on-my-grave feeling she got whenever the subject of their children came up. Lila had to be thinking the same thing she was: that it was a miracle Phoebe and Neal were even alive, much less prospering. "I'm happy for you. I really am." She reached over to squeeze Lila's hand, her eyes unexpectedly filling with tears.

"What is it, Abby? Is something wrong?" Lila eyed her with concern.

"Yes, but it's a good thing. Or rather, it will be." She told Lila then about her decision to step down as CEO, which had been a secret until now—the only person she'd taken into her confidence, for obvious reasons, had been Ellen Tsao. "It was time," she said. "I realized that in order to have a life, I'd have to start making one. And I couldn't do that working eighty-hour weeks. So . . . here I am. Not exactly footloose and fancy-free, but at least I'm not keeping that insane schedule."

Lila took it all in, wearing a thoughtful expression. "You know," she said, "when Neal told me he was moving out, it kind of threw me into a panic. But it didn't take me long to realize that I liked living alone after all those years of looking after other people. So I guess while he was out finding himself, I was finding myself, too." She gave a small, wry smile. "Actually, I'm going to miss all that in some ways. Especially the part where I get to stay up as late as I like reading in bed."

"I can't remember the last book I read cover to cover. Maybe now I'll finally have the time. Who knows? I might even decide to go on a trip," Abigail said, thinking back to what Ellen had suggested earlier.

"Funny you should mention it. Actually, that's why I called." Lila gave her the sly look that meant she had something up her sleeve.

"Oh?"

"I heard from Vaughn today. He said he e-mailed you but hadn't heard back."

Abigail wondered what any of this had to do with her going on a trip. "He wanted to know if we could get together when he's in town next week. The reason I haven't gotten back to him is because I wasn't sure if I could fit it into my schedule," she lied.

"That *was* the plan. But now it looks like he's stuck in Reykjavik."

Abigail felt unreasonably let down. Though it was stupid to feel this way, she told herself, when she hadn't even made up her mind whether or not to see him. "That's too bad. I'm sure you were looking forward to his visit." She maintained a casual tone, as if it had had less to do with her than with Lila.

"Actually, it was more of a disappointment for Vaughn. And it had nothing to do with me," Lila said, giving her a pointed look. "The one he was really looking forward to seeing was you."

Abigail felt her heart take flight, then just as quickly plummet back down to earth. Illusions could be dangerous, she knew, so she'd best keep a level head. "In that case, I don't know why you're the one telling me. He could have told me himself," she said somewhat irritably.

"Oh, he will. But he wants to do it face-to-face."

"I don't understand." Abigail frowned in confusion.

Lila pulled a slim blue envelope from the pile of papers on her desk: a round-trip ticket to Reykjavik in her name, Abigail saw upon closer examination. "What's this?" she demanded, though she could plainly see what it was.

"Vaughn had me book it for you," Lila explained. "He thought it would be harder for you to say no this way."

"No to what? Are you seriously suggesting I fly to *Reykjavik*, of all places? That's crazy," Abigail protested, as if it were a trip to the moon. The truth was, she'd have gone to the moon and back to be with Vaughn, but where would that leave her? Worse off than when she started, that was for damn sure. "Why would I travel halfway around the world to see a man I don't hear from for weeks at a time, and when he does write, it's usually just a line or two here and there?" Lines she'd read over and over again until she knew them by heart.

"I'm not suggesting anything," Lila replied, a smile playing at her lips. "It was all Vaughn's idea. So I should tell him you can't go? No problem. I'll just go ahead and cancel this." She snatched the envelope from Abigail's hand and made as if to rip it in half.

Abigail quickly snatched it back. "At least give me a chance to think about it."

Lila gave a knowing chuckle. In a sudden motion, she snapped forward in her spring-loaded Aeron chair, her face inches from Abigail's, to stage-whisper, "Ha! I'm on to you, Abby."

Abigail threw up her hands. "Okay, I admit it. I'd love nothing more than to spend eight hours on a plane, then be jet-lagged for a whole weekend before I have to fly home. All for the fun of spending forty-eight hours with someone I won't see again for at least another three months." The only times she could count on with Vaughn were when he had to fly home for his checkups.

"In other words, you're dying to go."

"What difference would it make if I were?" Abigail replied testily. "Scratching that particular itch isn't going to help. It'll only make it worse." If even meeting him for a drink could throw her into a tailspin for days afterward, what would she be like after a long weekend in the sack?

"I felt that way about Karim in the beginning," Lila reminded her.

"It's different with you and Karim. You share the same zip code. Anyway, I just went through a divorce. The last thing I need is to have my life disrupted all over again. You know what your brother's like. Do you really see us shacking up together someday?"

"Not every relationship has to be conventional." Lila leaned back in her chair and folded her hands under her chin. "Karim and I might share the same zip code, but we're from two very different cultures. And believe me, not a day goes by that I'm not reminded of that. The first time he stayed over? I walked in on him bowing to Mecca and thought he was looking for something he'd dropped. I even offered to help him find it." She laughed and shook her head. "If I were to make a list of the adjustments we've had to make, it would all sound like stupid little stuff, but it adds up. I have to keep my eye on the bigger picture."

"And what exactly is the bigger picture here?" Abigail asked with more than a touch of defiance.

"It's simple. You two love each other. And you know what they say: Love conquers all."

Abigail grunted in derision. "That's a pretty simplistic view, if you ask me." But it left her wondering. *Was* she missing something here? If so, the only place she had even a remote chance of finding it was in Reykjavik. "Suppose I were to use this ticket. What would I get out of it?"

"I can't answer that. I know what my brother's like, so I'm not fooling myself into thinking you, or anyone, can domesticate him," Lila told her. "But it's a *life* you're looking for, Abby, not a husband. Don't confuse the two. I'm not even sure you'd know what to do with a husband right now."

Abigail took a deep breath and let it out in a long exhalation. "You're right," she said. "I *don't* need a husband. What I need right now is to stop obsessing about this. Maybe a long weekend with your brother will cure me of him once and for all." *If it doesn't kill me first.*

Lila broke into a grin as Abigail tucked the ticket into her purse. "In that case, have a safe trip."

Exactly fourteen hours and twenty-seven minutes later, Abigail was on an Air Iceland flight to Reykjavik awaiting takeoff. Earlier in the day, she'd seen her daughter off to the airport, and now here she sat, buckled into her seat, feeling like a teenager herself heading off to parts unknown. And though she still wasn't convinced this was a good idea— in fact, she was pretty sure it was a terrible one— it was too late to back out now. The hatch hadn't been closed yet, so technically she could, but it seemed her heart had the upper hand here. It knew what it wanted, and it wasn't going to rest until it got it . . . or got broken.

She was dozing off by the time the plane taxied down the runway, thanks to the sleeping pill she'd taken as soon as she'd boarded: her usual routine when flying trans-Atlantic. She slept straight through the flight, only to be roused, eight and some hours later, by the pilot's announcing from the flight deck that the plane was beginning its descent. It was five A.M. in Iceland. She pushed up her window shade to peer groggily out at the eerily lit landscape far below, which at first glance, with its uninterrupted miles of barren gray tundra, looked so much like the ocean over which they'd just flown that she wondered if someone in the control tower was asleep at the wheel. Surely they were meant to touch down on dry land?

An hour later, cruising along the lone highway into Reykjavik in the hired car that had been waiting for her at the airport, Abigail still hadn't shaken the sense of having been plunked down in some alien landscape, one that at a cursory glance didn't seem capable of supporting life, human or otherwise. Reykjavik, by contrast, was like the Emerald City, a modern metropolis rising from the stark terrain surrounding it. Yet she found it, too, strangely deserted. Driving through its nearly empty streets, she recalled having read in the guidebook that she'd flipped through on the plane that Reykjavik was far less populated than other cities of equal size, but even taking that and the early hour into account, it seemed strange not to see more people about.

Running through the center of the city was a river. She was astonished to see a man fishing off a bridge. "Is it safe?" she asked, pointing him out to the limo driver as they drove slowly past.

"Safe? Ah," he said, catching her meaning. "Yes, is safe. Water is clean, so fish is good." Like most of the people she'd encountered so far, he spoke English—true of Scandinavians in general.

She thought, You'd be taking your life in your hands if you were to eat a fish that came out of the Hudson River anywhere south of the White-stone Bridge. She smiled to herself. Maybe it was a good sign. Maybe coming here hadn't been such a bad idea after all.

Minutes later, they were pulling up in front of the hotel, a modern structure that looked to be built almost entirely of glass. She recognized the lobby, as soon as she stepped through the revolving door, as the one in the postcard Vaughn had sent—all clean lines and sleek blond wood, the front desk a slab of glass the size of an ice floe, supported by a central pillar that made it appear to float in space. She was approaching it when a smiling blond bellhop, so strikingly handsome that in New York or LA he'd have instantly been identified as an aspiring actor, materialized at her side to take charge of her suitcase. "Mr. Meriwhether asked me to escort you to his room," he informed her in his flawless, accented English.

Abigail was aware of her heart pounding in time with the clacking of their footsteps as they made their way across the glass-floored lobby, which was lit from below, giving it an eerie, lunar glow. What would she find when she got to Vaughn's room? More reasons not to have come . . . or a reason to stay? Had he changed at all in the months since she'd seen him last? Had she?

In the glass elevator, her jet lag fell away with the floors she could see receding below her as it climbed. She felt as clearheaded as if she'd just emerged from a pool after an invigorating swim. It wasn't just that she was on her way to meet Vaughn, it was that she was doing so in this strange, otherworldly city, where the rules of the natural world appeared to have been suspended—summer was neither hot nor cold, it seemed, and morning and night were nearly interchangeable. She felt as though she'd slipped out of her old skin as if from a travel-worn set of clothing, every inch of her alive with sensation, down to the tiny hairs on her arms and neck, quivering like antennae.

The elevator glided to a stop on the eighteenth floor, where the young Robert Redford look-alike guided the way down a corridor before stopping at one of the identical blond-wood doors lining it. He tapped on it, then retreated so quickly that Abigail didn't have a chance to tip him.

A moment later, the door swung open.

"Abby!"

Caught in Vaughn's embrace, Abigail felt as though she were being swept up by a force of nature. She smelled something minty—toothpaste?—and underneath it the earthier scent that was Vaughn alone. When he released her, it was a moment before she could gasp, "That was some hello."

He grinned. "I'm good at hellos. It's the good-byes that still need work."

He looked none the worse for his long sea voyage; if anything, he appeared more robust than ever, deeply tanned, his cheeks ruddy from the outdoors. Gone were the protruding bones and hollows that had worried her so when he was ill. The only evidence of his ordeal was the deep lines scoring his face, which only served to make it more appealing somehow. In his vintage Black Sabbath T-shirt and faded jeans, she could see that his body had filled out as well. He was solid muscle, his jeans snug in all the right places.

It was an effort to tear her gaze away. "Nice digs," she commented, glancing around the room, which was painted in cool blues and grays and furnished in Scandinavian modern.

"Believe me, I'm used to a lot more rugged accommodations than this," he said. "It just so happens that the guy who's directing this film is friends with the manager of the hotel. We got the family rate."

"Lucky you." She brought her gaze back to him, drinking in the sight of him: his eyes, blue as the thermal springs depicted in the framed photo on the wall at his back; his hair, fully grown in now, that was a dozen different shades of blond; the faint scar that ran like a seam down one cheek, which always made her think of a package to be unwrapped, like the queerly marked brown-paper parcels that would show up in her mailbox from time to time, smelling vaguely of foreign lands and intrigue.

He gestured toward the small table by the window, which was set for two. "I figured you'd be hungry, so I ordered in. I hope you like smoked fish because that's pretty much what you get for breakfast, lunch, and dinner around here."

"That was thoughtful of you." She sank gratefully into the chair he'd pulled out for her. She hadn't eaten since the day before, and she was starving. She broke off a piece of roll and nibbled on it while he poured the coffee.

The miniaturized view of the city spread out below made her think of an architectural model—it was almost too perfect to be real. Its buildings, a mixture of old and new, were spotlessly maintained, and there didn't appear to be a speck of dirt anywhere. Even the snowcapped mountains in the distance, which looked almost close enough to touch, were as pristine as if scoured.

"Pretty amazing, isn't it?" Vaughn said, following her gaze.

"It's not what I expected," she told him. "I was imagining something a lot less cosmopolitan."

"Another day and you'll feel right at home," he predicted. "For one thing, almost everyone here speaks English."

"So I've noticed."

"The only thing I don't get is how anyone could be content to live here year-round. In summer, the sun never really sets, and it's dark all winter long. I've been here over a week, and I still haven't gotten used to it." Using his fork, he helped himself to a piece of herring from the platter of smoked fish and cheeses at the center of the table. "But I'm only here for a few more days. We set sail again on Tuesday." Their boat had needed some repairs and was currently in dry dock, he explained. He'd thought he could slip away to New York for a few days, but work on the boat was going more quickly than anticipated. "Damned Scandinavian efficiency," he said with an easy laugh. "It'll fox you up every time."

He looked so much in his element, this modern-day nomad whose home was wherever his bag was unpacked, that she felt something akin to despair. *I shouldn't be here. I shouldn't have come.* At the same time, after months of dining out on memories alone, having him in such close proximity made her want to tear his clothes off. And the way he was looking at her, as if it was taking every ounce of his restraint to keep from doing the same, wasn't helping any. Damn him. And damn his sister, too. If Lila hadn't bamboozled her into this, Abigail never would have made the trip.

Her hand trembled as she raised her coffee cup to her lips. "How long will you be out to sea this time?" She kept her tone casual.

"Another two, three weeks, tops," he said, popping a morsel of herring into his mouth. "Angus is determined to film a whale harvest in the Faroe Islands, and it's not like something you can just order up like an act at Sea World. Also, we ran into some bad weather and lost time due to that as well as the usual technical difficulties—problems with equipment, footage that had to be reshot, that sort of thing. And you wouldn't believe the challenges involved in sticking to a production schedule on an island where the phones are down half the time and there's no Internet."

"And after that? I suppose you already have another gig lined up." It was always another gig, another far-flung place. Time with Vaughn was measured in days, hours, moments, not years.

He set his cup down in its saucer with a deliberateness that caused her to tense. "That depends," he said, his blue eyes fixing on her.

"On what?" she asked.

"You."

Her heart began to race, sending a surge of blood up into her face. What did he mean? Was he suggesting that she had any say in the matter? That she could command him to heel and he'd obey?

"I'm not sure I know what you're getting at," she said.

"Oh, I don't know. I was just thinking we could use a real vacation, someplace warm. Tahiti maybe," he replied casually with a glance out the window at the frigid, blue-gray landscape.

So this was it? His grand declaration of love? She felt absurdly disappointed, though to have hoped for more was foolish. "I have a business to run. Where would I find the time?" She spoke lightly, not knowing how serious he was. Probably it was just a passing fancy, one that would blow over with his next gig. She was glad now that she hadn't told him about her decision to step down as CEO. Better to have him go on thinking they were two of a kind: both so absorbed in their work that they had little time or energy left over for a real relationship. It was easier than getting her heart broken.

A romantic weekend I can recover from, she thought. *Longer than that, and I'd be in big trouble.*

"I've missed you, Abby." At the dubious look she gave him, he smiled. "I know what you're thinking. But with you . . ." He reached for her hand. "Wherever I go, I can't seem to get you out of my mind."

She held perfectly still, as if a butterfly had landed on her arm and she didn't dare move or even breathe for fear it would fly away. "What are you saying, Vaughn?" she asked.

"That I'm glad you came. I wasn't sure you would. And that I don't want it to be this way forever, the two of us dancing around each other like a pair of mating cranes." He brought her hand to his mouth and, one by one, kissed each of her knuckles, chipping away at her resistance with each soft press of his lips. "Come away with me, Abby."

"For how long? A week? Two weeks?" she said, withdrawing her hand. "What about after that?"

"I can't make any promises, but I'm willing to meet you halfway. A man has a lot of time to think when he's out at sea, and I've realized that maybe I've been going about this ass-backward. There's no reason I can't spend more time with you and take fewer gigs instead of its being the other way around." He rose from his chair and walked over to her, drawing her to her feet. Then he had his arms around her, his face buried in her hair, and she could feel his lips moving against her neck as he murmured, "See how easy it is? A piece of cake. We can do this, Abby."

For a moment, she allowed herself to be lulled, eyes closed, as she was rocked gently from side to side in his arms. The owl and the pussycat went to sea in a beautiful pea-green boat. . . .

Then she drew back to look him in the eye. "Prove it."

"All right, I will. It just so happens the National Geographic channel wanted to fly me to Australia as soon as I finished this gig—some special on the Great Barrier Reef—and I turned them down flat. I told them I needed some time off."

She eyed him warily, not quite sure what to make of it. "Wow. That's a first. I'm impressed."

"You should be." He flashed her his most disarming smile. "Though you have to admit, you're not always so available yourself."

"That used to be the case, but not anymore." She told him then about resigning as CEO, emphasizing that it had been a decision that was entirely personal and in no way related to him. She added somewhat sternly, "This doesn't mean I'm free to take off whenever I feel like it. I still have responsibilities. Commitments. People who depend on me."

At this last, he raised a questioning brow. "Don't tell me you've met someone."

"You mean another man?" She laughed at the idea. There had never been anyone but Vaughn. Not really. Even with Kent, there had been a part of her that had held back. "No, in that respect, I'm free as a bird."

"Well, I guess that makes two of us, then."

"What, you don't have a girl in every port?" she teased.

"No, just one." He dropped a kiss onto her forehead. "In the city where the sun never sets."

"Maybe we could just pretend this was all one long day." She gave a wistful sigh, peering out the window at the eternal sun in its golden slipper of haze. "That way we'd never have to leave."

"Or we could just play it by ear," he said. "I could spend more time in New York, and you could join me on the road whenever possible. In between, we could go on trips. How does that sound?"

"Sounds like a plan to me." She let her head fall onto his chest, where she allowed it to rest as she dreamed with her eyes open, of a different kind of future than the one she'd always imagined. She recalled what Lila had said about not every relationship needing to be conventional and realized that, in some ways, her wanting that had been as much a figment of her imagination as the cozy, domestic persona she'd created for herself.

"So where to next?" Vaughn whispered in her ear.

She pictured them sunning themselves on some remote tropical beach, shimmering turquoise water beckoning offshore. But right now she had another, far better destination in mind.

She tipped her head back to give him a kiss that left no doubt as to her intentions. "Bed," she said.

EPILOGUE

LAS CRUCES, MEXICO

Not much had changed in the two years since she'd last returned to her village, except that it looked more prosperous. Small changes, for the most part, but they jumped out at her wherever she went: The house next door to where she used to live, which had worn the same blistering coat of paint for as long as she could recall and was now freshly whitewashed, its trim the festive red of a dried-chile wreath; the new tile-roofed building that had gone up in place of the crumbling former convent where Milagros had gone to school; the chapel of Sangre de Cristo, with its handsome new mosaic-tiled facade replacing the old adobe one; the sign in front of the tobacconist's where her husband Gustavo used to buy his cigarettes—*Juegos!*—advertising that you could now purchase lottery tickets there.

And, of course, there was the brand-new cinder-block structure in front of which she now stood, one that might have seemed ordinary to some but to Concepción was a shining monument: the Milagros Sánchez Clínica de Medicina. It was the reason she'd traveled all this way. The reason she'd risked getting on a plane, never mind Jesús's repeated assurances that her passport was perfectly legitimate and there was no reason to fear that she'd be denied reentry to the United States. She had wanted to see this with her own eyes. Eyes that shone now as she turned to her husband to say, in a voice filled to overflowing with emotion, "The angels must be smiling up in heaven today."

He squeezed her hand and nodded, looking a bit overcome himself. *"Sí, seguro."*

It wasn't much by big-city standards. Two examining rooms and a small dispensary, staffed by a lone doctor and nurse—a girl Milagros had gone to school with, in fact—but to the community, it was a godsend. Lives would be saved: ailing infants and *viejos* who wouldn't survive the daylong trip to the medical center in Hermosillo; young women who might otherwise bleed to death after a visit to the abortionist's in the dark of night; victims of accident and fire who would succumb to their injuries without immediate medical attention.

It was too late as far as her daughter was concerned, but for Concepción it was redemption of sorts: that of the Señora, who'd kept her promise, and possibly of herself. For she'd finally and fully forgiven the Señora. She'd come to see the truth in her *abuelita*'s words and know that in a heart filled with hatred, there'd have been no room for the blessings that had since come her way, blessings that would have been left shivering out in the cold like beggars denied shelter.

She could see the Señora up on the dais consulting with the mayor and the newly appointed director of the clinic, Dr. Gutierrez, before the commencement of the dedication ceremony. The canopy over the dais shielded them from the harshest of the sun's rays, but in the light that filtered through the loosely woven cloth, the Señora appeared to glow like one of the gilded statues in the chapel, where Concepción had knelt to pray earlier in the day. The Señora was no saint, for sure, but neither was she the devil Concepción had once imagined her to be. If nothing else, she'd had the ability to recognize where she'd failed and to try to rectify those errors. No, there would be no bringing Milagros back, but if not for the Señora, there wouldn't have been this clinic; nor would Concepción have known the quiet strength of this man at her side or—

Her thoughts were interrupted by the blare of trumpets and thrumming of guitars as the mariachi band under a thatched *palapa* in the plaza across the way launched into a spirited number. Concepción looked around her and saw that the small group gathered for the ceremony had swelled to more than a hundred. At the fringes of the crowd were vendors hawking their wares—steaming *tamales* wrapped in corn husks, fried *churros* dusted with sugar, peeled mangoes on sticks, sprinkled with chile powder, as well as all manner of trinkets and religious medallions. It might have been the festival of el Día de los Muertos rather than a tribute to something life-giving.

It was midmorning by the time the dedication ceremony commenced. Concepción, who had been standing for the better part of an hour, having arrived early with her husband to be assured the best view of the podium, shifted from one foot to the other, still weary even after two days of resting from their long trip. But excitement soon triumphed over exhaustion as the speeches began, the first one by the portly mayor, Señor Hidalgo, followed by the director of the clinic, Dr. Gutierrez, a boyish-looking man sporting an earring in one ear, who went on enthusiastically at some length about how deeply honored he was to be serving his own community.

The Señora was the last to speak. Watching as she approached the podium, Concepción thought she might have been a deity for the reverent hush that fell over the crowd. In that moment the Señora almost seemed to be one as she stood poised before them, so radiant she nearly glowed, her arms lifted as if to deliver a benediction rather than a speech. Certainly she looked like no one else in her white dress belted at the waist and stylish straw hat tied with a polka-dot ribbon.

Concepción found herself leaning forward expectantly along with the rest of the crowd, gripping her husband's arm while holding her shawl tightly wrapped around her with the other. She had declined the Señora's invitation to take part in the proceedings, despite her repeated urgings. Concepción hadn't wanted this day to be about her when, in her eyes, it belonged to her daughter alone. For, however tragic the origin, there would have been no clinic without Milagros.

The Señora leaned in to speak, but something was wrong with the microphone. It let out a series of squawks and squeals, and as the Señora stood by patiently waiting for the man fiddling with it to get it working again, Concepción found herself reflecting on the journey that had brought her full circle. The hellish trek through the desert . . . meeting Jesús . . . rescuing the Señora's daughter from the fire. She recalled little of the immediate aftermath of that fire, during which time she'd drifted in and out of consciousness for what she was later told was the better part of a week. Her only clear memories were of the Señora appearing at her bedside in the hospital from time to time: holding a glass of water to her chapped lips, fetching her an extra blanket when she was cold, bringing bouquets of flowers to brighten the room.

Then one day Concepción opened her eyes, and there was Jesús standing over her. She was so disoriented from the drugs they'd been giving her that her first thought was that she was dreaming.

"Jesús? *Estás tú?*" She'd touched him to make sure he was real.

"*Sí, mi corazón.*" He gently took hold of her hand, and though even that slight pressure caused her to wince—her bandages had been removed by then, but her hands were still red and swollen—she didn't pull it away. The sight of Jesús's dear face hovering over her, his brown eyes peering at her with a mixture of love and concern, was more healing than any medicine. "I got here as soon as I could," he told her. "It was only yesterday that I learned what had happened."

She nodded, her cracked lips forming a smile. "I'm glad you came."

"The doctor tells me you're being released tomorrow. I've come to take you home," he informed her.

At first she was confused. Home to her village? Was that where he was taking her? "It's a long way for you to travel," she rasped in her scratchy whisper of a voice.

To which he responded, with a smile, "And where else would you have me go? Don't I live there, too?"

Then she understood. He meant home to LA.

She shook her head. "I can't go with you."

His smile faded, his beautiful but not handsome face seeming to crumple into itself. *"Porqué no?"* he asked. "Did you not promise to come back to me when all this was finished?"

She hadn't promised that, exactly, but she didn't argue with him. Besides, there was now a different reason why she couldn't remain with Jesús. "I'm in this country illegally," she reminded him. "They know about it—a man from La Migra came to see me yesterday." A big, official-looking *gringo* holding a clipboard who had asked her a lot of questions in his rudimentary Spanish. "The Señora has said she will try and get me a green card, but there are no guarantees. And even if she succeeds, I'll most probably be sent home while the matter is being decided."

Jesús surprised her by bursting into laughter. He laughed so hard, tears squeezed from the corners of his eyes. When his laughter subsided, he said, shaking his head and dabbing at his eyes with his handkerchief, "Ah, *mi corazón.* Is that all that's worrying you? I was afraid it was something worse than that."

"Isn't that enough?" she asked, puzzled by his behavior.

He leaned closer to kiss her on the lips, whispering, "La Migra can't send you back when we are man and wife."

A week after they arrived back in LA, they were married at City Hall. And now Concepción was no longer the widow Delgado but Mrs. Jesús Ramírez, wife of a U.S. citizen, and as such, the proud possessor of the blue passport now safely tucked in her purse. She had her own home as well, the one that she and Jesús had moved into shortly after they had been married. It even had fruit trees in the backyard. Not only that, she was taking driving lessons so that she could someday drive her own car—though she'd made Jesús promise not to buy her one that was new or fancy, lest she be mistaken for a *gringa*. In short, she was living the life that her daughter had once dreamed of when Milagros used to talk of joining her husband in the Promised Land.

Concepción felt the old sorrow well up in her at the thought. How she'd have loved to share her newfound prosperity with Milagros! Briefly, she wondered about the Señora's daughter. How was she faring? Well, she was alive, at least. Which was more than Concepción could say of her child.

The microphone let out a final earsplitting squeal before the Señora's voice at last came floating forth on a sea of applause. For those who'd been expecting her to address the audience in English, Concepción among them, it came as a welcome surprise when, ignoring the translator who stood in readiness at her side, she did so in Spanish, albeit haltingly, eliciting approving murmurs from the crowd. *"Señores e señoras, estoy aquí en este día de tan importancia . . ."* She didn't wish to be thanked, she went on to say, this time with the aid of the translator (of which Concepción herself had no need, as her English had vastly improved over the past year or so). Instead, it was she who should be thanking the people of Las Cruces. None of this would have been possible, she reminded them, without the labor they'd provided, much of it free; she knew they had also worked hard to make the factory a success, which in part had enabled her to fund this worthy cause. Without their help, the dream of the clinic would never have been realized.

"There is one more person I would like to thank," she said in conclusion. "She would be up here with me if she weren't so modest, so I'll have to speak for her in saying that she wishes for her daughter's memory to live on with this clinic that bears her name." The Señora's eyes, bright with tears, scanned the crowd in search of Concepción. "I can honestly say I wouldn't be standing here today if not for this remarkable woman. She's the real reason for this clinic. Concepción Delgado—excuse me, *Ramírez*—I know the angels are smiling down from heaven today."

Concepción felt a light chill go through her, hearing the Señora echo the very words she herself had spoken to Jesús earlier on. Only for her, it wasn't the angels smiling down from heaven but one angel in particular.

She felt hands nudging her from behind. Mañuel and Magdalena Veléz, former neighbors of hers with whom she and Jesús had been staying. They were urging her to step forward and make her presence known.

They couldn't understand why she would prefer to remain in the shadows, for if they'd had any memory of the dark time when she had blamed the Señora for the death of her daughter, they had forgotten it. And now others who knew her were propelling her forward as well. Concepción looked to Jesús in mild panic, but he only smiled helplessly in return, as if to say, *We both knew this would happen. It's no use trying to escape.*

Becoming aware of the commotion, the crowd parted before her, and Concepción had no choice but to step forward, her shawl clutched tightly around her. People were cheering, but she ignored them. She would not use this occasion to reap glory for herself. She'd done nothing to deserve it. She had lost her child, and, as any mother could testify, there was no glory or honor in that.

When she reached the foot of the dais, she stopped, refusing to go any farther. She only turned and waved to the crowd, calling out, *"Gracias! Gracias por todo!"* A wave of applause broke over her, and then her moment in the spotlight was over, the crowd's attention diverted by the ribbon-cutting ceremony taking place at the entrance to the clinic. Minutes later, with the ceremony at an end and the crowd starting to disperse, she headed off in search of her husband. She hadn't gone more than a dozen steps when she was brought to a halt by a hand on her elbow. She turned to find herself face-to-face with the Señora. Her face was partially obscured from view by the wide brim of her hat, so all Concepción could see at first was her smile. White teeth and crimson lips.

"I'm glad I caught you," the Señora said a bit breathlessly. She turned to the tall man at her side. "I'd like you to meet my boyfriend, Vaughn. Vaughn, this is the very special lady I was telling you about." The boyfriend was rugged, like a mountaineer, with blue eyes and yellow hair bleached by the sun. Handsome for a *gringo*, Concepción supposed, though no match for Jesús in her eyes. And speaking of Jesús . . . She glanced about in search of him, but he was nowhere to be seen.

"I've heard a lot about you," the boyfriend said to her, smiling warmly at Concepción as he shook her hand before slipping an arm around the Señora's shoulders. "It's a pleasure to finally meet you."

"The pleasure is all mine, Señor," said Concepción politely. She felt awkward conversing with the Señora and her boyfriend. It was one thing to have forgiven her, another to be acting as though they were old friends.

But if she felt uncomfortable, the Señora didn't appear to notice. "It's wonderful, isn't it? I never thought I'd see this day. And here we all are, joined in celebration." She tilted her head back to look up at the clinic, and as her face came into full view, Concepción could see her eyes, which were shining with tears of joy. "I meant what I said up there. I owe it all to you," she said, bringing her gaze back to Concepción.

Concepción shook her head. "I did nothing."

"That's not true. If I hadn't met you, I wouldn't have known . . ." The Señora faltered a bit before continuing, "You made me realize that it wasn't enough to be sorry, that I needed to give back. Not that it could ever make up for—" She broke off, visibly distressed, and Concepción saw the boyfriend's arm tighten about her shoulders.

An awkward silence ensued, in which Concepción experienced a flurry of emotions. Pity. Anger. Sorrow. Most of all sorrow—which would always be with her, she knew, like a hard nugget of amber formed of sap that had once run freely. An image of Milagros's dear face rose in her mind, bringing a wave of longing so fierce it nearly bowled her over.

Something stirred beneath her shawl just then, and the silence was broken by a tiny, mewing cry. Concepción drew back the shawl to reveal the infant in a sling across her chest: a tiny girl with a tuft of black hair and eyes like two shiny coffee beans, now blinking up at her sleepily. Concepción smiled down tenderly at her child, feeling something hard and implacable inside her melt. She stroked the baby's cheek, cooing to her.

"Oh!" Abigail's eyes widened in surprise, and she leaned in for a closer look. "I didn't realize . . . Is she yours?"

Concepción nodded in response. She didn't blame the Señora for looking so astonished. She, too, had been thunderstruck to learn that she was with child at the relatively advanced age of forty-five. Then to have given birth to a healthy infant, a beautiful baby girl, after so many failed pregnancies and stillbirths—it could only be described as a miracle, a gift from God.

"Her name is Esperanza," she said. "It means 'hope.'"

"She's beautiful," said the boyfriend, smiling down at Esperanza.

Abigail merely stared at the infant in openmouthed wonder. When she finally tore her gaze away, she and Concepción exchanged a long look. That of two women with a shared knowledge of what it is to be a mother: the joy and the heartbreak, the wonder that never ceases, the fearsome burden of responsibility it brings and the knowing that at any given moment it can be snatched away.

"I wish . . ." the Señora started to say, the tears in her eyes spilling over.

Concepción nodded in understanding. The Señora wished this joy weren't colored by sorrow. But wasn't that true of most joys? Didn't they by their very nature shine in contrast to the darkness around them? Once more recalling her *abuelita*'s words, she placed her hand on the Señora's. *"Está bien."* She did a startling thing then, something that surprised her as much as it did the Señora. She leaned in to kiss the other woman's cheek. "The angels are indeed smiling," she said.